BLACK HAWK

AND OTHER TALES OF THE AMAZON

BLACK HAWK

AND OTHER TALES OF THE AMAZON

ARTHUR O. FRIEL

WILDSIDE PRESS

CONTENTS

BLACK HAWK

IN THE vast trackless solitudes of the Amazon jungle dwells the bird of evil omen — the black hawk.

Not the somber silent ghoul of the upper air which drops to rend and destroy after the hand of Death has struck — not the *urubu* vulture. Far more sinister is the black hawk, *caracara-i*. The vulture is but the follower of fate. The hawk is the harbinger of doom.

Out of the lethal labyrinths of tropical thicket the wide-winged portent floats to circle above some little Indian village, veering downward at length into the top of some tall tree. And there it whines.

Hour after hour its doleful plaint sounds, foreboding death to some inhabitant of the huts beneath; presaging, too, a sudden end to any weaker bird which, moved by the forlorn cry, flies near to seek the cause.

Not until it has made its kill or been attacked by a squad of the doughty little *bemlivi* flycatchers will it swerve again into the jungle fastness whence it came. And long after the black hawk has gone the copper-skinned men who have heard its querulous note bear in their hearts numb dread.

Yet, for all its menace, the *caracara-i* is only a bird, and of itself can do nothing to fulfil its warning to men. So, if the wanderer on the upper Amazon should by chance drift into the river-town of Viciado and speak there the name "Black Hawk," he might be surprised to see its hard-swearing, hard-drinking inhabitants, male and female both, glance nervously over their shoulders and hastily gulp another gourd of raw liquor. But in time he would learn that their qualms were due not so much to superstitious fear of a bird as to memory of another sort of Black Hawk.

He might hear, too — when the bacchanal bravos of the town had sufficiently fortified their courage — much braggadocio regarding their valiant deeds in connection with the passing of that Black Hawk. But these vaporings would be even less trustworthy than the tall talk born of drink usually is. They would be a mere mass of lies, told by men who had no hand in the removal of the worst menace their territory ever knew.

If the traveler would learn the facts, he might perhaps journey on westward to the river Javary, the flowing boundary between Brazil and Peru; and there he might seek out a straight-speaking, straight-shooting veteran of the Brazilian bush — one Lourenço Moraes. Then, if Lourenço liked the set of the stranger's jaw and the look in his eye, and if he happened to be at leisure and in reminiscent mood, the true tale would be told. And this is the tale:

I

OUR part in this affair of the Black Hawk began, *senhor*, in the office of my employer, Coronel Nunes, owner of the greatest rubber estate in this Javary jungle. It ended in the wilderness.

Four of us sat that hot afternoon in the room which the *coronel* uses for business. Three of us belonged there; the *coronel* and I and my comrade Pedro Andrada, who, like myself, drew pay as a *seringueiro* but much preferred to roam the bush as a scout. The fourth was a blond-bearded but deeply tanned North American who called himself "Thomas Gordon Mack of the U. S. A."

Though Thomas Gordon Mack — or, as Pedro and I called him, *Senhor* Tom — was a recent arrival at the headquarters of the *coronel*, he was no stranger to Brazil or to us two bushmen. He had been exploring the unmapped region to the southeast of us for the government authorities of Rio. This work had ended suddenly when a brutal tribe of cannibals killed all his assistants and carried him alive to their chief to be tortured.

Pedro and I, scouting for new rubber-trees, had found him in the hands of those beasts and managed not only to save him but also later to destroy his captors. And now he had returned with us to headquarters, where we two were to get a new outfit and report to the *coronel*.

For a time after finishing our tale we sat smoking. When the *coronel*'s long cigar had shrunk to a stub he spoke, first to *Senhor* Tom and then to us.

"*Senhor* Mack, your explorations have ended, or at least must be suspended until you can requisition new aids. Now I shall be greatly pleased if you will consider this poor house your headquarters and command my services in any way. There is much work to be done, I dare say, in preparing your report to the government; and if the facilities here are not too crude I trust that you will remain here to do that work and to enjoy whatever sport the river and the forest afford.

"Lourenço and Pedro, I sent you out to find several million milreis' worth of new rubber, and you only got yourselves into a fine fight — as usual. If all my men were as unreliable as you two scamps I should soon be ruined. Now I am going to sentence you —"

He paused, his eyes twinkling.

"To go back and find that rubber," Pedro smiled.

"Exactly. Either to do that or to go on another journey and find something else. You have your choice."

We sat up. Knowing our old *coronel* as we did, we suspected that the other journey he had in mind was likely to be dangerous. Otherwise he would not have given us a choice. It is his practise never to order a man to go on a hazardous mission. He lets the man know what he wants, and if the man refuses to take the risk the *coronel* neither blames him then nor holds the refusal against him afterward.

Unforeseen danger may, of course, come to any of us *seringueiros* in our daily work — risks of attack by snakes or wild beasts or savages — and we are expected to be ready to meet such things. But when perils are known beforehand, or even suspected, *Coronel* Nunes will drive no man among them.

"If there is rubber in the bush beyond where we have just been, *coronel*, it will still be there whenever we return," I said. "Rubber-trees do not ramble off. Let us hear of the other thing in your mind."

"Have you heard of *caracara-i*?" he asked.

We nodded.

"Certainly," I said. "The black hawk of death. Every bushman knows that bird."

"This is a bird of another feather," he told us, "though I suspect that it, too, is a hawk of death. A wingless hawk which lives on the ground, but which has sharp talons and a bloody beak.

"Word has come to me that in the jungle behind Viciado, on the Solimoes — By the way, do you men know that town?"

"I know where it is, and I know it has a bad name," I replied, "but I never have visited it. Have you, Pedro?"

My partner shook his head. Then up spoke *Senhor* Tom.

"I have. It looks worse than it sounds and it smells worse than it looks. Sets on a hill on the south shore of the Amazon, between the Javary and the Jutahy. Inhabited by Indians, half-breeds, and near-white bums. Men are a lot of booze-hounds, and the women — phew! As Kipling might have said, 'The female of the species is more rotten than the male.' Favorite indoor sport, as you might expect, is wife-beating. Some town!"

"A very good description of the place — though somewhat mild, if I may believe all I have heard of it," the *coronel* agreed. "I never have stopped there, nor do I wish to. As you say, it is on the south shore of the Solimoes — that is the name by which we Brazilians call the upper Amazon, *senhor* — and between this Javary of ours and the Jutahy. But it is not the town itself which interests me, but what lies behind it.

"I am told that there, miles back from the river, is a man called Black Hawk, or *Caracara-i*; that he is bad; and, more important, that he has ambitions to make himself a sort of jungle emperor. His idea, I understand, is to control the entire country between the Javary and the Jurua, the next river eastward from the Jutahy — a neat little empire of some seventy thousand square miles. Swamp-land, of course, covered with wild jungle, inhabited by aborigines; but capable of giving him a very respectable fortune in the shape of rubber, medicinal herbs, and such things.

"This would be well enough if he would let the rest of us live in peace — any man has the right to carve his fortune out of this jungle if he is man enough to do it. But that is not his plan. He boasts that every rubber owner, every trader, every man in this region who has any business or any money, must pay heavy tribute to him or die. That leaves us only two possibilities; to run or to fight."

Pedro and I laughed loudly.

"He is full of Viciado rum," Pedro scoffed. "I should like to see him come in here and try to scare you out, *coronel.* The poor fool!"

But the *coronel* did not laugh.

"It is not a joke, Pedro *meo,*" he frowned. "I do not take seriously such a matter unless it is serious. This Black Hawk is not confining himself to drunken dreaming, nor is he acting single-handed. He has made a beginning by terrorizing Viciado, robbing and murdering traders, and stealing women; and he has a small army of Indians which is increasing steadily. Once his army is big enough he will be able to carry out his plan."

"But he couldn't last long," objected *Senhor* Tom. "The government —"

"Is thousands of miles from here, *senhor,*" the *coronel* cut in. "And if this man presses all the Indians of this section into his service it will take even the government a long time to overthrow him. Jungle fighting is the hardest kind of fighting. And it does you no good to have the government execute a man for your murder. Better prevent him from committing the murder."

"True enough," nodded the blond man.

"What is more, *senhor*, we Brazilians have not forgotten the war of the Cabanos, though it took place nearly a hundred years ago — the revolt in which the blacks massacred the whites in the streets of Para. Para, as you know, is two thousand miles nearer to Rio than this place; yet it took the government nearly a year to suppress the rebellion, and it would have taken much longer if the Mundurucus and other Indians had not fought for the whites.

"Up here at the headwaters of the great river, any man who even makes a beginning of violence against white men is a serious menace. Indians are always ready to listen to talk of a race war."

"Is this Black Hawk an Indian?"

"My information is that he is a *cafuzo* — a half-breed of Indian and negro."

"Hm! Bad combination of bloods," said the North American. "Makes a merciless brute."

"Exactly, *senhor*. And Black Hawk has already shown that he is of that type. Now I have told you all I know of him — and I know this much only from reports which I believe to be trustworthy but which have passed through several mouths before reaching me. I should like to know more, and to hear it from my own men."

I made a new cigaret and tried to remember all I knew about the Indians of the country behind Viciado. It was not much, for nothing ever had happened which would take me into that place. Of the red men to the south and east, some of whom were cannibals and all of whom were wild, I knew a great deal, for chance had thrown me among them at various times.

But about all I could remember regarding those toward the Amazon was that they were of the Tucuna race and supposed to be tame; that they were more fond of drinking and dancing than of fighting or working, and that what work they did was mostly the making of clay jars and knitting bags from fiber-twine. Such people, it would seem, were hardly the sort to become warriors now. Yet I have noticed that sometimes men usually quiet and peaceable were more to be dreaded, when they did go on the warpath, than those who were always seeking trouble.

The more I thought about this fact, the more interested I became in the Tucunas and the man of the black name who would be a jungle king. So I glanced at Pedro and found his brown eyes gleaming with the same thought. For the moment I had forgotten about the North American. But as I turned toward the *coronel* I caught his steady gaze fixed on me, and the blue glimmer under his bushy brows spoke man-talk.

"You too, *Senhor* Tom?" I asked.

"Me too, old top!" he drawled. "I'm in on this play. Part of my official duties, you know. Something to add to the long-drawn report I'm going to write for the Rio chaps when I get around to it."

The *coronel* looked thoughtful. The North American eyed him keenly, blew a smoke-ring, and added:

"Don't take that remark too seriously, *coronel*. I'm not so bloated up over working for the government that I have to tell all I know. In fact, I took this exploring job only to satisfy my own curiosity as to what was in here.

"So if anything happens on this trip which needn't be reported to Rio — well, I can forget an awful lot in a remarkably short time. And if my presence is likely to handicap you fellows, Lourenço, go ahead without me. I'll just borrow a canoe and some grub and cartridges and go in there on my own."

"Ah — you understand, *senhor*, that the object of this trip is only to learn as much as possible concerning Black Hawk, not to attack him," said the *coronel*.

"I understand perfectly."

And *Senhor* Tom let one eyelid droop.

"We shall carry guns only for hunting purposes," he went on. "If any one accidentally gets shot it will be due to his own carelessness. What say, fellows? Do we go together or otherwise?"

"Together, certainly," I said, and Pedro grunted approval.

"Good. And how?"

We thought a while, and I asked Pedro whether he knew the bush in the direction of Viciado. He did not.

"If it were the season of high-water we could cross over by flood-channels to the Jutahy," I said then, "but it is not. So I suppose we must go to the Amazon and then inland."

"Poor plan," he disagreed. "Takes at least three hundred miles of water-travel to reach the town that way. Worse yet, Viciado is admittedly scared stiff by this Black Hawk, and he undoubtedly has more than one spy at work there. He'd know we were there long before we knew where he was. Our game is to work up on him from behind."

"How?" I demanded. "Have you a flying-machine which will put us behind him? Or are we to chop our way through a hundred miles of thick bush?"

"Neither. For once, I can show you jungle-rangers something. Remember, I came in here to explore. I have explored, especially west of the Jutahy; and I can show you the neatest little network of navigable creeks and rivers you ever saw, running from the Tecuahy eastward into the section we're after. They're not dried up now, either, and we can go by canoe. Wait till I get my maps."

He strode into his room. When he returned and put his maps on the *coronel*'s desk we found that he had spoken truth. His lines showed a network of water east of the Tecuahy, just as he said. If the maps were true — and he was ready to fight any man who said they were not — we could go by boat into the region we sought.

"You must know something of Black Hawk if you have been in there," Pedro suggested.

"Very little. Almost nothing. I heard there was a bad 'breed' somewhere in there, but never ran onto him and wasn't interested anyhow — didn't know he was ambitious to be king of the jungle. Haven't been at Viciado for five years, either, so haven't heard the Black Hawk gossip.

"Stopped there once when I was on my way down-river from the Marañon country. This time I went inland at the mouth of the Jutahy and worked west among the side-streams. But I sure am starting on the black gent's trail now. Let's see, what's the little bird that tackles the *caracara-i?*"

"The *bemlivi.*"

"Oh, sure. Well, that's us. The Bemlivi Brothers of the Brazilian Bush. Mister Black Hawk, you'd better tie a string around your tail-feathers. First thing you know you may get 'em yanked out."

II

IN A speedy but strong three-man canoe we left the headquarters on a windy morning. Out on the river the waves chased one another, and before we pushed out from the bank they slapped against the side of our dugout like hands.

"The river does not want us to go, Pedro," I said. "It is trying to drive us back on shore."

"You have it wrong," he disputed. "it is only giving us a friendly farewell and wishing us good fortune."

"That's the idea," *Senhor* Tom agreed. "Slapping us on the shoulder and saying, 'So long, fellows. Give 'em Hell !'"

"And so say I, *senhor*," nodded the *coronel*, who had walked down to the water to see us depart. "If you meet enemies, give them what you say. I regret that you leave me so soon, but we shall meet again. Perhaps when you return you will have had enough of roving for a time. Are you quite sure you can reach the Black Hawk country by way of the back-streams?"

"Dead sure," the blond man declared. "If these boys can put me on the Tecuahy I'll show the route from there. All we have to do is to hit the Ituhy, go down that to the Tecuahy, work over to the Capacete by creek, cut across to the Jundiatyba by other creeks, and then slide down that river toward the Amazon. Very simple."

Pedro and I blinked. The *coronel* chuckled.

"As you say, very simple," he echoed dryly. "It is all on the maps, yes? Then of course there can be no doubt. But the maps, I have noticed, are as thick with little lines as a monkey with hairs. If by any chance, *senhor*, you should get on the wrong hair — I mean the wrong line — let my men have their head. They are natural *matteiros* — woodsmen — and can smell their way through the thickest bush. *Adeos!* Go with God."

Out into the river we shoved the boat, and down-stream we rode into the wind. Looking back from the first turn, we saw the old *coronel* still standing there on the shore.

One white-sleeved arm went up as we watched, and we tossed our paddles in reply. Then the current bore us around the bend and we saw only the thick growth lining the banks.

Senhor Tom twitched his hat a little farther down on the sunny side of his face, thumped out a lively measure with his paddle on the bottom of the boat, splashed it over the side, and heaved so hard that the tough shaft bent in his hands.

"Off again on a new trail!" he cried. "Lord, but it's good to be moving again! Nothing much to look forward to except maybe a scrap with our little friend Black Hawk, but we're going somewhere anyhow. Suppose I ought to be back yonder drudging over that gosh-awful report of mine; but I'd rather paddle twenty miles than write twenty words. Why in thunder does a man have to be so restless all the time?"

"I do not know, *senhor*, unless it is because he is alive." I answered. "And he will have to be quiet a long time after he is dead."

"About as good a reason as any. Guess the only thing that will ever keep me quiet will be the old man with the scythe. Either that or getting married — from which may the good Lord deliver us."

And he twirled his paddle twice around his head and began to sing:

> *"Merrily we roll along,*
> *Roll along,*
> *Roll along,*
> *Merrily we roll along*
> *Down the Javaree!"*

Pedro, up in the bow, turned and grinned at me. We knew exactly how *Senhor* Tom felt, for we too were glad to be striking out on a new trail instead of attending to our regular duties as rubber-workers.

So it always is with us whose feet are restless; the start on a fresh venture finds us glad to be off, and the less we know about what lies ahead of us the more eager we are to go and see.

Now we timed our stroke to the singing of the blond man between us, and when he became silent we swung on with the same swift sway.

For hours we paddled around the loops of the crooked river. Then we slowed, watching the right bank. Ahead was a very sharp turn where the stream twisted abruptly from southeast to northwest before swinging eastward again; and at this turn a small, slow, but deep creek flowed in from the south. Over it the trees matted their branches so thickly that no sunlight came through, and the mouth of the narrow stream seemed only a gloomy cave in the bank.

"Here we say farewell to the river," I said. "We now start for the Tecuahy. This is our first cut-off — the Ygarapé da Morte."

"What's that? Ygarapé da Morte? Creek of Death?" exclaimed Mack. "You've picked a sweet-sounding stream to start in on. Looks as bad as it sounds, too. Any particular reason for the name?"

"Only that several men have gone up it and have not returned." I told him.

And I spoke of two men whom I knew, and others of whom I had heard, who had disappeared forever in that darkness. Each had gone in by canoe, and some time later the canoes had come out again — empty. And not one of the boats had shown bloodstains or other signs of attack.

"Umph! Spooky hole. Ever been in here yourself?"

I had. When the canoe of Moreira Macedo, one of the *coronel*'s men, had been seen stuck at the mouth of that creek and other men refused to go in to see what had happened, I had paddled up for some distance alone, but had found no sign.

At that time the creek had been quite full and the shores so muddy and soft that I found no place to land; so I had come out again believing that Moreira must have drowned. He never was seen again.

"Well," said *Senhor* Tom, moving his rifle nearer with one foot, "let's go. If there's a man-eating demon up here we may have an interesting afternoon. Otherwise we'll ramble on. All aboard for the Ituhy, Tecuahy, Capacete, Jundiatyba and way stations, via the Creek of Death!"

And we left the sunny wind-swept river for the still, dark stream that crawled snakily out of the jungle.

The Creek of Death was not a cheerful place at any time; and now, coming into its smooth-creeping water and its solemn gloom after being tossed by the lively waves and dazzled by dancing sunbeams, it seemed even more deathlike than usual. No wind touched us now, no bird-voices came to our ears, nothing stood out clearly in the vague dimness around. And not only the light of the sun but its heat also had left us. The damp air felt clammy.

For a little way we moved very slowly, waiting for our eyes to become used to the murk. When the thick mass on either side dissolved into small trees and dangling *cipos* we put more power into our strokes and began to make fair speed up the water-lane. The tangled banks slipped away behind us for some time, and no danger showed itself. At length, reaching a spot where the sunlight fell through a small gap, we decided to halt a while and eat.

Without leaving the canoe we munched on a few mouthfuls of sun-dried monkey-meat with farinha, washing it down with gourds of water from the stream, which was cool and fairly clean. Then we made cigarets and rested.

Senhor Tom's cigaret was about half-smoked when he twitched his shoulders, turned, and scowled at the bush behind him.

"Got a chill," he grumbled. "Queer sort of chill, too. Feel as if somebody was watching me."

We scanned the jungle growth, but saw only a tangle of trees and some *cipos* hanging down from above or twined around thick trunks.

"It is because we are still and the air is so damp," said Pedro. "It is easy to become chilly in such a place. Perhaps we had best move onward into the sun."

But the North American kept on watching for a few minutes, then twisted himself about to face the other way.

"Don't feel it now," he said presently. "Since I got my back to you fellows I'm warm enough. But something or other keeps telling me to go ashore. Guess I'll go see if there's anything —"

Pedro and I glanced swiftly at each other. Then we picked up our guns.

"Stay here, *senhor*," I said. "We have had that feeling once or twice in the past and found that there was a reason for it. Keep quiet and look closely at everything."

And we began searching every foot of ground with our eyes.

Minutes dragged past. Then Pedro made a murmuring sound.

"I can see it now," he said quietly. "And it is much too close to us. That leaning *tartarugeira* tree, Lourenço, with the big *cipo* twisted around it — look at the butt. We must get away before we shoot. Paddle backward slowly."

I looked at the gnarled turtle-tree and the thick climber hugging the trunk. A chill went down my own back. Softly I sunk my paddle in the water, and we drifted down-stream.

"What is it?" asked the North American. "I don't see —"

Pedro's rifle cut him short. At the crash of the report I heaved hard on the paddle and the dugout jumped backward. At the same instant the *cipo* around that tree jumped also. It flew downward in a collapsing coil, and from the ground sounded a horrible hiss.

Pedro's gun roared again. *Senhor Tom* snatched his own rifle, leaped up, fired over my squatting partner's head. The false *cipo* hissed again and thrashed about in awful fury. Bushes flew in the air and the creek splashed into angry waves as the writhing body and bullet-torn head of the great serpent beat against earth and water. The spot where we had taken our ease became a welter of mud and blood.

Not until the guns were empty did my comrades quit shooting. By that time the snake had buried its head under the water, but its thick barrel, drilled through by heavy bullets, and spouting red, still crushed down the surrounding bush in its death-agony. But we were out of its reach, and though the dugout rolled and pitched I had only to hang to a drooping branch and hold it safe.

"That, *senhor*, was what was calling you ashore," Pedro said coolly as he reloaded. "That was what chilled your back — the fixed gaze of the *sucuruju*. Did you not see its head on the ground?"

"By thunder, I didn't. And I was looking right at it, too. Couldn't see the blasted thing at all."

"That was because you were the one who was being summoned," I explained. "The power of the snake's eye was on you. We saw it because we were not called."

The explorer, still standing up and balancing to the roll of the boat, watched the struggle up ahead for a time before answering. Then, sitting down and feeding fresh cartridges into his magazine, he said —

"I've heard that stuff about snake-mesmerism before, but I never believed it."

"Yet you looked at it, less than twenty feet away, after Pedro had told you where it was — and could not see it."

"Uh-huh. I can see it plain enough now, anyhow. Say! We've wiped out the man-eater of the Creek of Death! Bet you he's the fellow that killed your friends!"

For the time we had forgotten where we were. Now, remembering the empty canoes which had come floating from this dismal stream, we nodded and looked with new hatred at the hideous thing twisting about on the bank.

"It must be so," I agreed. "Poor Moreira! Poor Affonso Costa! They could not draw their machetes in time."

Seeing that he looked a little puzzled, I explained.

"The machete, *senhor*, is your only hope if the *sucuruju* attacks you. He does not kill you instantly; he has to set himself to squeeze you dead. First he throws one swift loop around neck or body and sinks his fangs into your flesh in order to anchor himself. Then he coils around you and begins crushing — and you are gone.

"If you are not paralyzed with shock and fear by the sudden attack, you have a few seconds in which to chop him with your machete. He is scaly and hard, but if your knife is keen and your arm strong you can cut him enough to make him relax. Then chop again — attack him hard — and you can fight free. But you must work fast."

"And if his first loop nails your arms to your sides —"

"You die," Pedro finished.

Again *Senhor* Tom twitched his shoulders.

"Ugh!" he grunted. "Nice cheerful little place this, as I said before. Suppose now we'll have to stick here until this boneless wonder gets through doing the shimmy and lets us pass on. However, we have all the time in the world, and when we move we'll have a safe creek ahead."

He was not quite right. The Creek of Death was not yet safe. Nor will it ever be.

III

ANY men will tell you, *senhor,* that a snake, though killed, will "live" until sunset. It is an interesting story, but it is not true. I have killed many a snake, and, though some squirmed longer than others, I never have known one to writhe for any great length of time. Nor did the big *sucuruju* of the Ygarapé da Morte delay us very long.

True, the beast still was moving when we passed the point where stood the crooked turtle-tree, but its squirms had become only shivers toward the tail, and the red water above its buried head was quiet. In another half-hour or less we could have jabbed it with machetes without causing the slightest tremor.

On between the sloping bushy banks we drove, looping around turn after turn but steadily eating up the miles into the south. At times we found the water so shallow that we had to shorten our holds on the paddles; but we never quite scraped the bottom, and always the depth increased after a few rods. Our eyes now were so accustomed to the shadows that we could have spied instantly any menacing movement on either side, and our ears were ever alert for any sound. But no sound or movement except our own was on that lonely creek.

Hour after hour we forged ahead until at length camping time approached. Then, as we looked forward for a good place to sling our hammocks and make a palm-leaf shelter, we found the banks sinking and the creek broadening out. Soon we came into better light. The trees ended, the bush thinned, and the dropping sun shot long slanting shadows across tall grass covering level land through which the *ygarapé* flowed lazily.

Off to the right, a short gunshot away, rose a good-sized hill where lofty trees stood, and from those trees came the chattering of monkeys and parrots. It looked to be a good place to get fresh meat and make our camp.

But the creek did not flow close to the hill. Instead, it veered away to the left. In the wet season all this low *ygapo* would be far under water and the hill itself half-covered; but now the flat land must be crossed on foot before the height could be reached.

"Never like to get far from my canoe at night," said *Senhor* Tom. "A sudden rain, and you may wake up to find your boat gone. But that sure looks like a made-to-order camp-ground."

"I do not think we need fear losing the canoe tonight," Pedro replied. "We shall tie it with a long rope to allow for. any rise of water. I will go now and look at that hill. Ah, there is a path."

As he said a small path ran away from the edge of the water toward the hill. We pushed the canoe to it and looked at it before getting out. In it were no footmarks. Yet it was a track showing signs of use, leading straight into the high grass toward the trees.

"An animal runway of some kind," *Senhor* Tom judged. "Used by things up on the hill, most likely. Go ahead, Pedro. We'll get out the hammocks and other stuff."

Pedro stepped lightly away along the trail, rifle ready. We started to unload what few things we should need for the night.

As I stepped into the soft mud beside the path my feet sank slowly. I thought nothing of it, as I was accustomed to mud. I only spread my toes and leaned over the canoe, seeking the salt-bag and extra cartridges. The salt was not in sight, so I turned over several other food-bags and finally found it. By that time I had sunk half-way to my knees.

"Rotten mess of mud here," grumbled *Senhor* Tom. "Soft and sticky. Wonder where the bottom is. I'm still going down."

True enough, the mud had crawled up higher on his legs than on mine. With an irritated laugh he tried to pull up his feet. They stuck. And I too was still going down.

And then, from a place a little beyond us in the tall grass, came Pedro's voice. Cool and calm it was, but deadly serious.

"Comrades," it said, "do not land. This place is a death-trap. A *mondongo.*"

For the second time that day a chill crawled down my back. A *mondongo* is not land. It is only a crust, half-hardened by the sun, grown over with grass. Under it is mud so soft that it is almost water. Sink through that crust and the sucking, suffocating slime beneath it ends you and buries you both at once. The only animal with legs that can cross such places is the web-footed water-hog, the capybara. A death-trap in truth.

"*Senhor* Tom!" I gasped. "Grab the canoe and lift yourself by your arms! Quick!"

We both dropped everything into the boat and seized the sides. As it happened we had drawn the craft well up, and though it turned partly over beneath our weight it stayed where it was. The flat, broad side sank only an inch or two into the hardened upper crust, then held firm. With a heaving, gasping, kicking struggle we tore our legs out of the slimy grip of the lower mud and tumbled into the canoe.

"Pedro!" I shouted. "Where are you?"

"In the mud. Going down. Adeos, comrades."

His voice still was calm, but with the strained calmness of a man facing certain death.

"*Vive Deus!*" I yelled. "You do not go alone!"

And I scrambled up to jump toward him. But *Senhor* Tom seized me with an iron hand.

"One minute!" he snapped, the words coming like bullets. "Wait, Pedro! Are you in the path?"

"No. I stepped off. Do not come to me."

"Oh, we're coming. Don't fool yourself about that. Throw yourself as flat as possible and spread out."

"I have done that. It is useless."

"Not by a — sight it isn't! Hold hard!"

Then to me he said:

"The path! Keep in the path! It's firmer and may hold us. Go ahead."

With that he tore at the bags as if hunting something. I was out and away at once, running fast but as lightly as possible. The path was solid enough to hold me up, but I felt it quiver underfoot.

Only a few rods away I found Pedro. He was not more than ten feet off the path, but he had no more chance of reaching it than if those ten feet were ten miles. The sucking mud had drawn him down to his thighs, and slowly but steadily he was sinking deeper.

As he had told us, he had thrown his body flat, and lay with arms outstretched and fists gripping at the grass-roots. But the treacherous crust, though it held up his trunk, was settling under him so that he lay in a shallow trough which gradually grew deeper; and in spite of his clutch at the loosely rooted stalks the weight of his mired legs was pulling him backward and downward with a creeping slowness terrible to see.

He had stopped trying to kick his legs clear, realizing that this only made him sink faster. But he still was fighting stubbornly for life, pulling with his hands at the grass and the mud-crust and trying to overcome the downward drag at his feet by the power of his arms. Great drops of sweat rolled off his face and body, his muscles and his temple-veins stood out like cords under his skin, and he gasped as if locked in a death-grapple with some powerful human enemy.

For an instant I was on the point of throwing myself forward to grasp his hands and add my own strength to his. But he saw me and panted:

"Back! You will break through. Go!"

Sense enough remained in me to realize that I should indeed break through if I stepped out of the path, and I remained in it. Then came the North American running from the creek, carrying a coil of thin but strong rope.

"All right, old top!" he called, swiftly unrolling the coil. "We'll snake you out of there in a jiffy. When I get these loops made, work them down over your shoulders and under your arms."

With fast-working hands he made at each end of the rope a sliding noose. Then, holding the rope by the middle, he cast the nooses within reach of our trapped comrade.

"One arm at a time," he cautioned. "Keep your grip on the grass with the other hand. Get both loops around your chest. That's the stuff. Now don't move for a minute. Lourenço, get hold here! Now step away along the path. Spread your legs and set your feet so that the push on this crust won't all come at the same point. We've got to distribute the strain all we can."

As he commanded, I grasped the rope and went onward two or three yards, got a small loop around each hand, and braced myself. Pedro, letting go with one hand and then with the other, had shoved the nooses down around him. The rope now lay like a triangle, with one of us at each corner.

"Now, no yanking or heaving!" *Senhor* Tom warned. "It has to be a clean, strong, steady pull. If we yank we go through. Maybe we will anyway, but there's a chance that we won't if we hold steady. Pedro, you can kick and claw — help yourself any way you can. All set, Lourenço? Let's go!"

We settled back. Smoothly we put all our power into the steady pull that might win. In a few seconds I was tugging with all my strength. I heard the North American's bones and muscles crack with the strain of his draw. Pedro's face knotted with the pain of the cutting cord. He hooked his fingers into the grass-roots and pulled toward us. His back moved as he worked his legs in the lower muck. But for a long minute he stayed where he was.

Then, slowly, he slipped a little nearer to us. We strained backward farther. Again he slid an inch — three inches — more yet. With a squirming wriggle he got one leg partly clear.

Suddenly my left foot broke through the surface and plunged down almost to the knee.

I had to quit pulling. But my grip on the rope held me from falling backward, and for the moment I used it and Pedro's weight to draw my leg clear. Then I moved a little nearer to *Senhor* Tom, braced again, and renewed my drag at the cord.

The new pull was all Pedro needed. He came sliding forward more than a foot along his trough. His legs, smeared with black filth, came out into the air. As we took up the slack he gave a choked groan and shook his head, and when we eased up he scrambled toward us for a yard, then flattened and wrenched at the ropes around his chest. He loosed them enough to get more air into his pinched lungs before he moved on again. Then, still keeping flat, he worked his way to the path.

I suddenly felt weak. The strain of fear for my partner had taken far more of my strength than the bitter pulling at the rope. I wanted to sit down. But as I glanced downward I saw that I must move away. The crust had sunk under me so that I was standing in a shallow bowl, and it might let me through at any instant.

Senhor Tom also was in a bowl. He saw the danger and moved away.

"Out of here!" he snapped. "We'll all be in the soup in another minute. Move quick!"

As I could not move toward him without making his part of the path sink deeper, I stepped swiftly the other way until I was on new ground. Pedro, his breath rasping in his throat, still lay on the path until he had cast off one noose. And then, when we expected him to rise and get away from there, he turned and began creeping out again.

"Pedro! Are you mad?" I cried.

"I dropped my rifle," was all the answer he gave me.

And, working along in his prone position, he crawled over the bending crust, avoiding the hole from which he had just escaped until he reached his gun lying a yard farther on. With this in hand he came snaking back in the same way. Reaching the path, he sat up and laughed shakily.

"I think, comrades, that we had best not camp here tonight" he said. "Perhaps some day we shall all go into the Bottomless Pit, but we are not yet ready for it."

"Stop your foolishness and move!" I growled. "I will not break my back to pull you out of a second hole."

"I did not ask you to pull me out of this one," he grinned.

But he stood up, pulled the other noose off over his head, and began to walk toward me.

"The other way," I told him, thinking he had lost his sense of direction.

He kept on coming.

"I want to see what makes this path," he said. "I think I know, but I want to be sure."

"Well, you double fool!" the North American swore. "Haven't you brains enough to let well enough alone? Go drown yourself, then!"

And he turned back toward the boat, growling like a dog with a sore ear. Pedro grinned again.

"Go on, Lourenço," he said. "Let us look. We are safe enough as long as we stay on this track and keep moving."

I scolded, but I went ahead, realizing that he spoke sense. If the crust here was tough enough to stand the strain we had just put on it, we were in no danger now unless we stood still too long. As we went onward I asked why he had first left the path.

He said he had seen something moving the grass and had gone. toward it, finding nothing. Then he had stood still watching, and thinking nothing of the fact that he was sinking, until he found that instead of stopping he was going down faster. It then was too late to get out.

For perhaps a hundred feet we moved on toward the hill, finding the footing fairly firm. Then I stopped with a grunt.

"Ah. As I thought," said Pedro.

Before us the grass faded away, sweeping off to right and left and rimming the foulest hole I ever saw. The crust on which we walked came to an end, and beyond was a slimy mass of fluid muck in which only one kind of creature could live — the most loathsome creature known to man. The black ooze was packed with snakes.

It was a nest of *sucurujus*. Some were at least thirty feet long and nearly as thick-bodied as a man, others no bigger than eels Many of them were asleep, and none was active, though some were crawling lazily over others. They were tangled among one another so that it was hard to tell where any one of them began — a mass of hideous blue-gray bodies basking in the warmth of the sun-heated slime; death resting in death.

I lifted my rifle. But then I let it sink. It would take many precious cartridges to destroy half of those reptiles, and those cartridges must not be wasted. Besides, the crust on which we stood was thinner here at the hole, and already it was sinking too fast under our combined weight. We could not linger even if we wished to; and I had no wish to.

"Shoot the two largest ones," Pedro muttered over my shoulder. "Then get away fast. I will take that big one to the right. Ready?"

I aimed quickly at a huge head in the middle of the mass. Our guns crashed together. Instantly we wheeled and ran.

And we ran none too soon. The path rolled and shook under us and the grass all around swayed and dipped as the two serpents leaped and thrashed in their death-flurry. Hisses burst out, and the ugly tangle must have gone squirming in every direction from the hole. But we saw nothing of that. We dashed straight to the creek, and there we pushed out the canoe and tumbled aboard.

Senhor Tom asked no questions, but sank his paddle in the water and shoved the dugout up-stream. Not until we had gone a mile and found a passable camping-spot did we talk. Then we told him of what we had seen and done.

We knew now what had made that smooth trail. When the last flood had drained away toward the far-off eastern sea, and the sun had not yet hardened the top of the muck, the water-boas had sought that hole and made it their breeding-home; and from time to time they had crawled to the creek to hunt, their heavy bodies pressing down the half-dried mud into a rut which later became tougher than the loose matter on either side. Their path now had lured a man into the jaws of death, yet helped to save him.

"And I'm willing to bet," the explorer added when we spoke of this, "that the bones of more than one missing man are hidden in that black slime. The big snake down-stream may have got one or two, but not all. A lone man caught as you were, Pedro, would have no chance."

"No chance indeed, *senhor*," my comrade agreed. "This is truly a Creek of Death. When we come back we shall warn our mates at headquarters, and perhaps block up the mouth of this stream with trees, so that no man shall wander in here again."

"Good idea. I'll help — when we come back."

I V

IN THE next few days we worked slowly but steadily toward the little river Ituhy, which flows into the Tecuahy about seventy miles above its mouth, and itself is some forty miles long. To reach it we had to labor across from the Creek of Death to two other *ygarapés* in turn — the Iraité and the Rodrigues — traveling now almost due east and toiling along small wandering side-streams and through shrunken weedy lagoons.

More than once we had to use poles instead of paddles, and, a few times we even had to get out on shore and haul the canoe along the stream to deeper water. And at the head of the Rodrigues, where we again turned south to strike the source of the Ituhy, we had to make what the North American called "portages" — cut paths through the jungle with our machetes, carry everything except the canoe across in packs, then strew short poles in the paths and drag the boat over the poles to the next pool or little stream.

This was hot, hard work, and once *Senhor* Tom grumbled that we ought to have a light "canvas canoe" such as he said was used in his own country. But then he admitted that snags would ruin the bottom of such a craft, and that for our jungle the solid *itauba* stonewood dugouts were best, even though heavy.

And in spite of the time and toil it cost us to cross from stream to stream, we saved many miles of paddling and reached the mouth of the Ituhy days sooner than if we had gone down the Javary and then up the Tecuahy.

Pedro and I knew all that country west of the Tecuahy well enough to make no mistakes in moving about, whether the waters were high or low; and *Senhor* Tom never looked at any map until we had crossed the Tecuahy and camped on its eastern shore.

Then, as we smoked after breakfast, Pedro said:

"Now, *senhor*, your turn comes. We have traveled more than a hundred *milhas* without looking at hair-lines on paper, and we are here without mishap. Let us see now what your charts can do for us."

"Oh, very well," he smiled. "You fellows can grin all you want to at me and my maps, but if I don't set you spank on the Jundiatyba I'll lie down and let you kick me hard. The little old Jundiatyba will float us clear to the Amazon, if we want to go that far. No more boat-hauling after we're in it."

And he opened his map-case, glanced over a chart, measured a line with a fingernail, watched the flow of the Tecuahy a minute, and then told us that after four hours of easy paddling down-stream. we should find a creek opening on the east shore. There we should leave the river and head for the sources of the river Capacete.

We nodded; for we knew, though we had not told him so, that a creek did flow into the Tecuahy at the place of which he spoke. With no questions, we shoved off and slid away down the current.

Yet we did not reach the mouth of that creek in four hours, for we tarried nearly an hour at a lonely hut where we found a launch tied up to take aboard more wood for fuel.

It was the regular boat from Iquitos, Peru, which goes up the Tecuahy once a month to carry supplies to the few *seringales* scattered along its two-hundred-mile banks, and the little clearing where it had stopped was one of its usual places for getting wood.

Its crew and the old man who sold the fuel were the first men we had seen since leaving our own river, and naturally we wanted to talk — or rather to listen to their talk, since we had no intention of telling all the world what we planned to do.

We were asked, of course, what we did there, and I said we had been out on a rubber-scouting trip. This was perfectly true; we had been on such a trip — before the *coronel* sent us eastward.

When we were asked where we had been and what we had found, we only laughed and looked wise, so our questioners believed our tale and believed also that we had discovered something too good to tell about.

Then, like men fresh from the back-bush, we asked for any news of affairs down the river, and got what we wanted — a warning against Black Hawk.

It would be well, the boatmen said, for us to sleep on the western bank until we reached the Javary. The man called *Caracara-i* was somewhere in the jungle east of the river, and one could not tell what he might do. Certainly the North American *senhor* with us would be likely to die if Black Hawk met us, unless he could pay well for his life.

No, they did not know whether the *cafuzo* was near this river now; he might be many miles away; but the report was that he was not near Viciado, so he must be somewhere farther back.

When we pretended ignorance of Black Hawk, we heard almost the same tale the *coronel* had told us. All the big river was talking of him, the boatmen said, but nobody seemed to do anything but talk. Little was known now of what went on at the town of Viciado, for the Amazon steamers had stopped calling there.

The latest report — that Black Hawk now was away — had been brought by a man of Viciado who, with his woman, had fled upriver in a canoe because they dared not stay there longer.

The news that the big river-boats had quit stopping at Viciado made us ask why. We got an answer that made us scowl. Black Hawk was greedy for women. And the last steamer to call at Viciado had among its passengers an Englishman with a pretty daughter, who had insisted on going ashore to walk about the town. They disappeared as if the earth had swallowed them.

Before the boat went onward, its men searched the place so thoroughly that it seemed even a rat could not have evaded them. But no sign of the missing foreigners could be found, nor could any one who would admit knowing about them.

So the steamers stopped there no more, and the word was given out that until the people of the upper river produced either the missing pair or those who had made away with them, Viciado could remain cut off from the world. Not even the small trading-boats of the river would call there now.

The man and the woman who had recently deserted the place by canoe could not, or would not, tell what had happened to the English couple, we heard. They said they were both dead drunk at the time and knew nothing of the matter. Besides, they were such a lying worthless pair that even if they should happen to tell the truth nobody would know whether to believe it.

As we could learn no more, we resumed our paddling. For awhile we said nothing. Then *Senhor* Tom spoke in a hard, cold tone.

"I'm getting right interested in this Black Hawk. If we meet him I wouldn't be a danged bit surprized if something dropped."

"We are with you in that, *senhor,*" said Pedro, his voice even. "An Englishman more or less is nothing to me, but a foul black brute that steals white girls must die."

"Yet, to give the devil his due," I said, "there is no proof that Black Hawk had any hand in this affair. Judging from what I hear, the men of Viciado are not the kind to be trusted at the backs of a prosperous-looking stranger and a handsome young woman. It is quite possible that they know much more about the fate of those two than does Black Hawk himself."

"Oh, that Viciado bunch is only a pack of curs," scoffed the North American.

"Yet even a pack of curs is brave enough to jump at the back of an unsuspecting man," I persisted.

"True," he admitted. "All the same, I opine that Black Hawk ought to be rubbed out on general principles How do you vote on that proposition?"

"With you," I said.

And we paddled on in silence.

In the hot blaze of noonday we reached our creek and turned into its cool shade. And at sunset, after a forest journey which seemed easy after our work on the other side of the river, we camped on the western shore of a northward-flowing stream which our explorer-guide said was the Capacete.

"So far, so good," said *Senhor* Tom. "We never fell off the hair-line once, did we, Pedro? And tomorrow we'll be better off than we are to-day — we have two hairs to crawl on instead of one. Which will you have?"

He passed the map to us, but we could make little of it.

"All hairs look alike to me," said Pedro. "Choose your own, and we will try to creep along it."

"Oh, very well. We'll take this wabbly hair with knobs on it — the knobs being lagoons, if you want to know. For the next couple of days we have to twist around like drunken mud-worms, but after that we can straighten out and go somewhere."

He spoke truth. In following that wabbly hair with knobs on it we traveled in every direction known, except up into the treetops. The little stream was hardly more than a thread, and it wound all around itself in going from one lagoon to another. Yet it held water enough to float us along, and two days later we came out into a broad creek full of sunlight.

As we entered it Pedro held up a hand.

Out from the thick growth beyond us rose a clear, sweet song like the voice of a girl ringing out in wordless happiness. The tone changed smoothly into notes so like those of a flute that it seemed as if some one had taken the song from the lips of the girl and was pouring it from a musical instrument. Then came some long, slow, mellow tones as if a new song were beginning — and silence.

We listened, but heard it no more. Nothing but the harsh squawk of some distant parrots and the buzz of near-by mosquitoes came to us.

"*Realejo* — the organ-bird," Pedro explained.

"Right. I've heard it before," said the explorer. "And we now are on the Jundiatyba. This is its head. A clear trail now to the land of Black Hawk. Let's go."

But he did not dip his paddle at once. He looked across, sober-faced, at the place where that -girlish bird-voice had sung. Watching, I read his thought. Not long ago, before ever she saw Viciado, that young white girl on the steamer perhaps had sung as joyously and sweetly as the songster of the forest. And now —

V

WITH the seventy-league Jundiatyba flowing free under us, and the way to Black Hawk's nest open ahead, we became more bold and more cautious both at once. From sunrise until nearly sundown we paddled with long regular swing and with no attempt at concealment, ready to give fight to any one who wanted it. But at night we took pains to hide our camps and mask our fires.

The stream soon widened from a creek into a river of respectable depth, wandering on between the usual bush-grown banks and inhabited by numbers of birds which more than once made us cease paddling a moment and hold the blades ready for a blow.

They were those diving birds called snake-necks, which feed under water for a time and then suddenly shoot slender wriggling necks up for more than a foot above the surface, looking so much like snakes that at first sight a boatman can not see what they really are.

There were real snakes too in that water, and between them and the birds the upper part of the river seemed a little too reptilian to be pleasant. Yet no harm came to us, and for days we drove on toward the Amazon without seeing sign of man.

Then, up a little side-stream, we found Indians.

Late on a sweltering day, when we were looking along the shores for a good place to hide and make camp, we saw at the right a ravine which looked promising. Arriving there, we found that water ran a little way into it from the river and stopped. And at the farther end of the little cove, partly hidden under drooping brush, lay two canoes. From, these a little path led up the ravine.

We stood a minute looking along the valley, which now was dry but which in the flood season would be a deep *ygarapé*. It was the right place for an Indian settlement, and the fact that only two canoes lay there showed that it must be small.

"I think we had best visit these people," I said. "We are not yet near Black Hawk's headquarters, and Indians dwelling in such a quiet spot as this probably will be friendly. Let us see."

But we did not have to go to the settlement to find whether its people were sociable. As we pulled our bow up on shore a man appeared from behind a tree where he had been watching us.

Calmly he stepped down and stood near, looking at each of us in turn. And though I never before had been on this river, I recognized his tribe and knew we should be welcome. His skin was not dark, but a light red-brown; and on his face was tattooed a large square blue patch. He was a Passé.

The Passés are perhaps the highest type of Indians to be found in our upper Amazon country. Old men who could remember far back and who also carried in memory the talk of their fathers, have told me that once the Passés were a big, powerful tribe who controlled the river-lands from the Rio Negro to Peru.

Now they are few, and those few live usually in small settlements hidden in the bush along the smaller rivers, where they can be at peace and raise crops on their plantations. Always they have been friends to white men. And the pity of it is, *senhor*, that this friendliness has been their ruin.

One reason for this, I have heard, was that their women were handsome. White men coming into this wild country, having no women of their own race, took the shapely Passé girls for their wives, and so the number of mothers among the villages of that tribe steadily grew fewer.

Nor was that all. The children too were lured away from their homes to become servants of the big-river whites, and when they grew up they mated with white men or with *mestiços* of other Indian races. So the blood of the Passés slowly died out.

But this mingling of their blood with that of others was not the only cause of the passing of the Passés. Much more deadly to them was a disease brought upon them by the white men the *defluxo.*

To us Brazilians, *defluxo* is only a cold in the head; but to the Passés it is death. Where we should merely blow our noses and sneeze a few days and then be rid of our cold, the Passés get a slow fever which becomes *tisica* — consumption. And a queer thing is that these people often catch the disease from whites who themselves have no sign of a cold or other ailment. The very air around a white visitor to their settlements seems to hold death for them.

Yet the friendship of the Passés lasts to the end. Knowing that the white man is their doom, they still give welcome to him — even if he shows by red eyes and running nose that he brings the fatal disease.

If we whites found that Indians coming among us brought a plague we should drive them out, and if they still came we probably should shoot them on sight. But the Passés raise no hand against us. They only ask of visitors whether they bring the disease.

So it was now. The tall, middle-aged Indian looked us in the eyes and then spoke gravely in the Tupi *lengoa geral.*

"Do you bring *defluxo?* "

"No," I answered. "No *defluxo* rides in our canoe."

"It is well. Do you come to visit us?"

"We go to the great river. We are glad to meet our friends the Passés."

He nodded politely, turned back to the tree, and picked up a couple of good-sized fish. Then he walked before us up the ravine, and as he went he explained why he had taken cover on seeing us. He had been fishing from the bank, and with the sun in his eyes he could not at first tell whether we were *Cariwa camarah* or *Tapanyuh uyukahn* — friendly whites or a black enemy.

When he spoke of a black enemy we glanced at one another, but we said nothing at the time. We trailed behind him as he went on up the narrow valley and climbed its right side into a cleared space. There we found a couple of shed-like shelters and several small mud-walled houses, behind which lay a fair-sized plantation of mandioca, melons, corn and cane.

In that garden field a number of figures were moving about, and at a fire under one of the shelters a couple of women were busy cooking. The smoke drifted lazily away in the slanting sunshine, and from some bush beyond the houses rang the loud, cheerful notes of a musical *tanana* cricket tuning up for his night-song.

"A little idyl of content," said *Senhor* Tom.

And though we did not know just what sort of thing an idyl might be, we nodded; for to our jungle-weary eyes the peaceful little opening in the forest seemed filled with simple trust and faith and friendliness.

Up to the cooking-fires went our host to give the fish to the women. One of these was plump and no longer young, but far from bad-looking. The other was a slender maiden who gazed shyly at us from great dark eyes and then dropped her head.

To them the man said a few words which I did not catch, but which evidently told them we were friends; for the older woman smiled frankly at us and then began to talk so fast that I could make nothing of it.

When she stopped for breath I told her and the others that our names were Thomaz, Pedro, and Lourenço. In return we learned that the tall man's name was Lontra, meaning "Otter;" that the maiden was Merere, which in Tupi means "Arrow;" and that the talkative woman was called Itariapu. This last made us grin, for *itariapu* means a place where water comes rushing noisily over rocks — a rapid. And when she saw our smiles she started talking more rapidly than before.

The tall Otter grunted; and we followed him into another hut, leaving the woman still pouring out words. As we walked I saw Pedro glance back and smile, so I also looked back. As I expected, the girl was looking after my handsome comrade. She smiled too, then lowered her rosy face again to her work.

"Careful, Pedro!" I muttered. "Arrows are dangerous."

"But not fatal unless they strike the heart," he said.

Then we entered the house of the Otter. And there the rest of the little tribe came to meet us and give us respectful welcome.

In all they numbered not more than twenty, and none was old. About half of them were children, and of the five men living there only one was past thirty — a long, lean, silent Indian who was the brother of Lontra but did not appear to have Lontra's wiry strength.

By far the best-looking man of the lot was a straight, lithe young fellow with deep eyes who moved with the easy grace of a cat, and whose name fitted him well — Jawuah, or "Jaguar." I looked from him to Pedro, and from Pedro back at him, and it was hard to decide which of the two was the more manly in appearance. Jawuah himself gazed with interest at my comrade and then gave him a friendly smile.

There was not much talk at first. All stood or squatted around while the Otter poured gourds of a reddish liquor from a big clay jar and handed them to us, afterward motioning to a couple of hammocks in which

Senhor Tom and I sat down. Pedro remained standing while he drank some of the liquor from his gourd and then passed it to Jawuah.

The Jaguar took it, drained it, and laughed. And all the others, watching the two tall young fellows drink from the same gourd, broke out into laughing chatter and eyed my comrade approvingly. Pedro grinned back at them, then leaned against a roof-post and made a cigaret.

"Go on and start the palaver, Lourenço," said *Senhor* Tom. "I can talk the Tupi lingo all right, but you're probably more used to it than I."

So, seeing that Lontra was chief here, I began a talk with him.

"The family of the Otter is young and strong. I see no old or sick."

"The old are gone to their fathers. The *defluxo* took them," he explained.

"Better the *defluxo* than the hand of an enemy. Who is the black enemy who would harm the Otter?"

"No enemy will harm the Otter. The Otter knows how to dodge the hawk."

"The enemy then is a hawk? A black hawk?"

"It is so. *Caracara-i.* May he choke and fall dead on the dirt."

"Why should the hawk strike at the otter? They do not hunt on the same ground."

"True. But this Black Hawk of the north hunts young otters."

"She-otters?"

"It is so. He destroys the young shes. So the Otter must watch and hide the young from his evil claws."

"This Black Hawk has been here?"

"Not yet. But the word of him has gone through the forest, and in time he will come — he or his smaller hawks."

"So. And the Otter then will hide the young she-otters from his sight? Why does not the Otter kill him?"

Lontra frowned. It was not a fair question, and he gave me the answer I deserved.

"How?" he demanded. "We are few. We have no guns. *Caracara-i* has guns and many men. He rules the land. He drives the whites, who also have guns, into the great river.

"Once the Passés were great, and then they would have squashed this creature like a bug. Now they are weak, and soon they will be no more. Why do not the white men, who have taken the strength from the Passés, kill this Black Hawk instead of running from him? Have the white men too lost their strength?"

"No!" I denied. "They have only begun to notice this Black Hawk and to wonder what sort of creature he is. If any man tells the Otter that *Caracara-i* rules this land and drives white men into the river, that man speaks with a split tongue. Black Hawk is only a small bird who thinks himself great, and those who follow him are fools. Before long the white men will shoot him out of his tree."

Lontra looked me straight in the eyes, and I looked straight back at him. After a minute he turned his gaze to *Senhor* Tom. The North American nodded. He threw his rifle over his shoulder, aimed upward as if at a bird, let the gun sink, and moved his hand downward with a fluttering motion; then bent, reached as if picking a dead thing off the ground, and waved his hand aside with a sneer on his face.

Every eye watched him. And when he sat back, an approving growl broke from Jawuah. For the moment the Indians almost believed they had seen the white man kill the Black Hawk.

I did some thinking. These Passés hated Black Hawk. There must be other Passés in this Jundiatyba country. Perhaps the Tucunas also were not all under the control of the *cafuzo* who thought himself king. An idea began to grow in my head.

"Who follows *Caracara-i*?" I asked "Passés?"

"No Passés. Tucunas. We Passés always have been the white man's friends, and we join no enemy of the white man."

"And why is the hand of the Tucunas turned against the whites? What have the whites done to them?"

"Nothing. But they are told that soon many white men will come here to cut down the trees and make all this land a great plantation, on which the Tucunas must work as slaved or be beaten to death. But if they join together under Black Hawk they can drive out the whites who now are here and scare away those who intend to come here. So the land will be safe for them to live in as they always have lived."

"They are fools!" I repeated. "Such talk is lying talk. The white men do not want this land of flood and mud. But if the Tucunas make war on the whites, then the whites will fight back, and in the end the foolish Tucunas will be killed. Who told the Otter this tale?"

"A pair of Tucunas."

"Men of the Hawk?"

"I do not know. But they warned us to hide our young women from *Caracara-i*. They said many Tucunas hid their daughters from him."

His eyes traveled to one of the girls as he spoke. I saw that she was Metere, the shy young Arrow, who had stolen in to hear what was said. And I saw also that the lithe Jawuah was looking at her with sober gaze. My idea grew swiftly.

"So the Tucunas themselves dare not trust their leader. Again I say they are fools to follow him. When he becomes great and rules all, who shall be safe? He can hunt down all the young women, and the man who would defend his own daughter will be killed — or worse. Will you let Merere here be dragged away to please that foul brute for a week and then be murdered?"

Terror flashed into the face of Merere. Again a growl came from the men — a hoarse rumble of anger. At once I went on.

"You can save her and many other girls. The Tucunas and the Passés are friends, is it not so?"

"It is so."

"Then go among them and tell them the truth that we tell you; that the white man wishes them no harm, and that Black Hawk is a liar and their worst enemy. He grows great only because no man opposes him. By the time the white men make up their minds to destroy him he will be stronger — and your own young women may be his victims. Now is the time to act.

"We are the first white men to come against the Hawk. We go to learn what we can of him, so that the other white men outside may know. Will the Passés help us? Will the Otter and the Jaguar go with us to spread the truth among the Indians? Or will they hide here like scared monkeys in a hollow tree?"

Lontra and Jawuah looked at each other. They looked at Merere and at the other young girls. Slowly their faces flamed. And as one man they promised —

"We will go!"

VI

INTO the middle of our conference came Itariapu, talking so loudly that we had to turn to her. She had remained at her cooking work until she lost her temper — probably because there was nobody to talk to — and now she demanded help from every young one in the place. The girls went slowly to the fire, where we heard her still clattering on so fast that nobody had a chance to tell her what had been decided on.

We were quite as well satisfied to have the women out of the way, though I noticed again that young Jawuah's eyes followed the winsome maid Merere. When they were gone we again filled our gourds with the red *cauim* and drank success to ourselves and ruin to Black Hawk. Then we asked Lontra whether he had heard anything of a white man and a white girl who had come up the great river in one of the big fire-canoes and disappeared at Viciado.

He had not. He never went down to the big river, he said, and all he knew of matters outside his little home was what he heard from other Passés not many miles away. None of his neighbors had spoken of such a thing.

So then we asked about those other Passés of whom he spoke, and learned that they numbered perhaps thirty or forty. Besides these there were a few small tribes of the same dying race scattered around in various nooks between the Javary and the Jutahy, but altogether they probably would not total more than fifty or sixty men of fighting age. The Otter admitted this sadly, as if mourning the fact that his nation could not prove its friendship by bringing many spears and bows to back the whites.

But we told him his help and that of the other Passés in opening the eyes of the Tucunas to the truth would be worth far more than weapons of war, besides saving the lives of many who otherwise would perish. I took care to repeat over and over that the white men now had no enmity toward the Tucunas and that they would have none in future unless the Indians showed themselves to be foes; but that when the whites did strike they would strike hard, and the innocent must pay with the guilty. This was the most important thing to put into the ears of any Tucunas willing to listen, and I made sure that Lontra got it fixed firmly in mind.

Then we had to stop talking and eat, for Itariapu had prepared the night meal to suit herself and now insisted that all attend to the feast while everything was tasty. We were not sorry to do so, for our appetites were strong and the meal very good.

As the water now was low, the Indians had captured their yearly supply of turtles, and we were served with *sarapatel* — turtle soup boiled in the upper shell of the dead reptile — and sweet, tender turtle steaks cut from the breast.

There were also iguana eggs, eaten raw with *farinha* and salt, which Pedro and I liked well enough, though *Senhor* Tom did not relish them because they were too oily for his taste. Besides these we had large portions of the *acari* fish caught by the Otter, plenty of bananas, and all the *cauim* we cared to drink.

Itariapu fussed around us while we ate, so anxious to make sure we visitors had plenty that she became rather tiresome. She need not have worried about Pedro, for he was attended every minute by Merere, who took care that he got good portions of everything on the mats. If Jawuah noticed this he gave no sign of it. Indeed, he gave no sign of anything but hunger, shoveling away with both hands until I began to wonder where he put all his food.

By the time the meal was over, night had come, and the children soon were sent to bed in the mud-walled houses. The rest of us sat or squatted in the open shelter where we had eaten; we three travelers smoking and sipping more *cauim,* the Passé men talking among themselves, the young women watching us and smiling whenever they caught our eyes, and Itariapu — as usual — talking to everybody.

Just as I was beginning to pity Lontra for having to live with a woman whose tongue clattered so much, he turned calmly to her.

"Be still," he said.

The words were spoken so quietly that we hardly heard them. But the woman stopped as if hit by a club. I wasted no more pity on the Otter. He was master in his own house.

"The Otter and the Jaguar alone will go to carry the word," Lontra told us. "The brother of the Otter and his sons stay here to protect the young and the women. When the Otter and the Jaguar tell the Passés that they have looked into the eyes of the white men and seen there the light of truth, the Passés then will carry on the word from one to another and to the Tucunas also. So the number who hear shall grow wide, though only two speak at first."

"It is well," I answered. "The young otters and their mothers must be kept safe, and the tongues of the Otter and the Jaguar need no help to speak the truth. Where does Lontra go first?"

"Down the river to the town where are more Passés than here. The canoe of the white men shall go with ours. Then the Otter will turn aside into the Ypihah Aku — Warm Creek — to a place where dwell others. Do you go straight to the great river?"

"We go on until we find the place of Black Hawk, though we know not where that is."

Lontra nodded, his eyes on our rifles leaning against posts.

"The Otter does not know where *Caracara-i* can be found," he said, "but others may know."

And with that he stopped talking of Black Hawk and poured more *cauim.* We all drank again.

After that he began telling a tale of nearly being bitten by a snake. Jawuah followed with a story of killing with a spear a black jaguar which had sprung at him from a tree — and proved it by bringing in the hide of the creature and showing the spear-hole in it. Then Pedro, who had said hardly anything since we came, told of our experiences on the Creek of Death, describing them so well that all the Indians leaned forward with eyes wide.

Other tales followed as our tongues grew loose from the mild but mellow liquor. Even *Senhor* Tom told a story or two in the Tupi tongue, the Passés nodding gravely whenever he paused, and following his words with close attention.

To them, buried so far back in the bush that they saw few even of their own people, it was a wonderful evening when three white men stayed among them and told of things elsewhere. If we had not grown sleepy I believe they would gladly have stayed awake all night to listen to us.

But at length we yawned so often that we had to stop talking. Then Lontra offered us his own house for the night. But we told him we would rather sleep where we were, in the open shed, with a fire beside us. So, though he protested that the hammocks there were old, and that some evil might come to us if we slept outside walls, that was what we did.

A fire was laid and lit and piled high with slow-burning wood. The women took the little nut-oil lamps and went to the huts. The silent brother and nephews of Lontra followed. Only the Otter and the Jaguar remained — and Merere, who looked often at Pedro.

"Pedro, take your little lady friend around the corner and kiss her good night," said *Senhor* Tom. "That's what she's waiting for."

"Perhaps I would, *senhor,*" Pedro smiled, "But I think she is the Jaguar's girl, and I like the Jaguar." .

"Brother and sister, you boob!"

"No. He is the chief's son, and she is daughter to the chief's brother, I think. Cousins."

But then, still smiling, he spoke to the girl, wishing her pleasant dreams and calling her *hereui* — sister. She laughed very prettily, making no answer with her lips — though her big dark eyes said much.

At once my comrade turned to Jawuah, wished him also peaceful rest, and called him *hereneh* — brother. The tall fellow, who had looked rather sober again, smiled slightly and strode away toward the houses, the girl following. Lontra looked after them with eyes twinkling. Then, with no more words, he left us.

"Neatly done, old chap," said the North American. "She's a lovable little thing, if you ask me. But we have serious business ahead and no time for flirtations. Besides, we need the Jaguar in our business. And I have to hand it to you, Lourenço, for thinking up this scheme of starting a backfire against Black Hawk. It may make a big difference in the end."

"Perhaps so, *senhor,*" I said. "Or perhaps not. It was worth trying, so I tried it. And now, if that *cauim* is not all gone, let us have one more good gourdful and sleep."

The liquor was not all gone. We helped ourselves and lay down. And if any danger was near us in the night it did not disturb us. After my eyes closed I knew no more until day lay bright around us.

Then, with another hearty meal under our belts, we picked up our guns and said we were ready. For once we were not troubled by the talk of Itariapu, who was very quiet and often looked anxiously at her man, the chief.

Merere too lingered near us, unsmiling. Yet the girl seemed not so much concerned about her kinsman Jawuah as about Pedro's leaving, for she watched my comrade and gave the Jaguar hardly a glance.

As before, Jawuah gave little sign that he noticed this or cared. But Pedro, after looking from one to the other, muttered —

"I must say good-by to the maid — and see to it that she understands that it is good-by."

So, when we started for the canoe, he spoke to her.

"Farewell, little Arrow. We take with us our brother the Jaguar, but he will return soon to you. We do not return. A happy life to you, and a good man, and many handsome sons."

For a long minute she stood looking steadily at him. Then she answered, speaking soft and low.

"*Camarah - ikuana Tupana cirum.* Friend — go with God."

When we reached the top of the bank and turned to look back before dropping into the ravine she still stood there beside the hammocks we had left, and somehow she looked lonely and wistful. And as we went down the path in the gully I pondered on the fact that she had used the old form of farewell taught by the Jesuit missionaries, and that instead of giving Pedro the usual name of *Cariwa* (white man) she had called him *camarah* — friend. It was plain that Jawuah had not gained by our visit.

But that could not be helped, and nothing was said. At the water's edge we three spent a little time arranging our supplies in a way that suited us better, the Otter and the Jaguar meanwhile waiting patiently. Then we got aboard and pushed out into the river.

In the middle of the sluggish stream the two Indians turned their eyes back toward their homes. Only the screen of riverside bush and the narrow mouth of the dry creek were in sight. But all at once their faces showed sudden dread.

Puzzled, we looked at them and at the ravine. Then, listening, we knew what caused their dismay. Thinly from the direction of the clearing sounded a whining wail.

It was not the weeping of a woman or the cry of a child. It was worse. Into the tiny town which we had left, another visitor now had come, and from some tree close beside the huts it was pouring out its weird plaint; the black bird *caracara-i*, herald of death.

VII

WHILE we listened to that bird of evil omen the current was carrying us away, and soon the sound died out behind us.

"Let us go back and kill that infernal thing," I said.

But Pedro felt otherwise.

"It would do little good," he objected. "The death-message still would stay in the minds of the Indians. Worse yet, if these two should go back the women would beg them not to leave again, and they might decide to stay there and defend the others against the death which they would expect to come, whether we shot the bird or not. Then your plan of sending the word among the other Indians would be dead, unless you found others to do it."

"What's more," added *Senhor* Tom, "we might not bag the cussed bird after all. It might fly off, or we might miss our shot. Then these chaps sure would think the Black Hawk had the better of us. Now that we've made a start, let's go."

With which he resumed paddling. We sank our own blades in the water. Lontra and Jawuah, though with troubled faces, pushed on downstream with us.

"The Black Hawk is late," I said with a grin, trying to cheer them. "We were away and about our business before it woke up. Unless it shows more speed hereafter we shall soon have it hanging by the feet for the monkeys to jeer at."

But their faces remained solemn, and Lontra spoke the thing which I knew must be in his mind.

"The *caracara-i* spoke not to us but to those we leave behind. Death comes to the young otters."

"Death might come to them if the Otter did nothing to stop it, but already the Otter has gotten ahead of it," I retorted. "From the Black Hawk neither the Otter nor his people have anything to fear — it is too slow, and now it can only sit and whine because it knows its own death is not far off.

"Is not Lontra the head of his family? Does not every messenger, good or bad, talk to the head of the tribe? Of course. Then why did not the *caracara-i* speak before we left? Because it is a coward and a liar, and it waited until the Otter had left the land before it dared fly to the Otter's place and open its sniveling mouth. Death comes, yes. But it comes to the Black Hawk itself, and well the whining creature knows it."

This gave the Passé pair another side of the matter to think about, and though my argument was a poor one it seemed to comfort them. They still looked serious, but they stroked more heartily than before, and no more was said. Soon they pushed their canoe ahead of ours.

"Give them a race, comrades, and let them win," suggested Pedro. "It will take the trouble out of their minds."

Then to the Passés he added in Tupi —

"My brothers are strong paddlers, but we shall beat them to the next turn."

Jawuah grinned slowly and heaved hard. Lontra at once took up the challenge. We made a great show of desperate efforts to pass them, and it was not all pretense; for the Passé pair were born canoemen and well muscled, and we had to let ourselves out in order to make it look like a race.

By the time we reached the bend both dugouts were flying, and the Indians were on edge with excitement. Then, having beaten us with plenty of room to spare, they laughed like a couple of big boys. For the time, at least, their dread of the Black Hawk was gone.

For some hours we journeyed on at good speed, cheering up the Indians with another race whenever they seemed to be growing too serious. Then they slowed and swung toward a creek-mouth on the west shore.

"Ypihah Aku," said the Otter. "Warm Creek."

Their canoe drifted easily down to the entrance, went on inland, and kept going. We followed. Unlike the dry ravine leading to the town of the Otter, this little valley held a good depth of gently flowing water, and the village of the Passés living there was farther from the river.

As we paddled on up the stream we could see and feel why it was called warm, it ran nearly straight east and west, the trees did not interlock overhead, and the sunlight fell into it all day; so the air and the water both were heated.

For perhaps half a mile we kept on before reaching the town. Nowhere along the stream did we see or hear any human life. And even when we reached the clearing where the village stood we heard no children shouting or other noise of a town. For a moment we thought some disaster might have fallen on the place.

But then, after climbing the bank and looking about, we saw that plenty of people were there, even though quiet. At an open shelter, like the one where we had slept last night, a crowd was gathered, listening to some talk going on inside. And when we walked over to join the crowd we found that other visitors had arrived before us.

The Passés, with words of greeting to the Otter and the Jaguar and friendly smiles at us, opened a way into the center of their circle. There we found an old, very thin Passé who seemed to be chief, and five Indians who certainly were not Passés.

After one glance at them *Senhor* Tom grunted.

"Tucunas," he said.

Pedro and I looked with interest at the men of the tribe backing Black Hawk. They were not so much unlike the Passés as we had expected. Indeed, they resembled the Passés much more than the usual Indian type; for their skins were rather light, their mouths small, their lips thin and noses high. But they were thicker of body than the slim Passés, they lacked the dignity of Jawuah and Lontra, and their face-tattooing was much different; a number of straight lines instead of a square patch.

More important to us than these bodily differences, however, was the variance in their expressions and manners. They looked sullen, and instead of the friendly smiles and murmured greetings of the Warm Creek people, they gave us cold, slow stares. Yet their gaze was not hostile, even when they looked into the blue eyes of the North American.

"For once I do not know whether I am among friends or enemies," Pedro said, studying those five faces. "They might be either."

"Exactly," nodded *Senhor* Tom. "It runs in the Tucuna blood. They're not so loyal as most Indians. Mostly they're friendly enough toward whites, but they can change color without much difficulty."

"So much the better for us," I pointed out. "If they can turn against us they can also turn against Black Hawk."

Then the Otter began talking to the thin chief of Warm Creek, and all listened intently. Without any waste of words he told that we came into this country to learn more of Black Hawk; that we said the Hawk was a liar and those who followed him were fools; that the white men outside wished no harm to Passés or Tucunas, did not intend to make slaves of them as *caracara-i* said, and would not trouble them in any way unless forced to; but that if the men of this jungle made war on them they would come with many guns and sweep the land from end to end.

"The Passés and the white men always have been friends," he went on. "Never has war come between us. Many of the daughters of the Passés have blended their blood with that of the whites, and many of the whites who now live along the great river carry in their hearts the blood of the Passés. Now at the last, when the Passé nation fades into the grave, the brotherhood of Passé and white shall still hold strong and true. Uituh Aku — Warm Wind — has the Otter spoken well?"

"Well!" agreed Warm Wind.

And from all the Passés round about us sounded hearty approval. But the Tucunas said no word.

"Do the whites ask our help?" Warm Wind added.

Before Lontra could answer *Senhor* Tom spoke up.

"The whites ask no help. We can fight our own fight, if fighting must be. We ask only that the Passés carry the words of truth to one another and give no aid to that evil Black Hawk who feasts on women."

A rumble went around. Old Warm Wind answered:

"We give no aid to that one. The white man need not have asked."

"Warm Wind speaks truly," I broke in. "We know the hands of our brothers the Passés never will be lifted against us. Yet here are Tucunas. We hear that the Tucunas are men of Black Hawk. Why are the men of the Hawk in the town of our friends?"

The old chief let the Tucunas make their own reply. One of them, more muscular than the others, looked me boldly in the face as he spoke.

"We are no men of Black Hawk. We are no men of the whites. We are our own masters. We visit our friends the Passés."

"It is well," I answered. "We are glad to find Tucunas too wise to follow *Caracara-i*. Why do other Tucunas believe the lies of that creature and support him?"

"How do we know they are lies?" he retorted. "The Tucunas have known white men who spoke with a split tongue. They have known whites who robbed the men of the forest. How do we know you speak truth?"

Again *Senhor* Tom spoke first. He stepped forward, his face hard, his eyes gleaming, his blond beard bristling, his voice fierce.

"Take care, Tucuna! Say that again and I will twist your nose! I am Tupahn! Tupahn, who journeyed on the Jutahy and knows the Tucunas well. Did any Tucuna ever say Tupahn spoke lies?"

The bold-eyed Tucuna flinched under the American's glare. His mates glanced at one another as if the name Tupahn meant something to them. To me and to the Passés it meant only "thunder-storm," for that word is part of the Tupi language. But the five visitors now looked at him with respect.

"We have heard of Tupahn," one of them said. "No man has said the Thunderstorm talks falsely."

"And no man will be wise to say so," *Senhor* Tom declared, his voice booming now like the thunder whose name he carried. "I, Tupahn, say to you that the words you have heard from the Otter are truth. I say to you that the Tucunas who follow Black Hawk bring death on themselves.

"And nor only on themselves but on you and on all other Tucunas. When a great army of my white comrades pours in here with guns and knives, how shall they know who has been friend or foe? They can not know. So they will punish all."

The five looked at one another again, uneasily this time.

"There is yet time for the Tucunas to save themselves," the blond man went on. "Let them leave the Hawk and go to their homes and drink and dance in safety. Was there war and murder and girl-ruin here before Black Hawk poured his lies into the ears of the Tucunas? No. And there will be none after the Tucunas leave him. We white men will attend to him. The Tucunas will be at peace as before.

"Go tell your brothers the truth, and you save their lives and your own. Then the great white chiefs who live at the end of the great river shall hear that the Tucunas still are their friends, and so they will not turn the guns upon them. I, Tupahn, will tell them."

Once more the five looked around them; looked at us, at Lontra and Jawuah, at Warm Wind and the people of the Warm Creek. They muttered among themselves, glancing up now and then at *Senhor* Tom. And more than once we caught the words —

"Tupahn tells truth."

At length they nodded in agreement. The one who had done most of the talking spoke up in a tone of decision.

"We believe the words of Tupahn. It is true that the young women of the Tucunas were safe until *Caracara-i* came among us, and that now they are not safe. That is why we who are here have not followed that man. There are others like us. The Tucunas want peace and pleasure, not war. If Tupahn will tell the great white chiefs we still are friends, we shall talk to our brothers."

"Tupahn has spoken. What Tupahn says he will do, that he does. Now if our brother Warm Wind has *cauim,* let us drink to the peace and pleasure of the Passés and the Tucunas."

The eyes of the Tucunas glowed at the word cauim, and they glowed still more when the red drink came by the gourdful. But we did not purpose to spend the day there in drinking. So, after the Otter and the Jaguar and Warm Wind had talked among themselves for a while, we three told the rest we now would go on toward Black Hawk's roost, and asked whether any one went down-stream with us.

"The Tucunas said nothing and looked thirsty. But when Warm Wind said that eight men from his town would start at once to spread the word, and Lontra and Jawuah added that they would go with us some hours farther, the visitors saw that the chance of an all-day drinking match was gone. So they said they would go with us to a side-stream where they would find other Tucunas. And soon we turned our backs on the Warm Creek people, and paddled away toward the river, leaving behind us eight men preparing to travel the bush, and followed by the canoes of the Otter and the Tucunas.

At the mouth of the sunlit stream we paused and asked the Tucunas where the Hawk now was. They said he was somewhere lower down the river. Then we asked where his usual camp was, and were told they did not know, except that it was not many days away from Viciado. They never had been there, they said. This convinced us that they told truth when they said they were not men of *caracara-i*. So we asked about only one more matter.

"What has become of the white man and the white girl who were caught at Viciada?" I demanded.

"The man is dead."

"Dead? How?"

"Killed."

"And the girl?"

"No man knows."

"Black Hawk had her?"

"So we have heard."

"And she now is gone?"

"Gone."

We shoved away down-stream.

VIII

FOR a while we paddled in silence. As before, the two Passés led the way. We made no more show of racing, with them, but swung along at our usual cruising speed. Behind us came the two canoes of the Tucunas.

"*Senhor* Thunder-storm, how did you earn your name?" Pedro asked after a time.

The blond man, who had been plying his blade with an angry sort of punch, lifted his head as if bringing his thoughts back from some other place.

"Oh, by roaring at a Tucuna gang I had for a while. Tucunas mostly are slow movers, except when a boozing bout is on. Then they're fast workers. So when I wanted to throw a little pep into them I'd start rip-roaring around until I had them on the hop.

"The way to handle Tucunas is to treat 'em rough — only not too rough. Bawl 'em out, but don't give them the boot. Notice how quick they began to pull in their horns after I let loose my stand-out-from-under voice? Maybe you thought they were scared, but it wasn't that exactly. They just woke up to the fact that there was a boss in the place."

"Yet it was not your voice alone that moved them. They had heard other things of you."

"Oh well, I always treated my men square, of course. Paid them well and kept my word. An Indian might forgive you for killing his brother or swiping his squaw, but never for breaking your promise. And besides, I saved one chap's life after he got snake-bitten, and they appreciate little things like that. Looks as if my square-deal policy might pay dividends now."

"It is as you say, *senhor*," I agreed. "An Indian has a long memory. These Tucunas told truth when they said some white men lied and robbed them, for more than one *aviador* — roving trader — is a sneaking cheat. So if you had not been known here as honest we now should lack at least five of the fifteen men who are working for us. And these five are the most important."

"They are unless somebody side-tracks them with a jug of rum. But before we part I'll try to impress them again with the seriousness of matters. We need all the missionaries we can get, and then some."

Remembering the eagerness of the Tucunas to drink Warm Wind's liquor, and their slowness in leaving it, I could easily believe that they might tarry in any place where drink was free. But, drunk or sober, they would not be likely to forget to talk about us, and the word we gave them would spread as any news always does among Indians — slowly, perhaps, but steadily, as ripples on water go on and on until they reach the farthest shore.

And, thinking of this, I thought also of another thing; that now we had started the message to traveling, we must give it time to travel. So I spoke my thought to *Senhor* Tom and Pedro.

The North American scowled, but slowly nodded.

"You're right, I suppose," he admitted. "If we outrun our back-fire it won't do us much good. But, dang it —"

He broke off and chewed his mustache.

"I understand, *senhor*," I said. "You want to drive ahead and close with the Hawk before he does more harm. And you feel that by haste we might help that white girl in some way. But I fear we come far too late to do her any good. It has been some time since she and her father were caught, and whatever has happened to her is now over; she has disappeared, and no doubt she is dead.

"And since all the Amazon boats now avoid Viciado, there is little chance that any other whites will fall into the clutches of *Caracara-i* for some time to come. So neither we nor any one else will gain by our rushing ahead in impatience."

"Unless Black Hawk himself gains by it," added Pedro. "And that is not what we desire."

Senhor Tom paddled on for a few minutes before replying.

"Yes, you're right," he conceded then. "I'm in too much of a hurry. Usually am. Patience isn't my long suit. You fellows are the bosses on this expedition anyhow, so run the show your own way. What'll we do? Lie up somewhere while our word travels?"

"Not at all," I dissented. "We can not depend too much on the value of our message to the Tucunas, and we must do our own work. But we have almost forgotten our orders. We have grown to feel that we are here to hunt down this Black Hawk and kill him. The *coronel's* instructions were only to learn all we could, and not, as he said, to 'set ourselves into a fine fight.'

"So let us try first to find the camp of the *cafuzo,* scout around it, and find out all we can about it and about him. If we can smash him before we leave, so much the better. But our first duty is to get information that will help our *coronel* and carry it out to him."

"In other words, keep out of the hawk's claws until we can clip his wings for good," the blond man agreed. "That's sense. A scouting expedition has to watch its step if it's going to deliver the goods. All the same, here's hoping for a good crack at that black stinker."

To this we grunted agreement. Then we gave all our attention to paddling and watching the shores and the stream ahead.

A couple of hours later our Passé friends left us. At a place where a long point ran out into the river they said they now would go inland to talk with another tribe of their own people whose creek had dried up like their own; and from there They would make visits to other villages until they were sure the word had been carried to all the Passés and to neighboring Tucunas as well. So we paddled with them to the point, and said farewell.

"Always, Cariwa, the hand, of the Passés is joined with the hand of the white man," said the Otter, standing straight and dignified at the edge of the water, and speaking to *Senhor* Tom.

"The great white chiefs shall hear the words of the Otter," the blond man promised. "And when the Otter has gone to his fathers the white man will be the friend of the Jaguar and the Arrow and the others of the Otter people. Go with God."

"Ikuana Tupana cirum," the Jaguar answered, his eyes on Pedro. Then, as we moved on, they turned their faces to the forest.

For another hour or two the Tucunas trailed silently behind. At length they drove their canoes up to ours, and the man who had done the talking pointed to a knoll on the left bank, on which a giant *massaranduba* tree towered high above the rest of the forest growth.

"Tupahn, we go," he said.

Senhor Tom nodded, and we swung over toward the knoll, thinking an Indian village might be on it. But none was there. Instead, an inlet of water opened below the knoll, and into this the Tucuna dugouts turned.

The muscular spokesman said the inlet became a curving lagoon, at the farther end of which was a Tucuna town. He did not ask us to go to that town, and we did not care about visiting the place, as the sun now was sinking and we would rather sleep in a secret camp of our own. So there the five left us.

Before they went, however, *Senhor* Tom talked solemnly to them, declaring once more that unless the Tucunas came to their senses and deserted *Caracara-i* a terrible punishment would come upon them.

He also told them we had no time to go about warning all the Tucunas — we had other work to do; so it rested with them to spread the message, and if they failed theirs would be the blame for the deaths of many men later on. They made no answer, gave no word or other sign. But there was no doubt that they were impressed. Their faces and eyes showed that.

With no word of farewell they pushed their boats away and faded from sight around a turn in the channel. We squinted at the sun, dug our paddles in deep, and sped away down the Jundiatyba seeking a good camping-place.

Once more our canoe was alone on the river, driving on toward the Hawk's foul nest. The bush on both sides looked as empty of human life as before. But now in that bush men were moving out to east and west, carrying along hidden creek and dry ravine a message that would creep onward until it reached the ears of every jungle-man between the Javary and the Jutahy.

When we had found a snug little port and were resting in our hammocks under a palm-leaf *tambo*, *Senhor* Tom chuckled.

"Funny, when you come to think of it," he said. "Here we three chaps come breezing in here bold as brass, and start to knock the props out from under the jungle emperor before he gets his throne well warmed up. I don't know how big a following he's got, but it must be big enough to gobble us at one bite if it caught us. And yet, without even pulling a gun, we've begun to eat up his army. All done by spilling a few words in the right place."

"Yet that is how begot his army, *senhor*," said Pedro. "By words — lying words — he has drawn the Tucunas around him. After all, it is only the old fight between truth and falsehood. And truth always wins."

"In the end, yes. But a lie always gets off to a flying start, and sometimes it takes the truth an awful while to catch up. All the same, we've given old Lady Truth a pretty good getaway. Yesterday noon nobody around these parts would give her a boost, and now she's riding around on the tongues of at least fifteen men. By tomorrow night the number will be doubled. And if it doubles every day for two weeks it'll be — let's see, now."

He dug a pencil and a small note-book out of a shirt-pocket and went to work. In a few minutes he whistled.

"More than a hundred and twenty thousand! Judas, that's impossible, even if the figures do say so. Anyway, a lot of folks in this neck of the woods will be doing some tall thinking within a fortnight. Lourenço, you sure have started something. I hope all the people who are going to be worried over your talk to the Passés won't walk over your chest in dreams tonight. If they do you'll be trampled flat before morning."

I grinned, yawned, and said no dreams would trouble me. Yet after I slept I did dream. The things that passed through my mind that night were not such as *Senhor* Tom had joked about, but they made me awake in the darkness and wonder over them before sleeping again.

In that dream I walked through a dim forest of great trees until I came to slow-moving black water across which no fallen tree or other bridge lay. Up along the shore of this I went until the wide rounded trough of the stream pinched together into two steep hills, between which the creek flowed out through a narrow ravine. As I stood looking at it, from some place beyond sounded the whining cry of the black hawk *caracara-i*.

I hated that sound, and I climbed one of the hills and went on, hunting for the odious bird. Then I found myself in an open space, and there I saw two living things; a shriveled old woman, and, high overhead, a monstrous black hawk.

The hawk was not perched in a tree-top as usual, but sweeping around far up in the air, pouring out its wretched call as it wheeled, and watching the ground. The old woman looked up at it and shook her skinny hands in rage. And as I watched she began to scream:

"Come here and I will burn you! Come down and I will burn you!"

But the hawk did not come down. It kept on sweeping around. And it was so huge that though it was far above I could see its claws working as it flew, opening and closing like the fists of a man furious but afraid.

Then while I stood there like a fool, forgetting that I had a gun, another thing came floating and flitting across the open space — a great butterfly.

It was one of those splendid big insects, with glossy wings of dark blue and purple, which one often sees here on the upper Amazon; but it was much larger than any I ever had seen, and its wide wings flashed in the sunlight like gleams of blue fire. It swung around me a few times and then came to rest on my shoulder.

And as I looked up again at the hawk a voice spoke in my ear — a voice low but tuneful and vibrant as the strings of a guitar.

"Kill the hawk!" it said. "Kill quickly, or it will tear you apart!"

I turned my head to look at the talking butterfly, and saw that now it had the face of a beautiful girl with eyes so darkly blue that they seemed almost black. Before I could notice more, the red lips moved and the voice came again, quick and urgent.

"The hawk comes! Shoot!"

It was true. The huge hawk was swooping toward me. I threw up my gun and shot swift and straight. The bird swerved, screeched, then went flapping crazily away. And then all at once the place became full of peccaries — grunting, squealing animals which clashed their teeth and rushed around as if seeking something to rip to death. And the beasts had the faces of Tucunas.

The girl-butterfly darted out over the heads of the jungle pigs and disappeared. The old woman shrieked, the hawk's whining wail became a piercing whistle, and somewhere in the bush near me the shouts and shots of battling men broke out.

THEN all at once the whole scene blurred and faded. I found myself in my hammock.

Around me was the peace of a moonlit night. Somewhere far out in the forest a *guariba* monkey was howling at the moon, and beside me both my comrades were gently snoring, Pedro with soft gurgles and *Senhor* Tom with a tiny whistling noise. Outside our little *tambo* the deep shadows were splashed with silvery light, and among them moved nothing dangerous.

For some time I lay looking out, enjoying the damp coolness and thinking about what I had just heard and seen in my sleep. Then I told myself that it all came from hearing the night noises of the bush and the sounds of sleeping men. So I changed my position, closed my eyes, and soon drifted away again into rest.

But the time was not far off when I was to think more of that dream.

IX

FOR days after that we cruised on toward the Amazon. In those days we met no danger except a couple of sudden thunder-squalls which lashed the river into waves that gave us hard paddling to avoid upset. Of animals we saw little, and of men nothing at all.

Yet, though we spied no men, we knew well that we probably were seen. There are always eyes in the bush, and any wandering hunter or fisherman along either shore could not have failed to observe our canoe sliding down the water. But since nobody menaced us, we gave little attention to the creek-mouths which we passed each day.

On the morning after my queer dream I told my comrades of it. *Senhor* Tom laughed and advised me to plug my ears before going to sleep, and I threatened to put a split stick on his nose to stop his whistling snore.

But Pedro, though he too laughed, showed much interest in my story and asked many questions about it. And when I had told him everything I could remember he drank more coffee in an absent way and then sat puffing his cigaret as thoughtfully as if I had really seen those things instead of imagining them.

"Come out of it, Pedro!" *Senhor* Tom jeered. "Don't sit there in a clairvoyant trance. You don't believe in dreams, do you? That's old-woman stuff."

"Perhaps so, *senhor*," my partner said coolly. "Most dreams are foolishness. Yet I have known of dreams which meant something, and this one of Lourenço's is strange enough to be worth thinking about. That butterfly of yours, Lourenço — was her face that of an Indian girl or a white?"

"White," I told him. "I can not remember it well now, but it was not the face of any one I ever saw. It was not that of Merere, if that is what you mean."

He grinned, and *Senhor* Tom snickered. Then the American made more fun of him.

"If you're a dream-reader, translate this one. I had a most gosh-awful dream last night. I was a monkey, away up in a high tree, hanging off a branch by my tail and making faces at you down on the ground. After awhile I got tired of it and tried to get hold of the branch with my hind paws, but I couldn't make it.

"While I was scrambling around, my tail broke plumb off — made a noise just like a man tearing his pants, too — and I fell about three miles and landed kerplunk in the mud. Then I woke up and found I had rolled out of my hammock. Now what do you make of that?"

"That is easy, *Senhor* Tom," Pedro told him. "It means: Do not make a monkey of yourself."

The blond man blinked. Then he laughed.

"You win," he said. "I won't make any more faces at you. Come on, let's go."

And we left the camp for another day of paddling.

In the next few days Pedro spoke several times of that dream of mine, and *Senhor* Tom made fun of both of us. Then we said no more of it, for new work came up in our journey toward Black Hawk's lair. For the first time we learned how to reach the place we sought.

It was an old Tucuna who told us. Rounding a bend in the river, we saw him and a couple of small boys in a canoe moving slowly along in shallow water near shore, spearing fish. The two boys were using the paddles, while the old man stood at the bow with weapon ready.

Just as we came into sight he stabbed a good-sized fish and threw it into the dugout, and for a few minutes the three were so intent on their catch that they did not notice us. One of the boys spied us then, and the old man turned with the spear held as if he meant to throw it. But after a look at us he lowered it.

"Good day, *heramuhm* — grandfather," I greeted him. "Your spear is strong and your eye keen, but you do not need the spear for us. We are friends."

He looked at me so long that I thought he would not answer. But then he spoke, calling me *auah uhnyah* — young man — and asking where I journeyed.

"Where should any man journey on a stream flowing into the great river?" I asked in return.

He thought this over, and then said we were in a bad country for white men. If we would reach the great river safely, he told us, we must hasten and beware of all whom we met. If *Caracara-i* caught us we should die.

From his way of speaking we could see he had no hostility toward us and no love for Black Hawk. So I said we had no fear of the evil *cafuzo,* and that before long there would be no Black Hawk here. He asked what I meant.

"We white men are tired of Black Hawk's actions," I declared. "He has lived too long. He is a liar and a woman-destroyer. We hear that even the Tucunas, who once were our friends but now help our enemy, must hide their daughters from him. If the Tucunas were the men we have always thought them they would make an end of him. But since they will not, we must do it.

"You know the way of the white man, *heramuhm* — slow to move sometimes, but deadly in war. Soon we shall strike to kill. I hope your young men are not with that vile creature. If so, they die with him. Have you not heard the word which now travels the bush — that the Tucunas must leave *caracara-i* if they would save their lives?"

In his deliberate way he let my talk sink into his mind before replying. He said then that he had heard no word. I told him that soon he would hear it, and from the mouths of his own people. He looked at me with troubled gaze, then stared down the river.

"The young men are fools and will not listen to their elders," he said after a while. "I, who have been out on the great river and worked for the whites before I grew old and slow, have told our young men that we must lift no hand against them.

"But the black man has put a spell on them and made their ears deaf to sense. in my village now are no young men. All are with *caracara-i*. My heart is heavy for them. It would grow light again if that black one died before the white guns came here."

"The white guns are here now," I replied, lifting my rifle. "They do not seek the lives of the Tucunas. But our grandfather's heart might grow light even as he says, if these guns could find the Hawk's nest."

His eyes fixed on my big-bored weapon, and in them came a hard gleam.

"If the guns would find that nest let them go on until the sun once more stands in the middle of the sky," he told us. "Then let them go into an *ygarapé* on the right hand where stands a twisted *mandiroba* tree. Two days more toward the place where the sun comes up will bring them to slow black water crawling from the north. Up the black water is the place where *Caracara-i* sleeps."

"We shall remember," I promised. "And when we go out we shall tell our comrades that the young men of the Tucunas are held by the evil eye of the Hawk, and when that eye is shut they will again be friends of the white man. Perhaps that eye will shut before we reach the great river."

With that we passed on, leaving him staring solemnly after us.

"Tomorrow noon turn east into a creek marked by a twisted tree," *Senhor* Tom repeated. "Then two days east, up a black stream from the north — Hm! Must be hills in there, or the black water would run to the Amazon. Let's see."

He laid down his paddle and dug into his map-case. After a silent study of some papers he went on:

"Creek opens off this river about where he said. No hills shown there, though, and neither is the black-water stream. But we'll find them if they exist. Looks as if we were closing in on our *cafuzo.*"

The next noon we found the twisted *mandiroba* on the east shore. Beside it opened the *ygarapé* of which the old Tucuna had told. And into this we went, alert for any sign of foes.

Yet we traveled on eastward until sundown without meeting any man. Around us only the usual noises of the bush sounded, and nowhere along the sloping shores could we see even the mark of a human foot or of a canoe-bow. Nor did anything disturb our rest that night.

On the following day we traveled onward in the same way and with the same result.

The *ygarapé* wound along for mile after mile, broadened into a long weedy lagoon, narrowed again, and continued on as before. Over it hung the same feeling of loneliness, on its banks was the same lack of human signs.

Here and there along the way other streams flowed into it, and some were of dark water; but not one of them was large enough to make a by-path for canoes. We made our camp that night up one of those brooks which was wide enough to float our dugout, and well screened by undergrowth. When we had eaten we looked at one another with the same thought in our minds.

"It's all wrong," said *Senhor* Tom. "We're supposed to be closing in on a young army, but there's no trace. This place not only looks empty — it feels empty. No sign of anything or anybody. I suspect that old fisherman was an angel-faced liar, sending us off here on a wild-goose chase. Why? To get us bottled up, maybe, and then nail us from behind. What do you think?"

"I can hardly believe that," I disagreed. "I think he spoke the truth. When he said 'two days more' he must have meant two full days, from noon to noon. That would not bring us to the black-water stream until tomorrow noon. Yet I do not understand why we have seen no sign that men use this waterway."

"Nor I," Pedro admitted. "But I feel that we are on the right trail. Something tells me that tomorrow we shall find something beyond here."

"If we don't I'm going all the way back to give that old son-of-a-gun an earful," growled the blond man. "And I'll make him cough up the straight dope or wring his skinny neck. Meanwhile let's put our dreamers to work. Lourenço, see if you can't have a good one tonight. And if your butterfly lady lights on your shoulder again, grab her and hold her until you wake up. I'd like to see her."

But my butterfly girl did not visit any of us that night, nor any other dream. In the morning we ate in silence and moved on with a feeling that somehow we had gone astray since leaving the river.

This feeling, however, quickly left us. Only a little way beyond our hiding-place we spied what we had been looking for all the time; an old camp. Marks of canoes and many feet showed on the left bank, partly washed out by rains; and up at the top the bush was beaten down and cut away. We did not go up to inspect the place, for the blurred tracks in the clay showed that some time had passed since the men had stayed there. Now that we knew this creek had been used by a large body of men, we pushed on carefully.

Noon passed, and still we had not found the black water nor any more sign. But we had moved slowly, and so we felt quite sure the stream from the north was beyond us. This proved true. About two hours later Pedro hissed softly and pointed ahead with his paddle. A few more quiet strokes brought us to the mouth of black water flowing sluggishly in from the left.

There we hung in the *ygarapé* a little while, squinting up the shadowy lane and listening. Nothing moved, no sound came. We turned and went up the dark water toward Black Hawk's abode.

Sunset was near again when we checked our paddles. Just ahead of us the light was much brighter, and we knew an opening in the trees was there. Very slowly we worked around one more turn. Then the quiet stream widened, and we looked down a good-sized lake.

The lake lay in a bowl of hills. On its west side, perhaps half a mile away, smoke rose from the top of a hill higher than the others. Its sides were steep and so thinly wooded that we knew it had been cleared of all bush by fire and steel. But of the men on its top we could see nothing, for the heads of the trees still standing on the slopes hid them from us. We could judge their number only by the size of the smoke and the number of canoes floating at the base of the hill.

"Hm!" muttered *Senhor* Tom. "Where's all that big army? If there are more than enough to make three squads up there I'm cock-eyed. Only a handful of canoes in sight, and only enough fire to cook grub for twenty men."

We looked around at the other hills, but saw no more smoke. Nor did we find any more boats. Except for that one place the lake seemed deserted. Then Pedro guessed what we soon learned was the truth.

"We have found the Hawk's nest, but not the Hawk himself. He is away."

X

NIGHT came before we moved.

We could not go back and camp in a cove or up some side stream, as usual, because on that last stretch we had seen no break in the steep banks for an hour or more before reaching the lake; and of course we did not wish to make any marks on the clay slopes themselves to show we had been there.

Nor could we push out into the lake until darkness hid us from any eye on that hill. So we stayed where we were, screened behind thin undergrowth, until the sun dropped from sight. Meanwhile we studied the whole lake.

"There seems to be a narrow *enseada* down on the east shore," Pedro pointed out. "No doubt we can find a good spot there for our hammocks. And since we can make no fire tonight, we may as well eat now while we wait."

So, keeping watch both ahead and behind, we made a meal from our salt fish and *chibeh,* and even smoked our usual cigarets — though we did not throw our butts away after smoking; we touched the coals to the water and dropped the dead stubs into our pockets, to keep until we could tread them into the mud where they would never be seen.

By the time we had finished with them the sun was touching the edge of the western hills, and soon afterward we were creeping out on a lake of darkness.

After some slow paddling we floated into the narrow bay Pedro had picked, and down this we journeyed until we began to wonder where it would end. We could see very little around us, for the gloom was thick. Up on the shores it was so black that we decided to wait for moonrise before trying to find a place to sleep. We had not long to wait, and when the moon did sail up we changed our minds about staying there.

The bay was more than a bay; it was another creek. By the new light we saw that we were almost at the end of the *enseada* itself, but that from its tip the new creek stretched on eastward, wider and probably deeper than the one up which we had come. While we studied it *Senhor* Tom made a suggestion.

"Say, fellows," he said softly, "why not spend another hour or two cruising alongshore on the lake and getting the lay of the land? Keep away from the inhabited hill for tonight, but find out what's what elsewhere. This place doesn't look very good for a camp anyhow."

So we turned and went back, hugging the shore. Before reaching the lake we met a thing that made our trigger-fingers itch.

It was a jaguar drinking at the water's edge. We were very near before Pedro saw it and backed water. The creature lifted its head with a fierce snarl, and by the size of its blazing eyes we knew it must be a powerful animal. For a few seconds I thought it would jump at us. But, though it growled and we could hear its tail switch about in the leaves, it did not leap. Quietly we backed until out of reach.

"You old son-of-a-gun!" *Senhor* Tom muttered. "I'd give a dollar to slam a soft-nose right between those yellow moons of yours. But we're after bigger game than bush-cats. Go chase your tail!"

The jungle king did not understand him, of course, but after another minute of growling it hushed, and its eyes vanished. We made an outward loop before returning to the shore-line, and we saw the great cat no more.

"Perhaps it was as well that we did not land there in the dark," Pedro remarked. "There might have been some noise."

Then we rounded the point into the lake.

Still keeping close to land, we rowed along to the other end of the open water. Two short coves dented the shore-line, and we found that one of these curved around so that its end could not be seen from the outside. This we picked for our sleeping-spot. But we did not stop there then.

We kept on until we found at the north end a third creek, larger than either of the other two. There we halted, for the hill where the canoes lay was not far from us, and from it came noises that showed the men there were awake. Indeed, the shouts up there sounded as if all were getting drunk.

Back along the shore we traveled and around to the end of the curving cove. There we found firm ground and places to hang our nets. And there we smoked again and talked in low tones.

"Easy enough now to see why we found so little sign along our way in here," said *Senhor* Tom. "We came in by the back door. These other two creeks are bigger and better, and one runs north — toward Viciado,/ most likely — and the other east toward more thickly settled country. So they're used and the back way isn't, except by men coming in from up the Jundiatyba. The old boy up-stream told us the quickest route, and I hereby apologize to him for threatening to wring his neck."

"He has served us well," I agreed. "But now I would give much to know where Black Hawk is and when he will return."

"He is not expected to come back at once," said Pedro, "or those men on the hill would not be holding a drunken revel tonight. Now would be a good time for us to go and spy on their camp."

"Tomorrow would be better," I objected. "We can see much better by day. And I am tired."

"Me too," yawned *Senhor* Tom. "I'm going to pound my ear right now. See you in the morning, gents."

And he lay back and slept. So did we.

Darkness was still around us when Pedro's hand on my arm woke me. But it was the darkness just before dawn, and the noise of birds to the east told me that above the trees the light was coming.

"Let us move," said Pedro. "We ought to scout around that hill, and if we are to do it we must cross to the other shore before the mists rise. After that we can not move the canoe without being seen. Come."

"I am going to have some hot coffee first," I told him. "There will be plenty of time. That gang on the hill will sleep off the liquor before they can see anything."

So we made a small fire and had a hot breakfast — the last warm meal we were to have for some time to come. By the time it was finished the light was strong, but the morning fog still hung heavy on the water. We could see nothing a canoe-length away, but we knew just where the hill stood, and in our first careful study of the lake we had noted that between that hill and the small southern creek was a little bay. We planned to strike this and to hide our canoe there.

While Pedro and I were putting the hammocks into the boat, we heard a sharp click. As we turned toward *Senhor* Tom we found him sheathing his revolver. An instant later he snatched it out again, pulled trigger at a tree-trunk, jammed it back into the holster. Several times he did this. And he never moved the gun farther than his hip.

"Just practising hip-shot," he explained when we asked him what he was trying to do. "Gun's rusty, and so's my draw. Got to limber them both up. Might want to work fast sometime soon."

"Can you hit anything with your hand at your side?" I doubted.

"Can I? Well, here goes your right eye."

The weapon jumped from his leg again. It did not click this time, but 1 dodged. The big muzzle was looking me in the face.

"I believe you," I said. "Point it somewhere else."

He chuckled, swung out the cylinder, reloaded it, snapped it shut and holstered it.

"I'm slow on the draw, though," he grumbled. "Got to pick up speed. If I couldn't do any better than that in some places up home — the Big Bend in Texas, for one — I'd be dead six times before I got the gun out. Those boys shoot from both hips and the collar."

To us his speed in drawing the weapon seemed unbeatable, but he still worked his fingers as if they were lame. And when he picked up his paddle he scowled at it.

"That's what does it," he complained. "Hooking your hands around a paddle all day leaves your muscles stiff. Hereafter Mister Mack gives his hands a little set-up work twice a day. Not that a fifth of a second is likely to matter much down here, but you never can tell. Many a man has died because the other fellow-shaded him by a hair."

"And many a man has delayed too long in starting a journey," Pedro reminded both of us. "The fog will lift soon. If we are to cross this lake today —"

"Right! Let's go."

And we shoved away to the mouth of the inlet.

We moved none too soon. Before we were half-way across the lake the mists moved and grew streaky, and we put more power into our strokes to reach the other side in time. When we slipped into the small bay the sun had thinned the fog to a haze which would not have hidden even a bird. And while we looked around us for a spot where we could conceal the canoe the haze vanished and broad day lit up the water.

The banks of the bay were too steep to give our dugout any hiding-place, but at the farther end a small stream came in from a gently curving hollow between sloping hills. It was wide enough to give us good passage, and well screened by small drooping palms. We slid into it and found ourselves once more in gloom.

"So far, so good," said *Senhor* Tom. "Plenty of streams in and out of this lake. This one shows no sign of use either. Now to find a crack for the boat to lie in."

We soon found one — a tiny arm of water under the palms — and pushed into it. Then, leaving everything but our weapons, we began threading the bush toward the stronghold of the man who ruled this jungle.

As we went we noticed that this part of the forest was little trodden. Though the Hawk's hill was hardly more than a good gunshot away, and though many men must be there at times, we found hardly a human footprint in the cool depths of the virgin jungle through which we passed. The ground was a succession of knolls, all heavily timbered but not thick with undergrowth, between which ran clear, cold little brooks.

Here and there the sunlight fell hot through the branches, and in these warm spots bright butterflies fluttered about in pretty play. A man passing through that place without knowing of the sinister hill ahead would never suspect that danger was near.

But if he had walked with us that morning he would have realized the danger with sickening suddenness. For as we came out of that peaceful forest and looked up the side of the cleared hill, we stumbled over human bones.

They lay scattered around just as the vultures had left them, and among them we counted three skulls. They had been there for some time; some were partly covered by dry mud, and the rest were spattered with dirt splashed on them by rains. It was easy to see that the three bodies had been rolled and kicked down the slope as the easiest way to get them out of the camp. And I much doubted that they had been Indians.

"Do the Tucunas bury their dead?" I whispered.

The explorer nodded and whispered back:

"Chiefs are buried in big clay jars under their houses. Don't know whether common men get jars too, but I think they do. Anyway, they're buried."

After a searching look along the slope we gazed down again at the bones. Pedro pointed at a leg-bone, then at an arm-bone; then at another leg-bone. All had been broken. And as we glanced at others we found more broken ones.

"A slow death," he said. "Comrades, those men were broken up *pouco a pouco* — bit by bit. Your hawk is a cruel bird."

Our blond companion growled and his blue eyes glittered. Looking at him, I left unsaid the thing that came into my mind — that those bones might be those of women, not men. Neither did I think it well to speak of the Englishman and his daughter.

The thing I did say was that we could do nobody any good by standing there, and that we had best move on at once. Even as I muttered this there came to our nostrils a faint odor of wood-smoke, telling us that some of the men above us were awake and cooking breakfast.

We had reached the hill at a place well back from the water, and on the slope before us no path was visible from where we stood. The trees still growing on the hillside were few and too widely scattered to give any real cover, but we began crawling upward without seeking a place where the concealment might be better. From tree to tree we worked, pausing behind each butt - to watch and listen, until we had mounted to the upper edge.

There, hugging a charred stump big enough to hide all three of us, we gazed upon the camp of Black Hawk.

XI

BEFORE us stretched a long, fairly wide plateau on which stood a few huge trees, many stumps, and a straggling array of small huts.

The little shelters were only roofs of palm-leaves supported by poles or by the stumps left after clearing the ground, and they showed no orderly arrangement, seeming to stand wherever each builder happened to feel like putting up his roof. Most of these, as we could easily see, were empty.

But off to our right, near the bold front of the hill, about a dozen Tucunas were grouped around a couple of small fires, and in a number of the huts nearest them others were still lying in hammocks. So far as we could see, these were the only men in the camp.

Those who were awake were eating or squatting stupidly around the fires. None was talking, and all acted sluggish, as if still half drunk with the liquor swallowed last night.

"Tucunas who have come in to join Black Hawk but arrived after he left," Pedro guessed. "They have found liquor — or brought it with them — and are waiting for him to return."

"If they're drinking up the Hawk's private stock there'll be trouble for somebody when he comes back," muttered *Senhor* Tom. "But that's their own lookout. Let's move farther along."

Letting ourselves down until we were below the level of the edge, we worked away along the slope toward the rear of the place. Then we rose to the top and looked around again, saw nothing new, and stole downward once more. Repeating this move, we kept on until noon, when we had gone almost around the encampment and seen all that was worth while.

Then we retreated into the rolling ground through which we had come after leaving our canoe. The last we saw of the Tucunas showed them still loafing where we had first found them, taking a drink now and then from clay jars, and ignorant that other men were near them.

We had found that the flat top of the hill ran back westward for a long distance from the lake — how far we did not know, for we kept at the edge of the camp. Only enough ground had been cleared to make room for the closely crowded huts; and beyond these the forest still stood.

Through this untouched back-jungle ran a broad path, probably used by hunting-parties when the Hawk's gang was here. On the northern side the hill dropped much more steeply than where we had come up, and at the bottom on that side was marshland.

The place would be easy enough to attack, if men enough could be brought in to rush it from the rear and the southern side. But it would take a big force to do that, for we judged from the number of crude shelters that the Hawk's followers must number at least three hundred — probably more.

We had also found Black Hawk's foul nest. Not far from the spot where the Tucunas lounged, under a big tree, stood a low but long house with walls of woven withes — the only walled shelter in the town. Around it was a clear space, and on each side of its one low dark doorway were signs showing beyond doubt whose house it was: black wings of the bird *caracara-i*, pinned to the walls by thorns.

We had watched that house for some time, thinking perhaps some woman left behind by the *cafuzo* might show herself. But none appeared. Either the last woman to be kept captive there had been taken away with the gang or — more likely — she had been killed when her master tired of her. The house was empty.

Whether any more bones lay along the base of the hill we did not know, for we made no search there; but it was more than likely that others could have been found without much hunting. And though we did not return to the canoe by the same route and thus did not see those broken bones again, we had not forgotten them.

Our North American comrade's face was more grim than at any time since we left the river. And Pedro and I, once more squatting in our dugout and chewing our dry fish and farinha, looked at each other and said no word.

When *Senhor* Tom did speak, though, it was not of what had happened but of the future.

"Well, what next?" was his question.

Pedro still said nothing, but looked at the little stream flowing past the end of the canoe. It was black water.

"Let us find out more about the country on this side of the hill," I said. "There is not much use in our trying to explore the two large creeks to the north and east, at least not now. We know of one way into this lake — the way we came from the Jundiatyba; and that is enough for our purpose.

"When we go out perhaps we can go by the northern stream and see where it leads. But now, since this day is half gone, we can use it best by going up this little black water and perhaps finding a better camping-place."

Pedro nodded. But *Senhor* Tom looked toward the south.

"I'm more curious to look around between here and the little creek down south," he remarked. "Tell you what — let's split up. I'll spend the afternoon browsing around in the bush. You fellows take the canoe up-stream.

"If you find a good place, make camp. Come back here for me a little before sundown. You can't go very far on this little creek with the dugout, anyhow, so you won't have to travel far coming back. How about it?"

I objected to parting company with him, even though Black Hawk now was absent. But he snorted.

"Think I'll get lost? I'm no greenhorn in the bush. And there's no danger from those Tucunas yonder. They're too lazy to come prowling down here — as long as the booze holds out, anyway. If they did I'd scare them to death with my thunderstorm voice."

Pedro smiled, Then a queer light passed over his face, as if a sudden thought had come to him. I waited for him to speak. But all he said was:

"I want to see more of this stream, senior. So Lourenço and I will go up it and meet you later, just as you say. Will you take your maps, so that you can find this spot again?"

And he laughed.

"Humph! I've half a mind to bat you over the head for that. But the maps would be no good anyhow — this place isn't charted. If you fellows don't find me here when you come back, use that wonderful instinct your *coronel* bragged about and find me. You couldn't possibly miss me."

"Not as long as you wear boots," I retorted. "We could track your heels anywhere."

He grinned, but made no answer. We pushed the canoe out from its hiding-place, set him on the other shore, and watched him fade into the wilderness of big trees and creepers beyond. When he was gone we paddled slowly up the sober-colored stream.

It curved gradually around to the right, swung off to the left for perhaps fifty yards, and then became a fairly straight waterway leading back into the farther bush. The shores on both sides shelved upward at a gentle grade, and both were heavily grown with good-sized trees and dense smaller stuff.

The only openings we saw were low runways used by animals, and nowhere along it were any signs of men. Several good camping-spots were scattered along it, but we passed them by while we looked farther on.

After a time we reached a fallen tree which blocked our boat like a wall. Only the top of the tree was in the water, but its branches made an obstacle past which no canoe could go. Beyond it, however, the forest seemed quite clear of bush. So, having plenty of time, we pushed our craft up to the right shore, got out, walked under the big tree-trunk — held up off the ground by stout limbs — and stole on up the black-water stream.

Around us the forest was dim, cool, and quiet. Among the big tree-columns we passed for some distance, still finding only the traces of beasts and birds. At length I paused and said we might as well go back. But Pedro, looking ahead, said he was going farther.

"I am much interested in this creek and these woods," he said. "We may as well move on as go back and wait for the North American."

And he went ahead. I followed.

We had left the water, or rather it had left us; for it rambled off to the left, while we went straight on, expecting to find it looping back before long. Now we did find it again, and with it we found something else — a couple of empty banana-skins caught among weeds at a little curve.

Pedro pointed at them. We went onward more carefully, hunting now for the person who had eaten that fruit.

A little farther on the smoothly rolling valley which we had been following came to an end. Hills rose steep before us. Between them the stream lay at the bottom of a cleft gouged out by the weight of floodwaters in the wet season.

Somehow the spot looked familiar. But in my years of bush-roving I had seen such places more than once, and I gave no thought to it, for I knew I never had been here before. I only wondered whether the banana-eater lived beyond that ravine.

The question soon was answered. Silently we climbed the hill before us and passed on along the upper edge of the cleft. Then the ground lowered a little, the trees thinned, and we looked into a shallow bowl through which the little creek trickled lazily. In this bowl grew a few banana-trees, some peach-palms, mandioca, and corn. And working in the corn were two women.

I stood watching them in astonishment. And I was surprised not so much by seeing women as by the fact that they were clothed. Indian women of the bush, such as I was accustomed to seeing, wear only a *tanga* around the hips. But these two were covered from shoulders to knees by loose wrappers. Yet their brown skins showed them to be Indians.

Looking around for their house, I saw none. Still, a score of huts might be hidden among the big trees surrounding the place. The smallness of the corn-patch, though, showed that very few people could be living near.

Pedro coughed. He tried to smother the sound, but the women heard it. They jumped like frightened deer, whirling to face us after their first leap. We stepped out into plain sight, holding up our hands as signs of friendship, and advanced toward them.

They backed away, but did not run. One stopped and stood waiting, her head forward, and face wrinkled into a squint. The other kept retreating.

"Have no fear," I said in Tupi. "We come as friends, and our hearts are clean."

No answer came. Reaching the first one, we halted. Though we now were within six feet of her, the squinting wrinkles and frown remained on her face. They were wrinkles that never would fade until death took her. She was old.

For a few minutes we stood quiet, letting her look us over and glancing at the other, who now had stopped at some distance from us. In spite of her shapeless garment we could see that she was much younger than the woman near us, and she looked quite handsome. But we made no move to go toward her. Turning my eyes again to the old woman, I found her staring intently into our faces.

"We are friends, mother," I repeated. "Where are your men?"

She squinted at me for some time before answering. Then she began to mumble. No men were allowed here. This was the home of the *Mai d'Agoa* — Mother of Water. Any man coming here would be swallowed alive by the great snake unless he went away at once.

Yes, and she could put on us a curse that would turn our guns into worms and our bones into water, so that we could not run away when the great serpent came for us. She could burn us, too — burn us without fire. She could do other terrible things. Unless we left instantly she would do all of them.

By the time she was through with her threats I knew what she was — a mad old *feiticeira,* or witch. So I did not laugh at her. I told her to keep her snake and her fire and her curse to use against an evil bird which surely would carry off her handsome daughter if he ever saw her; the black *caracara-i* which lived on the hill by the lake.

If I had called her a crazy fool and other insulting names she could not have flown into a greater fury. Her old eyes blazed like those of a maddened cat. She spat like a cat, too, and her bony fingers worked like claws, Then she burst into curses of *Caracara-i.*

She used such language as I had never before heard from an Indian woman — talk that could only come from insane hatred, and words which no maiden ought to hear. It made me feel uncomfortable, and I glanced toward the younger woman to see whether she was still standing there and listening to the other's ravings. Then I felt better. She had moved on and disappeared among the trees.

The old woman paused a minute to catch her breath. Then, shaking her clenched hands at the air, she screamed:

"I will burn you! Come here, *Caracara-i,* and I will burn you!"

"If he comes here he is more likely to burn you," I started to say, but the words stuck on my tongue.

All at once there came over me again that queer feeling that I had been here before, and now even the words of the old woman seemed to be the same ones I had heard when I last visited this place. Without thinking why, I looked up into the air, half expecting to see there a huge hawk sweeping around.

Pedro chuckled.

"He has not yet come, Lourenço," he said, "but he may come soon. Now show me your beautiful butterfly. Do you know where you are? This is the place of your dream."

XII

I STARED around, unable to believe it. I had forgotten that dream, and Pedro had not spoken of it since we left the Jundiatyba. But he remembered it well, as his words proved.

"Through a dim forest of big trees to hills between which black water flows," he reminded me. "Over the hill to an open space where an old woman shrieks at the black hawk. That is how we have journeyed today, and this is the place. Now I am on fire to see the lovely white girl rest on your shoulder. You love the ladies so well that you surely will not omit that part."

"I am no lady-lover, and well you know it," I growled, still looking around and feeling queer.

He chuckled again. Then he asked the old woman a surprizing question.

"Where is the white girl?"

She drew her face into a tighter squint and peered at him as if wondering whether she heard right.

"Come, mother," he coaxed, "tell us. Soon we and other white men will destroy *Caracara-i*. But first let us take the white girl to a safer place. Where is she?"

Slowly the wrinkled face spread in a cunning grin.

"Kill *Caracara-i* first," she said. "Show me his head. Then ask for a white girl."

"Why do you want his head?" I asked. "What has he done to you?"

The grin disappeared and her face twisted in new fury. Again she cursed Black Hawk. Then, growing somewhat more quiet, she talked in a rapid, rambling way, saying some things which meant nothing to us along with other things which were fairly clear.

By listening and putting together what we could understand, we made out that she had lived long in this place before Black Hawk came; that before he made his camp on the hill by the lake a few Indians had had their homes there, all of whom were related to her by blood; that in some drunken rage he had killed several of them and driven the rest out, never to return.

So she hated him for destroying all her people. She would get his head; she would burn him without fire, and so on.

While she talked away we glanced up at the sun and saw that it was time for us to go. But first Pedro broke in to ask her again about a white girl. She snapped that no white girl was there. We decided then to look at her house, if we could find it, and learn anything we could from the Indian girl. So we pushed past her.

"Over here," Pedro directed. "I watched the girl go."

At once the old woman began to make new threats and order us away. But we went on, paying no attention to her, to the edge of the forest where Pedro had seen the girl disappear. There we found a short path, and at its end, between two huge trees, a small walled house in whose one little doorway stood the young woman. As we approached she retreated into the house.

We halted outside a minute, the old woman shrilly menacing us with all kinds of torture. Then I told her to be still, speaking so gruffly that she obeyed. With her noise stopped, Pedro called gently to the girl, telling her she need have no fear and that we should go as soon as we had looked around. With that we walked in.

The inside of the place was so dark that we could see little, but we did see that nobody except the Indian girl was there. She stood against the rear wall, holding an old machete ready to use. She was handsome, there was no question about that even in the dim light; but there was no question also that her skin was very brown.

We both spoke to her again in Tupi, asking a few questions about herself and about any white girl. But she made no answer at all. She only stood there, ready for anything, cool and silent. So, with a smile and a nod, we walked out again.

"Watch over your little one carefully, mother," I said as we turned away. "The claws of the Hawk are cruel, and he is not yet dead. Good day to you."

And with no more words we swung away toward the creek which had led us there.

Back along that black stream we hastened to reach our canoe in time to make a camp and meet *Senhor* Tom. We had no time for talking until we were paddling down toward the lake. Then Pedro said —

"The best part of your dream has not yet come true."

"Nor is it likely to," I scoffed. "Why did you ask that foolish question about a white girl?"

"Perhaps it was not so foolish. She promised me a white girl if Black Hawk was killed."

"She did not," I disputed. "She only told you to ask her for one; she did not say she would give you what you asked. She wants *Caracara-i* killed, so she let you bait yourself. Then later she snapped out the truth — that there is no white girl. And we saw for ourselves that none was there."

To that he made no answer.

At one of the places we had noticed on the way up, we stopped long enough to make a rough camp, slinging our hammocks and leaving our food in them. Soon after that we met *Senhor* Tom at the place agreed on.

"Thought you fellows never would show up," he greeted us in the low tone we had always used since reaching the lake. "I got scared without my maps, so I've been sitting here all afternoon waiting for you to come back."

The mud on his boots, though, showed that he had traveled a good deal that afternoon and returned very recently.

Without questions, we took him aboard and returned to the camp, where we had just enough time to eat and make all snug before darkness fell. Then, sitting close together in our hammocks, we told him of our discovery up the creek.

"Say, I don't mind having you fellows kid me about my maps," he said in a tired tone, "but when you try to string me with any such cock-and-bull yarn as that you're going too far. It's a bum joke."

"It is no joke at all," we insisted. "The place is there and the women are there, and you can go with us tomorrow and see them for yourself."

"All right, I'll do that. You've got to show me. I didn't find a thing worth while this afternoon with all my tramping — oh yes, I snooped all around between this creek and the one we came in by — so I might as well spend tomorrow in your dreamland as anywhere. Gee, I hope Black Hawk gets back soon. This country will be a slow place to hang around in if he stays away another month."

"Perhaps we may learn something about him by getting near enough to those Tucunas on the hill to hear their talk," I suggested.

He shook his head.

"No chance," he said. "They'd be with him if they knew where he was. And I can tell you without moving from this hammock what they talk about. Fellow with a thirst says, 'Pass the jug.' Fellow with the jug says, 'You go to — !' That's all."

"No, we could learn little from them," Pedro agreed. "But I have an idea, *senhor*, which may be foolish but can do no harm. You spoke today of scaring them with your thunder-storm voice. Why not do it? Hide somewhere and shout that death trails the Hawk. Then get away before they find you."

"What's the use?" objected the blond man.

"This is the use. The Hawk undoubtedly rules his men by fear. His lies about white men help him too, but I feel sure that many Tucunas follow him because they fear to refuse. Fear is a powerful weapon, but it is two-edged, and the man who uses it must beware lest it cut him.

"Now those Tucunas on the hill wait until the Hawk comes back, and if they are scared by a great voice predicting death to the *cafuzo* they surely will tell the rest about it when they see them. Perhaps we can even scare the army itself when it returns. And when they get the word from up the river that the white men will come against the Hawk —"

"I get you," *Senhor* Tom cut in. "Not such a bad idea. It'll be fun to kid those fellows anyhow. But they're likely to trail my boot-tracks, and that won't do."

Pedro laughed softly.

"They can not trail any man on water. Let your warning be given from the lake after dark, or in the foggy morning, when the canoe can not be seen. We two can paddle so softly that no sound of a boat will be heard. You can throw those deep chest-tones a long way, yes?"

The American began to laugh too as he thought about it.

"Sure I can! And to make it all the louder and more ghastly I'll make a megaphone. Roll up some bark into a horn, you know. It'll sound hollow and most gosh-awful. Say, let's do it now! What say?"

We were not only ready to do it but able to make the horn; for some of the trees around us were thin-barked and easily peeled. By lighting a few matches we soon succeeded in stripping a three-foot roll of bark and tying it into shape. And then, with *Senhor* Tom still chuckling, we got into the canoe and felt our way slowly down the stream.

Black though it was, we worked out to the little bay without bumping much against the shores. After traveling through that dense gloom the open lake seemed almost light, though no moon was up. But we knew the Tucunas on the hill, who probably were sitting around fires, would be unable to see us out on the water when they came to the edge; so we paddled on easily until we were a few hundred yards from their camp. There we stopped.

Senhor Tom lifted the bark roll to his mouth, and boomed out in the Tupi tongue —

"Beware!"

Deep, solemn, weirdly hollow, the word rolled out over the murky water and echoed from the hill.

"Beware! Death follows *Caracara-i*!"

In the long minute following the slow words we thought a thin yell of alarm sounded on the shore.

"Wo to the Hawk!

"Wo to his followers!

"All shall die!

"Beware!"

The message boomed outward and upward like the voice of doom. Faintly from the hill echoed the last words —

"Die! Beware!"

The horn sank. Silently, carefully, we slipped the dugout back toward the bay and our creek.

"And I guess that'll hold you for a while," *Senhor* Tom muttered. "If not, I'll hand you another earful at dawn."

And he did. After finding our way to camp again — which was not easy, for we traveled without light and could rely only on our judgment and the feel of the creek — we slept until the noise of birds woke us to the faint light of a new day. At once we drove down-stream to the lake and out into the heavy fog. And when we thought we were in the right place our companion spoke again in Tupi, using his deepest tones.

"*Caracara-i* is doomed!

"Death sweeps upon him!

"Wo to his men!"

No sound came from the camp. We waited for the time of three slow breaths, *Senhor* Tom still holding the bark roll at his lips. Then he spoke again.

"The white guns come!

"Beware!"

With that he nodded, and without noise we moved back to shore. We did not go just right, and had to hunt for the mouth of our bay. But we soon found it, and long before the mist lifted we had disappeared inland, leaving no trace behind.

"I've done all kinds of things," the explorer said when we had finished our breakfast, "but I never before tried to be the angel with the trumpet. If I could only watch those fellows roll their eyes and shiver it would be more fun.

"I know Tucunas pretty well, and I'll bet that bunch is covered with goose-flesh right now. Anything supernatural gives them chills. But now that I've qualified as an angel I'm all set to put the jinx on that witch of yours. Come on, let's go."

We went. Up to the fallen tree we paddled, and on to the split hill we tramped, and over to the edge of the open bowl we crept stealthily. The sun shone bright and hot into the garden-spot, and over it butterflies flitted and bees droned. But the women were not there.

Crossing to the little path, we walked to the small house, seeing nobody, hearing no human sound. At the door we stopped and spoke. Still no sound came. We looked in, went in, came out and stared around. Nobody was in the house.

Moreover, nothing else was in it. The hammocks, the machete we had seen in the girl's hand yesterday, the small cooking pots and the other little things needed in daily life — all were gone. There was no sign of violence or of hasty flight. But the inside of that house was as bare as the outside.

All around that open field we scouted, finding no other house or hiding-place. The only living things we saw were the butterflies dancing in the sun and a few parrots which flew over, two by two. And when we were back at the place where we had first stood, *Senhor* Tom looked hard at us.

"Humph!" he said, striding off on our back-trail.

We followed, saying nothing. There was nothing to say.

XIII

EIGHT days passed. Eight days of quiet and concealment in the bush. Then we found ourselves quite active.

Not that we spent those eight days lounging in our hidden camp. We moved around a good deal in that time, and once we even shifted the camp itself to a better place a little farther up-stream. We talked of returning to our curved cove across the lake, where we could make fires without so much risk of being traced by the smoke; but we decided against it.

Here we were near enough to the hill of the Hawk to reach it without much travel, yet far enough away to he quite unsuspected; and fires were hardly necessary, as we could not shoot any game without betraying ourselves and thus had no meat to cook. So we remained on the little black stream leading to "Dreamland," as *Senhor* Tom mockingly called the place where we had failed to show him the old witch.

Every night after dark and every morning in the mist we went out on the lake, and the blond man croaked hollowly into the ears of the Tucunas. We knew they now were expecting, and dreading, the voice of the great demon of the lake, and we never gave them hope that the demon had left the place.

After five days of these repeated warnings we had proof that they were taking effect. Eight men from that hilltop took to their canoes after the sun was well up, and paddled away fast, looking back as if fearing some awful monster would rise from the water and swallow them They went out by the wide creek to the east, and they did not come back.

The next day, watching from the shore, we saw four more quit the place in the same manner. These disappeared by the creek at the north; and, like the other eight, they did not return. Later in the day I sneaked up to the camp and counted those who remained. Only nine were there. So in six days we drove away more than half the men we had found on that hill, and ourselves remained undiscovered.

"Your weapon of fear proves sharp, Pedro," I said when we three were together again.

"Too sharp," *Senhor* Tom commented. "We don't want to drive all those chaps out, or they can't scare the rest later on. Guess I'd better ease up."

So, though he did not stop his ghostly talk from the lake, he did suspend his threats against the Tucunas. By dark and by dawn he spoke only one sentence —

"The white guns follow Black Hawk's trail."

When next I spied on the camp I could see only six of the nine who had last been there. Whether the other three had fled or only gone hunting in the forest to the rear I never learned. But at least six men stayed there to the end.

These warnings and spyings, however, took up only a short part of each day. The rest of the time we scouted around the hill, learning all there was to learn about the country on that side of the lake.

We followed the path leading from the back of the camp into the forest — Pedro and I stepping on *Senhor* Tom's tracks and treading out the marks of his boot-heels with our own bare feet — until we found that it broke into several faint *picadas,* or hunters' trails, which in turn faded into pathless ground.

We also traveled north to the upper creek. And once we crossed the lake in the early mist and spent the day prowling among the eastern hills.

These trips gained us nothing except a better knowledge of the country and a new map which the explorer drew on the back of an old one in his idle moments. Pedro and I grinned at each other over that map-work, for neither we nor the North American needed it, and we did not stop to consider that the time might come when other men might want such a chart.

But we took care not to let *Senhor* Tom see our grins, for we knew he would retort with some ridicule of our witch and our "dream-country," and we did not feel like being laughed at.

Pedro went once alone to that place where the old *feiticeira* and her daughter — or, more likely, her granddaughter — had lived. He slipped away without saying where he was going, and when he returned he told *Senhor* Tom only that he had been roving without result. But later he told me where he had been, adding that there was no sign of the women except that some one had been gathering food from the garden-patch within a few hours of his visit.

"The poor creatures fear us and are hiding in some secret hole of the forest," I said. "And it is not strange, even though we spoke kindly to them. We have not shaved for a long time, we look wild and rough, and for all they know we may be a pair of renegados who pretend honesty in order to spy on them and then betray them to *Caracara-i*. Let us keep away from that place in the future."

"Until we have taken Black Hawk's head," my comrade smiled. "Then I shall return there and shout until they come out, and I shall ask to see the splendid butterfly with the white girl's face."

I said no more; for, instead of the butterfly girl, my mind saw again the broken bones at the base of the Hawk's nest.

Yet we never went again to the little home of the witch of the black creek. Things soon came about which made such a trip useless.

On the afternoon of the ninth day we three were idling in the wilderness between our camp and the hill. We had been roving aimlessly among the timbered hills that day, unable to think of anything new to do, but too restless to pass the time lolling in our hammocks.

And now, in one of the prettiest little forest nooks we had yet found, we had bathed in a sparkling little cold brook and were lounging on the shore, watching the water swirl around our dangling feet. The brook made a pleasant little murmuring noise, the warm air from a sunlit space just beyond us crept around our bare bodies, and we sat silent and content.

Then suddenly Pedro lifted his head.

Into the quietness had come a murmur which was not that of the brook. It grew into a hum. It seemed to be at the north, behind us. We turned around and looked, but saw no life of any kind.

"Swarming bees?" suggested the North American.

We listened a moment longer. The hum still sounded, but it did not move. It remained at one place in the north, seeming to be up among the tree-tops.

"Not bees," Pedro decided. "Men."

"By Judas! The Hawk's gang!"

We jumped up, hastily pulled on our clothes, looked to our guns, and started northward, traveling quietly but losing no time.

Now our knowledge of the country helped us to make speed. We pushed rapidly over the rolling knolls, and as we went we worked somewhat westward. With the top of that hill swarming with men, we should be fools if we tried to scale its bald sides. Instead we headed for the rear of the camp, where we could climb amid the timber and watch from the thick cover on top.

As we neared the place the hum grew heavier, but not much louder; the low rumble of many male voices grunting and calling and disputing about their shelters. And among all those man-noises we could not hear one with a note of laughter. The sound was sullen and cheerless.

When we had reached a point at the edge of the upper forest where we could watch the movements and the faces of the nearest men, we found that our ears had not deceived us. They looked as sulky and sour as they sounded.

Stocky, dull-eyed, scowling at their crude huts, and growling at one another, they passed about and worked at small tasks with the sluggishness of men doing things only because they had to, dissatisfied with life and all things in it.

The faces were those of men not bad by nature; men who, left to themselves, might be easy-going, good-natured fellows with no ill will toward any one, but who now were slaves to fear and brute power. And on his bare chest every man of them carried the mark of his slavery — the shape of a hawk's wing, painted on the skin with the black dye of the *genipapa* plant.

Believing Black Hawk's lies and fearing servitude under white men, these Tucunas now found themselves in the grip of a worse master than any white ever would be.

If we had needed any proof of this after watching them a while we should not have been long in doubt. Just as I was wondering if it would be possible to dodge unseen along the hillside to a place where I could look at the house of Black Hawk, the infamous *cafuzo* himself appeared. And when he had gone back toward the lake he left behind him an example of his method of ruling his gang.

One of the Tucunas not far from us had been acting sick. He had sunk on his haunches in a narrow lane that ran the whole length of the camp, and there he squatted with head hanging. None of his mates gave him the slightest attention, except to step around him instead of shoving him out of the way. But now they did give attention to something up the lane.

A wave of low warnings came down the pathway. The men in it slunk aside among the huts, leaving the way clear. Down that lane came a man alone. The instant my eyes rested on him I knew he was the dreaded *caracara-i*.

Tall, gaunt, black of skin and hair and eye, with the hawk nose and lank hair of an Indian, but the thick lips and brutal jaw of the lowest kind of negro, he did not need the big circlet of black hawk plumes he wore around his head to prove him the cruel creature of whom fearful tales were told.

His face and his walk would tell that. He stepped along with the silence of a drifting bird of prey, his eyes darting from side to side, his head held forward as if seeking something to swoop at. And in the sick man who blocked his path he found his victim.

The wretched Tucuna still squatted there, perhaps too miserable to hear or understand the muttered warnings of the others. A foot away from him the Hawk stopped, eyes glittering, mouth curving downward in a malicious smile.

His hands rose to his hips and hung there motionless, curved like talons; and for the first time I noticed that he wore breeches and weapons. The breeches, cut off at the knee, were dyed black with *genipapa*. Under his left hand hung a machete in a black sheath; under his right, a black-butted revolver in a black holster.

For a long, still, tense minute his claws hovered over knife and gun as if he were deciding whether to shoot the poor creature in the back or cut his throat. Then they sank, empty. And the Hawk spoke —

"You whelp of a dog, stand before me."

The harsh voice held a sinister whining note like the treacherous cry of the bird of death. And if the squatting man had been at his home in his own village and heard that bird on his roof-peak he could not have been more fear-struck. His eyes opened in terror, his jaw fell and worked quiveringly, he lurched as if his legs had lost all strength, and he fell over on hip and hand.

"I am sick," he gasped.

"Sick," the Hawk echoed; the whine becoming a snarl. "I will give you something to be sick about."

Like a flash he stooped and clutched a limp arm. He yanked the man staggering to his feet. They stood so close now that I could not see just what hold the Hawk had had on the arm, but from the victim's face I saw he was in torment. He moaned, gasped, then screamed out sharply.

Something cracked.

Another scream rang in our ears. Then the man was free. He reeled away, sobbing with pain. His arm hung limp.

The other Indians cowered back, gray-faced. Black Hawk peered around, his mouth still curved in that merciless downward smile. Then, as no man moved, he came onward a few steps, looked about the end of the camp, finished his inspection, and returned toward the front of the place. Not until he was lost down the lane did any one come from the huts. Then they gathered around the broken man, who had stumbled into a hammock.

Nobody spoke.

We three looked into one another's hard faces. For the first time I realized that *Senhor* Tom was gripping my gun, holding it down, and that I had been trying to lift it. Now he released it.

"All in good time, all in good time," he whispered. "But not now. Let's go."

We went. As we slipped away into the dimness behind, and then dodged down the hill and swung away over the knolls, we heard no sound behind. The hum of voices was stilled.

And as we went, we let *Senhor* Tom get some distance ahead.

Then Pedro poke hoarsely.

"Ai Jesu! Think of a helpless girl in the claws of that fiend!"

XIV

BACK in our camp, *Senhor* Tom leaned against a tree and smoked slowly and thoughtfully. When his cigaret was finished and stamped into the ground, he flipped his revolver from its holster, emptied it of cartridges, and took his usual "hip-shot" practise.

He had been doing this twice each day, just as he had said he would; and he had improved. Remembering the first time we had watched him, we could see that his draw had been a little stiff at the time. But it was smooth enough now, and fast as a snake-strike besides. Yet this day, after drawing and sheathing a dozen times, he frowned as if not quite satisfied with himself.

"Lourenço, give me a try-out, will you?" he asked. "Stand in front of me. Hold your right hand so. Drop it as suddenly as you can."

Wondering, I did so. Holding my right hand at my hip, I dropped it again and again. And each time his gun was out and on me before I had more than started the movement. Yet he never looked at my hand. His eyes always bored into mine.

"All right. Now, Pedro, try this one. Hold your hand behind your back. Don't move your arm. Just shut your fist suddenly. Lourenço, see if he gets the jump on me."

Standing where I could see my comrade's hidden hand and the explorer's gun, I watched them try this new trick. The revolver jumped from its scabbard before Pedro's hand could close.

"Por Deus, senhor!" I exclaimed. "You must have a devil's eye. How can you do that?"

He smiled, reloaded the weapon, and rolled another smoke.

"Guess I'll get by," he said. "I did it by watching your eyes. That's what I was after — to see if I could spot your move before you made it. Speed of the hand is all right, but the ability to read the signs is more important. When you can let the other fellow go for his gun, and then beat him to the bullet, you're fairly good. D'you know, I'm sort of glad the Black Hawk packs a gun. It may simplify things."

"What do you mean?" Pedro asked.

"Oh, I don't know. Only when a chap straps a gun onto his leg he's expected to know how to use it."

"Are you going to challenge him to a duel?" I puzzled.

"Oh, no. My gosh, no. I'm absolutely terrified by the mere thought of such a thing. You forget that I'm an angel and my weapon is a trumpet. I'm just going to preach from the lake a few days more, and maybe then the Hawk will get religion."

With, that he chuckled, looked at his watch, and said we had better eat. When we had done so he spoke more seriously.

"You fellows saw what happened this afternoon. You saw how dispirited and grouchy the men were before that. They realize pretty well now what they're up against, but they haven't the spunk to break loose from this self-constituted 'king' of theirs, nor the vision to look ahead and see that the future will be worse than the present. So they stick.

"Your guess a while ago, Pedro, was correct; Black Hawk rules now by fear alone. But, as you very aptly put it, fear is double-edged and likely to cut the man using it. Our little job for the next few days is to throw fear into the whole gang with our demon stunt.

"It's a safe bet that those Tucunas who have already heard us have started the news trickling around the camp before now. When we've given our usual performance this evening all the newcomers will be doing a lot of talking under their breath, and I'm betting desertions will start before we're three days older. Best of all, we'll undermine the nerve of that nigger-Indian himself — I never knew one yet who wasn't afraid of spooks.

"I don't think there will be many more recruits to the Hawk ranks. The word we sent out through the Passés on our way down will fix that. On the other hand, I doubt if that word will reach as far as this lake. So now we've just got to concentrate on this gang here and carry on a war of attrition, if you know what that is — wearing away the enemy. When we've got the Hawk where we want him — well, then we'll see."

Then he took down from the ridge-pole where it hung, the flaring roll of bark which long before this had been made into a real speaking-trumpet and carefully bound with bushcord. In the fading light of sunset we glided down-stream on our nightly trip. Just inside the mouth of the creek we lurked until all the lake was wrapped in gloom. And after a stealthy journey to the outer end of the bay and a careful scrutiny of all the open water we could see, we floated out to our usual place.

There, pointing the horn high, so that his voice would seem to come from the upper air rather than from the surface of the lake, the North American croaked his slow prophesy of doom,

"Death follows *Caracara-i*!

"Wo to him, slayer of men and slayer of women!

"Wo to all men who follow him!

"The white guns come and Black Hawk falls!

"Beware!

"Beware!"

And, as ever, back came the hollow echo from the hill:

"Beware! Beware!"

Back to our bay we slid. There, at the mouth, we floated motionless, watching the outer water.

"Now if you're a he man, Mister Black Hawk," muttered *Senhor* Tom, "you'll go out there hunting the demon. But if you're the cowardly brute I think you are, you'll stay on land and sweat cold. And as sure as you do that, your grip on your men begins to slip."

We waited long, but no sound came to us. No paddles dipped on the lake, no voices spoke. The blond man murmured in a satisfied way. We floated inland and paddled back up the black creek, which we now knew so well that we never bumped the bank even in deepest darkness.

In our hammocks we talked for a while about the necessity for keeping under cover at all times. Much against our wishes, we decided not to spy again on the camp for several days to come. The chances of being spied upon in return by some one of the many men up there, or of being traced by some wandering hunter, were too great.

We had taken pains at all times before this to make as few tracks as possible in our roamings, being particularly careful to cover the North

American's boot-marks; and to make new ones just now would be not only useless but perhaps fatal to our plan.

It was not so much a matter of protecting our lives as of carrying out our purpose of breaking the Hawk's hold on his men. To succeed, we must let nobody know strangers were here. We must be ghosts, demons, heard but never seen.

We also discussed the possibility of being caught on the lake by canoes concealed alongshore to trap us when we voiced our warnings.

"No chance of that," the explorer declared. "The Hawk showed tonight that he hasn't the nerve to come out himself against the demon, and if I know anything at all about Tucunas he can't drive his men to do it either.

"Even if he did force them to, they'd get ashore as soon as they were well away from camp, hide in the bush, nearly die of heart-failure when they beard the voice, and later report either that nothing appeared or that they saw a gosh-awful monster standing in the middle of the lake. They're not white men, remember.

"No, what he'll do will be to increase his savagery to cover his own yellow streak, and make his serfs fear him all the more. The psychology of brutes is the same everywhere. Those boys are going to have a tough time, and I'm sort of sorry for them; but they may as well get a stiff dose of terrorism now, and be driven into quitting him, as to live all the rest of their lives in despair.

"From now on it's a finish fight between the Fear Brothers — fear of the brute versus fear of the infernal. I'm backing the latter. I'm betting a gold double-eagle against your tobacco that the Hawk will be busted flat within a fortnight without our firing a shot. Want to take that up?"

We did not bet. Yet if we had, we should have won. More. than one shot was fired, and within less than half the time he set. Like many another good plan, ours was upset by that snaky thing on which no honest man counts — treachery. And even while we talked the treachery had been done.

The next five days were very long. We were confined to that creek like prisoners, and we felt like prisoners. We could not hunt, we could not tramp, we could not make any noise.

Only in the early mist and the darkness did we leave that little stream and sound our blood-chilling warning through the hollow horn. On those journeys we never saw or heard any sign of any one seeking us, and if any man came near our camp during the long hours between our trips he failed to find it.

The only times when we saw the Tucunas were when we grew so desperate from inaction that we drifted down to the end of the creek and, hidden there, watched an occasional canoe float past the bay-mouth in search of fish.

Then we observed that even in broad daylight the men looked around often in a scared way, as if fearing a demon of water or jungle. And, seeing this, we grinned at one another. Our weapon of fear was steadily cutting deeper.

On the sixth day we could no longer stand the slow strain of waiting in ignorance. I declared that, tracks or no tracks, I was going to find out what result our campaign had brought. The others were as eager as I.

We decided first to paddle down to the little nook where we had first hidden our canoe on this stream, then work through the bush to the mouth of the bay and look out along the lake to see how any men on it were acting. After that we would steal slowly to the hill.

But when we stood on the ground above the lake, we spied something that made us drop our caution and go tearing madly northward. It was a pair of canoes, which must have passed by our bay while we were moving through the tangle to the point, and which now were some distance beyond us.

In those dugouts were six people. Only four were paddling — two in each boat. They looked around and ahead like men newly arrived, and paddled as if a little in doubt. The other two seemed to be wounded, sick, or prisoners. They sat amidships, bowed over with either weakness or despair. And though the paddlers were Tucunas, the passengers were not.

"Por Deus!" Pedro muttered, squinting in the sun-glare thrown up from the water. "New Tucunas come, bringing captives to the Hawk. Lourenço — this light blinds me — are those prisoners white?"

I peered under one hand at the receding dugouts. The glare hurt my eyes too, but something about those two pairs of drooping shoulders made my tongue stick a moment. Then I got my voice.

"Sunburned whites or Passés — I can not tell which. But the one in the second canoe is a woman!"

"By Judas!" snapped *Senhor* Tom. "You're right! A morsel for the Hawk. A virgin being carried to the sacrifice. But, by the living — this is going to be the bloodiest sacrifice that beast over yonder ever saw! Come on!"

He hurled himself headlong into the bush. We crashed after him. Then we were in open ground under the big trees. With all speed we dashed for the hill of the Hawk.

XV

PANTING, we stopped in the edge of the jungle at the base of the hill. We had run blindly, caring little where we might come out. The arrival of that woman captive meant the end of our career as ghosts. To help her we must become men. So, as 1 say, we reached the hill at the point to which chance led us. And that point was the spot where lay the broken human bones.

At sight of those grim reminders of Black Hawk's cruelty *Senhor* Tom snarled like a maddened jaguar. His yellow beard bristled. We too growled. Yet we stood quiet a couple of minutes to control our loud breathing.

Looking upward, we saw a few Tucunas in open spaces along the edge. If they stayed there they would see us when we started to climb. But, as it happened, they did not; for before we emerged from our cover they all turned, looked beyond them, and then faded out of sight. We knew the prisoners had been brought into camp.

"Straight up," said the blond man.

With no word of reply we left our cover and climbed. Nor did we hug the trees along the way. We gave no thought to concealment until we reached the top, and we needed none; for nobody now was looking down that hillside.

As we reached the edge we found plenty of men in sight, but all were looking away from us. And after working along toward the lake a little farther, we found a place where we could stand beside a stump and see what they saw.

Quietly the men of the Hawk had drifted toward the house of their ruler. But none dared approach it too closely; and before the house was an open space where stood the newcomers and the *cafuzo* himself.

The paddlers of the two dugouts were standing between us and the pair of prisoners so that we could not see the faces of the captives. But we could see their sides, their bound hands, and the backs of their heads. And we knew they were a man and a woman of the Passés.

Black Hawk, head forward and curving hands resting on his hip-bones, was smiling that downward grin of his — a grim smile more evil than that we had seen when he tortured the sick man; the merciless leer of the vile brute into whose power a pure young woman has fallen.

He made no move. He looked at the girl and listened to the men who had brought her. And so quiet was the place that we could hear most of what those betrayers said.

Their spokesman was telling that he and his fellows were there to join Black Hawk against the white men. He said these Passés were enemies of the great Hawk. All the Passés, he added, were saying white men would soon come to destroy the Hawk and all who fought for him.

At this I saw a sudden movement of heads among the rest of the Tucunas; man looking at man with the same thought in mind — the warning of the demon of the lake.

The *cafuzo*, too, suddenly shifted his gaze, looking from the woman to the man prisoner. His hideous grin faded; his face sharpened with rage.

The Tucuna went on to say he and his mates did not believe such talk. So they had killed one man who brought that lying word, killed also others of his family, and brought to the Hawk the handsomest girl and strongest man of that family for his amusement.

The Hawk spoke.

"Well done. *Caracara-i* will amuse himself well with these two. He will bend them to his will — until they break! Ha-ha-ha!"

The whining screech of his laugh chilled me. It chilled his own men too; I saw them shrink back. But then the Passé man spoke out, brave even in despair.

"*Caracara-i*, you die. The white men come. These Tucunas speak with split tongues. They are no warriors but snakes. They killed my people by sneaking murder. They killed my father asleep. They caught me asleep. They are not men. No other Tucunas come to you. Only the white men come. You die."

Something in the voice pulled at my memory. I had heard it somewhere. Then the four Tucunas, snarling, turned on him. As they moved he swung to face them. We saw who he was; Jawuah, son of the Otter.

And the girl was the winsome Merere, the Arrow.

Pedro hissed through his teeth. His rifle rose.

"Not yet, Pedro!" harshly whispered *Senhor* Tom. "Plenty of time. We're all in this game. Wait!"

My comrade growled, but did not shoot. Black Hawk moved. We saw the traitorous Tucunas shoved back. The hateful whining voice of the *cafuzo* sounded.

"Back, dogs! Black Hawk will amuse himself. Passé, your bones are strong? Soon you will dance on boneless legs for me while your woman —"

He stopped. His head went forward a little farther, peering beyond the Passés and the Tucunas. Other heads turned to look in the same direction.

Several men were coming nearer among the huts from the rear of the camp. The others made way. Then into the open space came three more Tucunas — men on whose breasts the black-hawk wing showed. And they dragged with them another woman.

"Vive Deus!" I whispered. "The Hawk's men have caught the girl of the witch!"

It was so. Pedro and I recognized at once the shapeless garment and brown but handsome face of the girl of the black creek. She was fighting to hold back, struggling to get away, but making no outcry.

Her captors shoved her forward to stand beside Merere. For an instant the two girls looked into each others eyes, sisters in misery. Then the whining screech of the Hawk's laugh made them, and us too, look at him.

His face now held an evil joy which had not been there even when he gloated on Merere. His yellow teeth showed between his coarse lips. One hand shot out, grabbed the new girl by an arm, and yanked her toward him.

"The white men come? Ha-ha! No, but their women come! The blue-eyed girl turns Indian but she comes back to the Hawk! Ha ha ha! Now *Caracara-i* has two slaves in one day, and a man whose bones shall crack — crack — crack! Let the white men come — and bring their women to the Hawk! Let them come —"

He yelped again in his terrible mirth.

"All right, you!" grated *Senhor* Tom, "Here comes one white man! Pedro, Lourenço, I'm going in. You stay here and cover my back. Lie low. Take this rifle."

He strode away from the stump.

"We go with you!" Pedro snapped.

"Shut up! Stay here until you're needed. Over there you're two white men — here you're a dozen or a hundred. Keep down!"

We caught his idea and, unwillingly, obeyed. Without coming to the edge, no man could know how many of us might be here. We would keep them from coming to the edge. Just what he intended to do we did not know, but we realized we were more valuable behind him than with him. We dropped, guns ready:

Alone, carrying no rifle, he strode straight for the Hawk.

Tucunas, seeing him pass, stared in blank amazement. Black Hawk's laugh froze. The two girls turned toward us, and as they saw the blond-bearded man swinging toward them, both cried out — little gasping cries of wonder and hope. And Jawuah, his somber face suddenly gleaming, spoke again loud and clear.

"The white men come!"

The swaggering walk of that lone white man was in itself enough to convince all who saw him that more were at hand. Though every Indian along his way was painted with the sign of enmity to whites, he gave them no more attention than if they had been worms. He did not put a hand to machete or revolver.

He tramped along with a gait as easy and contemptuous as if backed by a thousand rifles. And when he reached the little group standing before the Hawk he shoved a couple of the traitorous Tucunas aside as arrogantly as if he, not the Hawk, were master of that jungle.

And no man laid a hand on him. Even the men he shoved away stepped farther aside of their own accord after one look at him. For the moment the only one in all that camp who showed any sign of fight was Black Hawk himself. His hands rose and hung over his weapons in that hovering, ready, but waiting way of his.

"Por Deus! What a man!" Pedro breathed as the North American halted and glared into the vicious black face of his enemy.

Then out boomed the thunder-storm voice of the blond man himself.

"Yes, the white men come! And Black Hawk dies! Passé, you speak truth. No more Tucunas come to this camp. We whites have seen to that. Now we are here to see to the filthy black beast who lies about us to the Tucunas, wrecks women, tortures prisoners and murders the helpless. Black Hawk, whine your last whine!"

Motionless, wordless, the Hawk poised with eyes boring into those of the white man. And the explorer, his own eyes never leaving those of his foe, spoke on in that great voice which all heard.

"Tucunas, hear me. The great white chiefs who live where the water is salt know that you have been deceived by lying words. They are patient with their red brothers. They will not punish those who go to their homes and live in peace as before. They, allow no man, white or black, to make slaves of the Tucunas. Only those shall be punished who have stolen women or who now fight against us. All others go free —"

One of the four traitors who had brought the two Passés, and who now heard the promise of punishment for their deed, began sneaking behind *Senhor* Tom. He gripped a short spear. His stealthy step foretold murder.

We fired.

At the double crash of our big-bored rifles every man jumped — except *Senhor* Tom. The assassin dropped, dead before he struck the earth. The Hawk's hands darted to his weapons. But he did not draw. His face jerked toward us, then back to the dead man on the ground. And *Senhor* Tom, though his right hand now hung ready at his belt, did not touch his gun-butt. Nor did he look at what lay behind him.

For a long minute, while the men of the Hawk stared fearfully toward our stump and then back at their master, there was no sound. The black man's head lifted, and again his eyes fixed on the blond-bearded face before him. Savagely *Senhor* Tom roared his challenge.

"*Caracara-i*, liar and murderer, shoot! Here stands one white man. Your hand is on your gun. You dare not draw it. You can only lie about white men — you dare not fight one. Hawk? Bah! Dog — snakebeast of the mud! Crawl on your belly and show your men what a slobbering coward you are! Down!"

One instant longer Black Hawk waited. In that instant his power over his men vanished. Every eye was on him, and every eye saw that fear gripped him. Then, with a gasping snarl, he jerked his revolver upward.

Flame stabbed from the blond man's hip. A shot roared.

The Hawk's gun spat — downward. He staggered — tottered — fell. As he went down, his revolver cracked again uselessly. Face in the dirt, he lay still.

X V

SENHOR TOM whirled on the prisoners. In the Tupi tongue which he had been speaking he snapped to the women —

"Into the house! Quick!"

As he spoke he sheathed his gun, drew his machete, cut the cords on the wrists of the Jaguar, gave the long knife to him. Instantly he faced around again, his gun out once more.

"Tucunas," he roared, "go to your homes in peace! The man who made you slaves lies dead by the hand of the white man. All who fight us shall follow him in death."

They stood as if stunned, staring at the black thing which had been the terror of their jungle. The witch's girl, too, stood as if not understanding the command of *Senhor* Tom to go in. But Merere seized her arm and pulled her away, and the pair disappeared through the doorway.

The Tucunas stirred then and looked at one another. Perhaps they might have obeyed the white man and gone without trouble, if not attacked. But Jawuah spoiled that chance.

Gripping the machete, he sprang with a yell of hate at the three living Tucunas who had killed his people and brought Merere to worse than death. For a second they shrank back.

His knife chopped into the neck of the nearest, and the man fell asprawl. The other two closed with him. Grappling, cutting, stabbing, clawing, they went wheeling and stumbling around in a death-lock.

And though some men of the Hawk realized that the Passé was avenging himself only on those who had cruelly wronged him, others who were slower of thought and still bewildered saw only a light-skinned man destroying those of their own tribe.

A rumble ran among those men, and they turned toward their shelters for weapons. At that all the others did the same. Yells of rage arose, and the camp became a whirlpool of rushing men.

We sprang up and dashed for the house of the dead Hawk. Men who blundered into our way we knocked spinning. Blows fell on us, but we wasted no time in stopping to return them. We held our gait, and very soon we were beside *Senhor* Tom.

"Thanks!" he grunted, snatching his rifle from my left hand. "Looks stormy. By thunder, though, we've got a chance! Look there! They're fighting one another!"

It was so. Men who did not want to fight us were falling foul of men who did. Knots of struggling Tucunas wrestled and showed and struck. Flimsy huts fell apart and came down on the heads of those thrown against the poles. Machetes fell and rose dripping red. Spears flew in air. Shots sounded bluntly from old rifles. The whole camp boiled with fight.

Panting, red from wounds, the Jaguar came running to stand beside us. His two foes were down; one with throat slashed, the other with a great hole in the body. His eyes glared like those of the fierce jungle animal whose name he bore. But even in his lust for more Tucuna blood he remembered his duty to white men, and instead of leaping at more antagonists he stood shoulder to shoulder with us, and waited.

He did not have to wait long. Before he got his breath a small mob of howling Tucunas charged at us with spears.

We opened fire. The first ones fell. Others stumbled over them. We shot as fast as we could pump our levers. The ground became paved with dead. Then our hammers clicked down on empty magazines. And still a few men came on.

Senhor Tom dropped his rifle and fought on with his revolver. Jawuah jumped forward with machete whirling and struck. We jammed fresh cartridges into our receivers and shot down the last men in that attacking force. When our rifles were empty again *Senhor* Tom had reloaded both his guns and was ready to carry on the fight. But no more fighting was needed.

Jawuah came striding back, leaving behind him two more dead Tucunas. Beyond the corpse-strewn space the fighting among the Hawk's men was dying down. The struggle with one another, the rapid roar of our guns, and the sight of their mates falling dead before us had driven some sense into them. Soon the conflict among them ended.

They hung back, glowering at us. They saw plainly enough that we were only four. But they saw what we four had done. Before they could decide whether to quit or attack us anew *Senhor* Tom settled the question for them.

"Peace, fools!" he boomed. "Why destroy yourselves? We are your friends. Wash the sign of this dead bird off you and go home. If you fight more we shall wash off that sign with your blood."

They stared at us. They stared at the dead. They shifted their feet and looked at one another. The only sound now was that of hoarse breathing.

"Let those who want peace stand to the right. Those who want war with the white guns move to the left," commanded *Senhor* Tom.

Many men moved to the right. Others followed more slowly. Soon all were massed together.

"It is well," the blond man approved, letting his rifle-butt sink to the ground. "The great white chiefs shall know you are once more their friends. See that you remain their friends for all time. Throw this dead thing —" he pointed to Black Hawk — "into the lake for the alligators. That is all it ever was good for. But first bring here the men who dragged into camp from the forest the brown girl wearing a long shirt."

The Tucunas moved about. Voices called, asked questions, gave answers. We waited patiently, but the men were not brought. At length a couple of Indians came forward and began looking at the faces of the dead. When they had looked at all, they stood before us and one spoke.

"The girl who lived with the devil-woman brought death to those who touched her. All those men, Cariwa, died before your guns. They were this man and that one and that."

He pointed to each in turn. As he faced us again we looked into his eyes and saw that he spoke truth.

"It is well," repeated *Senhor* Tom. "So die all who abuse helpless women. Now bury your dead and go. Let night find you on your way home. And carry to your people the word that Black Hawk is food for the alligators, and the white man your friend."

"So it shall be, Cariwa," the man answered, and the pair turned back to their mates.

"Watch them," directed *Senhor* Tom. "I've got important business in the house."

He grinned suddenly and turned away. A minute later we heard his voice beyond the doorway. But he was no longer using the tones of Tupahn the Thunder-storm, and what he was saying we could not hear dearly. Besides, we were too busy watching and listening to the Indians to pay attention to what went on behind us.

The menace had died out of their faces now, and none muttered any threat. But we let them see that our guns were ready, and we spoke no word to them, even though some grinned at us in a shamefaced way as if wanting to show friendship.

Men came forward and, after peering at Black Hawk as if still afraid of him, turned him face upward. The sight of the big bullet-hole between his ribs left no doubt that he was dead. Yanking at his arms, they hauled him away toward the lake, his head hanging back, his dingy hawk-plumes dragging in the dirt, his revolver trailing beside him in the death-clutch of the hand that had been too slow.

And that was the last we ever saw of the merciless creature who would have made himself king of all the jungle between the Jurua and the Javary — bumping along through the camp-refuse on his way to the jaws of the ugly beasts of the mud.

Other men gathered up the bodies of their fallen comrades and bore them away toward the forest at the rear. And when the ground before us again was clear the rest of the army of the Hawk turned to gather up what few things they owned before starting homeward.

A hum of talk grew among them. Their voices became more cheerful. Peace and freedom and safety for their women again had come to their country, and already they were forgetting what was past and looking forward to the drinking and dancing when they should be once more at home.

But they had not forgotten the demon of the lake. Sunset was creeping nearer all the time, and repeatedly we heard the word *"anyi,"* which means "devil." No man there wanted to stay another night on that hill, even though the white men now were there to protect them from the demon.

And though we made no attempt to count them, we saw easily that their number had shrunk much since we first spied on their swarming camp. During the past five days many Tucunas must have sneaked quietly away into the bush, afraid to stay longer near Black Hawk and the awful voice which croaked so hollowly from the dark waters. Now the rest lost no time in deserting that accursed spot forever.

Past us went a straggling procession heading for the water and the canoes. Some eyed us somberly, some marched with gaze fixed before them, some slunk past as if ashamed, some laughed and called us friends and bade us farewell. To these we gave the old Tupi godspeed, *"Ikuana Tupana deirum."* Before long the last man had faded from sight over the edge of the hill. The army of Black Hawk was no more.

Then we turned to the long low house on which the dingy hawk-wings had hung as the badge of the power of the *cafuzo*. They hung there no longer. Jawuah had torn them off, and the last sign of the rule of *Caracara-i* lay on the dirt.

The Jaguar himself, gashed and battered and smeared with red from face to feet, but paying no attention whatever to his hurts, stood beside the black doorway looking silently down at Merere, whose big eyes were on us two. Leaning against the wall on the other side of the opening, *Senhor* Tom was coolly smoking a cigaret.

"*Senhor* Tupahn," said Pedro, "your name here now will be not Thunder but Lightning. You blasted the Hawk so swiftly that no man could see your hand move. Where is the daughter of the witch?"

"It's a poor thunder-storm that hasn't a little lightning," the explorer laughed. "As for witches' daughters, I haven't seen any."

"But the brown girl —"

"Ah, yes. The *senhorita* is inside — removing her brown skin, most likely. I gave her a chance to weep on my manly chest and all that, but all I got was a polite request to take the air."

"*Por Deus!*" I cried. "She is white? The English girl?"

"No, not English —" he started to say, when a new, face appeared in the doorway.

We looked again on the brown girl, now no longer brown. The stain which had made her an Indian was washed away, and the black hair which had hung about her face was caught up in a hasty coil around her head. Without the paint her skin seemed rather pale, but her lips were like a red flower and her eyes like the night sky — deep, dark blue. Handsome before, she now was beautiful.

"*Nossa senhora!*" I muttered. "The butterfly girl! The blue-black butterfly of the dark creek!"

"I agree that she is a dream," said *Senhor* Tom.

Then, changing from Portuguese to English, he went on:

"Miss Marshall, allow me to present the three men to whom the overthrow of Black Hawk is directly due; the *senhor*es Lourenço Moraes and Pedro Andrada, and Jawuah the Jaguar, of — er — various places in the United States of Brazil. Also the little lady whom you have previously met — Merere the Arrow, of the Rio Jundiatyba. Brothers and sister, this is Miss Marion Marshall, of the United States of North America."

XVII

MORNING dawned again on the lake, the hill of the Hawk, and our camp on the black creek. But this time no hollow voice spoke doom from the mists, and when those mists were gone the sun did not shine down on the camp of the Hawk's army. That camp, like the army, was gone forever. The top of the hill now was covered only with the ashes of the shelters which we had fired before paddling away in canoes left behind by the departing Tucunas.

But if the Hawk's hill was empty, our camp was crowded. Before this we had been three; now we were six. We had given up two of our hammocks and the whole *tambo* to the two girls, slinging the third hammock among the trees and sleeping in it by turns while those who were awake kept fires going and saw that no beast of the forest came too near.

In those cool dark hours of the night-watches we had talked with Jawuah and heard his tale of murder and capture. He and his father, the Otter, had visited several scattered villages of the Passés and two in which lived Tucunas. The Passés all had gladly accepted the message and sent it on.

The Tucunas had received it rather sourly, but those in the first town, after some wrangling, had decided to keep away from the Hawk. It was in the second Tucuna settlement — a drunken little place of a few huts — that treachery had ended the Otter's life just as he was planning to return to his own village.

There, while Lontra and his son slept, some Tucuna had crushed the Otter's head with a club. The Jaguar, roused by the sound of the blow, had been struck and stunned while springing up.

When his senses came back he found himself tightly tied, and heard the murderers of his father say that, as they were going to join Black Hawk, they would take him there for punishment by the Hawk himself. They would take also the handsomest girl of the Otter's family to please the black "king." And, leaving him closely guarded by older men, they went up the river.

Six of them went. Four returned with Merere. The other two, he learned from her, had been killed after the party entered the village as friends and then suddenly attacked their hosts. But the three Passé men there also had been killed, and so had Itariapu, who tried to protect Merere. The other women and the children had fled to the bush, and Merere had been carried down-stream and, with the bound Jaguar, brought to the Hawk.

So the death-warning of the black bird *caracara-i* on the morning of our departure from the Otter's home had come true. Jawuah spoke quietly of it all, showing no bitterness now that he had avenged his wrong on the traitors; but we knew his heart was heavy.

We knew, too, that it was heavier because, even after his splendid fighting, the lovely little Merere still looked far more at Pedro than at him. But that was a thing which none of as could help. A maid looks where she will, not always where she should.

This was the simple tale of the Passé pair. But the story of the other girl, recently an Indian of the back-bush, but now a North American beauty, still was untold. She had spoken hardly a dozen words since leaving the Hawk's hut, and then her voice, though low and musical, had sounded very tired.

After what she had been through, we could hardly wonder at this, and we had swallowed our questions until she could rest. But now, with the new day streaking the trees, and no danger near, we looked for her to explain why she was here.

We waited, however, for some time. Under the shadow of the tambo she slept on long after the rest of us were astir. We breakfasted quietly, little Merere smiling shyly at Pedro now and then as the meal went on, Jawuah solemn as ever, and we three pretending not to see the condition of affairs between the two Passés.

I began to wonder whether the Arrow would willingly go back to the Jundiatyba jungle with the big stout-hearted fellow who was her fit mate. But when we had finished eating and our tobacco-smoke was drifting in the air, Pedro settled the question.

"Today we go," he said in Tupi. "My brother the Jaguar, who now is the chief and the only man of the Otter people, must return to protect them with his strength."

"It is so, Cariwa," agreed Jawuah.

"The young ones must not be left long unguarded," Pedro went on. "My own heart is anxious for the safety of my woman and my little sons on the Javary. Now I return to them with all speed."

His gaze was over the heads of the Indian pair, as if he looked at something far away. Jawuah started and gave him a long stare. The girl's eyes widened; her lips opened as if to speak, quivered, closed again without a word. She dropped her head and looked long into the dying fire. We three smoked on.

"I have thought," added Pedro, "that now, since the Otter has gone to his fathers and the Jaguar is the one man left, it would be wise for the Jaguar to take his people to the Ypihah Aku and live there among the men of Warm Wind.

"My brother is strong and brave and terrible toward his enemies, as I have seen. Yet death lurks ever ready in the jungle, and at its own time it strikes us all. My heart would be lighter about my brother and my sister if I knew they and the little jaguars who shall come to them were with the men of the Warm Creek."

The Jaguar's steady eyes went to the Arrow's face. After a time he said:

"My brother's words are good. And since the Jaguar can help the white men no more, he returns now to those who need him."

He arose, stepped to the canoe in which he had come from the camp of the Hawk, and stood waiting, his gaze fixed on the creek. Slowly then Merere stood up and took a step toward him. We three straightened. She paused and looked up for the last time into Pedro's face.

"Hereneh, ikuana Tupana deirum," she whispered.

"Go with God, my sister," he echoed. "And make happy the life of my brother whose heart you have pierced."

She passed on to the canoe. In it she picked up a paddle. Jawuah settled himself, sank another paddle into the dark water, and pushed gently away. With no backward look they floated down-stream and out of our lives.

"And there they go, paddling their own canoe," *Senhor* Tom approved. "Pedro, have you really a wife and children?"

"None, *senhor*. But it was the best way."

"You're right. Well, about all that's left now is to break camp after Miss Marshall has her sleep out. We'll have to go north and see that she gets a steamer, of course. While we're waiting, how about some fresh meat?"

"We were thinking of that," I answered. "We two will get some. You are her countryman, so you had best stay here with her."

And we took our rifles and went seeking some of the game which had been teasing us during our days of silence and stealth.

When we came back, bringing a big *mutum* bird and a couple of fine fat *pacas* which we had scared out of their burrows, we found the white girl sitting in her hammock and sipping hot coffee. *Senhor* Tom was gathering more wood for the fire.

"Good morning, *senhorita,*" Pedro greeted her in English. "You look as fresh and dainty as an orchid after a night of rain."

Her deep blue eyes looked coolly into his smiling brown ones. Soon an answering smile grew on her red mouth.

"Hardly that, I fear," she replied. "But I do feel ever so much better. Last night I seemed to be absolutely dead."

"You will soon feel better yet," he promised. "You have lived too long on corn and bananas. Here is meat — a *mutum* and *pacas*. They will give you new strength."

She looked rather doubtfully at the dead things.

Senhor Tom spoke up.

"How would broiled turkey and roast suckling-pig taste, Miss Marshall? Sounds tantalizing, eh? Well, that's about what you're going to get, minus the fixings. We neglected to bring along the garnish, I'm sorry to say."

"How very careless of you! But I'll forgive you if you will prepare the rest of it at once."

"Right! Hop to it, boys, before the lady expires from starvation. She couldn't eat a mouthful last night, remember."

We remembered, and we "hopped to it." While we roasted the meat I looked often at her and wondered; wondered not so much about how she came there as at the unconscious dignity of her manner.

Barefoot, bare-armed, clothed only in that ugly floppy shirt-like thing, she still seemed queenly. Yet she was not big and stately; she was just a slender, graceful girl whose head would hardly reach up to the jaw of my tall comrade Pedro.

"De puro sangue," muttered Pedro.

"Thoroughbred. That's it," *Senhor* Tom agreed in an undertone.

Then, loading up a bark plate with fragrant meat, he presented it to her with a bow. But she arose and told him to put the bark on the ground.

"I have learned to eat in the jungle fashion," she said. "And you must all eat with me. Yes, I dare say you have breakfasted, but you must be as hungry for meat as I. And I know I am going to make a perfect pig of myself, so I want company in my disgrace."

"Well, if you put it that way —" said *Senhor* Tom.

"We shall all be pigs together," I finished. I thought it quite a clever remark, but when every one laughed at me I decided to use my mouth only for eating. And while we four squatted in a circle and ate heartily, and afterward when she sat again in the hammock and *Senhor* Tom talked, I said nothing.

We still asked no questions. But *Senhor* Tom told the tale of how we had come there, giving me and Pedro much more credit than was necessary. When he had finished she told us what we had waited for.

She was the English girl of whom we had heard, but she was neither English nor the daughter of the man who had brought her there. Her home was in a place called Virginia, in North America. The man was her mother's brother, and he was English; a wealthy man who was very fond of traveling and had been in almost every country of the world.

The girl also was fond of roaming about and seeing new things, and she and her English uncle had traveled together more than once in North America. Then, while visiting her home before starting to South America to see some places where he had not previously been, he had asked her if she cared to go with him. She did.

The first place they visited in Brazil was Para. There he decided to make the long trip up the Amazon to Iquitos, in Peru. The pair came up on one of the big boats, going ashore wherever the steamer stopped, but finding the journey rather dull.

In time they reached Viciado, and there they were advised not to land because the town was not worth seeing and some harm might come to them. But the Englishman would neither listen to any advice nor allow any one to go with him to protect him. He went ashore, and with him went the girl, feeling safe at his side.

When they were well away from the river and out of sight from the boat, they stopped to give a few coins to some children. Suddenly a thick cloth was thrown over the girl's head from behind and she heard a hard blow, a gasp, and low coarse voices. Before she could cry out, she was choked, lifted, and carried for some distance by several men.

Then she was dropped among bushes and kept there a long time with a man's hand always on her throat, choking her whenever she tried to call or struggle away. She heard the steamer whistling, then heard it no more.

After that voices talked loudly, the cloth and the choking hand were taken away, and she found herself in the jungle among evil-looking men who seemed to be half-breeds. Near her lay her uncle, dead and robbed.

He had been struck from behind so hard that his skull was broken. After making sure he was dead, searching him again, and even taking his clothes, the men pitched him into water near-by and turned on her.

They took her rings and watch and little gold necklace, tore her clothes nearly off in a hunt for other valuables, and then, after an argument which she could not understand because she knew nothing of Portuguese, forced her into a canoe. Two of them took up the paddles and drove the canoe away.

They traveled three days, keeping her always under watch, or tied so tightly that she could not escape. Then they dragged her up the hill of the Hawk and handed her over to the vile cafuzo.

It was almost dark when she reached the camp. After one look at the Hawk she tried to run and throw herself into the lake. But he caught her, dug his fingers into her arms until she nearly fainted from pain, dragged her to his door, and struck her so hard that she fell stunned inside.

As it happened, she upset a jar of water in her fall, and the water rushed over her head, reviving her almost at once. He remained outside a few minutes talking to the men who had brought her there. Before he entered the dark house she was up and had found a rifle.

She knew how to handle a rifle, and she was cool enough to examine this one to see whether it was loaded. It was not. So she used it as a club. When he came inside and peered around the floor to find her she struck him on the back of the head, knocking him senseless.

Then night fell. In the darkness she slipped down the hillside into the jungle. And there, with no food, easy prey to any forest beast which might find her, she wandered all that night and for two days after that.

Somewhere she had heard of walking in water to leave no trail, and she waded long distances in the little brooks. She slept wherever she fell exhausted. She grew so faint that she lost all sense except the will to keep going. Then at last she found herself in an open place with an old Indian woman bending over her.

This old woman cared for her, brought back her strength, stained her skin brown and gave her the bark-cloth robe which she still wore. The girl could not understand her talk, but she could see that she was mad. In spite of this they got on well together, and after a time the girl learned that she was almost safe under the old woman's care.

Several Tucunas with the black-hawk wing on their breasts came there, but when the old woman walked at them with fingers wriggling and eyes staring, they fled, yelling with fear. And from that day until Pedro and I came she saw no man.

Then, because she did not know the Tupi language we spoke, she could not understand us and did not trust us. After we went, the pair fled and hid in a great hollow tree well back from the clearing. But yesterday afternoon, while the girl was getting food from the garden, she heard a thundering sound in the forest; and when she reached their tree she found that it had fallen and killed the old woman under it.

She ran from the place — and ran into the clutches of three Black Hawk hunters who were prowling the woods. They dragged her away to their chief. Then we came, and the Hawk fell.

"And now —" she said, and paused.

"Now you go home, plucky girl," said *Senhor* Tom. "We go to the Amazon, and I'll see you safe on a steamer. Don't worry about the transportation. Before we burned the Hawk's house last night we ransacked it, and we found money enough to carry you around the world — deluxe style, too. We've decided that it's yours. So that's all right."

"But it is not all right, Mr. Mack," she objected, smiling but shaking her head decidedly.

"I can not permit that. If you will be so kind as to advance my transportation — and enable me to clothe myself more becomingly — I shall be very grateful. But I will accept nothing more. I am eternally indebted to you three —"

"Oh, forget it!" snapped *senhor* Tom. "We just happened around at the right time, and you don't owe us a danged nickel. Now —"

" — and the money you found should be divided among you as the spoils of war," she continued very coolly. "I shall accept nothing except absolute necessities. That is final."

Their eyes fought. Then he laughed and rubbed his jaw.

"Oh, very well. Anything you say. We three will divide the swag after subtracting your share. But since clothes are more or less necessary, will you accept my spare kit until we hit the river? I always carry one, and I don't need it now, and you sure do. You look a fright in that dowdy thing."

Then she laughed — a merry little laugh that was music to us and made her altogether lovely.

"So I do not look like an orchid dripping with dew? Mr. Andrada, you are a very gallant fibber. Mr. Mack, your spare kit will be very welcome and much more comfortable than this garment."

Senhor Tom laid out his extra khaki. We walked away for a while. When we came back and looked at her we almost whistled.

In the snug breeches, loose shirt open at the throat, and laced boots, with her glossy black hair newly coiled and pinned up with tough twigs, her deep eyes shining mischievously under curving brows and her face aglow with the new life given by long sleep and strong food, she made a picture to tug at a man's heart. And if she knew it, who can blame her for that?

"By thunder!" Senhor Tom said in Portuguese. "A man's woman! I say, *amigos* — er — I am not going back to headquarters with you. Something might happen to this lady, and — I am a Brazilian government official in a way, and — it becomes my official duty — er — well —"

"We understand perfectly, *senhor*," Pedro laughed. "A new trail opens before you."

"Just so. And I'm going to stick on it like a bloodhound. Tell the *coronel* to send the things I left behind to me at Rio. I may write up that cursed report of mine some time, but for a while I expect to be quite busy."

Then in English he said:

"Since you have made yourself presentable, Miss Marshall, I will permit you to ride in my canoe. Let's go."

"So kind of you," she smiled. "I shall work my passage. I really am not bad at a paddle."

"Glad to hear it. I think we'll make a good team. That is — er — Well, what are you fellows snickering about? Load up!"

We loaded and pushed out, leaving behind us an empty *tambo* and the shapeless bark-cloth garment that was the last sign of the Indian girl of the black creek.

Down that creek we swung, and up across the silent lake, and out along the wide stream leading north. And as the hill of Black Hawk vanished behind us *Senhor* Tom took his eyes off the slender back swaying before him, glanced around, and boomed out the song he had sung far back on the Javary; the same song, but with slightly different words.

> *"Merrily we roll along,*
> *Roll along,*
> *Roll along,*
> *Merrily we roll along*
> *Toward the deep blue sea!"*

THE TAPIR

THAT is a queer thing, *senhores.* You say that the tapir, so common here in South America, is found in no other continent except Asia, and there only in a section which you call Malaysia; and that place is thousands of miles from our Brazil and across a vast ocean. How could our tapir have gotten there? He never could swim so far!

Oh, I see. Pardon my foolish question. Long ago there were tapirs all over the world, but now they have died out almost everywhere? Yes, I can believe that, for the tapir has no defense except his thick hide and his habit of jumping into water when attacked; and both animals and men must be able to defend themselves, or they will be wiped out by others which are more fierce and better armed. So perhaps the odd part of it is not that there are so few tapirs on earth now, but rather that there are any at all.

He is a shy fellow, the tapir. He needs to be, for he is hunted both by beasts and by men. Among the wild Indians of our jungle, as you perhaps know, the greatest hunter is he who can find and kill that big thick-skinned animal with funny nose. The prowling jaguar, too, is always eager to make a meal from him. Possibly you two North Americans also, during your explorations here at the Amazon headwaters, have slain a tapir or two for the sake of fresh meat. Yes? Then I need not tell you any more about that animal, for you probably know as much about him as I.

Still, I can tell you a tale of a tapir tonight, while this steamer slides along down the Amazon, which probably will amuse you. You have seen the tapir, observed his ways and tasted his flesh. But did you ever find one up in a tree, moaning and weeping from love?

Yes, it sounds ridiculous. But let me tell you, *senhores,* if ever I meet another love-sick tapir I shall go straight away and leave him, unless I am willing to get myself into trouble. And this is why:

One day in the flood season I was paddling down a swollen little river among wild hills in the Javary region — whether it was in Brazil or in Peru I do not know, for I had been on a long rambling trip into unknown country and neither knew nor cared where the boundary might be. With me was a fearless young comrade named Pedro, who, like myself, was a rubber-worker on the great, *seringal* of the Coronel Nunes. The floods having stopped our work in the swampy lowlands, we had taken a canoe and gone out to seek adventures — and had found them. And now, having used up nearly all our cartridges in a battle with headhunting savages, we were on our way back to the headquarters of the *coronel*, paddling with our regular long distance stroke and expecting nothing at all to happen. But suddenly from the jungle near us came a mournful sound.

We held our paddles and looked. Only a few feet away was the hilly western shore of the stream, thick with bush. The sound had come from there, seeming to be a little distance away from the water and quite high up in the trees. We could not see anything in the tangle overhead, nor hear anything moving there. So after a minute I said softly to Pedro —

"Only a sick monkey grunting to himself."

He nodded slowly, as if in doubt, and continued squinting upward. I stroked again with my paddle, intending to go on. But before I put any power into the push the noise came again. I halted my arms.

"O-ho-o-o!" wailed a voice. "Oho-oo! Boo-hoo-hoo!"

We looked and listened. There was no sign of any man being in this place, but the voice was that of a man crying. It was a heavy voice, which ought to belong to a strong man; yet it was snuffling and sobbing there in the bush like that of a woman. To me, and I think also to Pedro, that sound was more dreadful than a cry of pain or a scream of fear; for it seemed that the man must be in a terrible condition to break down in that way. We turned the canoe, which had been drifting down the current, and silently paddled back.

Pedro, in the bow, jerked his head toward the shore. Looking closely, I saw what I had not noticed before — a quiet creek almost hidden by big drooping palm-leaves. We slipped the canoe through these leaves and stopped short. A few feet ahead of us was another canoe.

Then the voice came again. It was up over our heads.

"Oho-oo! What shall I do? I cannot live!" it sobbed.

More than twenty feet above the ground we spied a sort of house built in the branches of a big tree — a hut made from split palm logs and palm leaves. Up the trunk of the tree ran a stout notched pole making a ladder, such as we rubber-workers use in high tapping.

"The man must be dying alone up there, poor fellow," said Pedro.

I nodded. We stepped out on shore and went to the pole.

"What is the matter, friend?" Pedro called.

No answer came. There was a dead silence. Then we heard a slight movement up there, and out from a doorway at the top of the ladder came a head. We saw a dark face, with black hair and eyes. It peered down at us, and we started back. Then, without replying, the man swung himself out of the hut and came down the pole.

"*Por Deus!*" muttered Pedro. "He is not dying, nor even sick. He is as big and healthy as — as a tapir."

It was so. The fellow was so broad and heavy that it seemed as if the pole, stout though it was, ought to snap under him. Yet he was not clumsy; he came down so easily that we knew his muscles were strong and worked smoothly. I began to believe that there must be some one else up in that house, for it did not seem likely that this big man would have been moaning and blubbering so. But when he stood on the ground I saw that his eyes were wet and his face streaked, and the corners of his mouth turned down as if he were ready to start crying again.

As I looked at him I could not help grinning — partly because I was relieved, partly because his doleful face looked funny to me, and partly because Pedro's chance remark about a tapir was so near the truth. Above his heavy body and thick neck was the face of a tapir: for it was much narrower at the jaws than above the eyes, and the nose was so long and curving that it seemed to be not a nose but a snout. And, as I have said, the face was very dark, as the face of a tapir would be. He was a *caboclo,* with some white blood in him. Still, he looked like a good-natured young fellow, and he was not enough of an Indian to keep from showing his grief.

"What is the matter with you?" Pedro repeated. "We thought you were dying."

The other's mouth worked, and he sniffled.

"Maybe I am," he said in a choked tone. "I think I shall die. Oh, my poor little Bellie! Ah-hoo-wow!" He began to bawl.

"Your poor little belly?" demanded Pedro. "What ails your belly? It looks very healthy to me. Have you swallowed a live turtle?"

I snickered, and the tapir-man himself laughed. In the middle of a wail he changed his noise to a snort, and that in turn became heavy laughter. But then his mouth turned down again.

"You do not understand," he said. "I have lost my so-beautiful Bellie. It is a great misfortune, and not a thing to laugh about."

"Lost your appetite, do you mean?" asked my comrade. "That is nothing to make so much noise over. And I do not think your belly is so beautiful. It sticks out too much."

"No, no, you have it wrong!" the Tapir protested. "It is true I have no appetite — I have eaten nothing today, except some *chibeh* and a few handfuls of *pirarucu*-fish and some monkey-meat and a few other things. But that is because they have shut up my little Bellie for so long and will not let me have her. Even when they let her out I cannot have her — ah-hoo!"

"Stop that noise!" I ordered. "And stop your weeping also — it is wet enough here from the rains. Now tell us, what is this Bellie that gives you so much trouble? The matter must be serious if, as you say, you cannot eat more than two men need."

He nodded as quickly as his thick neck would let him, and told us:

"Indeed it is serious. My Bellie is a girl who has come to womanhood and should be given in marriage, but her father has not made ready for the feast, and so she is shut up. And the father does not favor me, but will give her to Gastoa. So you see it is a terrible misfortune."

"So I see," I said, "although I do not yet know just what you are talking about. Why is your girl shut up, and what has the feast to do with it? Tell us all about this matter. We are Pedro and Lourenço, *seringueiros* of Coronel Nunes. Perhaps we can help you."

He looked at us as if a little doubtful.

"I do not think you can help me," he said. "What I, Deodoro Maia, cannot do for myself is something no strangers can do for me. And perhaps even if we could free my Bellie I still should lose her. She likes men who are tall and handsome."

He looked at Pedro as he spoke. Pedro made a very low bow.

"Thank you, friend Deodoro," he laughed. "But have no fear. Girls do not interest me much. And if they did, I think perhaps I could get one without stealing her from another man."

Deodoro thought this over and nodded again.

"I think that is true," he admitted. After looking at both of us a while longer, he said: "Yes, I will tell you all about it. Will you come up into my house? I have some *cachassa,* but no tobacco."

"And we have tobacco but no *cachassa,*" I replied. "It is a fair exchange — a smoke for a drink."

So I climbed the ladder and entered his house. He and Pedro followed.

It was dark inside the place, for it had only one small window-hole, its doorway was hardly big enough to let the tapir-man in, and the daylight outside was dull. Yet the hut was comfortable enough, and it was dry. When we were all inside Deodoro lifted a jug from a dim corner and passed it to us. After a good pull at the *cachassa* which it contained we sat down on the floor, with our backs to the wall, and tossed him the makings of a smoke. He could hardly wait to roll the cigarette before he lit it.

"Ah, that is good!" he grunted, sucking a huge drag of smoke down into his lungs and blowing it slowly out. "I have not had a smoke for days."

"That may be one reason why you have felt so badly," I told him. "It is a mistake to be without tobacco when you are in trouble. A drink and a smoke will go far toward easing any kind of pain."

"That is so," he agreed. "But I have been so miserable that I did not think of it. Besides, there is only one place where I can get tobacco — that is at the town; and Gastoa and his brothers and Bernardo, the father of my Bellie, drive me away from there."

We said nothing, but waited. Sitting in his big hammock, he puffed at the cigarette until it burned his fingers. The tobacco soothed him, as we knew it would; and with the smoke, another drink, and somebody to talk to, he became quite cheerful. Then he told us of his trouble.

He, Deodoro Maia, was a native of a small *caboclo* village some miles to the west, on another little river. The people of this town were jealous of their women and watched them closely. The young girls, who were only children, had nearly as much freedom as the boys; but from the time when a girl reached womanhood until she was married she was watched continually — and after marriage too, for that matter. And it was the custom among these people, when a girl was old enough to take a man, for her parents to make a feast, and a celebration was held and everyone was told that the girl now could marry.

Now this custom, like many others, had both a good and a bad side. Whenever a girl grew up the whole village could have a merry time at the celebration. But the rule of having a feast at that time was so strong that unless the girls' parents were able to give that feast she could not be declared marriageable. In that case she was in a bad position; for she was no longer a child, with the child's freedom, nor yet a woman in the eyes of her people — she was nothing at all. Because of this, and also to keep her always guarded, her father would shut her up until he could give the usual feast.

This did not mean that she only had to stay in the house. A cage would be built — a tight, strong cage of woven cane inside the house — and she would be put into that cage and kept there like a beast. She might have to stay in that thing for many days; there was no escape for her until the feast was ready. Deodoro told us that sometimes a girl would be shut up so long that when she came out her copper-colored skin had faded almost to white.

Now Bernardo, father of the girl whom Deodoro wanted, was lazy and drunken, and meant to use his pretty daughter for his own benefit. So he intended to give her to a fellow named Gastoa, who was considered rich in his own village and had brothers who might help support the old drunkard in idleness; at least that was the father's plan. The man Gastoa was known to be cruel, and the girl feared and hated him; but that made no difference to old Bernardo, who thought only of an easy life for him-self. He was so worthless, though, that when his girl-child turned into a woman he had nothing with which he could give the feast. Worse yet, he would not do enough hunting to get the monkey-meat usually dried and kept for the celebration. He only shut the girl into a cage and kept on drinking and sleeping.

So the moons came and went, and poor Bella — or Bellie, as the Tapir called her — was still a caged woman with no prospect of release.

The girl's mother did all she could for her. She worked hard to grow enough green foods for the feasting, and she tried to get Gastoa and his brothers to kill monkeys and salt away fish. But Gastoa was so sure he would have Bella in the end that he could not see any use in doing so much work for her, and so he and his family only laughed and sneered and did nothing.

And then a misfortune came to the crops. A herd of peccaries got into them and tore up almost everything, so that Bella's family had hardly enough left to live on, and all hope of the celebration was destroyed until new crops could grow.

When this happened Bernardo flew into a drunken rage. As might be expected, he vented his spleen on those who were not to blame. He beat his wife, and then he dragged his daughter out of her cage and beat her too because she was causing so much trouble to him. While he was still ugly Deodoro came in. A fight followed.

Deodoro, hoping to win the girl for himself, had done the thing which both Bernardo and Gastoa refused to do — he had hunted monkeys, birds, and fish, and dried or salted their meat. He had been very quiet about this, doing his work here at this house which he had built up in the tree, where nobody would be likely to find him. Now, with some of the best pieces of meat, he had gone back to the village to tell Bernardo he would give all he had toward the feast if he could have Bella for his own. But he came at a bad time, for, as I have said, Bernardo was ugly.

When he heard the young man's proposition he called him a vile name and kicked the meat into the dirt, where some dogs snatched it and ran off with it. Then he ordered Deodoro out; and when Deodoro hesitated he struck him. This was too much for even the slow, good-humored tapir-man to stand. He hit back and then started in to give the old fool the best thrashing of his life.

If he had been let alone he might have beaten some sense into Bernardo. But Bernardo, getting the worst of it, yelled for Gastoa to help him. Gastoa came, and his brothers with him, and jumped on Deodoro. They gave him such a beating that he was lucky to escape alive. Then they threw him out of the village, warning him not to come back.

In spite of this, Deodoro went back — though he took care not to go openly. Several times he went by moonlight, late at night when he knew the village was asleep. He even succeeded in talking a little with the girl through the thin cane wall of the house, and offered to cut a hole there and take her away with him. But, though she hated to be shut up so, still she wanted to be made a woman with the usual ceremony, and she would not consent to running off to some unknown place where she could not see the people whom she had always known. Besides, she did not think very seriously of Deodoro. Nobody did, he said.

When we asked him why this was, he said it was partly because of his white blood. He was neither a full-blooded *caboclo* nor a white man. His mother's father, he said, had been a white Brazilian trader who stayed for a time on that river while buying sarsaparilla for the market. Before his mother was born this man sailed away, and he never came back. So the girl was laughed at by the others because she had no father, and when she grew up she was sneered at because she was half white. In the same way her son Deodoro was laughed at in his turn, though his own father was a *caboclo*. The only one who did not jeer at him, he said, was the girl Bella, who sympathized with him when the rest mocked him.

This story made us sorry and angry — sorry for the young fellow and angry at those who had treated him so. We saw that he was not by nature a fighter, and that, with the whole town against him and the girl unwilling, he felt that there was nothing he could do but stay in his tree and be miserable. He was much in need of help.

"The big question is, does the girl care for you?" said Pedro. "Does she want you more than another?"

Deodoro stared out of the door awhile before he answered.

"I do not know just what she wants," he said then. "I do not think she knows either. She has not seemed to think much about men. I know she likes me as well as any one, and much better than she likes Gastoa. She does not like him at all."

"She likes you but she does not admire you," said Pedro. "Then you have two things to do — to free her and to make her respect you. Women admire men who are strong and bold. Be strong and bold, friend, and she will realize that you are a man. Now she thinks of you as a boy. Am I right?"

The Tapir thought again and agreed.

"You have it right," he said. "But what can I do? I can not go into the town and shoot everybody that tries to stop me from taking her away. My bullets are all gone."

We laughed.

"Of course you can not," said Pedro. "That would be a blundering way. Even if you shot down the whole town you would not win what you want most — the girl herself. She would then fear you more than she fears Gastoa. "You want her to admire you, not to be afraid of you. Now let us try to make a plan."

So we talked about different ideas that came to us, but none of them got us anywhere. At length I said:

"We are wasting time. You and I, Pedro, have never been at this place where Deodoro lived, and all we know about it is what he tells us. We might sit here and talk for a week, and then go there and have our great idea smashed by some little thing none of us had thought of. The one thing we are sure about is that first the girl must be gotten out of her cage. The best way to get that done is to go ahead and do it."

Deodoro nodded seriously, as if I had said a very wise thing. Pedro laughed, but he agreed.

"That is the best plan of all," he said. "Let us go with God and trust to luck."

We arose and turned toward the door. But Deodoro halted us.

"Wait," he said. "I am feeling much better, and I think I can eat something before we start. I have all the meat I saved for the feast — except the few pieces I lost at Bernardo's house — and now I shall not give any of it to those who have not treated me well, but will keep it for myself and Bellie and my friends Pedro and Lourenço. I think we had better have some of it now."

"You have spoken most wisely, friend," Pedro answered with a grin. "My comrade and I have not been eating much for the last few days. We have been on a long trip and our supplies are nearly gone. So we shall not throw your meat to the dogs as Bernardo did. But where do you keep it?"

"Since you are my friends, I will show you," he replied with a sly look.

Lifting a couple of the split palms that made his floor, he brought out meat.

"See, my floor is double," he explained. "The big branches of this tree hold up my house, and between the branches I have made boxes, and then covered branches and all with my floor. It is a good way to hide things."

"Deodoro, you are one of the cleverest fellows I ever met," said Pedro. "Few men would have thought of such a thing."

Deodoro's face beamed. Probably it was the first time anybody had ever praised him; and somehow he seemed to grow bigger as he thought about it. Pedro gave me a slight wink, and I saw what he was trying to do — to make this shy, downcast fellow think well of himself. And indeed, *senhores,* that is a thing that has much power to help or harm a man; for if he does not feel himself to be the equal of other men, who else will believe him to be so? Seeing Pedro's thought and realizing its value, I changed my own manner toward the young tapir-man and no longer treated him as a boy.

We went down the pole, built a little fire and ate. Pedro and I were hungry, and we did not spare the meat; but I do not believe that both of us together ate as much as Deodoro put away alone. When the food was gone he was still hungry, and he climbed the ladder and brought down more. This time he brought down his jug also. We found that it held more *cachassa* than we had thought, but we emptied it. Then, feeling quite merry, we got into our canoes and pushed out into the river.

With our new comrade leading, we paddled downstream until he swerved to the left. Up another quiet creek we followed him. The stream widened into a long swampy lake which seemed to have no end, for it wound along among the low hills so that whenever we thought we had reached the end we found that there was more of it. At length, when we had about concluded that it was no lake but a flooded arm of the river ahead, Deodoro led us into another narrow stream. Down this we went, and soon we came out into another river.

"It is not far now," said Deodoro in a low tone. "It is only a short paddle upstream."

"Very good," Pedro replied. "But why do you speak so quietly? You are not afraid if the whole world hears you."

Again Deodoro seemed to swell.

"No!" he agreed, and his heavy voice boomed like a gun. "I do not fear any man!"

He began paddling again with a bold stroke.

As he said, it was not far to the town. We heard it before we saw it. Shouts and laughter came to us, and then some one began to beat a drum in Indian time. Deodoro suddenly stopped paddling.

"There is a celebration," he said. "I wonder — it can not be — it is not possible that Bernardo has made the feast!"

"If there is a feast, so much the better," I said. "Everyone will get drunk. Is it not so?"

He nodded.

"Then it will be easier for us to do what we come for," I explained. "When all are drunk, who shall stop us?"

He made no answer. We saw that he was worried, thinking the noise might mean that his girl was given to the man Gastoa.

"Come, comrade," said Pedro. "We are slopping here as if we were afraid."

The hint was enough. Deodoro's head came up, and he swung into his stroke as if he owned the river. Pedro let out a yell, and we joined in. Shouting and paddling hard, we surged up to the town like men sure of a welcome.

Like all towns in that region, it was on a hill above the reach of any floods. In the dry time it probably was some distance from the stream, but now the high water made it easy for boatmen to land beside it. As we stepped out on shore the drum-beating stopped. Several men came to meet us, and some barking dogs rushed at us.

Pedro knocked the dogs aside with his rifle. I had no gun, for I had broken mine and lost it in that fight with the headhunters of which I have told you. But I had two good feet in heavy boots, and I used them. One of the dogs, an ugly brute, snarled as if about to spring at me, but I kicked him again so hard that he yelped and retreated. At this, one of the men scowled at me in evil fashion.

"Kick my dog again and you will get yourself into trouble," he growled.

"I am used to trouble," I retorted. "And I kick an ugly dog wherever I meet him — whether he stands on four legs or on two."

He glared and took a step toward me. Then he halted as if not quite sure of himself. After glowering at me for a minute he shifted his gaze to Deodoro.

"You Deodoro!" he snarled. "Did I not tell you not to come back here?"

"You did, Gastoa," answered the tapir-man. "But you see I am back. I think I shall stay, too." His voice was strong and steady.

Three other men scowled when they heard this. I judged that they were the brothers of Gastoa, who had helped to beat Deodoro and drive him out. More *caboclos* had gathered around us now, and among them I noticed a short, piggish-looking man of middle age who seemed quite drunk. Pointing at Deodoro, this man yelled:

"Throw that one into the river! Throw the others in! Drown them all! What business have they here?"

Gastoa and his brothers growled again, but they did not quite dare to rush us. We stood shoulder to shoulder, and they could easily see that we did not intend to be driven away without a fight. Before they could decide just what to do Pedro spoke.

"Is your name Bernardo?" he asked.

The drunken man blinked at him.

"Yes, I am Bernardo."

"I thought so," said Pedro. "I had heard that in this town lived a man named Bernardo who was a know-nothing and a drunkard. I knew you must be the one, because nobody but a drunken fool would try to drown strangers who came to trade and make his town rich."

Bernardo became furious. He screeched that Pedro lied. But the other men looked at us with a new expression in their faces. Then one of them roughly told Bernardo to be quiet; and when he kept on yelling two others shoved him away. By this time everyone in the place was there at the shore. They all stood staring, and I saw some whispering to one another.

"Is that the truth?" demanded Gastoa. "Have you come to trade?"

"You do not think we came to look at your handsome face, do you?" sneered Pedro. "Who is the head man here?" I will do my business with him."

The crowd opened, and out stepped a man who was rather old but looked strong and shrewd.

"I am chief," he said. "I, Araujo."

His sharp eyes went to our canoe, which now held only the few supplies that remained after our long trip.

"If you come to trade, where are your trade goods?" he asked.

"Greetings to you, *compadre*," said Pedro, as if the head man were no better than the rest. "Surely you do not think we would bring our goods in that little canoe. It will take a big *batelao* to carry the things we have for you — that is, if we decide to trade with you. This is not a small matter of wax and salt fish."

His insolent manner made Araujo frown, but I could see that he and all the rest were impressed by it and by his big talk. I had no idea of what tale Pedro intended to tell, but I saw he had made a good beginning; so I tried to look like an important trader, instead of what I was — a bush-tramp with hardly enough food and cartridges to get home on. The thought came to me that Deodoro might show surprise and betray us. But a glance at him showed me he had more sense than that. His face was like wood, and he was looking straight ahead.

"What do you want for this *batelao* full of riches?" asked the head man.

"We will talk alone with you about that," Pedro told him. "We do not do our business on the riverbank. And before we do any business at all we want food for ourselves and this guide of ours, Deodoro."

Araujo looked as all over again, staring hard at Deodoro, who stared back at him. Then he nodded and turned away. We followed him, and I noticed that the crowd now was looking in friendly fashion at our Tapir companion and sourly at Gastoa. The reason was easy to see; they believed Deodoro had brought us there to make them rich, and that Gastoa had angered us and might have lost them their chance to trade. I had hard work to keep from grinning.

"You have come in time to eat at the feast," said Araujo. "This is a feast-day here. A girl has come to womanhood."

"What girl?" asked the Tapir.

"Not the one you are thinking of," the old man answered. "It is the youngest daughter of Fontoura."

"Oho! So you have a girl here, Deodoro!" teased Pedro, as if he had not heard of it. "You sly fellow, why did you not tell us?"

Deodoro looked queerly at him, but made no answer. The head man chuckled.

"There are several men between him and his girl," he explained. "And the girl has not yet been made a woman. So I would not say that he has any."

We had gotten away from the crowd by this time, and he stopped.

"Now you can tell me your business," he said.

"*Amanha* — tomorrow," Pedro answered, "I never do business on a feast-day; and since we have been lucky enough to come at a time of merry-making, we will join you in it. Tomorrow, when I have rested, we can talk of this matter."

Araujo scowled again. So Pedro added —

"Today it is enough to ask you whether you can get sarsaparilla roots, and perhaps Peruvian bark, for us from the forest near here."

The face of the chief brightened.

"Yes, yes! There is much in the hills above here."

"Then our guide has not lied to us," said Pedro, as if well pleased. "Perhaps you have heard of the big new company of Englishmen who now are working out of Tabatinga and preparing to buy these medical things for the markets in Europe?"

Araujo had not. Neither had I, and neither had Pedro. But the chief now thought he understood.

"And you are the scouts of this company," he guessed. "You are very welcome. We can make much trade for you. What do you give for those roots?"

But Pedro shook his head.

"*Amanha*," he said again.

So, seeing that he would talk no more of business that day, Araujo told us the town was ours.

The drum started up again, and others joined in. Men came to us with liquor and meat, and we ate and drank well — for we had paddled several miles since eating at Deodoro's tree-hut, and our appetites again were strong. Everyone made us welcome — that is, all but Bernardo and Gastoa and his gang. They stayed by themselves, talking angrily and drinking much.

I was glad to see that they drank, for I felt that they were the ones whom we needed to watch most, and hoped that in the end they would make themselves senseless. If we waited until night, I thought, it should be quite easy to get the girl out of her prison and escape with her. But Deodoro spoiled that plan.

Before long the *caboclos* formed for a dance around the drummers. It was not much of a dance. They only trotted around and around, yelling and laughing, and dropping out one by one for a drink now and then. Araujo, the chief, trotted with the rest, tooting solemnly on a little tin whistle he had gotten somewhere. Some of the men shouted to us to join in, and I saw several young women making eyes at Pedro; but we said we were tired and squatted by ourselves, smoking and watching. Then Pedro said to Deodoro:

"Now is a good time for you, comrade, to slip away and talk to your girl. She must feel very badly at hearing all this merriment, knowing that it is for another girl, while she remains cooped up. She ought to be ready to run away with you now. If she is, tell her that at the right time we will take her where she can be happy."

The young fellow started to rise. Pedro grabbed him and pulled him down.

"Not like that!" he cautioned. "Do not get up and walk away in plain sight. Creep around behind us and then crawl behind this house at our backs. After that you can walk."

The big fellow grunted and obeyed. Like the tapir he resembled, he was not very good at creeping. He made some noise as he went. But nobody seemed to notice his going. Between the liquor and the dancing, the *caboclos* now were getting quite drunk and thinking of nothing but their own fun. So our companion got away without being seen.

We sat for a while longer watching the circling crowd. Then Pedro said:

"They are a worthless lot, Lourenço. Even if we were the traders they think us to be I doubt if I should want to do business with them. They look lazy, mean and treacherous. They have no welcome to a stranger unless they hope to make something from him, and their laughter now is only the kind born of drink and drums. I shall be glad when we are out of this place. This is the first time I ever took a hand in a woman-stealing."

"That is the way I feel too," I agreed. "I am not afraid of them, but I dislike them all. And unless Deodoro's girl is better than the women I have seen here she is hardly worth our time and trouble."

"He thinks she is," he laughed. "And every man must be his own judge in such matters. But I wish he would come back. I want to get up and walk around — those drums make me restless. If we do that, though, the *caboclos* will notice that he is gone."

It did seem that Deodoro had been gone for some time, and as the throbbing of the drums went on I too wished I could move around. A few minutes later I was moving around more than I had expected to.

A yell broke out. The dancers stopped. We hopped up. Then, before a house near the water, we saw men fighting and a girl running toward the stream.

"The fool!" snorted Pedro. "He has let her out too soon!"

We ran toward the struggle. So did everyone else. One of the fighting men broke away and dashed after the girl. Another fell backward and lay still. But there were four of them left, and three of them were attacking Deodoro. They were Gastoa and two of his brothers. The man on the ground was the third brother.

As we reached them, Gastoa himself went down. The Tapir was fighting only with his hands, but those hands were terrible enough.

He got a clumsy swing into Gastoa's face, and it cracked like flat wood hitting water. Gastoa fell like a dead man. After he was down I caught a glimpse of his face. It looked as if a real tapir had jumped on it — mashed flat.

Pedro and I knocked down the other two men and yelled to Deodoro to run. All three of us jumped for our canoes. We ran into the girl and the man who had seized her. She was screaming and trying to escape. The man was her father, and he was striking her brutally in the face and body.

Pedro, the quickest of us three, reached them first. He jolted Bernardo in the head with his rifle-butt, and the drunkard fell sprawling. Without a pause Pedro snatched the girl off the ground and kept on running. But the crowd was almost on us, and as we slowed at the water's edge they caught us.

"Go!" I grunted to Pedro. Then I yanked his gun from his fist, whirled and struck around me. Men fell, but others swarmed in. I heard grunts and blows beside me and knew somebody was helping me to fight, but I had no time to see who it was. I thought it must be Pedro. Later I was surprised to find that it was Deodoro.

Pedro had hastily pushed the girl into our canoe and then turned back. But Deodoro, thinking only of getting the girl away, shoved Pedro backward so that he tumbled into the canoe, and then he heaved the boat out into the river. In falling, Pedro hit his head hard against the bottom of the canoe, and the blow stunned him so that he lay there a few minutes while he and the girl drifted away downstream. Then the fighting Tapir wheeled back to help me hold off the furious crowd.

Between us we did some rough work. But we were outnumbered; and to tell truth, *senhores,* I never got such a beating in my life. I have fought hard before and since that time, and have had far more serious wounds than I received then; but those *caboclos* knew how to hit where it would hurt. If they had had their weapons they would have cut me to pieces. But none of them had stopped to pick up a knife, and now they could fight only with hands, feet and teeth. Those were enough.

Somehow I did not think of shooting. I could not have shot well if I had tried, for they were too close. They wrenched at the gun while they beat me, and how I kept it I do not know. But I did keep it, and slugged around me with muzzle and butt. Finally, though, they knocked my legs out from under me. I fell hard, and they jumped all over me.

I kicked and squirmed and bit, but they had me. Then suddenly I felt a tremendous tug at one foot. I went sliding and bumping down the bank with two men hanging to me. Blows sounded and the men fell away. Somebody tumbled me head first into a canoe. The canoe slid outward.

A raging yell sounded behind me. Sitting up, I found myself afloat. With me was the Tapir. His face was battered and his big snout was gushing red, but he was as strong as ever. He had grabbed a paddle and was shoving the boat downstream with strokes so powerful that the dugout seemed to leap from the water. As I looked at him he grinned through split lips.

"I had to pull hard to get you out of that tangle," he said. "You seemed stuck to the ground."

I tried to answer, but all I could do was to make a wheezing sound. The wind was beaten out of me. So I sat still while my breath came back and my head grew clear. I saw that the *caboclos* were jumping into boats and coming after us. Then we caught up with my own canoe, where the girl was crouching and Pedro was getting up and reaching for a paddle. Pedro had a surprised look, as if wondering how he had come there, but he wasted no time in talk. Scooping up a handful of water, he threw it on his head and then began to paddle hard.

I looked for a paddle too, but there was none. Deodoro was using the only one in this canoe. I still had the rifle, though; and, seeing that the maddened men behind were gaining on us, I began shooting. I did not shoot to kill, for I do not like to kill men if it can be avoided. At the same time, I shot close enough to make them think I meant death.

Aiming carefully, I sent several bullets thumping along the sides of their dugouts. They slowed up at once. Some yelled to stop, others shouted to go on, and they paddled both ways at once — some trying to keep after us and others backing water. While this was going on we drew away fast.

The Tapir swerved into the bank and up the same stream we had traveled before. Pedro followed. For some time we kept on at the same rate of speed, and then we came out into the long crooked lake. There we stopped, listened — and heard nothing.

"They have given up," panted Pedro.

The Tapir shook his head.

"They have gone back for guns, and they follow," he said. "But we can dodge them. There is more than one way out of this lake."

Looking around as if to get his bearings, he pushed on again. Down around a bushy point we went, and there turned sharp to the right. A short arm of water ran that way, and we traveled down this until we seemed about to bump the shore. Then he swung to the left, and we were in a quiet, winding stream. There we stopped.

I got up with grunts and groans, for I had been sitting still and my bruised muscles had stiffened so that each one had a pain of its own. Deodoro grinned again. The grin annoyed me.

"Now," I demanded, "tell me why you got us into all this trouble. Why did you not come back to us and wait until we were ready?"

"You said yourself that the first thing to do was to free Bellie, and that the quickest way to free her was to go ahead and do it," he answered. "So I went and did it. And your comrade Pedro told me to be strong and bold. Have I not been strong and bold?"

His face and voice were so serious that Pedro and I laughed.

"More bold than we wanted you to be," I told him.

"I am sorry you got hurt," he said. "But I went and talked to Bellie and found her mad to get out at once. So I thought I had better take her before she changed her mind, and I cut a hole and pulled her through. If Gastoa and his brothers had not sneaked up just then we should have gotten away without trouble. And nobody would have thought you two traders had anything to do with it, because you were sitting in plain sight all the time."

"I see," I said. "And now that we are all here I think you had better take your girl and let me get into my own canoe."

We had been holding to bushes while we talked, and now Pedro drew our canoe up beside me. For the first time I had a good look at the girl, and after that look I did not blame Deodoro for wanting her. She was very pretty. True, she looked thin and weak, and her skin seemed pale; but I remembered that she had been caged for a long time, and knew that a healthy life outdoors and plenty to eat would quickly make her plump and strong. Her eyes and mouth were beautiful, and she looked no more like the other women we had seen than a butterfly looks like a mud-worm. Remembering the evil face of Gastoa and the brutality of her father, I was glad I had gone to help her, even though I now was full of aches and pains.

Then I noticed something that was not so pleasing. She did not want to leave Pedro and come to Deodoro. She looked long at Pedro, then glanced at the tapir-man and wrinkled her nose. I too looked at both the men, and saw what a difference there was. Pedro was a graceful fellow, with merry brown eyes and curly hair; and he had not been hit during the fight, so his face was not marked at all. Deodoro, with his clumsy-looking body and lank hair and big nose, was not a beauty at any time; and now his eyes were swollen so that they peered through slits, and his whole face was bruised and bloody.

It came to me, too, that though Deodoro had given the girl her chance to escape from the house, it was Pedro who had attacked Bernardo when she was being beaten and had run with her in his arms to the water; so that she might easily feel that it was the handsome stranger who had saved her. Besides, she had not seen Deodoro's one fight at the house, because then she was running for the river. And she probably did not know much about his battle on the bank, for then she was floating away and we were all tangled up in a lighting knot. Poor Deodoro! Everything seemed to be against him.

Whether he saw all this I did not know, but I hoped not. When the girl made no move to change canoes I spoke gruffly to her, telling her to make room for me. She rose then though slowly, and took my place without a word.

As I settled down and picked up my paddle I heard voices out on the lake. We slipped the canoes silently downstream and looked. The Tapir was right — two boatloads of armed *caboclos* were passing, the men working hard and looking ahead. Others came behind them. We kept very quiet until they were gone.

"They will go down the lake to the end hunting us," said the Tapir. "Then they will work back and search all the coves. We shall be at my house long before they have finished here. Are you not glad to be free, Bellie?"

The girl made no answer. Her eyes came again to Pedro's face, and then she looked down into the water. Deodoro looked long at her, then at Pedro, then at me. His face grew sad. With a deep sigh he pushed his canoe against the slow current, and we passed silently up the creek.

After a time we came into a network of winding water courses without any current that I could see. Deodoro hesitated several times, but seemed always to pick the right one. At length we found ourselves again in flowing water, and now we went downstream instead of up. At length we entered the river on which Pedro and I had been traveling that morning.

There our leader turned downward, and we saw that he had brought us out above his house. Keeping near the left shore and watching sharply for *caboclos,* we soon reached the little inlet masked by the palms.

"Now you are safe, Bella," I said when we stepped out on shore. "See the fine house Deodoro has built for you up here in the tree, where you can always be dry and comfortable. It is much better than any house in your town, and you will never have to live in a cage again. He has much meat too, and you and he will have plenty to eat. You will be very happy here."

"Do you two stay here also?" she asked.

"No," I said. "This is Deodoro's place. We must go on, for we live far from here."

She glanced once more at the house in the tree. Then she cried:

"I do not want to stay here, I will not stay here! Take me away!"

We all stood silent, staring at her. I wanted to scold her, but knew that would do no good. So I said the first thing that seemed best.

"We cannot take you away today, Bella — it will soon be night. And we two are not going until tomorrow. We shall rest and eat here. Tomorrow we shall see what is best to be done. Now go up and see what a fine house that is."

She stood still, stubbornly, until Pedro also told her to mount the ladder. Then she obeyed, climbing as if afraid she would fall, but going upward until she got into the hut.

"*Nossa Senhora!*" muttered Pedro. "Now this is a pretty mess! After all our trouble she wants to go back home."

Slowly the Tapir shook his head. His face was full of pain.

"No, it is not that," he said. "It is as I told you before we went. She likes tall handsome men, and I am not tall nor handsome."

He swallowed hard, as if trying to keep from crying. And then, through his teeth, he added:

"She wants to — to go with you, Pedro. If she will — be happier with you, comrade, then — then you had better take her with you."

He choked and turned away.

For an instant Pedro stared. Then he sprang and caught him by the shoulder.

"*Par Deus*, you are a man!" he said. "Why, comrade, I do not want your girl! I do not want any girl at all. And you are wrong — she does not want me either. She may be interested in me because I am a new man whom she has not seen before, but after I am gone she will quickly forget me."

But Deodoro shook his head again, and so did I. I had seen women fall swiftly in love with Pedro before this — women who knew more about men than this little girl-woman knew; and I felt that Bella would not forget him so quickly as he said, and that neither she nor Deodoro would be happy because of this. When Pedro asked me if I did not agree with him, I said no.

"There is some truth in what Deodoro says," I told him, "If she had not seen you she might have been happy with him. I think our work is only half-done. We have freed her, but how are we to make her satisfied?"

He scowled and stood thinking. Then his eyes began to twinkle, and he threw up his head and laughed.

"Deodoro, let me talk to you," he said. "Lourenço, climb up and talk with her so that she will not overhear us. Ask her if she would like to go away with me — but try to show her that she would be foolish to do such a thing."

I did as he said. Up the pole I went, and in the hammock I found the girl, looking very small and sad and dissatisfied. When I came in she brightened up and glanced beyond me as if expecting someone else. Seeing that nobody followed, she seemed disappointed.

"The others will be up soon," I informed her.

Then I sat down against the wall, grunting from the pain of my stiff muscles.

"I am very lame," I went on. "Still, I am glad I am alive to feel lame. If it had not been for the splendid fighting of Deodoro I should probably be dead — and you would be back in your cage, to be beaten by your father and given to Gastoa."

She turned more pale at that thought, but looked surprised too. And she asked what Deodoro had done that was so brave. So I saw that I was right — she did not realize what a fight he had made. Taking care not to praise him over-much, I told her how he had fought off the gang of Gastoa and then battled beside me so that she could get away, and how he had pulled me out when I was down. Her big dark eyes grew larger as I talked.

Then, when her mind was full of this new fighting Deodoro, I suddenly asked her whether she would like to go away with us.

"My friend Pedro likes you," I said, "and if you want to go with him we can fool Deodoro in some way. You might not be happy with Pedro, but —"

"Why not?" she cut in.

"Well, of course he is a handsome man," I pointed out, "and other girls like him very well, and you could not expect him to give all his time to you. He would not stay with you as this simple Deodoro would do. And he likes his fun with men too, and so he would drink and gamble with them. And he is restless and will not stay long in one place — and you know he would not want you trailing after him everywhere. If you expected him to be as faithful to you as Deodoro would be, you might not be happy. But if you are willing to be reasonable about those things we can take you away when we go. He is keeping Deodoro down below while I ask you about this."

Senhores, that gave her a good deal to think about. At first she looked as if she wanted to cry, and I felt sorry for her — but I did not let her see that. Then, she asked the question I expected.

"If he wants me, why does he not talk to me himself instead of sending you?"

I laughed as if that were a foolish question.

"Because Deodoro would probably fight to keep you, and Pedro knows how hard he would fight. Pedro probably would get his handsome face hurt. And besides, what is the sense of fighting over a woman? Deodoro thinks you are the only pretty woman in the world, but Pedro and I know you are not."

She looked at me then as if beginning to dislike me. Before we could talk more we heard Pedro's voice down below, and it was loud and ugly.

"Then if you have more *cachassa,* why did you not say so?" he demanded. "I want a drink and I want it now! After we have gone to that dirty town of yours and brought back that female for you, I call it shabby treatment to try to hide your liquor!"

"You can have a drink if you want it," came the voice of the Tapir. "But do not speak so of my girl. She is not the kind of girl that a man like you ought to talk about."

"Bah! The world is full of girls, and not one of them is worth anything. I want that drink!"

"Then come up and you shall have it."

I stuck my head out of the door beside me and looked down. Deodoro, I noticed, had washed his face and looked much better. As he came upward and saw me he grinned. Pedro, behind him, winked at me. But when they came into the house their expressions had changed. Deodoro looked very serious, and Pedro scowled.

The Tapir lifted part of his floor again, and this time he pulled up a jar which he handed Pedro. My partner seemed to take a huge drink. When he passed the jar to me, however, I found that very little of the liquor was gone. I took as much as I wanted, and then held it out toward Deodoro. But Pedro snatched it and appeared to swallow about half of what was left, making a guzzling noise and letting some of the *cachassa* drip off his chin. The girl watched all this, and a look of disgust crept across her face. The thought came to me that my comrade's actions must remind her of her drunken, worthless father.

Then Pedro slumped down beside me and rolled a cigarette. Usually he was very deft at making a smoke, but now his fingers seemed clumsy. He spilled most of his tobacco, and then he snarled. He tried again, and made a worse mess than before. Finally he ordered me to make his cigarette for him. I did so, but I took my time about it. Then he abused me because I was so slow, and growled once more at Deodoro because he had not been more free with his liquor. After the cigarette was lit and going well, though, he quieted somewhat.

None of us spoke while he smoked, Deodoro watched us solemnly, and I saw the girl studying him and Pedro in turn. Pedro's face grew more heavy, as if the *cachassa* were working on him. Presently he began to leer at Bella.

"Think I will take you downriver with me, girl," he said roughly. "You do not want to stay here and you do not want to go back to your cage. You have to go somewhere, so come with me."

She looked him straight in the eyes. Then she said —

"I do not think I want to go with you."

"What!" snapped Pedro. "Do not be a little fool!" He looked at Deodoro and grinned in a nasty way, as if the liquor had given him courage which he had lacked before. "You, Deodoro, you can stay here with your *cachassa.* I am going away with this woman of yours. I am going now!"

He lurched up and staggered toward the girl.

Then the Tapir moved. He swooped at the rifle Pedro had left leaning against the wall. He jammed the muzzle into my comrade's stomach, and I heard the hammer click back.

"Stop where you are!" he ordered. "You shall not take her away. She is too good for you."

Pedro stood very still, staring down at the gun as if stricken with fear. I got up as quickly as I could, drawing my machete, for I did not like the sound of that hammer going back. But before I could get within arm's length of Deodoro the girl jumped at me.

She came so suddenly and swiftly that before I realized it she had knocked my bush-knife from my hands. With another lightning move she threw it out of the door, and I heard it thump on the ground below. Then, her face full of fury, she warned me —

"Keep back or I will tear your eyes out!"

I kept back. Her nails were very long, and I had seen how quick she was. Her sudden action had taken us all by surprise, and we stood staring at her. Then Deodoro spoke again to Pedro.

"If she wished to go with you and if you would be kind to her I would let her go. But I know you have other women. You boasted about it when you first came here and drank my *cachassa.* You said you only played with women, and that when you tired of one you left her and got another. You will not do so with Bellie."

Pedro made no answer. He looked at Bella. She looked back, at him as if now she hated him. To Deodoro she said:

"You are the only honest man I know, Deodoro. I will stay with you and be your good girl. Drive these two into the river! This one is no better than the other." She pointed at me. "He wanted me to fool you and run away with them. Drive them out!"

"Get down the pole!" grunted the Tapir savagely. "Bellie, stay here!"

Pedro glanced at me and jerked his head toward the door. We went down the pole, Deodoro still covering us.

"Do not touch that machete!" he warned, as I stepped toward my knife. "Go to your canoe."

"Come, Lourenço," whispered Pedro. "He will follow."

So we got into our canoe. Deodoro came down, picked up my weapon and. stepped into his own boat.

"Out into the river!" he commanded.

Pedro, looking much afraid, splashed his paddle quickly into the water and we moved outward. Behind us came the Tapir.

As we went downstream I felt the canoe shaking. I could not understand this until I looked at Pedro.

The drunken look was gone from his face, and, though he made no sound, he was laughing so hard that he could scarcely use his paddle.

"Over to the right, where you see that *massaranduba* tree," came the voice of the Tapir.

We turned to the place. Below the tree we found a little cove which twisted around like a hook. At its end, where it could not be seen from the river, was a small hut.

There we got out. Pedro leaned on his paddle and laughed again. The Tapir, grinning, handed us our weapons.

"You can sleep dry here, comrades," he said. "I built this place while I was hunting monkey-meat, I do not think the men from the town will come to this river until tomorrow — the darkness is coming. If they should come, they will not find you here."

"Be careful that they do not find you either, friend," Pedro answered.

"They will not find us. If they do they will be sorry,"

He spoke with a calm strength that made me think what a difference a few hours had made in him. That morning he had been a blubbering boy. Now, with the knowledge that Bella was his own and that he could thrash any two of those *caboclos* who had made his life and hers so wretched, he was a man. Rather slow of thought, perhaps, but able to take care of himself from this time on — that was the new Deodoro who now talked so surely and called us "comrades." His eye was steady and his head was up, and he feared no man.

"I am sorry that I had to drive you out in such a way," he went on. "You are the first men who ever did anything for me, and you have done the greatest thing any man could do for me. So I do not like to seem ungrateful, even though you understand and know that I am not. If ever I can do anything for you, Pedro and Lourenço, call on me and I will do it, not matter what it is."

He grinned again.

"That was a very wise plan of yours, Pedro — you know women better than I do. But Bellie nearly spoiled it all when she jumped at Lourenço. I almost forgot everything you had told me to say and do."

"So did I," admitted my partner, "After she did that it was not really necessary to talk about the women I had abandoned — ha ha ha! I nearly laughed in your face. But she is all yours now, friend. Treat her well — but be strong and bold, strong and bold!"

"I will," the Tapir promised earnestly. "*Adeos!*"

He stepped back into his canoe and left us. Pedro took cartridges from a pocket and reloaded his rifle.

THE PATHLESS TRAIL

I

SONS OF THE NORTH

Three men stood ankle deep in mud on the shore of a jungle river, silently watching a ribbon of smoke drift and dissolve above the somber mass of trees to the northwest.

Three men of widely different types they were, yet all cradled in the same far-off northern land. The tallest, lean bodied but broad shouldered, black of hair and gray of eye, held himself in soldierly fashion and gazed unmoved. His two mates — one stocky, red faced and red headed; the other slender, bronzed and blond — betrayed their thoughts in their blue eyes. The red man squinted quizzically at the smoke feather as if it mattered little to him where he was. The blond watched it with the wistfulness of one who sees the last sign of his own world fade out.

Behind them, at a respectful distance, a number of swarthy individuals of both sexes in nondescript garments smoked and stared at the trio with the interest always accorded strangers by the dwellers of the Out Places. They eyed the uncompromising back of the tall one, the easy lounge of the red one, the thoughtful attitude of the light one. The copper-faced men peered at the rifles hanging in the right hands of the newcomers, their knee boots, khaki clothing, and wide hats. The women let their eyes rove over the boxes and bundles reposing in the mud beside the three.

"*Ingles?*" hazarded a woman, speaking through the stem of the black pipe clutched in her filed teeth.

"*Notre-Americano,*" asserted a man, nodding toward the broad hats. "Englishmen would wear the round helmets of pith."

"*Mercadores?* Traders?" suggested the woman, hopefully running an eye again over the bundles.

"*Exploradores,*" the man corrected. "Explorers of the bush. Have you no eyes? Do you not see the guns and high boots?"

The woman subsided. The others continued what seemed to be their only occupation — smoking.

The smoke streamer in the north vanished. As if moved by the same impulse, the three strangers turned their heads and looked south-westward, upriver. The red-haired man spoke.

"So we've lit at last, as the feller said when him and his airyplane landed in a sewer. Faith, I dunno but he was better off than us, at that — he wasn't two thousand miles from nowheres like we are. The steamer's gone, and us three pore li'l' boys are left a long ways from home."

Then, assuming the tone of a showman, he went on:

"Before ye, girls, ye see the well known Ja-va-ree River, which I never seen before and comes from gosh-knows-where and ends in the Ammyzon. Over there on t'other side the water is Peru. Yer feet are in the mud of Brazil. This other river to yer left is the Tickywahoo —"

"Tecuahy," the blond man corrected, grinning.

"Yeah. And behind ye is the last town in the world and the place that God forgot. What d'ye call this here, now, city?"

"Remate de Males. Which means 'Culmination of Evils.'"

"Yeah. It looks it. Wonder if it's anything like Hell's Kitchen, up in li'l' old N'Yawk."

They turned and looked dubiously at the town — a row of perhaps seventy iron-walled and palm-roofed houses set on high palm-trunk poles, each with its ladder dropping from the doorway to the one muddy street. Then spoke the tall man.

"Before you see it again, Tim, you'll think it's quite a town. Above here is nothing but a few rubber estates, seven hundred miles of un-known river, and empty jungle."

"Empty, huh? Then they kidded us on the boat. From what they said it's fair crawlin' with snakes and jaggers and lizards and bloody vam-pires and spiders as big as yer fist. And the water is full o' man-eatin' fish and the bush full o' man-eatin' Injuns. If that's what ye call empty, Cap, don't take me no place where it's crowded."

A slight smile twitched the set lips of the tall "cap."

"They're all here, Tim, though maybe not so thick as you expect. Lots of other things too. Who's this?"

Through the knot of pipe-puffing idlers came a portly coppery man in uniform.

"Well, I'll be — Say, he's the same chap who came onto the boat in a police uniform. Now he's in army rig," the light-haired member of the trio exclaimed. "O Lordy! I've got it! He's the police force and the army! The whole blooming works! Ha!"

Tim snickered and stepped forward.

"Hullo, buddy!" he greeted. "What's on yer mind?"

"*Boa dia*, senhor," responded the official, affably. With the words he deftly slipped an arm around Tim's waist and lifted the other hand toward his shoulder. But that hand stopped short, then flew wildly out into the air.

Tim gave a grunt and a heave. The official went skidding and slither-ing six feet through the mud, clutching at nothing and contorting himself in a frantic effort to keep from sprawling in the muck. By a margin thin as an eyelash he succeeded in preserving his balance and stood where he stopped, amazement and anger in his face.

"Lay off that stuff!" growled Tim, head forward and jaw out. "If ye want trouble come and git it like a man, not sneak up with a grin and then clinch. Don't reach for no knife, now, or I'll drill ye —"

"Tim!" barked the black-haired one. "Ten-*shun!*"

Automatically Tim's head snapped erect and his shoulders went back. He relaxed again almost at once. But in the meantime the tall man had stepped forward and faced the raging representative of the government of Brazil.

"Pardon, comrade," he said with an engaging smile. "My friend is a stranger to Brazil and not acquainted with your manner of welcome. In our own country men never put the arm around one another except in combat. He has been a soldier. You are a soldier. So you can understand that a fighting man may be a little abrupt when he does not understand."

The smile, the apology, and most of all the subtle flattery of being treated as an equal by a man whose manner betokened the North American army officer, mollified the aggrieved official at once. The hot gleam died out of his eyes. Punctiliously he saluted. The salute was as punctiliously returned.

"It is forgotten, Capitao. As the capitao says, we soldiers are sometimes overquick. I come to give you welcome to Remate de Males. My services are at your disposal."

"We thank you. Why do you call me capitao?"

"My eyes know a capitao when they see him."

"But this is not a military expedition, my friend. Nor are any of us soldiers now — though we all have been."

"Once a capitao, always a capitao," the Brazilian insisted. Then he hinted: "If the capitao and his friends wish to call upon the superintendente they will find him in the intendencia, the blue building beyond the hotel. It will soon be closed for the day."

The tall American's keen gray eyes roved down the street to the weather-beaten house whose peeling walls once might have been blue. He nodded shortly.

"Better go down there," he said. "Come on, Merry. Tim, stick here and keep an eye on the stuff. And don't start another war while we're gone."

"Right, Cap." Tim deftly swung his rifle to his right shoulder. "I'll walk me post in a military manner, keepin' always on the alert and observin' everything that takes place within sight or hearin', accordin' to Gin'ral Order Number Two. There won't be no war unless somebody starts somethin'. Hey, there, buddy, would ye smoke a God's-country cigarette if I give ye one?"

"*Si*," grinned the soldier-policeman, all animosity gone. And as the other two men tramped away through the mud they also grinned, looking back at the North and the South American pacing side by side in sentry-go, blowing smoke and conversing like brothers in arms.

"Tim likes to remember his 'general orders,' but he's forgotten Number Five," laughed the blond man.

"Five? 'To talk to no one except in line of duty.' Don't need it here, Merry."

"Nope. The *entente cordiale* is the thing. Here's hoping nobody makes Tim remember his 'Gin'ral Order Number Thirteen' while we're gone, Rod."

He of the black hair smiled again as his mate, mimicking Tim's gruff voice, quoted:

"'Gin'ral Order Number Thirteen: In case o' doubt, bust the other guy quick.'"

II

AT SUNDOWN

Past the loungers in the street, past others in the doorways, past children and dogs and goats, the pair marched briskly to the faded blue house whence the federal superintendent ruled the town with tropic indolence. There they found a thin, fever-worn, gravely courteous gentleman awaiting them.

"Sit, senhores," he urged, with a languid wave of the hand toward chairs. "I am honored by your visit, as is all Remate de Males. In what way can I serve you?"

The blond answered:

"We have come, sir, both for the pleasure of making your acquaintance and for a little information. First permit me to introduce my friend Mr. Roderick McKay, lately a captain in the United States army. I am Meredith Knowlton. There is a third member of our party, Mr. Timothy Ryan, who remained on the river bank to talk with — er — a soldier of Brazil."

The federal official nodded, a slight smile in his eyes.

"We are here ostensibly for exploration," Knowlton continued, candidly, "but actually to find a certain man. I think it quite probable that we shall have to do considerable exploring before finding him."

"Ah," the other murmured, shrewdly. "It is a matter of police work, perhaps?"

"No — and yes. The man we seek is not wanted by the law, and yet he is. He has committed no crime, and so cannot be arrested. But the law wants him badly because the settlement of a certain big estate hinges upon the question of whether he is alive or dead. If alive, he is heir to more than a million. If not — the money goes elsewhere."

"Ah," repeated the official, thoughtfully.

"I might add," McKay broke in with a touch of stiffness, "that neither I nor either of my companions would profit in any way by this man's death. Quite the contrary."

"Ah," reiterated the other, his face clearing. "You are commissioned, perhaps, to find and produce this man."

"Exactly," Knowlton nodded. "From our own financial standpoint he is worth much more alive than dead. On the other hand, any absolute proof of his death — proof which would stand in a court of law — is worth something also. Our task is to produce either the man himself or indisputable proof that he no longer lives.

"The man's name is David Dawson Rand. If alive, he now is thirty-three years old. Height five feet nine. Weight about one hundred sixty. Hair dark, though not black. Eyes grayish green. Chief distinguishing marks are the green eyes, a broken nose — caused by being struck in the face by a baseball — and a patch of snow-white hair the size of a thumb ball, two inches above the left ear. Accustomed to having his own way, not at all considerate of others. Yet not a bad fellow as men go — merely a man spoiled by too much mothering in boyhood and by the fact that he never had to work. This is he."

From a breast pocket he drew a small grain-leather notebook, from which he extracted an unmounted photograph. The superintendent looked into the pictured face of a full-cheeked, wide-mouthed, square-jawed man with a slightly blasé expression and a half-cynical smile. After studying it a minute he nodded and handed it back.

"As you say, senhor, a man who never has had to work."

"Exactly. For five years this man has been regarded as dead. It was his habit to start off suddenly for any place where his whims drew him, notifying nobody of his departure. But a few days later he would always write, cable, or telegraph his relatives, so that his general whereabouts would soon become known. On his last trip he sent a radio message from a steamer, out at sea, saying he was bound for Rio Janeiro. That was the last ever heard from him."

"Rio is far from here," suggested the Brazilian.

"Just so. We look for Rand at the headwaters of the Amazon, instead of in Rio, because Rio yields no clew and because of one other thing which I shall speak of presently.

"It has been learned that he reached Rio safely, but there his trail ended. As he had several thousand dollars on his person, it was concluded that he was murdered for his money and his body disposed of. This belief has been held until quite recently, when a new book of travel was published — *The Mother of Waters*, by Dwight Dexter, an explorer of considerable reputation."

The Brazilian's brows lifted.

"Senhor Dexter? I remember Senhor Dexter. He stopped here for a short time, ill with fever. So he has published a book?"

"Yes. It deals mainly with his travels and observations in Peru, along the Marañon, Huallaga, and Ucayali. But it includes a short chapter regarding the Javary, and in that chapter occurs the following, which I have copied verbatim."

From the notebook he read:

"'It falls to the lot of the explorer at times to meet not only hitherto unclassified species of fauna and flora, but also strange specimens of the *genus homo*. Such a creature came suddenly upon my camp one day just before a serious and well-nigh fatal attack of fever compelled me to relinquish my intention to proceed farther up the Javary.

"'While my Indian cook was preparing the afternoon meal, out from the dense jungle strode a bearded, shaggy-haired, painted white man, totally nude save for a narrow breechclout and a quiver containing several long hunting arrows. In one hand he carried a strong bow of really excellent workmanship. This was his only weapon. He wore no ornament, unless streaks of brilliant red paint be considered ornaments. He was wild and savage in appearance and manner as any cannibal Indian. Yet he was indubitably white.

"'To my somewhat startled greeting he made no response. Neither did he speak at any time during his unceremonious visit. Bolt upright, he stood beside my crude table until the Indian stolidly brought in my food. Then, without a by-your-leave, the wild man rapidly wolfed down the entire meal, feeding himself with one hand and holding his bow ready in the other. Though I questioned him and sought to draw him into conversation, he honored me with not so much as a grunt or a gesture. When the table was bare he stalked out again and vanished into the dim forest.

"'After he had gone my Indian urged that we leave the place at once. The man, he said, was "The Raposa" — a word which denotes a species of wild dog sometimes found on the upper Amazon. He knew nothing of this "Raposa" except that he apparently belonged to a wild tribe living far back in the forest, perhaps allied with the cannibal Mayorunas, who were very fierce; and that he appeared sometimes at Indian settlements, where, without ever speaking, he would help himself to the best food and then leave. My man seemed to fear that now some great misfortune would come to us unless we shifted our base. When the fever came upon me soon afterward, the superstitious fellow was convinced that the illness was attributable directly to the visit of the human "wild dog."

"'Aside from the nudity and barbarism of the mysterious stranger, certain personal peculiarities struck me. One was that his eyes were green. Another was a streak of snow-white hair above one ear. Furthermore, the red paint on his body outlined his skeleton. His ribs, spine, arm- and leg-bones all were portrayed on his tanned skin by those brilliant red streaks. In this connection my Indian asserted that in the tribe to which "The Raposa" probably belonged it was the custom to preserve the bones of the dead and to paint them with this same red dye, after which the bones were hung up in the huts of the deceased instead of being given burial. Beyond this my informant knew nothing of the "Red Bone" people, except that to enter their country was death.'"

Knowlton returned the book to his pocket and carefully buttoned the flap.

"When that appeared," he continued, "efforts were made to get hold of Dexter, with the idea of showing him the photograph of the missing man and learning any additional details. Unfortunately, by the time the book was published Dexter had gone to Africa to seek a race of dwarfs said to exist in the Igidi Desert, and thus was totally out of reach. Then we were called upon to follow up this clew and find the Raposa if possible. Men with green eyes and patches of white hair above one ear are not common. So, though our knowledge of this strange wild man is confined to those few words of Dexter's, we are here to learn more of him and to get him if we can."

He looked expectantly at the official. The latter, after staring out through the doorway for a time, shook his head slightly.

"Something of this Raposa and of those red-streaked people has come to my ears, senhores, but only as rumors," he said, slowly. "And one does not place great faith in rumors. Yet I have repeatedly been surprised to learn, after dismissing a story as an empty Indian tale, that the tale was true.

"Of the Mayorunas more is known. They are eaters of human flesh, inhabiting both sides of the Javary, deadly when angered, and very easily angered. Their country is not many days distant from here, but as they never attack us we do not attack them. It is an armed neutrality, as you senhores would say. True, we have to be careful in drinking water, for they sometimes poison the streams against real or imaginary enemies, and the poisoned waters flow down to us, causing those who drink it to die of a fever like the typhoid. Yet," and he smiled, "there is a saying, is there not, that water is made not to drink, but to bathe in?"

Knowlton laughed. McKay's eyes twinkled.

"I'm sorry to say that water's about all a fellow can get to drink in the States now," the blond man said, ruefully. "That is, of course, unless a man knows where to go."

"*Si*. It is a pity. But here in Brazil one need not drink water unless he wishes, and often it is better not to. Of the Mayorunas, senhor — you do not intend to go among them, seeking this wild man of the red bones? If you should do so it would be a matter of regret to me."

"Meaning that we should not come out again? That's a risk we have to face. We go wherever it is necessary."

"I am sorry. I regret also that I can give you no definite information. Yet I wish you all success, senhores, and a safe return. This much I can do and gladly will do: I can send word to another white man who now is in the town and who knows much of the upper river. He may be able to assist you, and without doubt will be eager to do so. He is staying at the hotel, just below here — Senhor Schwandorf."

The eyes of the two Americans narrowed. The official coughed.

"Senhor McKay has been a soldier. And Senhor Knowlton —"

"I was a lieutenant."

"Ah! But the war has passed, senhores. Senhor Schwandorf was not a soldier of Germany — he has been in Brazil for more than six years."

"War's over. That's right," McKay agreed. "But don't bother to send word. We'll find him if he's at the hotel. Going there ourselves. Glad to have met you, sir. Good luck!"

"And to you also luck, Capitao and Tenente," smiled the official. McKay and Knowlton strode out.

"Guess this is the hotel," hazarded McKay, glancing at a house which rose slightly above the others. "I'll go in and charter rooms. You get Tim and have somebody rustle our impedimenta up here."

He turned aside. Knowlton trudged on through the glare of sunset to the river bank where Tim and the army of Remate de Males still loafed up and down, the admired of all beholders.

"All right, Tim. We're moving to the hotel. No more war, I see."

"Lord love ye, no," grinned Tim. "Me and this feller are gittin' on fine. He's Joey — I forgit the rest of his names; he's got about a dozen more and they sound like stones rattlin' around inside a can. But Joey's a right guy. After me tour o' duty ends he's goin' to buy me a drink and maybe introjuce me to a lady friend o' his. Want to join the party, Looey?"

"Not unless the ladies are better looking than these," laughed the ex-lieutenant, moving his head toward the pipe-smoking females.

"Faith, I was thinkin' that same meself. Unless he can dig up somethin' fancier 'n what I see so far, I'd as soon have Mademoiselle."

"Who?"

"Mademoiselle of Armentières. Sure, ye know that one, Looey. Goes to the tune o' 'Parley-Voo.'"

Wherewith he lifted up a foghorn voice and, much to the edification of "Joey" (whose name really was Joao) and the rest of Remate de Males, burst into song:

> *"Mademoiselle of Armenteers,*
> *Pa-a-arley-voo!*
> *She smoked our butts and bummed our beers,*
> *Pa-a-arley-voo!*
> *She had cockeyes and jackass ears*
> *And she hadn't been kissed for forty years,*
> *Rinkydinky-parley-voo!"*

As his musical effort ended, out from the dense jungle hemming in the town burst a hideous roaring howl. Again and again it sounded in a horrible crash of noise.

"Holy Saint Pat!" gasped Tim, throwing his rifle to port and bracing his feet. "Now look what I went and done! Is that the echo, or a couple dozen jaggers all fightin' to oncet?"

"Guariba, Senhor Ree-ann," snickered Joao. "Not jaguars — no. Only one little guariba monkey. The howler."

"G'wan! Ye're kiddin'!"

"But no, *amigo*. It is as I tell you. One monkey. It is sunset, and the jungle awakes."

"My gosh! I'll say it does. Sounds like a Sat'day night row in a Second Av'noo saloon, except there ain't no shootin'. Guess you boys have some night life, too, even if ye are away back in the bush."

"Time for us to move, Tim," laughed Knowlton. "It'll be dark in no time. Joao, will you have our baggage moved to the hotel?"

"*Si*, senhor. *Immediatamente.* Antonio — Jorge — Rosario! And you, too, Meldo — *vem cà*! Carry the bundles of the gentlemen to the hotel, presto! Proceed, senhores. I, Joao d'Almeida Magalhaes Nabuco Pestana da Fonseca, will remain here on guard until all your possessions have been transported. Proceed without fear."

III

THE VOICE OF THE WILDS

McKay, eyes twinkling again, awaited them at the top of the hotel's street ladder.

"Rooms any good, Rod?" hailed Knowlton.

"Best in the house, Merry."

"See any insects in the beds?"

"Nary a bug — in the beds." The twinkle grew. "Didn't look in the bureaus or behind the mirrors. Come look 'em over."

Entering a sizable room evidently used for dining — for its chief articles of furniture were two tables made from planed palm trunks — McKay waved a hand toward a row of four doorways on the right.

"First three are ours," he explained. "Only vacancies here. Eight rooms in this hotel — the other four over there." He pointed across the room, on the other side of which opened four similar doors. "They're occupied by two sick men, one drunk — hear him snore? — and one she-goat which is kidding."

"Huh?" Tim snorted, suspiciously. "I think ye're the one that's kiddin', Cap."

"Not a bit. I looked. The last room on this side is the Dutchman's, and these are ours. Take your pick. They're all alike."

Knowlton stepped to the nearest and looked in. For a moment he said no word. Then he softly muttered:

"Well, I'll be spread-eagled!"

"Me, too," seconded Tim, who had been craning his neck.

The room was absolutely empty. No bed, no chair, no bureau, no rug — nothing at all was in it except two iron hooks. Its floor consisted of split palm logs, round side up, between which opened inch-wide spaces. Its walls were rusty corrugated iron, guiltless of mirrors or pictures, which did not reach to the roof.

"Observe the excellent ventilation," grinned McKay. "Wind blows up through the floor — if there is any wind — and then loops over the partition into the next fellow's room."

"Yeah. And I'll say any guy that drops his collar button is out o' luck. It goes plunk into the mud, seven foot down under the house. But say, Cap, how the heck do we sleep? Hang ourselves up on them hooks?"

"Exactly."

"Kind o' rough on a feller's shirt, ain't it? And the shirt would likely pull off over yer head before mornin'."

"Yes, probably would. But the secret is this — you're supposed to hang your hammock on those hooks. You provide the hammock. The hotel provides the hooks. What more can you ask of a modern hotel?"

"Huh! And if a guy wants a bath, there's the river, all full o' 'gators and cattawampuses and things. And if ye eat, I s'pose ye rustle yer own grub and pay for eatin' it off that slab table there. There's jest one thing ye can say for this dump — a feller can spit on the floor. But with all them cracks in it he might not hit it, at that. Mother of mine! To think Missus Ryan's li'l' boy should ever git caught stayin' in a hole like this, along o' drunks and skiddin' she-goats and — did ye say a Dutchman?"

"German. Chap named Schwandorf."

"Yeah?" Tim's tone was sinister. "Say, Cap, gimme the room next that guy. And if ye hear anybody yowlin' before mornin' don't git worried. It won't be me."

"None of that, Tim," warned Knowlton. "The war's over —"

"Since when? There wasn't no peace treaty signed when we left the States."

"Er — ahum! Well, technically you're right. But this fellow may be useful to us. He knows the upper river, they say."

"Aw, well, if ye can use him I'll lay off him. Where is he?"

"Out somewhere," answered McKay. "I haven't seen him yet. Want this first room, Merry?"

"Just to play safe, I'll take the one next the German. And if I hear any war in the night, Tim, I'm coming over the top with both hands going."

"Grrrumph!" growled Tim.

"That goes, Tim," warned McKay. "I'll take this room and you can have the one between us. Here comes the baggage train with our stuff. In here, men!"

Puffing and grunting, Antonio and Jorge and Rosario and Meldo shuffled in with the boxes and bundles. Under the directions of McKay and Knowlton, these were stowed in the bare rooms. Then the four shuffled out again, grinning happily over a small roll of Brazilian paper reis which McKay had peeled from a much larger roll and handed to them. Immediately following their departure, in came a youth carrying three new hammocks.

"Our beds," McKay explained. "I sent this lad to a trader's store for them. He's the proprietor's son. Thank you, Thomaz. Tell your father to put these on our bill, and take for yourself this small token of our appreciation."

More reis changed hands. The young Brazilian, with a flash of teeth, informed them that the evening meal would soon be ready and disappeared through a rear door.

"Do they really feed us at this here, now, hotel?" Tim demanded. "Then the goat's safe."

"Meaning?" puzzled Knowlton.

"Meanin' I didn't know but we had to kill our supper, and I was goin' to git the cap'n's goat. That is, the goat the cap'n's kiddin' — I mean the goat that's kiddin' the cap — the skiddin' she-goat — Aw, rats! ye know what I'm drivin' at. Me tongue so dry it don't work right."

Wherewith Tim retreated in disorder to his room and began wrestling with his new hammock and the iron hooks.

Swift darkness filled the rooms. The sun had slid down below the bulge of the fast-rolling world. Thomaz re-entered, lit candles stuck in empty bottles, and, with a bow, placed one of these crude illuminants at the door of each of the strangers. By the flickering lights McKay and Knowlton disposed their effects according to their individual desires, bearing in mind Tim's observation that any small article dropped on the floor would land in the mud under the house, whence sounded the grunts of pigs. Their work was soon completed, and they sauntered together to the small piazza.

"Nice quiet little place," commented Knowlton. "Make a good sanitarium for nervous folks."

The comment was made in a tone which, in the daytime, would carry half a mile. McKay nodded to save a similar effort. The outbreak of the howling monkey which so startled Tim had been only the first note of the night concert of the jungle. Now that the sun was gone the chorus was in full swing.

Beasts of the village, the jungle, the river, all hurled their voices into the uproar. From the gloom around the houses rose the bellowing of cows and calves, the howls and yelps of dogs, the yowling of cats, the grunts and squeals of hogs. In the black river, flowing past within a stone's throw of the hotel door, sounded the loud snorts of dolphins and the hideous night call of the foul beast of the mud — the alligator. Out from the matted tangle of trees and brush and great snakelike vines behind the town rolled the appalling roars of guaribas, raucous bird calls, dismal hoots, sudden scattered screams. And over all, whelming all other sound by the sheer might of its penetrating power, throbbed the rapid-fire hammering of millions of frogs.

"Frogs sound like a machine-gun barrage," the blond man added.

"Or thousands of riveting hammers pounding steel."

"Queer how much worse it is when you're right in it. We've heard it all the way up two thousand miles of Amazon, but —"

"But you're right beside the orchestra now. Position is everything in life."

The double-edged jest made Knowlton glance sidelong at his mate. Of the tall, eagle-faced Scot's past he knew little beyond what he had seen of him in war, where he had met him and learned to respect him whole-heartedly. From occasional remarks he had learned that McKay had been in all sorts of places between Buenos Aires and Nome; and from a few intangible hints he suspected that his "position in life" had once been much higher socially than at present. But he asked no questions.

"Some orchestra, all right," he responded, casually. "Plenty of jazz. It'll quiet down after a while."

For a time they stood leaning against the wall, staring abstractedly out at the dark. One by one the domestic animals ceased their clamor and settled themselves for the night. The jungle din, too, seemed to diminish, though perhaps this was because the ears of the men had become accustomed to it. At length through the discordant symphony boomed the voice of Tim.

"By cripes! I know now what folks mean when they talk about a howlin' wilderness. Always thought 'twas one o' them figgers o' speech, but I'll tell the world it ain't no joke! Gosh! Think of all the things that's layin' out there and bellerin' and waitin' for us pore li'l' fellers to come in amongst 'em and git et up."

"You'll find the same things in the cities up home," said Knowlton, a bit cynically. "Different bodies and different methods of attack, but the same merciless animals under the skin. Snakes in silk suits — foul-mouthed alligators in dinner jackets— hunting-cats and vampires, painted and powdered — and all the rest of it."

"Yeah. Ye said a mouthful, Looey. But say, Tommy's shovin' some grub on the table. Mebbe we better hop to it before the flies git it all."

After a glance at the vicious attack already begun by the aforesaid flies, the pair adopted Tim's suggestion and hopped to it. Manfully they assailed the rubbery jerked beef, black beans, rice, farinha, and thick, black, unsweetened coffee which comprised the meal. All three were wrestling with chunks of the meat when Tim, facing the door, stopped chewing long enough to mutter:

"Dutchland overalls. Here's the goose stepper."

The heads of the other two involuntarily moved a little. Then their necks stiffened and they continued eating. Tim alone stared straight at a burly, black-whiskered Teuton who had halted in the outer doorway. And

Tim alone saw the ugly look crossing the newcomer's visage as he gazed at the khaki shirts, the broad shoulders under them, and the unmistakably Irish — and hostile — face of Tim himself.

Catching the hard stare of the red-haired man, he of the black beard advanced at once, his eyes veering to the door of his own room. Straight to that room he marched with heavy tread. He opened the door with a kick, shut it behind him with a slam. The three at the table glanced at one another.

"Say what ye like," grumbled Tim, "but me and that guy don't hold no mush party. I don't like his map. I don't like his manners. And he looks too much like the Fritz that shot me in the back with a kamerad gun after surrenderin'. I was in hospital three months. D'ye mind that time, Looey?"

Knowlton nodded. He remembered also that Tim, shot down from behind and almost killed, had reeled up to his feet and bayoneted his man before falling the second time. Wherefore he replied:

"He isn't the same one, Tim."

"Nope," grimly. "That one won't never come back. All the same, if you gents want to chew the fat with this feller I'm goin' slummin' with me friend Joey Mouthgargle Nabisco Whoozis. Then I won't be round here to make no sour-caustic remarks and gum up yer party."

"Might be a good idea," McKay conceded.

"There he is now, the li'l' darlin'! Hullo, Joey, old sock! Stick around a minute while I scoop a few more beans. Be with ye toot sweet — vite — presto — P.D.Q."

Wherewith he demolished the rest of his meal with military dispatch, proceeded doorward, smote the grinning army of Remate de Males a buffet on the shoulder, and vanished into the night. A moment later his stentorian voice rolled back through the nocturnal racket in an impromptu paraphrase of an old and highly improper army song:

"We're in the jungle now,
We ain't behind the plow;
We'll never git rich,
We'll die with the itch.
We're in the jungle now!"

IV

THE GERMAN

The door of the German's room opened. The German came out and marched to the table. Two paces away he halted and faced the Americans, ready to speak if spoken to, equally ready to sit and ignore them if not greeted. McKay and Knowlton rose.

"Herr von Schwandorf?" inquired Knowlton.

"Schwandorf. Neither Herr nor von. Plain Schwandorf."

The reply came in excellent English, though with a slight throaty accent.

"Knowlton is my name. Mr. McKay. The third member of our party, Mr. Ryan, has just left."

Schwandorf bowed stiffly from the waist.

"It is a pleasure to meet you. White men are all too few here."

Seating himself at a place beyond that just vacated by Tim, he continued, "You stay here for a time?"

"Not long." They reseated themselves. "We go up the river as soon as we can arrange transportation."

The black brows lifted slightly.

"It is a dangerous river. You would do well to travel elsewhere unless you have some pressing reason to explore this stream."

With an accustomed sweep of the hand he shooed the flies from the bean dish and helped himself to a big portion. Over the legumes he poured farinha in the Brazilian fashion.

"We have. We are seeking a tribe of people who paint their bones red."

Schwandorf's hand, conveying the first mouthful of beans upward, stopped in air. His black eyes fixed the Americans with an astounded stare. He lowered the beans, stabbed absently at a chunk of beef, sawed it apart, popped a piece of it into his mouth, and sat for a time chewing. When the meat was down he spoke bluntly:

"Are there not ways enough to kill yourselves at home instead of traveling to this place to do it?"

McKay smiled. The directness of the man amused him.

"As bad as that?" asked Knowlton.

"As bad as that. Blow your head off if you like. Cut your throat. Take poison. Jump into the river among the alligators. Step on a snake. But keep away from the Red Bones."

"Why?" shot McKay.

"Cannibals — and worse."

"Worse?"

"Truly. Most of the Brazilian savages do not torture. The Red Bones do."

"Pleasant prospect."

"Very. Nothing to be gained among them, either. If you're hunting gold, try the hills over west of the Huallaga. None here."

Knowlton filled and lit a pipe. McKay slowly drank the last of his syrupy coffee and rolled a cigarette. Schwandorf continued shoveling food into his capacious mouth.

"Know anything about the Raposa?" Knowlton asked.

The Teuton's eyelashes flickered. He ground another chunk of meat between his jaws before answering.

"Of course," he said then. "Wild dog. Sharp snout, gray hair, bushy tail. I've shot a couple of them."

"This one is a man. Green eyes, streak of white hair over the left ear. Paints himself like the Red Bones, as you call them, but is a white man."

"Oh! That one? Heard of him, yes. Wild man of the jungle. Want to catch him and put him in a circus?"

"Maybe. We'd like to see him, anyhow. Heard about him awhile ago. Any way to get him that you know of?"

"Might try a steel trap," the German suggested, callously. "But I don't know where you'd set it. Best way to get a wild dog is to shoot him, and he isn't much good dead. Or would this one be worth something — dead?" A swift sidelong glance accompanied the question.

"Not a cent!" snapped McKay.

"And perhaps he'd be worth nothing alive," added Knowlton. "But we have a healthy curiosity to look him over. Guess the Red Bone country would be the likeliest place. How far is it from here?"

"Keep out of it," was the stubborn reply.

The Americans rose.

"We are not going to keep out of it," Knowlton declared, coldly. "We are going straight into it. Thank you for your assistance."

"Not so fast," Schwandorf protested. "If you are determined to go I will help you if I can. Shall we sit on the piazza with a small bottle to aid digestion? So! Thomaz! Bring from my stock the kümmel. Or would you prefer whisky, gentlemen?"

"Ginger-ale highballs are my favorite fruit," admitted Knowlton. "Can ginger ale be bought here?"

"Indeed yes. At one milrei a bottle."

"Cheap enough. Thomaz, three bottles of ginger ale and one of North American whisky — the best. Cigars also. Out on the piazza."

"Si, senhores."

Schwandorf got up.

"If you will pardon me, I will drink my kümmel. Frankly, I do not like whisky."

"And frankly, we do not like kümmel. All a matter of taste."

"Truly. So let each of us drink his own preference. I will join you in a moment."

The Americans sauntered to the door, while the German strode into his room.

"Blunt sort of cuss," Knowlton commented.

"Ay, blunt. But not candid. Knows more than he's telling."

Disposing themselves comfortably, they sat watching the lights of the town and the jungle — the first pouring from windows and open doors, the latter streaking across the darkness where the big fire beetles of the tropics winged their way. As Knowlton had predicted, the night noise of forest and stream had diminished; but now from the village itself rose a new discord — a babel of vocal and instrumental efforts at music emanating from the badly worn records of dozens of cheap phonographs grinding away in the stilt-poled huts.

"Good Lord!" groaned McKay. "Even here at the end of the world one can't get away from those beastly instruments."

A throaty chuckle from the doorway followed the words. Schwandorf emerged, carrying a big bottle.

"Yet there is one thing to be thankful for, gentlemen," he said. "In all this town there is not one man who attempts to play a trombone."

The others laughed. Thomaz appeared with bottles and thick cups. Corks were drawn, liquids gurgled, matches flared, cigars glowed. Without warning Schwandorf shot a question through the gloom:

"Have you seen Cabral — the superintendent?"

"Yes."

"Ask him about the wild man?"

"Yes."

"Get any information?"

"Nothing definite. He suggested that we see you."

"So."

A pause, while Schwandorf's cigar end glowed like a flaming eye.

"The Red Bones live well up the river," he began, abruptly. "Twenty-four days by canoe, five days through the bush on the east shore. That would bring you to their main settlement — if you were not wiped out before then. They're a big tribe, as tribes go. Ever been here before?"

"No. Not here," Knowlton told him. "I've been in Rio, and McKay here has knocked around in —"

A stealthy kick from McKay halted him an instant. Then, deftly shifting the sentence, he concluded, "— in a number of places."

"So." Another pause. "Then I should explain about tribes. Tribes here generally consist of from fifty to five hundred or more persons living in big houses called '*malocas*.' Unless the tribe is very big, one house holds them all. There may be any number of *malocas*, the inhabitants of which are all of the same racial stock; yet each *maloca* is, as far as government is concerned, a tribe to itself, controlled by a chief. No *maloca* owes any duty to any other *maloca*. There is no supreme ruler over all, nor even a federation among them. They live merely as neighbors — distant neighbors. At times they fight like neighbors. You understand."

"'When Greek meets Greek —'" quoted McKay.

"Just so. When I say, then, that the Red Bones are a big tribe, I mean that there are about five hundred — maybe more — individuals in their main settlement. They live in huts, not in one big tribe-house like the Mayorunas. They are not Mayorunas, in fact; they paint differently, are darker of skin, and more cruel.

"The Mayorunas, by the way, are not so debased as you might think. Though cannibals, they do not kill for the sake of eating 'long pig,' like the cannibals of the South Seas. Neither do they eat the whole body. Only the hands and feet of their dead enemies are devoured. These are carefully cooked and eaten as delicacies along with monkey meat, birds, fish, and other things prepared for a feast in honor of a victory. The eating of human flesh seems to be symbolism rather than savagery. Furthermore, they do not range the jungle hunting for victims. They eat only those who come against them as enemies.

"So it is quite possible, you see, that strangers might go among them and escape death. It would depend largely on the ability of the strangers to convince the savages that they were friends. The difficulty is that the savages consider all strangers to be enemies until friendship is proved."

"A sizable difficulty," McKay remarked.

"Almost insurmountable. Yet it might be done. Mind, I speak now of the Mayorunas, not of the Red Bones. I tell you again that the Red Bone country is closed."

"And where is the Mayoruna region?"

"In the same general section. The Mayorunas are much more widely distributed. They are on both banks of the Javary and extend as far west as the Ucayali.

"Now if I sought to enter the Red Bone region — and again I say I would not — this would be my way of going at it. I would go first among the Mayorunas near the Red Bones and seek to convince them that I was their friend. I would make the Mayoruna chief as friendly to me as possible. I might even take a Mayoruna woman for a time — some of them are handsome, and such a step would make me almost a Mayoruna myself in their eyes. Then I would persuade the chief to send messengers to the Red Bones with word of me and a request that I be allowed to visit their settlement. The request, coming from the Mayoruna chief, probably would be granted. I would then go in with a bodyguard of Mayorunas, do my business, and come out via the Mayoruna route."

A thoughtful silence ensued. Bottle necks clinked against the cups.

"Something in that idea," conceded Knowlton. "A good deal in it. Barring the woman part, of course."

"Ay," spoke McKay, his tone casual as ever. "When you came out what would you do with your woman, *mein Herr*?"

Schwandorf, tongue loosened a bit by his kümmel, chuckled.

"Ho-ho! The woman? Leave her, of course, when she had served my purpose. Why bother about a woman here and there?"

"I see." McKay's face, indistinct in the gloom, was unreadable, but his tone had a caustic edge.

Schwandorf laughed again. "You are fresh from the woman-worshiping United States and you disapprove. But this is the jungle, and all is different. '*Cada terra com seu uso*,' as these Brazilians say — each land with its own ways. Perhaps when you have met the Mayoruna women, looked on their handsome faces and shapely forms — they wear no clothing, by the way — you will change your ideas. More than one man along this border has risked his life to win one of those women. But that rests with you. And now if you will excuse me, gentlemen, I have an engagement with a man at the other end of town."

"Certainly. We are indebted to you for your interest."

"It is nothing. Remember that I strongly advise you not to go. But if you will go, I shall gladly do whatever lies in my power to aid you in preparing for the trip. Do not hesitate to call on me."

He passed into the house, returning almost at once.

"By the way," he added, "one of you has the room next mine?"

"I have it," said Knowlton.

"Yes. Are you a good sleeper? I sometimes snore most atrociously, I am told. So perhaps —"

"Don't worry. I can sleep in the middle of a bombardment."

"You are fortunate. Good evening, gentlemen."

When he was gone they sat for a time smoking, sipping now and then at their highballs. At length McKay said, "Humph!"

"Amen. Pretty square sort of chap, though, don't you think?"

"I'm not saying," was the Scot's cautious answer. "Seems to be trying to discourage us and egg us on at the same time. Something up his sleeve, perhaps."

"Can't tell. But his line of talk rings true so far. Checks up all right with what we've heard about the Mayorunas and so on. And that scheme of working in through the Mayoruna country sounds about as sensible as anything. Desperate chance and all that, but it might work. Say, why did you kick me when I was going to tell him you'd been in British Guiana?"

"Don't know exactly. Had a hunch. Seems to me I've seen that fellow before somewhere, but I can't place him. None of his business where I've been, anyhow. We're boobs from the States hunting for a wild man. That's all he needs to know."

But it was not enough for Schwandorf to know. At that very moment he was on his way to the home of Superintendent Cabral, with whom he had no engagement whatever, to learn all he could concerning the business of these military-appearing strangers; also to impress on that official the fact that he had sought to dissuade them from starting on their mad quest.

And much later that night, when Knowlton was making good his boast that he was a sound sleeper, a black-bearded face rose silently above the iron partition between his room and that of the German. A hand gripping a small electric flashlight followed. A white ray searched the room, halting on the khaki shirt lying over a box. A tough withe with a barb at one end came over like a slender tentacle, hooked the shirt neatly, drew it stealthily up to the top. Shirt, stick, lamp, hand, face all dissolved into darkness.

After a time they reappeared. The shirt came down, swung slowly back and forth, was dropped deftly where it had previously lain. The breast pocket holding the grain-leather notebook and the photograph of David Dawson Rand was buttoned as it had been, and the notebook bulged the cloth slightly as before. But the contents of that book and the pictured face of Rand now were stamped on the brain of Schwandorf. A sneering, snarling smile curled the heavy mouth of Schwandorf. And softly, so softly that none could hear it but himself, sounded the ironical benediction of Schwandorf:

"Sleep well, *offizier americanisch*! Dream on, poor fool! In time you will wake up. *Ja*, you will wake up!"

V

INTO THE BUSH

Sleepy eyed and frowzy haired, with shirt unbuttoned and breeches and boots unlaced, Tim emerged from his iron-walled cell into the cool-shadowed main room, blinked at McKay and Knowlton lounging over their morning coffee and cigarettes, stretched his hairy arms, and advanced sluggishly to the table.

"Yow-oo-hum!" he yawned. "Ain't they cute! All dressed and shaved like they was goin' to visit the C. O. And here's pore Timmy Ryan lookin' like a 'drunk and dirty' jest throwed into the guardhouse, and feelin' worse. Top o' the mornin' to ye, gents!"

"Same to you, Tim," McKay nodded.

"Who hit you?" asked Knowlton, squinting at bumps and scratches on Tim's forehead.

"Nobody. Couple fellers tried to, but they was out o' luck. Oh, I see what ye mean! I done that meself while I was gittin' to bed."

"Waves must have been running high on the ocean last night. Better drink some coffee. Thomaz, another cup — big and black."

"Thanks, Looey. 'Twas kind of an active night, at that."

"I heard you come in," vouchsafed McKay. "Were you trying some high diving in your room?"

"Faith, I done some divin' without tryin', but 'twas ragged work — I pulled a belly smacker every time. I got to tame that hammick o' mine. It threwed me four times hand-running and the only way I could hold it down was to unhook it and lay it on the floor."

"Sleep well then?"

"I did not. Cap, I thought I knowed somethin' about cooties, but I take it back — I never knowed nothin' about them insecks till last night. Where they come from I dunno, but I'll tell the world they come, and if they wasn't half an inch long I'll eat 'em. They darn near dragged me off whole, and all the sleep I got ye could stick in a flea's eye. Lookit here."

He extended an arm dotted with swollen red spots.

"Ants!" said McKay, after one glance. "Ants, not cooties. They're everywhere. Especially under the floor. That's one reason why folks sleep in hammocks down here. Even then they're likely to come down the hammock cords and drive you out."

"Ants, hey? Never thought o' that. And I'd sooner spend another night fightin' all the man-eatin' jaggers in the jungle than them bugs. It's the little things that count, as the feller said when his wife give him his fourteenth baby."

He downed the thick coffee brought by Thomaz, demanded another cup, accepted cigarette and light from Knowlton, and sighed heavily.

"Who tried to hit you?" Knowlton persisted.

"Aw, I dunno. Two-three fellers took swipes at me with bottles and things. Me and Joey went to a place where they's card games and so on — only place in town where the village sports can git action. Joey offers to buy, and does. Stuff tastes kind o' moldy to me, so I asks have they got any American beer. They have. It's bottled and warm, but it's beer and tastes like home. It goes down so slick I buy another round, and then one more, lettin' in a thirsty-lookin' stranger on the third round. That makes seven bottles altogether. Then I think mebbe I better pay up now before I lose track. Looey, guess what them seven bottles o' suds come to in American money."

"M-m-m! Well, say about three and a half or four dollars."

"That's what I figgered," mourned Tim. "But them highbinders want thirty-two dollars and twenty cents, American gold."

"What!"

"Sad but true. Seems the stuff sells here for four bucks and sixty cents a bottle. Thinkin' I'm gittin' rooked because I'm a tenderfoot, I raise a row to oncet and start to climb the guy. Other folks mix in and things git lively right off. But after I've dropped a couple o' fellers Joey winds himself round me and begs me not to make him arrest me, and also tells me I'm all wrong — that's the regular price. So o'course that makes me out a cheap skate unless I come acrost, and I do the right thing."

"Lucky you had the money on you," said McKay, eying him a bit oddly.

"I didn't," chuckled Tim. "All the dough I had was one pore lonesome ten-spot — the one I got from ye yesterday, Cap. But I don't tell 'em that. I jest wave my hand like thirty-two plunks wasn't nothin' in my young life, and start to work meself out o' the hole. After the two guys on the floor are brought back to their senses I order up drinks for all hands and git popular again. Then I git out the bones."

"Oh! I see!" McKay laughed silently.

"Sure. Remember they told us on the boat that these guys will gamble on anything? And that a feller without shoes on may be some rubber worker packin' a roll that would choke a horse? Wal, I make a few passes with them dice o' mine and their eyes light up like somebody had switched on the current. Then I scrabble me hand around in me pants pocket, like I was peelin' a bill off a roll so big I didn't want to flash the whole wad, and haul out that pore li'l' ten and ask would anybody like to play a man's game.

"They would. I'll say they would. And they got the coin to back up their play, too. Before I come home I was buyin' beer by the case instead o' the bottle. And it's all paid for, and I got more 'n a hundred dollars left, besides givin' Joey a fistful o' money jest for bein' a good feller. This ain't a bad town at all, gents. Outside o' that buckin'-broncho hammick and the man-eatin' ants I had a lovely evenin'."

"How about Joao's lady friend?" quizzed Knowlton.

"Huh? Oh, I didn't git to see her. When bones and beer are rollin' high and handsome I got no time for women. Besides, I found out she was mostly Injun and fat as a hog. Nothin' like that for li'l' Timmy Ryan. Oh, say, before I forgit it — I asked Joey about this Dutchman here, and he says —"

McKay scowled, shook his head, pointed toward the closed door of Schwandorf. Tim lifted his brows, winked understanding, and went on with a break: "— that this guy Sworn-off is a reg'lar feller and knows this river like a book. Says he's one fine guy and a man from hair to heels."

Following which he grimaced as if something smelled bad, adding in a barely audible whisper, "And that's the worst lie I ever told."

"We met Mr. Schwandorf last night after you went," Knowlton said, easily, drawing down one eyelid. "Very likable sort of chap. He's going to help us get started upriver."

"Uh-huh. When do we go? Today?"

"If possible."

"Glad of it. This big-town sportin' life would be the ruination of a simple country kid like me. Yo-hum! Wonder how all our neighbors are this mornin' — the goat and the drunk and the two sick fellers. Kind o' quiet over that side o' the room."

Thomaz entered just then with more coffee. Knowlton turned to him.

"Are the sick men better today, Thomaz?"

"Much better, senhor," the lad said, carelessly. "They are dead."

"Huh?" Tim grunted, explosively.

"Dead," the youth repeated. "They were taken out at dawn. Do not be alarmed. It was the swamp fever, which is not — what you say? — catching."

"Humph! Sort of a reg'lar thing to die of fever here, hey?"

Thomaz shrugged as if hearing a foolish question.

"*Si.* Swamp fever, yellow fever, smallpox, beriberi — today we live, tomorrow we are dead."

"True for ye. They's allays somethin' hidin' round the corner waitin' to jump ye, no matter where ye are. If 'tain't one thing, it's another."

Despite his philosophical answer, however, Tim fell silent, his eyes going to the doors of the rooms where Death had stalked last night while he was gambling. Like most men in whose veins red blood runs bold and free, he had no fear of the sort of death befitting a fighter — sudden and violent — but a deep repugnance for those two assassins against which a victim could not fight back — disease and poison. The Brazilian youth's nonchalant fatalism aroused him to the fact that here both those forms of death were very near him; the one in the air, the other on the ground — fever and snakes.

For the moment he was depressed. Then curiosity awoke.

"If this here, now, Javary fever ain't catchin', how does a feller git it?"

"Mosquitoes," McKay enlightened him. "The *anopheles*. It bites a man who has fever, then bites a well man and leaves the fever in him. Inside of ten days he's sick, unless he takes a huge dose of quinine right away. Mosquito attacks perpendicular to the skin. That is, it stands on its head. If you ever notice one of them biting that way get busy with the quinine."

"Huh! Fat chance a feller's got o' seein' just how all these bugs bite him. And one muskeeter standin' on its head does all that, hey?"

"So they say. Also they say it's only the female that bites."

"Yeah. I believe it. I been stung more 'n once by females before now. How about the yeller fever? Git that the same way?"

"Same way, only a different mosquito — the *stegomyia*. When you begin to vomit black you're gone. And if you get beriberi you're gone, too. First symptoms of that are numbness of the fingers and toes. Muscular paralysis goes on until your heart stops."

"Uh-huh. Nice cheerful place to die in, this Ammyzon jungle. Aw well, what's the odds?"

Wherewith he inhaled more coffee, flipped his cigarette butt at a small lizard on the floor not far away, yawned once more, and swaggered out to the piazza, bawling:

> *"And when I die*
> *Don't bury me a-tall,*
> *But pickle me bones*
> *In alky-hawl —"*

When his roar had subsided and the two former officers had sat silent a moment, smiling over his nocturnal adventures, the door of Schwandorf's room opened abruptly and the German stepped out.

"*Morgen*," he grunted, striding to the table. "Thomaz!"

"*Si*, Senhor Sssondoff." The youth faded away into the kitchen quarters.

"Always feel grumpy until I eat," grumbled the blackbeard. "None of this coffee-cigarette breakfast for me. A real meal, coffee with gin in it, a cigar — then I feel human. Sleep well?"

His bold gaze never flickered as it encountered Knowlton's.

"Fine. If you snored I didn't know it. Didn't hear the bodies taken out this morning, either."

"Bodies! Oh! Those fellows dead?" He tilted his head toward the doors behind which the sick men had lain. "Glad of it. Best for them and everybody else. Hate to have sick people in the place."

The Americans said nothing. They lit new cigarettes and waited for the other to become "human." And when his substantial breakfast was down, his gin-flavored coffee had disappeared, and his big cigar was aglow, he did.

"Well, gentlemen, have you decided to take good advice and let your Raposa alone?" he asked, affably.

"Who ever follows good advice?" Knowlton countered. Schwandorf chuckled.

"*Niemand.* Nobody. So you will go." He shook his head solemnly. "I have said all I can without offense. But if you persist I can only help you to start. If possible I should like to go with you up the river to the place where you will take to the bush; but I must go to Iquitos, in Peru, on the monthly launch which is due in a day or two, so all my business is in the other direction. If now I can aid in the matter of a crew —"

"That is what we were about to ask of you."

"So. Then let us be about it. I have been thinking, since you showed your determination last night, and have made inquiries about men. There are now in Nazareth, the little Peruvian town across the river, several men from whom you can pick an excellent crew. Men of the river and the bush, not worthless loafers like these townsmen here. Men who are not afraid of hell or high water, as the saying is. Not remarkable for either beauty or brains, but good men for your work — by far the best you can obtain. I would suggest a large canoe and six or eight of those men as crew."

The others smoked thoughtfully. Then McKay said, "We should prefer Brazilians."

"Not if you knew the people hereabouts as well as I. It, of course, makes no personal difference to me what sort of crew you get, but I tell you that these men are best. What does it matter which side of the river they come from? Men are men."

"True," McKay conceded.

"Can't be too fussy here," Knowlton added. "Let's see the men."

All rose. But then Schwandorf suggested:

"No need of your going to Nazareth. Better stay here, unless you want to go through a great deal of ceremonious foolishness over there. It's Peruvian ground and the barefooted ignoramuses of officials may insist on showing their importance by demanding your papers and all that. I can go across, get the men, and be back here before you'd be half through the preliminaries. Saves time."

"All right, if it's not too much trouble."

"A good deal less trouble than if you went, to be frank. I'm known, and I can go straight about the business. So sit down and wait. Thomaz! My hat!"

Out he tramped to the piazza, where he paused a moment to run a swift eye over the disheveled figure of Tim, who had fallen sound asleep in a chair. Then, without a further word or glance, he descended the ladder and swung away down the street. The Americans, watching him from the doorway, observed that children in his path hastened to get out of it, and that he spoke to nobody.

"Prussian," rasped McKay.

"M-hm! Done time in the Kaiser's army, too, even if he has been here since before the war. But he's treating us pretty white."

The captain made no answer. Their eyes followed the big figure until they saw it go sliding away toward Peru in a canoe propelled by two languid townsmen. Then McKay dropped a hand on Tim's shoulder. The red-lashed eyes flew open instantly.

Briefly, quietly, Knowlton told of what had passed while he napped, then asked what information he had gleaned from Joao.

"He says," answered Tim, "this guy is a queer duck. Been around here quite a while, but Joey don't know what's his game. He goes off on trips upriver, stays quite a while, comes back unexpected, and nobody knows where he's been or why. He don't use Brazilian boatmen — gits his men on the other side. And the Peru boys themselves dunno where he goes, or, anyways, they say they don't.

"Two of 'em come over here awhile back and got drunk, and Joey tried to pump 'em, but all the dope he got was that this here Fritz goes away upstream to a li'l' camp, and from there he goes off into the bush alone, and the Peru guys jest hang around the camp till he gits back. Sounds kind o' fishy to me, and Joey says it does to him, too, but he couldn't work nothin' more out o' the drunks because about that time Sworn-off himself comes buttin' in and asks these guys what they think they're doin' on this side the river, and they beat it back to Peru toot sweet. He's got their goat, all right, and I wouldn't wonder if he's got

Joey's, too. Anyways, Joey tells me he's off this geezer and advises me to lay off him, too, though he can't name a thing against him."

"Queer," said Knowlton, looking again at the canoe out on the water.

"Gun running?" suggested McKay.

"Nope," Tim contradicted. "I thought o' that, but Joey says they's nothin' to it; they watched this sourkrout close, and he don't never git no guns from nowheres. Besides, they's nobody up there to run guns to but Injuns, and them Injuns are so wild they don't want no guns; they stick to the bow and arrer and such stuff, which they sure know how to use. Whatever his game is, he plays a lone hand as far's this town knows. Got no pals here, and nobody wants to walk on his corns."

"May be perfectly all right, too," mused Knowlton. "A little gold cache or something — though he said there was none in this region. Oh, well, what do we care? We have our hands full with our own business, and all assistance is appreciated."

An hour drifted past. Men of the town lounged by, looking curiously at the strangers, some nodding and voicing a friendly, "*Boa dia.*" Women, too, watched them from windows and doors, and children slyly peeped around corners until something more important — such as a cat, a goat, or a gorgeous butterfly — came their way. Tim went inside and slicked up a bit by buttoning and lacing his clothes and combing his rebellious hair. At length a long boat put out from the farther shore and came surging across the sun-gleaming river.

"Handle themselves well," McKay approved, noting the easy grace of the crew. In the bow a tall, slender fellow stood with arms folded, balancing himself to the sway of the rather clumsy craft and watching the water ahead. In the stern, on a little platform whence he could look over the heads of the others and catch any signal from the lookout, a squat, dark-faced steersman lounged against his crude rudder. Between these two the paddlers stood, each with one foot on the bottom of the long dugout and the other on the gunwale, swinging in nonchalant unison as their blades moved fore and aft. Under the curving roof of a rough-and-ready cabin, open at the sides to allow free play of air, Schwandorf lolled like some old-time barbarian king.

Down to the landing place trudged the three Americans, and there the employers and the prospective employees looked one another over with interest. Eight men had come with Schwandorf, and a hard gang they were. The bowman, hawk nosed, slant eyed, black mustached, with hairy chest showing under his unbuttoned cotton shirt, had the face and bearing of a buccaneer chieftain; and the effect was intensified by a flaring red handkerchief around his head and the haft of a knife protruding from his waistband. The rowers behind him, though of varying degrees of swarthiness and height, all had the same sinewy build, the same bold stare, the same devil-may-care insolence of manner; and though none but the lookout wore the piratical red around his brow, more than one knife hilt showed at their waists. The steersman, whose copper-brown skin and flat face betokened a heavy strain of Indian blood, gazed stolidly at the Americans with the unwinking, expressionless eyes of a snake. Back into the minds of McKay and Knowlton came Schwandorf's words, "Men not afraid of hell or high water." They looked it.

"Here they are," announced the German, stepping ashore deliberately. "José, the *puntero*" — his hand indicated the lookout — "Francisco, the *popero*" — pointing to the steersman — "and six *bogas*. Good men."

McKay ran a cold eye along the line of faces, his gaze plumbing each. Under that chill scrutiny the third man's stare wavered and dropped. That of the next also veered aside. The rest fronted him eye to eye.

"Two of them will not do," he asserted, in the brusque tone of a captain inspecting his company. "Numbers Three and Four — fall out!"

Literal obedience would have put Three and Four into the river, wherefore they stood fast. But, though they did not quite understand the meaning of the words, they grasped the fact that they were not wanted. One laughed impudently, the other slid a poisonous glance at the bleak-faced officer. The squat Francisco scowled. So did Schwandorf.

"No man who cannot look me in the eye is needed on this trip," McKay declared. "Also, six men are enough. If necessary we will bear a hand at the paddles ourselves. José, you have been told by Senhor Schwandorf what we want?"

"*Si.*"

"You can start at once?"

"*Si.*"

"What pay?"

"We leave that to you."

"Um! A dollar a day for each man?"

"Money or goods?"

"American gold."

"*Si. Bueno.*"

"Very well. Take those two men back to Nazareth, get what belongings you need, return here, and report to me at the hotel. I am captain. Understand?"

"*Si* — Capitan."

"All right. On your way!"

As the boat drew out the two rejected men bade the Americans an ironical "*adios*," and one spat in the stream. In the faces of the others, however, showed something like respect for the crisp-spoken captain, and José snarled something at the ill-mannered Three and Four.

"You might need those men," mumbled Schwandorf.

"Guess not," McKay answered, serenely, turning toward the hotel. "Come on, boys. Let's get our stuff ready to ride."

Less than two hours later their rooms were vacant, their duffle was stowed in the long dugout, the Peruvian crew stood arrogantly eying the Brazilians who had gathered to witness the departure, and the Americans were bidding good-by to Remate de Males in general and its German resident in particular.

"Mr. Schwandorf, we thank you for your efficient aid," said Knowlton, extending a hearty hand. "You have helped us to get going with all dispatch, and we trust that we can repay the favor soon."

"You owe me no thanks," was the curt reply. "I would expect you to do as much for me if our positions were reversed. I wish you luck."

"Get aboard, Tim!" McKay ordered, setting the example himself. Tim obeyed, first giving the important Joao d'Almeida Magalhaes Nabuco Pestana da Fonseca a real American handgrip and getting in return a double embrace from that worthy official. Whereafter he winked and grinned expansively at several women garbed in violent hues of red, yellow, and green, frowned slightly at Schwandorf, lit the last cigar he was to smoke for many a long day, and, as the dugout began to move, erupted into a more or less musical farewell to the females of the species:

> *"The Yanks are goin' away,*
> *Pa-a-arley-voo!*
> *They're movin' on today,*
> *Pa-a-arley-voo!*
> *The Yanks are goin' away, they say,*
> *Leavin' the girls in a heartless way,*
> *Rinkydinky-parley-voo!"*

With one final wave of his cigar to the gesticulating Joao and the grinning women he turned his back on the town and faced the little-known river and the inscrutable jungle. But neither his eyes nor his thoughts traveled beyond the bow of the boat. Through narrowed lids he studied the swaying paddlers and the piratical José. And in his mind echoed the whispered warning of Joao, delivered during the effusive embrace at parting:

"Comrade, watch those *bastardos Peruanos*."

VI

IN THE NIGHT WATCH

Day by day the long canoe crawled into the vast unknown. Day by day the down-flowing jungle river pushed steadily, sullenly against its prow, as if striving to repel the invasion of its secret places by the fair-skinned men of another continent. Day by day it slid past in resentful impotence, conquered by the swinging blades of the Peruvian *bogas*. And day by day the close companionship of canoe and camp seemed to weld the voyagers into one compact unit.

Through hours of blazing sun, when the mercury of the thermometer which Knowlton had hung inside the shady *toldo* cabin fluctuated well above 100 degrees, the hardy crew forged on. Through drenching rains they still hung doggedly to their work, suspending it only when the water fell in such drowning quantities that they were forced to tie up hastily to shore and seek cover in order to breathe. When sunset neared they picked with unerring eye a spot fit for camping, attacked the bush with whirling machetes, cleared a space, threw up pole frameworks, swiftly thatched them with great palm leaves, and thus created from the jungle two crude but efficient huts — one for themselves and one for their *patrones*. When night had shut down and all hands squatted around the fire in a nightly smoke talk they regaled their employers with wild tales of adventures in bush and town, some of which were not at all polite, but all of which were mightily interesting. And despite all discomforts, fatigue, and the minor incidents and accidents which often lead fellow travelers in the wilderness to bickering and bitterness, no friction developed between the men of the north and the men of the south.

Not that the Peruvians were at all obsequious or servile. They were a reckless, lawless, Godless gang, perpetually bearing themselves with the careless insolence which had characterized them at first, blasphemous of speech toward one another — but never toward the North Americans. Disputes arose among them with volcanic suddenness, and more than once knives were half drawn, only to be slipped back under the tongue-lashing of the hawk-nosed *puntero*, José, who damned the disputants completely and promised to cut out the bowels of any man daring to lift his blade clear of its sheath. Five minutes afterward the fire eaters would be on as good terms as ever, shrugging and grinning at their passengers — particularly Tim, who, shaking his head disgustedly, would grumble:

"Aw, pickles! Another frog fight gone bust!"

Yet Tim, for all his disparagement of these abortive spats, knew full well that any one of them held the makings of a deadly duel and that José's lurid threats were no mere Latin hyperbole. He realized that the red-crowned bowman ruled his crew exactly as any of the old-time buccaneers whom he resembled had governed their free-booting gangs — by the iron hand; and that, though these men sailed no Spanish Main and flew no black flag, the iron-hand government was needed. He saw also that the rough-and-ready courtesy of this crowd toward their passengers was due largely to the attitude of Captain McKay, who had enforced their respect at the start by his soldierly bearing and retained it ever since by his military management.

For the captain, experienced in directing men, conducted himself at all times as a commanding officer should: he saw all, said little, treated José as a subordinate officer, and left the handling of the crew entirely to him. His aloofness forestalled any of that familiarity which, with such a gang, would have led to contempt. On the other hand, his avoidance of any assumption of meddlesome authority prevented the irritation and dislike which free men inevitably feel for the self-important type of leader. Thus he cannily steered himself and his mates between the two rocks which might have wrecked the expedition before it was well started. And Knowlton, ex-lieutenant, and Tim, ex-sergeant, seeing and understanding, followed his example.

So the days and nights rolled by, the miles of never-ending jungle shore fell away behind, and, save for the occasional outbreaks between members of the crew, all was serene. To all appearances the Peruvians were whole-heartedly interested in serving their employers faithfully, and the North Americans were gliding onward with no thought of insecurity. Yet appearances frequently are deceptive.

In the heat of the day — in fact, before the broiling sun neared the zenith — Tim and Knowlton habitually fell asleep inside the *toldo*, not to awake until two hours before sunset, when, according to the routine agreed upon, the night's camping place would be sought and two or three of the Peruvians would go into the bush with rifles, seeking fresh meat. McKay never slept during the day's traverse. Nothing escaped his eye from the time when he emerged from his mosquito net in the misty morning until he entered it again by firelight. The men in the boat; the floating alligators and wading birds of the water; the flashing parrots, jacamars, toucans, trogons, and hummers of the air; the yard-long lizards and nervous spider monkeys of the tangled tree branches alongshore — all these he watched quietly as the boat forged on. And the sinister Francisco, watching him in turn, and the paddlers throwing occasional glances his way, came to regard him as the only alert member of the trio. Wherein they erred.

The truth was that every one of the three adventurers was on his guard. Tim had not forgotten the last words of his boon companion, Joao, and at the first opportunity he had quietly passed on that warning. Moreover, McKay and Knowlton, without discussing the matter, had meditated on the unexpected assistance of Schwandorf, the speed with which the crew had been obtained, the promptness of José to accept the first payment offered, and other things. Wherefore it had come about that at no hour of the twenty-four was every eye and ear closed. And the real reason why red Tim and blond Knowlton slept by day was that they thus made up the slumber lost at night.

Not that either of them patrolled the camp in sentry go. So far as the Peruvians knew, they slept as soundly as McKay. But, lying in their hammocks, they divided the night watches between them on a schedule as regular as that of a military camp, though the shifts necessarily were longer. As sunset came always at six o'clock and all hands sought their hanging beds two hours later, Tim's "tour of duty" lasted until one in the morning. When the phosphorescent hands of his watch pointed to that hour he stealthily reached out and jabbed Knowlton, sleeping beside him. When a barely audible "All right" reached his ears he was officially relieved.

Night followed night, became a week, lengthened into a fortnight. Still, so far as the crew was concerned, nothing happened. A little rough banter among them as they smoked their last cigarettes, then sleep and snores; and that was all until morning. Men less experienced in night vigils than the ex-soldiers would have abandoned their watches long before this — if, indeed, they had ever adopted them. But these three were schooled in patience. Moreover, neither Tim nor Knowlton had ever before penetrated the jungle, and at times the light of the waxing moon revealed to their eyes strange things which they never would have seen by day. So the tedium of the long hours of wakefulness might be broken at any moment.

Once they camped close to a conical hillock of compact earth, some four feet high and almost stone hard, from which radiated narrow covered galleries — the citadel and viaducts of a community of termites. Tim, still harboring vivid recollections of his ant battle at Remate de Males — though by this time he had trained himself to sleep in his hammock, where he was comparatively safe — looked askance at it when told what it was, and was only partly reassured by the information that termites were eaters of wood rather than of flesh. After sleep had embraced the rest of the camp he still was uneasy, lifting his net at long intervals and squinting at the moonlit mound as if expecting a horde of pincer-jawed insects to erupt from it and charge him. And during one of these inspections he saw something totally unexpected.

From the black shadows of the forest had emerged another shadow, so grotesque and misshapen that it seemed a figment of indigestion and weird dreams — a thing from whose shaggy body protruded what appeared to be only a long tubular snout where a head should be, and which looked to be overbalanced at the other end by a great mass of hair. It stood stone still, and for the moment Tim could not decide which end of it was head and which was tail, or even whether it were not double-tailed and headless. Then, slowly, the apparition moved.

Into that hard-packed earth it dug huge hooked claws, and from its tapering muzzle a wormlike tongue licked about, gathering the outrushing white ants into its gullet. For minutes Tim lay blinking at it, wondering if he really saw it.

Then, picking up his rifle, he slipped outside his net and advanced on the creature.

The animal turned, sat back on its great tail, lifted its terrible claws, and waited. Six feet away, just out of its reach, Tim stopped and stared anew. Then he grinned.

"You win, feller," he informed the beast. "What ye are I dunno, but any critter that's got the guts to ramble right into camp and offer to gimme a battle is too good a sport for me to shoot. Help yourself to all the ants in the world, for all o' me. I'm goin' back to bed. Bon sewer, monseer."

Wherewith, still grinning, but warily watching, he backed until sure the big invader would not spring at him. Knowing nothing of ant bears, he did not know it was hardly a springing animal.

Its claws looked sufficiently formidable to disembowel a man — as, indeed, they were, if the man came near enough. But when Tim had withdrawn and the sluggish brute had decided that it would not need to defend itself, it sank to all-fours and passed stiffly away into the shades whence it had come.

On another night, when Tim slept, Knowlton detected a creeping, slithering sound which made him slip off the safety catch of his heavy-bulleted pistol and peer at the hut where slept the crew. No man was moving there. Still the sound persisted. Lifting his net, he spied beyond the hut of the Peruvians a moving mass on the ground — a cylindrical bulk which looked to be two feet thick, and which glided past like a solid stream of dark water flowing along above the dirt. Its beginning and end were hidden in the bush, and not until it tapered into nothing and was gone did he realize fully that he had been gazing at an enormous anaconda. Then he kicked himself for not shooting it. But before long he congratulated himself for letting it go.

Perhaps an hour later the startled forest resounded with an agonized scream, so piercing and so appallingly human that all the camp sprang awake. The outcry came but once, sounding from some place not far off, near the water's edge, and in the direction toward which the huge serpent had disappeared. Before the watcher had time to tell the others of what he had seen, one of the boatmen discovered the rut left in the soft ground by the reptile. Thereafter Knowlton kept his own counsel, listening to the excited curses of the men and observing their pallor and their nervous scanning of the shadows. José said the screech undoubtedly was the death shriek of some animal caught and crushed in the snake's tremendous coil. McKay concurred with a nod. And when Knowlton casually said it was tough that nobody had been awake to shoot the thing as it passed the camp, José emphatically disagreed.

A bullet fired into that fiendish giant, he averred, would have meant death to one or more men; for the serpent's writhing coils and lashing tail would have knocked down the sleeping-hut and shattered the spines of any men they struck. No, let Señor Knowlton thank the saints that the awful master of the swamps had gone its way unmolested. For the rest of that night Knowlton kept his watch openly, accompanied by José and three of the paddlers, who refused to sleep again until they should be miles away from the vicinity of that dread monster.

Two nights afterward the camp was aroused again. Tim alone saw the start of the disturbance, and he kept mum about it because he did not choose to let the Peruvians know he had been on the alert. Out from the gloom and straight past the huts a thick-bodied, curve-snouted animal came charging madly for the river, carrying on its back a ferocious cat creature whose fangs were buried deep in its steed's neck — a tapir attacked by a jaguar. With a resounding plunge the elephantine quarry struck the water and was gone. The tiger cat, forced to relinquish its hold or drown, swam hurriedly back to the bank below the encampment, where it roared and spat and squalled in a blood-chilling paroxysm of baffled fury. And though every man was awakened, not one left the flimsy shelter of his net. Nor did anyone so much as speak until Tim, wearying of the noise, announced his intention to "go bust that critter in the nose and give him somethin' to yowl about."

The proposal met with instant and peremptory veto.

"As you were!" snapped McKay. "Let him alone! You wouldn't have a Chinaman's chance in that black bush. A jaguar is bad all the time, and when he's mad he's deadly. Never fool with one of those beasts, Tim. I've met them before and I know what they can do."

To which José agreed with many picturesque oaths, declaring that a jaguar was no mere beast — it was a devil. Tim, grumbling, obeyed orders. The jaguar, hearing their voices, stopped its noise and probably reconnoitered the camp. But no man saw the brute, and its next roar sounded from some spot far off in the jungle.

Other things, too, passed within Tim's range of vision from time to time in the moonlit hours: a queer bony creature which he took for some new kind of turtle, but which really was an armadillo; a monstrous hairy spider which slid like a streak up his net, hung there for a time, decided to go elsewhere, and departed with such speed that the man inside rubbed his eyes and wondered if he was "seein' things that ain't"; a couple of vampires which flitted in from nowhere like ghoulish ghosts, wheeled and floated silently on wide wings, seeking an exposed foot protruding from the hammocks, found none, rested a moment on the roof poles, chirping hoarsely, and veered out again into the night.

To Knowlton's watch came a strange owl-faced little monkey with great staring eyes and face ringed with pale fur — one of those night apes seldom seen by man; a small troop of kinkajous, slender, long-tailed animals which looked to be monkeys, but were not, and which leaped deftly among the branches like frolicsome little devils let loose to play under the jungle moon; a big scaly iguana, its back ridged with saw teeth and its pendulous throat pouch dangling grotesquely under its jaw; and more than one deadly snake and huge alligator, the first gliding past with venomous head raised and cold eye glinting, the second lying quiescent except for occasional openings of horrific jaws.

To the ears of both the hammock sentinels came the mournful sounds of living things unseen. From the depths beyond drifted the weird plaint of the sloth, crying in the night, "Oh me, poor sloth, oh-oh-oh-oh!" Goat suckers repeated by the hour their monotonous refrains, "Quao quao," or "Cho-co-co-cao," while a third earnestly exhorted, "Joao corta pao!" ("John, cut wood!"). Tree frogs and crickets clacked and drummed and hoo-hooed, guaribas poured their awful discord into the air, and on one bright breathless night there sounded over and over a call freighted with wretchedness and despair — the wail of that lonely owl known to the bushmen as "the mother of the moon," whose dreadful cry portends evil to those who hear it.

Sometimes the air shook with the thunderous concussion of some great falling tree which, long since bled to death by parasitical plant growths, now at last toppled crashing back into the dank soil whence it had forced its way up into a place in the sun. Other noises, infrequent and unexplainable, also drifted at long intervals from the mysterious blackness. And in all the medley of night sounds not one was cheerful. The burden of the jungle's cacophonic cantanta ever was the same — despair, disaster, death.

Then came the fifteenth day. It dawned red, the sun fighting an ensanguined battle with the heavy morning mists and throwing on the faces of the early-rising travelers a sinister crimson hue. Before that sun should rise again some of those faces were to be stained a deeper red.

VII

COLD STEEL

Some two hours after the start, while Knowlton and Tim loafed at the fore end of the cabin, enjoying the comparative coolness of the early day, another boat hove in sight up ahead — a longish craft manned by eight paddlers and without a cabin.

As it came into view its bowman tossed his paddle in greeting. The Peruvians ignored the salutation. The bowman, after shading his eyes and peering at the flamboyant figure of José, resumed paddling without further ceremony, evidently intending to pass in silence. But then McKay arose, waved a hand, and told José to steer for the newcomers. José, with a slightly sour look, gave the signal to Francisco, and the course changed.

The other canoe slowed and waited. Its men watched the tall figure of McKay. Tim and Knowlton scanned the bronzed faces of those men and liked them at once. The paddlers evidently were Brazilians, but of a different type from the sluggish townsmen of Remate de Males — alert, active-looking fellows, steady of eye, honest of face, muscular of arm — in all, a more clean-cut set of men than the Peruvians. All three of the Americans noticed that no word was exchanged between the two crews.

"*Boa dia, amigos!*" spoke McKay. "Who are you and whence do you come?"

"We are rubber workers of Coronel Nunes, senhor," the bowman answered, civilly. "We go to make a new camp. This land is a part of the *seringel* of the coronel, and we left his headquarters yesterday."

"Ah! Then the headquarters is above here?"

"One more day's journey," the man nodded.

"I thank you. Good fortune go with you."

"And with you, senhor. May God protect you."

With the words the Brazilian glanced along the line of Peruvian faces and his eyes narrowed. Though his words were only a respectful farewell, his expressive face indicated that McKay might be badly in need of divine protection at no distant date. As his paddle dipped and his men nodded their leave-taking, Francisco, the *popero*; sneered raucously:

"Hah! Mere *caucheros*! Workers! Slaves!"

And he spat at the Brazilian boat.

Fire shot into the eyes of the bowman and his comrades. Their muscles tensed.

"Better be slaves — better be dogs — than Peruvian cutthroats!" one retorted. "Go your way, and keep to your own side of the river."

"We go where we will, and no misborn Brazilians can stop us," snarled Francisco. To which he added obscene epithets directed against Brazilians in general and the men of Coronel Nunes in particular.

The unprovoked insults angered the Americans as well as the Brazilians. Knowlton leaped through the *toldo* and confronted Francisco.

"Shut your dirty mouth!" he blazed.

For reply, the evil-eyed steersman spat at him the vilest name known to man.

An instant later, his lips split, he sprawled dazedly on his platform, perilously close to the edge. Knowlton, the knuckles of his left fist bleeding from impact with the other's teeth, stood over him in white fury. Francisco's right hand fumbled for his knife. Knowlton promptly stamped on that hand with a heavy boot heel.

"Good eye, Looey!" rumbled Tim's voice at his back. "Boot him some more for luck. Hey, you! Back up or I'll drill ye for keeps!" This to a pair of the Peruvian paddlers who had come scrambling through the cabin.

After one searching stare into Tim's hard blue eyes and a glance at his fist curled around the butt of his belt gun, the *bogas* backed up. A moment later they were thrown boldly into their own part of the boat by José, who blistered them with the profanity of three languages at once. Then McKay came through and took charge.

"That'll do, Tim! Same goes for you, Merry! José, I'll handle this. You, Francisco! Get up!"

The curt commands struck like blows. Every man obeyed. And when the squat steersman again stood up McKay went after him roughshod. In the colloquial Spanish of Mexico and the Argentine, in the man talk of American army camps, he flayed that offender alive. José himself, efficient man handler though he was, stared at his captain in awe. And Francisco, though not given to cringing, skulked like a beaten dog when the verbal flagellation was finished.

Turning then to the Brazilians, McKay formally apologized for the insults to them.

"It is nothing, senhor," coolly answered the bowman — though his glance at the Peruvians said plainly that it would have been something but for the swift punishment by the Americans. "Again I say — may God protect you! Adeos!"

The Brazilian boat glided away. The Peruvian craft crawled on upstream in silence.

When the next camp was made all apparently had forgotten the affair. The men badgered one another as usual, though none mentioned Francisco's split mouth; and Francisco, himself, albeit sulky, betrayed no sign of enmity. After nightfall the regular camp-fire meeting was held and at the usual time all turned in. One more night of listening to the sounds of the tropical wilderness seemed all that lay ahead of the secret sentinels.

Sleep enveloped the huts. Snores and gurgles rose and fell. Tim himself, for the sake of effect, snored heartily at intervals, though his eyes never closed. Through his mosquito bar he could see only vaguely, but he knew any man walking from the crew's quarters must cast a very visible shadow across that net, and to him the shadow would be as good a warning as a clear view of the substance. But the hours crept on and no shadow came.

At length, however, a small sound reached his alert ear — a sound different from the regular noises of the bush — a stealthy, creeping noise like that of a big snake or a huge lizard. It came from the ground a few feet away, and it seemed to be gradually advancing toward his own hammock. Whatever the creature was that made it, its method of progress was not human, but reptilian. Puzzled, suspicious, yet doubtful, Tim lifted the rear side of his net, on which no moonlight fell. Head out, he watched for the crawling thing to come close.

It came, and for an instant he was in doubt as to its character, for around it lay the deep shadow of some treetops which at that point blocked off the moon. It inched along on its stomach, its black head seeming round and minus a face, its body broad but flat — a thing that looked to be a man but not a man. Then, pausing, it raised its head and peered toward the hammock of Knowlton. With that movement Tim's doubts vanished. The lifting of the head showed the face — the face of Francisco, the face of murder. In its teeth was clamped a bare knife.

Forthwith Tim applied General Order Number Thirteen.

In one bound he was outside his net, colliding with Knowlton, who awoke instantly. In another he was beside the assassin, who, with a lightning grab at the knife in his mouth, had started to spring up. Tim wasted no time in grappling or clinching. He kicked.

His heavy boot, backed by the power of a hundred and ninety pounds of brawn, thudded into the Indian's chest. Francisco was hurled over sidewise on his back. Another kick crashed against his head above the ear. He went limp.

"Ye lousy snake!" grated Tim. "Crawlin' on yer belly to knife a slee-pin' man, hey? Blast yer rotten heart —"

"What's up?" barked McKay from his hammock.

"Night attack, Cap. If ye're comin' out bring along yer gat. Hey, Looey, got yer gun on? Some o' these other guys might git gay. They're comin' now."

True enough, the Peruvian gang was jumping from its hut. With an-other glance at the prostrate Francisco to make sure he was unconscious, Tim whirled to meet them, fist on gun.

"Halt!" he roared. "First guy passin' this corner post gits shot. Back up!"

The impact of his voice, the menace of his ready gun hand, the sight of Knowlton and McKay leaping out with pistols drawn, stopped the rush at the designated post. But swift hands dropped, and when they rose again the moonlight glinted on cold steel.

"Capitan, what happens here?" demanded José, ominously quiet.

"Knife work," McKay replied, curtly. "Your man Francisco attempted to creep in and murder Señor Knowlton. If you and the rest have similar intentions, now's your time to try. If not, put away those knives."

"Knives! *Por Dios*, what do you mean?"

"Look behind you."

José looked. At once he snarled curses and commands. Slowly the knives slipped out of sight. The paddlers edged backward to their own shack, leaving their *puntero* alone.

"The capitan has it wrong," asserted José. "We awake to find our *popero* being kicked in the head. We want to know why. If Francisco has done what you say I will deal with him. That I may be sure, allow me to look."

"Very well. Look."

José advanced, stooped, studied the ground, the position of Francis-co's body, the knife still clutched in the nerveless hand. Tim growlingly vouchsafed a brief explanation of the incident. When José straightened up, his mouth was a hard line and his eyes hot coals.

"*Si. Es verdad.* Tomorrow we shall have a new *popero*."

With which he stooped again, grasped the prone man by the hair, dragged him into the moonlit space between the huts, and flung him down. "Juan, bring water!" he ordered.

One of the paddlers, looking queerly at him, did so. José deluged the senseless man. Francisco, reviving, sat up and scowled about him. His eyes rested on the three Americans standing grimly ready, shoulder to shoulder, before their hut; veered to his mates bunched in sinister silence beside their own quarters; shifted again to meet the baleful glare of José. His hand stole to his empty sheath.

"Your knife, Francisco *mio*?" queried José, a menacing purr in his tone. "I have it. It seems that you are in haste to use it. Too much haste, Francisco. But if you will stand instead of crawling as before, you may have your knife again — and use it, too."

Francisco, staring sullenly up, seemed to read in the words more than was evident to the Americans. He lurched to his feet, staggered, caught his balance, braced himself, stood waiting.

"You know who commands here," José went on. "You disobey. You seek to stab in the night —"

"Now or later — what is the difference?"

"— and now the boat is too small for both of us." José ignored the interruption. "Here is your knife. Now use it!"

He flipped the weapon at the other, who caught it deftly. José dropped his right hand to his waist. An instant later naked steel licked out at Francisco's throat.

The steersman's knife flashed up, caught the reaching blade, knocked it with a scraping clink. For a few seconds the two weapons seemed welded together, their owners each striving to bear down the other's wrist. Then they parted as the combatants sprang back.

José side-stepped twice to his right. Francisco, turning to preserve his guard, now had the light full in his face. But the moon rode so high that the steersman's disadvantage was negligible, and the next assault of the *puntero* was blocked as before. And this time the wrist of the *popero* proved a bit the better; he threw the attacking steel aside and struck in a slashing sweep at his antagonist's stomach.

A convulsive inward movement of the bowman's middle, coupled with a swift back-step, made the slash miss by a hair's breadth. With the quickness of light José was in again. His knife hand, still outstretched sidewise, stopped with a light smack of flesh on flesh. Then it jerked outward. His steel now was red to the hilt.

One more rapid step back, a keen glance at his opponent, and José stood at ease. From Francisco burst a bubbling groan. He staggered. His knife dropped. His hands rose fumblingly toward his neck. Suddenly his knees gave way and he toppled backward to the ground. The silvery moonlight disclosed a dark flood welling from his severed jugular.

With the utmost coolness José ran two fingers down his wet blade, snapped the fingers in air, and spoke to his crew:

"As I said, we shall have a new *popero*. Tomorrow, Julio, you will take the platform."

A rumble ran among the men. Their eyes lifted from Francisco to the Americans, and in them shone a wolfish gleam. The bowman turned sharply and faced them.

"Who growls?" he rasped. "You, Julio?"

"*Si, yo soy,*" Julio answered, harshly, fingering his knife. "I will be steersman, but I steer downstream, not up. Francisco spoke the truth. Now or later — what is the difference? Let it be now!"

A louder growl from the others followed his words. One stepped back into the shadow of the hut.

"*Perros amarillos!* Yellow dogs! You go upstream, fools! The Americans must be taken —"

A raucous sneer from Julio interrupted him. Simultaneously the paddler's hand leaped upward, poising a knife.

"The gringos stay here — and you, too, you Yanqui cur!"

The poised knife hissed through the air at José.

Out from the crew house shot a streak of fire and a smashing rifle report.

José dodged, staggered, screeched in feline fury, the knife buried in his left arm.

McKay grunted suddenly, fell, lay still.

"God!" yelled Tim. "Cap's gone! Clean 'em, Looey!"

With the words he leaped aside and pulled his pistol, just as another rifle flare stabbed out from the other hut and a bullet whisked through the space where he had stood. An instant later he was pouring a stream of lead at the spot whence the burning powder had leaped.

Knives flashing, teeth gleaming, the other paddlers charged across the ten-foot space between the huts.

José, his left arm helpless, but his deadly right hand still gripping his knife, hurled himself on Julio, who had seized a machete from somewhere.

Knowlton slammed a bullet between the eyes of the foremost *boga*, who pitched headlong. He swung the muzzle to the other man's chest — yanked at the trigger — got no response. The gun was jammed.

With a triumphant snarl the blood-crazed Peruvian closed in, slashing for the throat. Knowlton slipped aside, evaded the thrust, swung the pistol down hard on his assailant's head. The man reeled, thrust again blindly, missed. Knowlton crashed his dumb gun down again. It struck fair on the temple. The man collapsed.

Tim was charging across the open at the crew house. José and Julio were locked in a death grapple. No other living man, except Knowlton, still stood upright. Stooping, he peered into the red-dyed face of McKay.

Then he laid a hand on the captain's chest. Faint but regular, he felt the heart beating.

"Thank God!" he breathed. With a wary eye on the battling Peruvians he swiftly raised the captain and put him into Tim's hammock. As he turned back to the fight Tim emerged from the other hut, carrying a body, which he dropped and swiftly inspected. At the same moment the fight of José and Julio ended.

With a choked scream Julio dropped, writhed, doubled up. Then he lay still. José, his face ghastly, stared around him. His mouth stretched in a terrible smile.

"So this ends it," he croaked, his gaze dropping to Julio. "*Adios*, Julio! The machete is not — so good as the knife — unless one has — room to — swing it —"

He chuckled hoarsely and sank down.

For an instant Knowlton hesitated, his glance going back and forth between McKay and José. Swiftly then he ran his finger tips over McKay's head. With a murmur of satisfaction he turned from his comrade and hurried to the motionless bowman, over whom Tim now bent.

"Bleedin' to death, Looey," informed Tim. "Ain't cut bad excep' that arm. That flyin' knife must have got an artery. Can we pull him through? He's a good skate."

"I'll try. You look after Cap. He's only knocked out — bullet creased him —"

"Glory be! He's all right, huh? Sure I'll fix him up. Everybody else dead? I got that guy in the bunk house — drilled him three times."

"Look out for that fellow over there. Maybe I brained him, but I'm not sure."

Knowlton was already down on his knees beside José, working fast to loop a tourniquet and stop the flow from the pierced arm. With a handkerchief and his pistol barrel he shut off the pulsating stream.

"Yeah, he's done," judged Tim, rising from the man whom Knowlton had downed at last. "Skull's caved in. What'd ye paste him with?"

"Gun. Cursed thing stuck."

"Uh-huh. Them automats are cranky. Say, lookit the mess Hozy made o' that guy Hooley-o."

Knowlton glanced at Julio and whistled. José's oft-repeated threat to disembowel a refractory member of the crew had at last been literally fulfilled.

But the lieutenant had seen worse sights in the shell-torn trenches of France, and now he kept his mind on his work. Wedging the gun to hold the tourniquet tight, he lifted his patient from the red-smeared mud and bore him to the nearest hammock in the crew quarters. Striding back, he found Tim alternately bathing McKay's head and giving him brandy. In a moment the captain's eyes opened.

"Some bean ye got, Cap," congratulated Tim, vastly relieved at sight of McKay's gray stare. "Bullet bounced right off. Here, take another swaller. Attaboy! Hey, Looey, we better pack this crease o' Cap's, huh? She keeps leakin'."

"Yep. Dip up the surgical kit. And give José a drink. I'll have to tie his artery, too. How do you feel, old chap?"

"Dizzy," McKay confessed. "What's happened?"

"Lost our crew," was the laconic answer. "All gone west but José, and he's bled white. We'll have to paddle our own canoe now."

For a time after his head was bandaged McKay lay quiet, staring out at the tiny battlefield and at his two mates working silently on the wounded arm of José. When they came back he spoke one word.

"Schwandorf."

"Yeah! He's the nigger in the woodpile, I bet my shirt. But why? What's his lay, d'ye s'pose?"

"Perhaps José knows," suggested Knowlton. "But he's in no shape to talk now. Let's see. Schwandorf said he was going to Iquitos?"

"Yes, but that doesn't mean anything."

"Probably not. Well, maybe José can explain."

There were some things, however, which José could not have told if he would, for he himself did not know them. One was that Schwandorf really had gone to Iquitos, where was a radio station. Another was that from that radio station to Puerto Bermudez, thence over the Andes to the coast, and northward to a New York address memorized from Knowlton's notebook, already had gone this message:

McKay expedition killed by Indians. Rand search most dangerous, but if empowered I attempt locate him for fifty thousand gold payable on safe delivery Rand at Manaos. Reply soon a possible.

Karl Schwandorf.

VIII

THE DOUBLE-CROSS

Noon, sweltering hot. A blazing sun pouring vertical rays down on a blinding river. A long canoe wearily creeping up the glaring waters, minus a lookout, heedless of the ever-present danger of sunken tree trunks; propelled by three sun-blistered white men, one of whom wore a bandage around his head; steered perfunctorily by a pallid pirate whose left arm hung in a sling. Atop the right bank an unbroken, endless tangle of jungle growth. Ahead, on the left shore, a gap gouged out of the forest and a number of boats at the water's edge.

"Guess that's it," panted Knowlton, shielding his eyes and squinting at the clearing. "One more day's journey, the Brazilian chap said. We've been two and a half."

"One day's journey for six hardened rivermen, señor," corrected José. "Not for three men doing six men's work and hampered by a cripple."

"Aw, ye're no crip, Hozy," dissented Tim. "Any guy that can steer a tub like this here one-handed after losin' a couple gallons o' juice is in good shape yet, I'll say. If ye had both legs shot off and yer arms broke and yer head stove in, now, ye might call yourself sort o' helpless. Ease her over to the left a li'l' more, so's we'll hit the bank right at the corner o' that gap. Me, I don't want to take one stroke more 'n I have to. Every muscle in me is so sore it squeaks."

"Same here," admitted Knowlton. "I'm one solid ache."

José nodded. The clumsy craft veered a bit. The three put a little more punch into their lagging strokes, noting, as they neared the steep bank, that a couple of men had appeared at its top and were staring at them. Gradually the long dugout worked in to the muddy shore, where the paddlers stabbed their blades into the clay and held it firm.

"Ahoy, up there! This the Nunes *seringal*?"

From the edge, some thirty feet above, the taller of the two watchers answered:

"*Si*, senhor. The headquarters of the coronel. Do you come to visit him?"

"Right."

"Then permit me to help you. The path is a little ahead. Pull up and tie to this stake."

The tall fellow came dropping swiftly downward. At the same time the other Brazilian stepped back and was gone.

With a dexterous twist the man of Nunes moored the boat to the designated stake. Then he reached a hand toward Tim to help him out.

"I ain't no old woman, feller," Tim refused, and hopped aground unassisted. McKay and Knowlton followed. But José, after moving languidly forward and contemplating the sharp slope, hesitated and then shrugged his shoulders.

"I am tired, señores," he said. "And perhaps it would be well for one to stay here and watch."

The tall Brazilian's eyes narrowed.

"There is no danger of loss," he asserted, with dignity. "We men of the coronel are not thieves."

The slight emphasis of his last sentence might have been taken as an intimation that some one else not far away would bear watching. José's mouth tightened. For a moment Brazilian and Peruvian eyed each other in obvious dislike. Then, with a glance at his crippled arm, José shrugged again.

"Better come along, José," McKay said. "Stuff's safe enough."

"As you will, Capitan."

He lounged to the edge, hesitated, wavered slightly. At once the Brazilian darted out a hand and gave him support. And while the four clambered up the slope he retained a grip on the Peruvian's arm, aiding him to the top. When they emerged on the level, however, he dropped his hand immediately. José gave him a half-mocking bow of thanks, to which he replied with a short nod. Then he stepped back and let the Peruvian precede him toward a number of substantial pole-supported houses a hundred yards away.

"No love lost between them two," thought Tim, who had watched it all. "Good skate, though, this new feller. Ready to help a guy that needs it, whether he likes him or not; ready to knock his block off, too, if he needs that. Bet he'd be a hellion in a scrap. Dang good-lookin' lad, too."

Wherewith he introduced himself.

"Don't git sore because I growled at ye down below," he said, with a friendly grin. "Sounded rough, mebbe, but that's my style. I'm Tim Ryan, from the States. I bark more 'n I bite."

The overture met with instant response — a quick smile and a twinkle in the warm eyes.

"It is not words that give offense, senhor, but the way they are spoken — and the man who speaks them. One man may growl, but you like him. Another may speak smoothly, but you itch to strike him. Is it not so? I am Pedro Andrada, a *seringueiro* who should be tapping trees instead of loafing here. But my partner and I have just come in from a long trip into the *sertao* — wilderness — and are resting."

"Yeah? Was that yer buddy I seen with ye?"

"My — ah — buddee? Partner? Yes, that was he — Lourenço Moraes, the best comrade one ever had. He has gone to tell the coronel of your arrival. Have you met with an accident downriver?"

He moved a thumb meaningly toward the only remaining member of the crew.

"Yeah," grimly. "Bad accident."

Tim tapped his pistol significantly, raised five fingers, winked, and twitched his head toward the Peruvian. Pedro lifted his brows, nodded quick understanding, pointed to the bad arm of José, and made motions as if pulling a trigger. Tim shook his head and enacted the pantomime of drawing and throwing a knife. Whereat the Brazilian, aware that José was not a prisoner and probably knowing that North Americans were not knife throwers, looked much puzzled. But their sign manual went no farther, for they now approached the house which evidently formed the dwelling and office of Coronel Nunes.

At the foot of the ladder stood a broad-shouldered, square-jawed, thick-muscled, deeply tanned man, who, without speaking, pointed a thumb upward. Above, in the doorway, waited an elderly Brazilian of medium height and spare figure, standing with soldierly erectness and garbed in white duck of semimilitary cut. He beamed down at McKay and Knowlton, but as his black eyes encountered those of José they seemed suddenly to become very sharp. Then his gaze rested on Tim's broad face and he smiled again.

"Enter, gentlemen," he invited. "*Esta casa e a suas ordenes* — this house is at your disposal."

McKay, with a bow, climbed the ladder, followed by Knowlton. José, with a swaggering stare at the wide-shouldered man, who stared straight back without facial change, also went up. Tim came fourth and last, for Pedro stopped beside his countryman, who evidently was Lourenço.

The travelers found themselves in a room which, in view of its distance from civilization, seemed palatial. Its floor was tight, its furniture modern, its walls decorated with a few excellent pictures, of which the largest was a superb view of the rugged harbor of Rio de Janeiro. Comfortable chairs were ranged along the walls, and the middle of the room was occupied by a massive square-cornered table on which lay a jumble of hand-written business papers, a number of books, a high-grade violin and bow. Beyond the table stood a swivel chair, evidently the usual seat of the coronel. Table and chair were so arranged that the master of this house sat always with his back to a wall and his face toward the door. And on a couple of hooks on that wall, ready for instant service, hung a high-power rifle.

On their way up the river the Americans had passed, at long intervals, a few small rubber estates, whose headquarters consisted mainly of a crude shack or two, hardly better than the dingy houses of Remate de Males. This place was more imposing. They had observed, while crossing the cleared space, that it was at least half a mile square; that its warehouse for supplies was big and solid; that a goodly number of *barracaos*, or rubber workers' huts, surrounded the house of the master at a respectful distance; and that the owner's home was no one-room cabin, but big enough to contain six or eight rooms. This well-appointed reception room and the formal yet sincere courtesy of its owner showed that Coronel Nunes was no mere native of the frontier. Later they were to learn that he was a gentleman of Rio who, exiling himself from the capital after the death of his wife, had carved from this forbidding jungle a fortune in the rubber trade.

With the correct touch of Latin punctilio McKay spoke the introductions and stated that they were on their way upriver to explore the hinterland. With equal politeness the coronel bowed and begged his illustrious guests to be seated. Then he touched a small bell. A door at one side opened and a white-suited negro appeared.

"Café," the coronel ordered. As speedily as if these visitors had been long expected, the servant brought in a tray bearing cups of syrupy coffee. Each of the guests accepted one. Whereafter the decorum of the occasion was shattered by Tim, who, at the imminent risk of scalding himself, gulped his refreshment and vociferated his satisfaction.

"O-o-oh boy! That hits right where I live! Gimme another one, feller, and make it man's size!"

The black fellow struggled with his quick mirth and then laughed outright — the throaty, infectious laugh of his race. The coronel's eyes twinkled. And when Tim fished a damp cigarette from his shirt, nonchalantly scraped a match on his host's table, blew a cloud of smoke, and sprawled back with one leg dangling over a chair arm, formality went a-glimmering.

"*A quem madruga Deus ajuda*," laughed the coronel. "Or, as you North Americans put it, 'God helps those who help themselves.' Let us not be ceremonious, gentlemen. 'Tonio, bring more coffee. And cigars. And —"

Down behind his table, where only the servant saw the motion, he twitched a finger as if pulling a cork. 'Tonio, his ebony countenance split by a grin, ducked his head and vanished into the other room.

"How is the rubber market, sir?" asked Knowlton, seeking to divert attention from Tim.

"Not so good," the old gentleman replied, with a deprecatory gesture. "In truth, it is very poor since the war — so poor that soon I shall abandon this *seringal* and go out to spend the rest of my life on the coast. With rubber selling at a mere five hundred dollars a ton in New York and the artificial plantations of the Far East growing greater yearly, there is no longer much profit in bleeding the wild trees of our jungle. I really do not know why I stay here now, unless it is because I have become so much accustomed to this life."

"Why, I understood that there was much money in rubber!"

"You speak truth — there was. Now there is not. The world moves and times change. Years ago foreigners came into Brazil, helped themselves to the seed of our wild trees, and planted it in Ceylon and the

Malay region. That seed now bears such fruit that the world is flooded with rubber. Ten years ago, senhores, a ton sold for six thousand five hundred dollars. Now, in this year nineteen-twenty, the price is only one-thirteenth of what it was in those days. It scarcely pays for the gathering. I hope you have not come expecting to make fortunes in rubber."

"No. We are here to find a race of men known as Red Bones."

The coronel's brows lifted. They kept on lifting, and he opened his lips twice without speaking. After a long stare at Knowlton he looked at McKay, at Tim, and finally at José. A frown grew on his face. And the Americans, following his look at the Peruvian, were surprised to see that José himself was staring blankly at the speaker.

"José Martinez!" snapped the coronel, leveling a finger pistollike at the *puntero*. "What devil's game are you working now?"

José recovered himself and lifted his coffee cup.

"I do not understand you, Nunes," he replied, languidly. "I am but the humble *puntero* of the crew engaged by these señores. My only work has been to earn my pay. And you may ask *el capitan* whether I have earned it."

"Ay, he has," corroborated McKay. "Killed two of his own crew in our defense."

The coronel's jaw dropped. He blinked as if disbelieving his ears.

"He — José? Not possible!" he stuttered. "José — this man — defended you against his companions?"

"Exactly."

The Brazilian slowly shook his head. Then suddenly he nodded as if an illuminating thought had crossed his mind.

"I see. José is very well paid."

"One dollar a day," was McKay's dry retort.

At that moment 'Tonio re-entered with a larger tray than before, bearing more coffee, long cigars, and squat glasses in which glowed a golden liquid. Tim sat up with a grunt and helped himself with both hands. When the coronel's turn came he disregarded the drinks, but lit the cigar as if he needed it.

"*De noite todos os gatos sao pardos*," he said. "At night all cats are gray. I am much in the dark, gentlemen. If you would be so good as to enlighten me —"

He paused, looking sidewise again at José as if the *puntero* had suddenly grown wings or horns.

"All right," nodded Knowlton, biting and lighting his cigar. "We are somewhat in the dark ourselves as to why José has been so zealous, for he has been very taciturn since the recent fight at our camp. Perhaps José also is a bit hazy about our expedition — he looked rather surprised just now. So here is the situation."

Briefly then he outlined the object of the search, stating that the identity of the mysterious Raposa was a matter of some concern to certain persons in the United States and that the expedition had been formed with the view of settling the question. From the time of the landing at Remate de Males, however, he narrated events more fully, giving complete details of Schwandorf's activities, Francisco's offense, and the final attack by the crew. While he talked the coronel's frown deepened. Also, José gradually assumed the expression of a thundercloud. And when the tale was done the *puntero* exploded.

"*Sangre de Cristo!*" he yelled. "*El Aleman* — the German — he told you we would go among the cannibals? We? Peruvians? *Madre de Dios!* If ever I get within knife length of him! Nunes, you see, do you not?"

The coronel nodded grimly.

"I see that he planned to have all of you destroyed. Senhor Knowlton, that black-bearded and black-hearted man suggested that you take Mayoruna women? He told you they were shapely of body and tried to put into your minds the thought of making them your paramours? The snake!

"He did not tell you, then, that the Mayoruna men allow no trifling with their women; that any alien man attempting to embrace one of them would be killed. But it is true. If you should succeed in establishing friendly relations with the men — which is not at all likely — you would forfeit all friendship, and your lives as well, by the slightest dalliance with any of the women.

"He told you that more than one man has risked his life to win a Mayoruna woman? That is true. But he gave you a false impression as to the way in which the risk was incurred. He did not tell you that Peruvian *caucheros* have sometimes raided small isolated *melocas* of the Mayorunas, shooting down the men and carrying off the girls to be victims of their bestial lust. He did not tell you that for this reason any Peruvian is considered their enemy and is killed without mercy wherever found. Yet he tried to send you with Peruvian guides into their country. He knew the Peruvians would be killed on sight — and you with them."

IX

FIDDLERS THREE

Black looks passed among the men as the duplicity of Schwandorf lay plain before their eyes. Tim growled. José hissed curses. The coronel whirled to him.

"José! What was his object in trying to destroy you and your crew? You have been his man. You know much about him. He wanted to stop your mouth, yes? Dead men tell no tales."

The *puntero's* eyes glittered. For a moment the others thought he was about to reveal important secrets. Then his face changed.

"I know no reason why we should be killed," he declared.

"I do not believe you," the coronel declared, bluntly.

José shrugged, calmly drank the coronel's wine, lighted the coronel's cigar, leaned back in the coronel's chair, and eyed the coronel with imperturbable insolence.

"See here, José," demanded McKay, "you've had something up your sleeve all along. Now come clean! What is it?"

José puffed airily at the cigar, saying nothing.

"What orders did Schwandorf give you?"

This time the reply came readily enough.

"To take you twenty-four days up the river and put you ashore. To prevent any trouble before that time."

"Ah! And after that?"

"Nothing. At least, nothing to me. What may have been said to the other men I do not know. Schwandorf came to me last, after he had picked all the others."

"And what do you know about Schwandorf?"

"What is between me and Schwandorf will be settled between me and Schwandorf. My duty to you señores lies only in handling the crew. Now that there is no crew my duty ends. Also, Capitan, I would like my pay now."

"You quit?"

"Why not? I have done my best. I can do no more. I am crippled. I am of no further use to you. Give me my pay, a little food, a small canoe, and I go."

"It is possible, Senhor José," spoke the coronel, with ironic politeness, "that you may not go so soon. You have killed two men recently. You refuse to reveal some things which should be known about the German. Perhaps the law —"

José burst into a jeering laugh.

"Law? You speak of law? There is no law up the river but the law of the gun and the knife. And if there were, señor, what then? I killed in a fair fight. I killed men who would do murder. I killed on the west bank of the river — Peru. Neither you nor any other Brazilian can lay hand on me. And though I now have only one good arm, it will not be well for anyone to try to hold me. My knife and my right hand still are ready."

"By cripes! the lad's right!" Tim blurted, impulsively. "And I'll tell the world I'm for him. He's got a right to keep his mouth shut if he wants to. He don't owe us nothin'. Mebbe he's got somethin' up his sleeve, at that; but he stuck with us in the pinch, and —"

"And we'll give him a square deal, of course," Knowlton cut in. "José, your own wages to this point, at a dollar a day, are eighteen dollars. The wages of the five other men to the place where they — quit — would aggregate seventy-five dollars. Grand total, ninety-three. The others chose to take their pay in lead instead of gold, so their account is closed. Therefore I suggest that their pay go to you as *puntero*, *popero*, and good sport. What say, Rod?"

"Make it a hundred flat," McKay agreed.

"Right. A hundred in gold. Satisfy you, José?"

"Indeed yes, señor. I did not expect such generosity."

"That's all right, then. We'll fix you up before we move on, and — Say! Are you in Schwandorf's pay, too?"

José hesitated. Then he replied:

"Since you mention it, I will admit that *el Aleman* offered me certain inducements to make this journey. I now see that he had no intention of meeting his promises. But you can leave it to me to collect from him whatever may be due."

Even the coronel nodded at this. The gleam in the Peruvian's eyes presaged unpleasantness for Schwandorf.

"You gentlemen, of course, will not attempt to continue your journey for the present," the coronel suggested. "You are fatigued and I shall greatly appreciate the pleasure of your companionship. New arrangements also will be necessary in the matter of a boat and men."

"We've been wondering about getting another boat and a new crew," Knowlton said, frankly. "The canoe we have is too big for three men to handle, and I'll admit we're tired. José, too, is in no shape to travel yet —"

"José, of course, is my guest also," the old gentleman interrupted. "The question of new men can be solved. But there is time for everything, and now is the time for all of you to rest. As our proverb has it, '*Devagar se vae ao longe*' — he goes far who goes slowly."

McKay arose, glass in hand.

"To our host," he bowed. The toast was drunk standing. Whereafter the host tapped the bell twice and 'Tonio reappeared with a tray of fresh glasses. A toast to the United States by the coronel followed, and as soon as the black man arrived with a third round the Republic of Brazil was pledged. Then the coronel directed the servant:

"'Tonio, if Pedro and Lourenço are outside, ask them to move the belongings of the gentlemen from the canoe. And make ready rooms for the guests."

'Tonio disappeared down the ladder. The coronel raised the violin, tendered it to the others, accepted their pleas to play it himself, and for the next half hour acquitted himself with no mean ability. Snatches of long-forgotten operas and improvisations of his own flowed from the strings in smooth harmony, hinting at bygone years amid far different surroundings for which his soul now hungered and to which he would return. Pedro and Lourenço, transporting the equipment, passed in and out soft-footed and almost unnoticed. At length the player, with a deprecatory smile and a half apology for "boring his guests," extended the instrument again toward the visitors. And McKay, silent McKay, took it.

Sweet and low, out welled the haunting melody of "Annie Laurie." Tim, who had listened with casual interest to the coronel's music, now grinned happily. And when the plaintive Scotch song became "Kathleen Mavourneen" he closed his eyes and lay back in pure enjoyment. "The River Shannon" flowed into "The Suwanee River," and this in turn blended into other heart-tugging airs of Dixieland. When the last strain died and the captain reached for his half-smoked cigar the room was silent for minutes.

Then, to the astonishment of all, José spoke:

"Señores, there was a time when I, too, could draw music from the violin. If I may —" His eyes rested longingly on the instrument.

"Certamente, if you can use the arm," the coronel acquiesced. With a little difficulty José drew his arm from the sling, balanced his left elbow on the chair arm, and poised the violin. A half smile showed in the eyes of the coronel as he glanced at his guests. He, and they as well, expected a discordant, uncouth attempt to scrape out some obscene ditty of the frontier.

But as José, after jockeying a bit, began drifting the bow across the strings, the suppressed smiles faded and eyes opened. Here was a man who, as he said, once could play. And he wasted no time on airs composed by others and known to half the world. Under his touch the mellow wood began to talk, and in the minds of the listeners grew pictures.

City streets, blank-walled houses, patios, the rattle of the hoofs of burros over cobbles, the shuffle of human feet, the toll of bells from a convent tower. Gay little bits of music, laughter, flashing eyes, a voluptuous love song repeated over and over. A sudden wild outbreak, fighting men, shots, the clash of steel — again a tolling bell and a requiem for the dead. A horse galloping in the night. Mountain winds crooning mournfully, rising to the scream of tempest and the crash of thunder. Dreary uplands, the hiss of rain, the sough of drifting snow, the patient plod of a mule along a perilous trail. And then the jungle: its discordant uproar, its hammering of frogs, its hoots and howls, the dismal swash of flood waters. A monotonous ebb and flow of life, punctuated by sudden flares of fight. Then a long, mournful wail — and silence.

His bow still on the strings, José sat for a minute like a stone image, his eyes straight ahead, his pale face drawn, his red kerchief glowing dully in the semishadow like a cap of blood. For once his face was empty of all insolence, changed by a pathetic wistfulness that made it tragic. Then, wordless, he lowered the violin, held it out to the coronel, fumbled absently at his sling, and slowly incased his wounded arm. When he looked up his old mocking expression had come back and he once more looked the reckless buccaneer.

For a time no one spoke. Each felt that he had glimpsed something of this man's past; felt, too, that he who now was a bloody-handed borderer had once been a *caballero*, moving in a much higher circle. Certainly he could not play like this unless he had been of the upper class in his youth. The coronel's face was thoughtful as he took back the violin. When at length he began to talk, however, it was on a topic as remote as possible from music and present personalities — the reconstruction of Europe as the result of the World War.

With this and kindred subjects, aided by the attentive ministrations of 'Tonio, the afternoon passed swiftly. Dinner proved a feast, the *pièce de résistance* being tender, well-cooked meat which the Americans took for roast beef, but which really was roast tapir. More cigars, coupled with the fatigue of the past two days of paddling, eventually caused the visitors to seek their rooms, where McKay and Knowlton paired off and Tim took José as his "bunkie."

When Tim awoke the next morning he found himself deserted.

To Knowlton, who drew from the small gold-chest the hundred dollars allotted to José and handed it to him before redressing his wound, the *puntero* quietly revealed his intention to go before sunrise.

"Say nothing, señor," he requested. "You need know nothing of it, if you like. I am here tonight — I am gone tomorrow — that is all. I am of no further use to you, I am unwelcome in this house of Nunes, and I go. Oh, have no fear for me! I have my gun, my knife, and my good right arm, and I can take care of myself very well. No doubt the coronel will be astonished to find that on leaving tonight I have neither cut anyone's throat nor stolen anything — ha! I have a black name on this river, and it is well earned, perhaps. Yet few men are as bad as those who dislike them think they are. I may borrow a small canoe, but any Indian would do the same. An unoccupied canoe is any man's property.

"Before our ways part, señor, let me say that as José Martinez never forgets his enemies, so he never forgets friends. Where some men would have turned me loose like a sick dog with my eighteen dollars, you and Señor McKay give me a hundred. And far more than that, you saved my life at a time when many men would have said, 'Bah! let the bloody one die! He is nothing but scum of the border and leader of that murdering crew.' You had only to let me lie a few minutes longer and you would be rid of me. No, José does not forget.

"That is all, except — if you will, in parting, take the hand of a man known as a killer and other things —"

Knowlton gripped that hand with swift heartiness. He would have protested against such a departure, but the other's steady gaze betokened inflexible purpose. So he merely said:

"Then good luck, old chap! And if you meet Schwandorf give him our affectionate regards."

"*Si*, señor," was the sardonic answer. "I will do that thing. And here is something that may be of interest to you. I happen to know that before we left Remate de Males a swift one-man canoe left Nazareth, and that the man in it was an Indian who is in the German's control. It went upstream while we were loading your supplies, and it has not returned. By this time it must be many hours above this place. I do not know what message that Indian carries, nor where he goes. But he is a short man, and his left leg is crooked. If you meet such a one make him talk. Good-by, señor."

Just how and when the *puntero* cat-footed his way out that night none ever knew but himself. But before the next dawn he had vanished from the Brazilian shore.

X

BY THE LIGHT OF STORM

"One thing I can't understand," Knowlton said, toying with his coffee cup the next morning, "is why Schwandorf should double-cross us. We never did anything to him. Another thing I don't quite get is how he expected to have the Peruvians wiped out when he knew blamed well they were aware of the enmity of the cannibals. They'd hardly be likely to go into the bush with us under those circumstances."

"My guess is this," McKay replied. "He set a trap. He is on a friendly footing with some of the savages above here, no doubt. He dispatched that Indian messenger to stir them up with some false tale and bring them to some place where they'd be pretty sure to get us. He primed the crew to jump us at the same place, perhaps. Then the crew would kill us or we'd kill them, and whichever side won would be smeared by the Indians. Sort of a trap within a trap. Why he did it doesn't matter much. He double-crossed us, he double-crossed the crew, he double-crossed José. First thing he knows he'll find he's double-crossed himself."

"Yeah," Tim grunted. "He better beat it before we git back!"

"He wanted no killing before we reached the cannibal country," McKay went on, "because then it would all be blamed on the savages and he could show clean hands. Francisco's vengefulness tipped over his cart."

"Still, he might have known we'd stop here for a call on the coronel, and that there was a big chance for us to be warned here about the feud between Mayorunas and Peruvians."

"That probably was provided for. Crew doubtless had orders to prevent any such visit, by lying to us or in other ways. We probably would have gone surging past here at top speed."

"Wal, it don't git us nothin' to talk about things that ain't happened," interposed the practical Tim. "Question is, where do we go from here? And how?"

All eyes went to the coronel, who sat languidly smoking his morning cigar.

"Coronel, we are in your hands," McKay said, bluntly. "Your men, I presume, are all out at work in various parts of the bush. We want a crew and, if possible, guides. Can you help us?"

The coronel flicked off an ash and spoke slowly:

"I have two men, senhores, who have no peers as bushmen. They are the two whom you saw yesterday. Frankly, they are most valuable to me, and I hesitate about sending them on so dangerous a mission as yours. Yet they might succeed where most men would fail, for they have repeatedly gone into the bush on risky journeys and returned unharmed. Their adventures would fill books.

"The older of these two, Lourenço Moraes, has been more than once among the cannibals of this region, and so he knows something of them. Naturally he did not live long among them; he left them as soon as he could. But he has the faculty of extricating himself from hopeless positions — or perhaps it would be better to say that his cool head and good fortune together have preserved him thus far. '*Tanta vez vae o cantaro a fonte ate gue um dia la fica*' — the pitcher may go often to the spring, but some day it remains there.

"Pedro Andrada, the younger, is not so steady and cool-headed as Lourenço. Yet he is a most capable man, and the two together — they are always together — make a very efficient team."

"I bet they do," Tim concurred, heartily. "I like that Pedro lad fine."

"So do I," the coronel smiled. "Now, gentlemen, I will not order these men to go with you. If they go it must be of their own choice. They have only recently returned from a hazardous mission and they are entitled to rest. Yet I have little doubt that they will jump at the chance to risk their lives in a new venture. If they choose to go, I suggest that you place yourselves entirely in their hands and give them free rein. You would look far for better men."

"And we're lucky to get them," Knowlton acquiesced. "To them and to you we shall be greatly indebted."

"Not to me, senhor," the coronel demurred "I do nothing but bring you men together. Theirs is the risk. 'Tonio! Find Pedro and Lourenço. Shall we go into the office, gentlemen?"

Chairs scraped back and an exodus from the dining room ensued. Outside, the lusty voice of the negro bawled. Soon he was back, and at his heels strode the lithe Pedro and the quiet Lourenço. They ran their eyes over the group, then stood looking inquiringly at their employer.

"Be seated, men. Roll cigarettes if you like," said the coronel. Coolly they did both. Pedro, catching Tim's friendly grin, flashed a quick smile in return. Lourenço, unsmiling, looked squarely into each man's face in turn and seemed satisfied with what he saw. Both then glanced around as if missing some one.

"Your friend José has left us," the coronel informed them, dryly, interpreting the look. "He disappeared in the night."

"Ah! That is why one of our canoes is gone," said Pedro. "We are ready to start."

"You mistake," the old gentleman laughed. "We do not want him back. Nothing else is missing."

Whereat Pedro looked slightly surprised. Lourenço's lips curved in a faint grin. Neither made any further comment.

The coronel plunged at once into the business for which they had been summoned. Succinctly he stated the purpose of the North Americans in coming here, pointed out their need of guides — and stopped there. He said nothing of the dangers ahead, mentioned no reward, did not even ask the men whether they would go. He merely lit a fresh cigar and leaned back in his chair.

A silence followed. Again Lourenço looked searchingly into the face of each American. Pedro contemplated the opposite wall, taking occasional puffs from his cigarette. At length Knowlton suggested, tentatively:

"We will pay well —"

Both the bushmen frowned. The coronel spoke in a tone of mild reproof:

"Senhor, it is not a matter of pay. These men can make plenty of money as *seringueiros*."

"Pardon," said Knowlton, and thereafter held his tongue.

Deliberately Lourenço finished his smoke, pinched the coal between a hard thumb and forefinger, and spoke for the first time.

"May I ask, senhor, if you are the commander?" His gaze rested on McKay.

"I am."

"And do I understand that we shall at all times be subject to your orders?"

"In case any orders are necessary — yes. But I assume that you will not need commands."

A quiet smile showed in the bushman's eyes. He glanced at Pedro. The latter met the look from the corner of his eye, without wink, nod, or other sign. But when Lourenço turned again to McKay he spoke as if all were arranged.

"When do we start, Capitao?"

Tim slapped his leg and cackled.

"By cripes! there ain't no lost motion with these guys. Hey, Cap?"

McKay smiled approvingly.

"We shall get on together" he said. "Lourenço and Pedro, this is not a one-man party. We are three comrades, who now become five. If at any time one man needs to command, I, as senior officer, will take that command. Otherwise we are all on an equal footing."

"Just so," Lourenço agreed. "If it were otherwise you would still be three men — not five. Since that is plain, let me say frankly that your big canoe had best stay here, also everything you do not need in the bush. Two light canoes are faster, easier to handle and to hide. Pedro and I have our own canoe and will provide our own supplies. We will pick out a three-man boat for you and load it with what you select from your equipment. After that every man swings his own paddle."

"*Cada qual por si e Deus por todos.* Each for himself and God for us all," Pedro summarized.

"That's the dope," applauded Tim. "Now say, Renzo, old feller, what d'ye know about these here, now, Red Bones up above here? And have ye got anything on that Raposy guy?"

Lourenço shook his head.

"I know little of the Red Bone people, for I have never met them. That is one reason why I now should like to meet them. I have heard of them, yes; and the things I have heard are not pleasant. Yet it may be that the tales are worse than the people. I have also heard terrible stories of the light-skinned cannibals, the Mayorunas; yet I have been among the cannibals and found them not so bad — though it is true that they eat the flesh of their enemies; I have seen it done. But it makes a very great difference how they are approached and who the men are who approach them. It is possible that we may go unharmed among even *los Ossos Vermelhos* — the Red Bones. We shall see.

"Of the Raposa I think I do know something. I have seen him."

Everyone except Pedro sat up with a start.

"You have seen him?" exclaimed the coronel. "When? Where? How? Why have you not spoken of it?"

"Because, Coronel, I forgot it until now. It meant nothing to us — yes, Pedro was with me — except that it was one more queer thing in the bush. In time I might have remembered it and told you. But you know we have been busy."

"True. But go on."

"It was only a little time ago. We were returning from the scouting trip on which you sent us to locate new rubber trees. We were seven — eight — seven —"

"Eight days' journey from here," prompted Pedro.

"*Si.* We were in our canoe when a sudden storm broke and we got ashore to wait until it was over. The place was on an *ygarapé* — a creek — about two days away from the river. The trees were large and the ground free from bush. In a flash of lightning we saw a man peering out at us from a hollow tree.

"He was naked and streaked with paint — that was all we saw in the flashes that came and went. The rain was heavy, and we stayed where we were until it ended. Then we ordered that man to come out.

"He came, and he held bow and arrow ready to shoot. We, too, were ready to shoot, but we held back our bullets and he held back his arrow. We saw that his paint was red and that it traced his bones; that his skin was that of a tanned white man and his hair was dark with a white streak over one ear. No, we did not notice the color of his eyes — the light was not good and he stood well away from us.

"We looked around for other men, but saw none. We asked him who he was and what he wanted, but he gave no answer. He looked at us for a long time, and we at him. Then he began walking away sidewise, watching us steadily, holding his arrow always ready. Finally he disappeared among the trees and we saw him no more. But we heard him, senhores; twice before we lost sight of him he spoke out in a queer voice like that of a parrot. And the thing he said was, 'Poor Davey!'"

McKay thumped a fist on his chair.

"Davey! David Rand!"

"Perhaps so, Capitao. I do not know. But he spoke English."

"By thunder! David Rand! Merry, where's that picture?"

Knowlton was already unbuttoning his pocket flap. Quickly he produced the photograph.

"That the fellow?"

Lourenço studied the face. The eagerly anticipated affirmative did not come.

"I cannot say surely. This is a full-faced, clean-shaven man with hair close trimmed. That one's face was gaunt, covered partly with beard and partly by long hair, and we were not close to him, as I have said. I would not say the two were the same until I could have a better look at the wild man."

"You didn't follow him?"

"No. Why should we? He had done nothing to us and we let him go his way. We did look at his hollow tree, though. But it was only an empty tree, not his home; a place where he had stepped in out of the storm. We had other things to do, so we got into our canoe again and paddled off."

"You can find the place again?"

"Yes. But I much doubt if we shall find him there."

"Never mind. We've something to start with now, and that's worth a lot. Get busy with your boats and supplies, boys, right away. Tim and Merry, let's dig out our essentials and start. We're on a hot trail at last. Let's go!"

XI

OUT OF THE AIR

Again the sun fought the mists of a new day, casting a pallid, watery light on the livid green roof of the limitless jungle. High up under that roof, more than a hundred feet above the ground, the morning alarm clock went off with a scream, the sudden chorus of monkeys and macaws awaking after a few hours of silence. Down on the eastern shore of the river, in a little natural port where the shadows still lay thick, men stirred under their black mosquito nets, yawned, and waited for more light before starting another day's journey.

To three of the five men housed under those flimsy coverings the somber hue of their nets was new. On leaving Remate de Males the insect bars had been clean white; and though they had grown somewhat soiled from daily handling, they never had approached the drab dinginess of the barriers draping the hammocks of the Peruvian rivermen. In fact, their owners had been at some pains to keep them as clean as possible, folding them each morning with military precision and stowing them carefully. Wherefore they were somewhat taken aback when informed that nice white nets were decidedly not the thing in this part of the world.

"Up to this place, senhores, they have done no harm," Pedro said, before leaving the coronel's grounds. "But from here on they will not do at all. The weakest moonlight — yes, even starlight — would make them stand out in the darkness like tombstones. A few days more and we shall be in the cannibal country. And it is an old trick of those eaters of men to skulk along the shore by night, watching a camp until all are asleep, and then sneak up with spears ready. A rush and a swift stab of the spears into those white nets, and you are dead or dying from the poisoned points. I would no more sleep under a white net than I would lie in my hammock and blow a horn to show where I was. Your light nets must stay here. We will find dark ones for you."

Thus the voyagers learned another of those little things on which sometimes hinges life or death. Even McKay, with his experience of other jungles, had never thought it necessary to drape himself in invisibility at night. But when his attention was called to it he recognized its value at once, and the white nets were forthwith abandoned.

Now, on the first morning out from the Nunes place, the three Americans stretched themselves in lazy enjoyment after a night passed without a sentinel. The stretching evoked sundry grunts due to the discovery that their muscles still were lame. The long steamer journey from their own land, followed by the daily confinement of the Peruvian canoe, had afforded scant opportunity for keeping themselves fit, and the sudden necessity for doing their own paddling had found every man soft. But they now were hardening fast, and the steady swing of the paddles was proving a physical joy. These were men ill accustomed to sitting in enforced idleness for weeks on end.

Matches flared under the nets and cigarette smoke drifted into the air, rousing to fresh activity the mosquitoes humming hungrily outside. Gradually the shadows paled and the weak light reflecting from the fog-shrouded water beyond grew into day. The nets lifted and the bloodthirsty insects swooped in vicious triumph on the emerging men. But again matches blazed, flame licked up among kindlings, a fire grew, and in its smoke screen the voyagers found some surcease from the bug hordes. Soon the fragrance of coffee floated into the air.

Tim yawned, coughed explosively, and swore.

"Fellers can't even take a gape for himself without gittin' these cussed bugs down his throat," he complained, and coughed again. "Gimme some coffee! I got one skeeter the size of a devil's darnin' needle stuck in me windpipe."

"A devil's darning needle? What is that, Senhor Tim?" inquired Pedro, passing him a cup of hot coffee. When the liquid — and the "skeeter" — had passed into Tim's stomach he enlightened the inquirer.

"Ye dunno what's a devil's darnin' needle? Gosh! I'm s'prised at ye. I seen lots of 'em right on this here river. He's a bug about so long" — he stuck out a finger — "and he's got jaws like a crab and a long limber tail a with reg'lar needle in the end, and inside him is a roll o' tough silk — tough as spider web. And he's death on liars. Any time a feller tells a lie he's got to look out, or all to oncet one o' them bugs'll come scootin' at him and grab him by the nose with them jaws. Then he'll curl up his tail — the bug, I mean — and run his needle and thread right through the feller's lips and sew his mouth up tight. Then he flies off lookin' for another liar."

"*Por Deus!* And the liar starves to death?"

"Wal, no. O' course he can git somebody to cut the stitches. But the needle is a good thick one and it leaves a row o' holes all along the feller's lips. Any time ye see a guy with li'l' round scars around his mouth, Pedro, ye'll know he's such an awful liar the devil bug got him."

McKay coughed. Knowlton blew his nose into a big handkerchief. Lourenço squinted sidewise at Tim, who was solemn as an owl. Pedro, his eyes twinkling, bent forward and scrutinized Tim's mouth.

"You have been fortunate, senhor," he said, simply — and stepped around to the other side of the fire.

"Huh? Say, lookit here, ye long-legged gorilla —"

Knowlton exploded. McKay and Lourenço snickered.

"It's on you, Tim!" vociferated Knowlton. "You dug the hole yourself. Now crawl in and pull it in after you."

Tim snorted wrathfully, but his eyes laughed.

"Aw, what's the use o' trying to educate you guys?"

"You swallowed a mosquito just now, but I cannot swallow that devil bug," Pedro grinned.

Tim rumbled something, solaced himself with a cigarette, then squatted and joined the others in their frugal breakfast of coffee and *chibeh* — a handful of farinha mixed with water in a gourd. When it was finished McKay, who never smoked in the morning until he had eaten, filled a pipe and suggested:

"Guess we'd better plan our campaign. We didn't take time yesterday. In case we find no trace of the Raposa at the place where you fellows saw him, what's your idea?"

Lourenço, puffing thoughtfully, stared into the fire.

"There will be time enough to decide that, Capitao, after we have visited that place," he said, slowly. "Still, perhaps it is best to make some plan; it can be changed at any time."

For a moment longer he looked at the dying flame. Then, dropping his cigarette stub into it, he continued:

"If I were going alone to find a man among the Red Bones, I should go first to the Mayorunas and work through them to make sure of a friendly reception by the other people. I would —"

"Why, that's the very thing Schwandorf suggested!"

"Yes? I have not heard what he said. Tell me."

McKay did so. Lourenço smiled.

"Sometimes, Capitao, the devil puts into the hands of men a weapon which is turned against himself. So it is now. That *Allemao*, Schwandorf, never expected you to reach the people you seek, but the plan is good. It would not be good if you followed it exactly as he laid it out, but things have changed; and what you could not do with Peruvian companions, or alone, you perhaps can do with us. I will show you.

"It happens that I have been twice among the cannibals living in a certain *maloca* which I can find again. Perhaps you know that those people live in scattered *malocas*, each ruled by its own chief —"

"Yes, we know about that."

"Good. Now if we went to any *maloca* where we were not known we might be killed at once. But at that *maloca* of which I speak I am known to the chief and all his fighting men, for I once led them on a raid into Peru. So they will remember me —"

"What's that?" Knowlton interrupted, in amazement. "You led a cannibal tribe on the warpath?"

"Just so, senhor. It is a long story, but these are the facts:

"There was in Peru a gang of killers, robbers — and worse — who called themselves the Peccaries. They raided one of the coronel's camps where I was in charge, killed all my gang except myself and one other, and used us two as slaves and beasts of burden.

"The other man died from poison. I lived only to revenge myself on those foul outlaws. There was much rubber of the coronel's, worth much money at that time, in the camp they had raided. So, after driving me like a beast to their stronghold in the hills of Peru, they came back with boats and Indian porters to get out that rubber.

"On that return journey I tried to kill the leader, who was called El Amarillo — yellow-skinned. I failed, and he had me nailed with long thorns to a tree where I might hang in torment for days, dying slowly. See. Here are the marks."

All three of the Americans had noticed on the previous day that each of Lourenço's hands was disfigured by a scar which looked as if a spike had been driven through. Now he held those hands forward for their inspection. Then he pulled off his loose shirt and rolled up his trousers. They saw other scars in the big muscles before the armpits, in the soft flesh under the ribs, in the thighs and calves.

"The dirty Hun!" Tim grated.

"That was not all, Senhor Tim. They also put fire ants on me, which bit so cruelly that I nearly lost my mind from pain. Then they went on, intending to have more sport with me when they came back with the rubber. But after they left me two hunters of the cannibal tribe who had been following a tapir's track found me and took me down from the tree.

"Now the Peccaries before this had stolen some women from a May-oruna *maloca* and were treating them like dogs — I saw one of those women brutally murdered while I was captive in the outlaw camp. I managed to tell the two hunters I could lead them to the Peccary stronghold and give them revenge. They carried me to their *maloca* — I could not walk — and told their chief what I had said. The chief caused my hurts to be cured, and then I kept my promise.

"I guided the savages to the outlaw camp; they surrounded it, and in the fight that followed every Peccary was killed except their leader. Now that cannibal chief has not forgotten me —"

"Wait a minute," protested Knowlton. "Did that Peccary leader escape?"

"No. He was kept alive until a big herd of peccaries was met. Then, because he called himself 'King of the Peccaries,' he was nailed to a tree, as I had been, and told to make the peccaries take out the thorns. The wild pigs tore him into ribbons with their tusks."

Calmly he donned his shirt again. Tim, staring at him, twitched his shoulders as if a chill had gone down his back.

"Ugh!" muttered Knowlton.

"So now," Lourenço resumed, "if I can find that chief again — he may have been killed in some tribal fight before now — he may be friendly to all of us. Or he may not. Savages cannot be relied on with much certainty. But if any of the Mayorunas will help us, he will. It is worth trying."

"And if he is not friendly —" Knowlton paused.

"We do not come back," Pedro finished. "Have you a better plan?"

All shook their heads.

"Laurenco's idea is excellent," said McKay. "I was thinking along the same line, though I did not know he had any such friendly relations with a chief. That makes it all the more advisable to try it, unless we find the Raposa first. We, of course, will not land at the place where Schwandorf told us to go ashore, seven days from here."

"By no means," Lourenço concurred. "In five days we leave the river and travel along the *ygarapé*. If we go to the *maloca* it will be from another direction than the river."

He began preparing to travel. The others also went about the work of breaking camp. By the time the canoes were loaded the mists had lifted and the river lay open and empty before them. In the bush around and beyond, gloom still lay thick and the forest life yelped, howled, clattered, and wailed. But out on the water it was broad day, and far overhead sounded the harsh cries of unseen parrots flying two by two in the sunlight above the matted branches. The world of the pathless tropic wilderness, ever dying, ever living, was about its daily business. The five invaders were about theirs.

As the paddlers dipped, however, Knowlton held back.

"Say, Rod, we didn't tell these fellows about Schwandorf's Indian. Hold up a second, men."

While all rested on their paddles he spoke of the mysterious messenger dispatched from Nazareth. Pedro and Lourenço contemplated the river, then frowned.

"That may be of importance, senhores," said Lourenço. "It may change everything for us. We saw a lone Indian go past the coronel's place, traveling fast, three days before you came. I would give much to know where he is now and what word he carries. A short man with a bad left leg, you say. We shall keep watch for such a man. Perhaps we may meet him."

Wherein he predicted more accurately than he knew.

The canoes swung out and the paddlers settled into the steady stroke to which they were growing accustomed. Hour after hour they forged on, the Brazilians adjusting their speed to that of the Americans, who had not yet attained the muscular ease of habitual canoemen. The miles flowed slowly but surely behind them, the sun rolled higher and hotter, the silence of approaching noon crept over the jungle on either side. Then, as the time drew near when they would land for a more hearty meal than that of the morning, Pedro pointed ahead.

Up out of the bush on the Peruvian shore rose a vulture. It flapped sullenly away as if disappointed. The bushmen, quick to note anything that might be a sign, paid no attention to the bird's flight, but marked with unerring eye the spot whence it had taken wing.

"Let us cross, comrades, and see what we may see," Pedro called. "If nothing is there, we can eat."

But something was there. All saw it before they landed — the stern of a small, speedy canoe almost concealed in a narrow rift at the bottom of the bank. In the soil of the rising slope were the prints of bare feet. And Pedro, scanning the tracks narrowly after he and the others reached shore, asserted, "These were not made today."

Up the bank they climbed, silent and watchful. At the top Lourenço took the lead. In under big trees the five passed in file. A short distance from the edge Lourenço stopped, looking at the ground. The others spread out and stared at the thing he had found.

Between the buttress roots of a tall tree was a crude shelter of palm leaves. Before this lay the scattered bones of a man. The skull had been crushed by a mighty blow.

The bones were picked clean — had been stripped and torn asunder days before, and the vulture which had just left had gotten nothing for its belated visit. Among them were remnants of cloth, a belt and a machete, and strands of coarse black hair. A few feet away lay a cheap "trade" gun. Lourenço inspected the weapon and laid it back.

"Did he shoot before he was downed?" asked Knowlton.

"No. The gun is loaded. His death came from above." The bushman ran his eye up the towering tree, then pointed to a large dark object on the ground near by.

"Castanha — Brazil-nut tree," he explained. "That heavy nut fell and smashed the Indian's skull like an egg. Indian, yes. His gun, his shelter, and his hair show that. And" — stooping and pointing at one of the bones — "that bone shows who he was. See, Capitao."

McKay looked down on a leg bone. At some time the leg had been broken and badly set, if set at all. The bone was crooked.

"A short Indian with a crooked leg. Schwandorf's messenger!"

"*Si*. No man will ever receive the message he bore. He camped here days ago. Now he camps here forever."

XII

THE ARROW

Slowly, silently, two canoes glided along the still, dark water of a gloomy creek over-arched by the interlaced limbs of lofty trees.

The first, propelled by the slow-dipping blades of two Brazilian bushmen, seemed to be seeking something; for it nosed along with frequent pauses of the paddles, during which it drifted almost to a stop while its crew searched the solemn jungle depths reaching away from the right-hand shore. The second, carrying three bronzed and bearded men of another continent, was only trailing the leader. It moved and paused like the first, but the recurrent scrutiny of the farther gloom by its paddlers was that of men who saw only a meaningless, monotonous bulk of buttresses and trunks and tangle of looping lianas. In this dimness and bewildering chaos the trio might as well have been blind. The eyes of the tiny fleet were in the first boat.

The progress of the dugouts was almost stealthy. Not a paddle thumped or splashed, not a voice spoke. They moved with the alert caution born not of fear, but of wary readiness for any sudden event — like prowling jungle creatures which, themselves seeking quarry, must be ever on guard lest they become the hunted instead of the hunters.

For the past two days they had moved thus. The last fresh meat had been shot miles down the river, where a well-placed bullet from the rifle of McKay had downed a fat swamp deer. Since that day not a gun had been fired. The rations now were tough jerked beef and monkey meat, slabs of salt pirarucu fish, and farinha, varied by tinned delicacies from the stores of the Americans. Henceforth gunfire was taboo unless it should become necessary in self-defense.

At length the fore canoe halted with an abruptness that told of back strokes of the blades hidden under water. McKay, bowman of the trailing craft, also backed water, while his mates held their paddles rigid. The two boats drifted together.

"This is the place," Lourenço said, speaking low.

The Americans, scanning the shore, saw nothing to differentiate the spot from the rest of the wilderness growth. Yet Lourenço's tone was sure. Pedro's face also showed recognition of his surroundings. With no apparent motion of the paddles — though the wrists of the paddlers moved almost imperceptibly — the canoe of the bushmen floated to the bank. They picked up their rifles, twitched their bow up on land, and turned their faces to the forest.

"Stay here," was Pedro's subdued command, "until you hear the bird-call which we taught you down the river."

He and Lourenço faded into the dimness and were gone.

"Beats me how them guys find their way 'round," muttered Tim. "I could land here twenty times hand-runnin', but if I went away and then come back I'd never know the place."

"It's all in the feel of it," was McKay's low-toned explanation. "They find places and travel the bush as an Indian does — by a sixth sense. Take them to New York City, guide them around, then turn them loose — and they'd be hopelessly lost in ten minutes."

The others nodded agreement and sat watching. In the shadows no creature moved. Afar off some bird cried mournfully like a lost soul condemned to wander forever alone in the grim green solitudes. No other sound came to the listeners save the ever-present hum of the big forest mosquitoes, to which they now had become indifferent. For all they could see or hear of their two guides, they might as well have been alone. Yet they knew the Brazilians were not far away, threading the maze with sure step and scouting hawk-eyed for any sign of danger.

At length a long soft whistle sounded in the bush ahead. Any Indian hunter hearing that sound would straightway have begun scanning the high branches, for the liquid call was that of the mutum, or curassow turkey. But the waiting trio knew it for Pedro's signal that all was clear. At once they slid their canoe to shore, lifted its bow to a firm grip on the clay, and, after plumbing the shadows, quietly advanced in squad column.

A few steps, and they halted suddenly and whirled. A voice had spoken just behind them. There, squatting leisurely between the root buttresses of a huge tree, Lourenço looked up at them in amusement. They had passed within rifle length of him without seeing him.

"Of what use are your eyes, comrades?" he chaffed. "In the bush one should see in all directions at once. You were looking at that patch of sunlight just ahead, yes? But danger lurks in the shadows, not in the glaring light."

Without awaiting an answer, he arose and took the lead. At the edge of the small sunlit space beyond he halted.

"You were heading for the right place," he added then. "Look around. Do you see anything?"

Swiftly they scrutinized the gap left by the fall of a great tree whose gigantic trunk had bludgeoned weaker trees away in its crushing descent. Seeing nothing unusual, they then peered around them. Tim suddenly snapped up his rifle.

"Holler tree there — and a man in it! Hey! come out o' there!"

"Your eyes improve," Lourenço complimented. "But the man is Pedro."

Tim lowered the gun as Pedro, grinning, came out of his concealment.

"That is the tree of the Raposa," Lourenço went on. "The lightning flashing in from above showed us the man. But now, senhores, I think we must tramp the bush for some time before we find that Raposa again. There is no trace of him here."

"Hm!" said Knowlton. Striding to the hollow tree, he peered about inside it. The cavity was almost big enough to sling a hammock in, but it was empty of any indication of habitation, human or otherwise. A temporary refuge — that was all.

"No sign anywhere around here, eh?" queried McKay.

"We have found none. We shall look farther, but I have small hope. If you senhores will make the camp this time we shall start at once and stay out until dark. Build no fire until we return. And if you hear the call of the mutum, pay no attention to it; we may use it to locate each other if we separate, and also perhaps as a decoy. Any wild man, red or white, hearing that call would seek the bird making it, for a fine fat mutum is well worth killing. Keep quiet and be on guard."

"Right. Go ahead."

The bushmen turned at once and stole away. The others returned to the canoes, transported the necessary duffle to the base of the hollow tree, made camp with a few poles, and squatted against the trunk to smoke, watch, and wait. Several times they heard mutum calls receding in the distance. Then came silence.

The sun-thrown shadows in the gap crawled steadily eastward. Knowlton tested the feed of his automatic, which, since its balkiness in the fight with the Peruvians, he had kept carefully oiled and free from the slightest speck of rust. Tim arose at intervals and paced up and down in sentry go, eyes and ears alert — a useless activity, but one which provided an outlet for his restless energy. McKay let his gaze rove over the small area visible from their post, studying the contours of the towering trunks, the prone giant whose fall had opened the hole in the leafy roof, the parasitical vines twined about other trees, the thin, outflung buttresses supporting the mighty columns — all familiar sights to him, but the only things to occupy his vision. So limned on his brain did the scene become that after a time he could close his eyes and see it in every important detail.

It might have been two hours after Pedro and Lourenço had departed — the shadows had grown much longer — when over McKay stole the feeling that he was being watched. He glanced at his companions and found that neither of them was looking at him. Knowlton, sitting with hands clasped around updrawn knees, was dozing. Tim, though wide awake, was staring absently at a fungus. The captain's eyes searched the short vistas all about, spying nothing new. Still the feeling persisted. Then all at once his roaming gaze stopped, became fixed on a point some forty feet away.

There rose a rough-barked red-brown tree, and from it, near the ground, projected a blackish bole. McKay was very sure the protuberance had not been there before. He had stared steadily at that tree more than once, and its shape was quite clear in his mind. Was that bump an insensate wood growth now revealed for the first time by the changing sun slant, or —

For minutes he watched it. It did not move. Then Tim, restless again, rose directly in McKay's line of sight, yawned silently, swung his gun to his shoulder, and began another slow parade of his self-appointed post. When he had stepped aside McKay looked again for the puzzling bole.

It was gone.

With a bound the captain was up and dashing toward the tree, drawing his pistol as he ran. But within three strides he went down. A tough vine, unnoticed on the ground, looped snakily around one ankle and threw him hard. His gun flew from his hand. As he fell a tiny whispering sound flitted past, followed by a small blow somewhere behind him. Ensued a gruff grunt from Tim and the swift clatter of a breech bolt.

Raging, McKay kicked his foot loose and heaved himself up. Empty handed, he continued his rush for the tree. But when he reached it he found nothing behind it. If anything had been there it now was gone, and the vacant shadows beyond were as inscrutable as ever.

Feet padded behind him and Tim and Knowlton halted on either side. A moment of silent searching, and Tim broke into reproach.

"Cap, don't never do that again! If ye take a tumble in my line o' fire, for the love o' Mike stay down till I shoot! I come so near drillin' ye when ye hopped up that I'm sweatin' blood right now."

In truth, the veteran was pale around the mouth and his broad face was beaded with cold drops.

"I seen more 'n one time in France when I felt like shootin' my s'perior officer, but I never come so near doin' it as jest now. I had finger to trigger and had took up the slack, and a hair's weight more pull would have spattered yer head all around. And besides givin' me heart failure ye let that guy git away. We'll never find him —"

"You saw him?" McKay cut in.

"I seen somethin' beyond ye — couldn't make out what 'twas, but from the way ye was goin' over the top I knowed it must be a man. And then when the arrer come —"

"Arrow?"

"Sure. Missed ye when ye took that flop, and stuck in the tree over yonder. What'd ye rush the guy for, anyways? Whyn't ye drill him from where ye was?"

In the reaction from his sudden fright Tim was as wrathfully ready to "bawl out" his captain as if he were some raw rookie. McKay, with a cool smile, explained his abrupt action, meanwhile reconnoitering the dimness for any further sign of the vanished assailant. None showed.

While Tim stood vigilant guard the other two stooped and moved around the base of the tree, narrowly examining the ground. Beyond it they paused at one spot, fingered the soil lightly, and lit a match or two.

"No ghost," said Knowlton. "Barefoot man. Didn't leave much trace, but enough to show he was here. Let's look at that arrow."

Back to the hollow tree they went, retrieving McKay's pistol on the way. About a yard above the earth a long shaft projected from the bark. Knowlton reached for it, but McKay held him back and drew it out.

"M-hm! Thought so!" he muttered. "Poisoned."

"Oof! Nice, gentle sort of a cuss," rumbled Tim. "That smear on the point — is that poison?"

"Poison. Quickest and deadliest kind of poison. Mixes instantly with blood. Paralysis — convulsions — death. The least scratch and you're gone. Wicked head on this thing, too: looks like a piece of serrated bone. See all those little barbs along the edges? War arrow, all right."

"Meanin' that we'll be jumped pretty soon by more Injuns. If that guy's on the warpath he ain't alone."

"Wouldn't be a bad idea to take cover," nodded McKay. Turning the five-foot shaft downward, he plunged its head into the soft ground and left it sticking there, harmless.

"Tim, go down and guard the canoes. Merry, lie in between these roots and keep watch off that way. I'll go over to that tree where the spy hid."

For another hour the camp was silent. Each in his covert, finger on trigger, the trio watched with ceaseless vigilance, expecting each instant to detect dusky forms crawling up from tree to tree. Yet nothing of the sort came. Nor did any hostile sound reach them. Somewhere parrots squawked, somewhere else the puppylike yapping of toucans disturbed the solitude; nothing else.

The wan light faded. The sun crawled up the trees, leaving all the ground in shadow. Then, not far off, sounded the soft whistle of the mutum. Suspicious, the watchers held their places until, with another whistle, Pedro came into view, followed by Lourenço.

McKay arose, met them, and briefly explained the situation. They nodded, but seemed undisturbed.

"We can start a fire now, Capitao," Lourenço said. "Night comes and we are hungry. There will be no danger before another dawn."

With which he leaned his rifle against a tree and started immediate preparations for a meal. Pedro continued on to the canoes, made sure they were drawn up high enough to remain in place in case of any sudden rain, and returned with Tim. Around them now resounded the swiftly rising roar of the nightly outbreak of animal life. The sun vanished. At once blackness whelmed all except the little fire.

"See anything while you were out?" asked McKay.

"We found no trace of the Raposa," Lourenço evaded.

"What do you plan to do now?"

"Eat — smoke — talk — sleep."

McKay eyed the bushman keenly, feeling that he was holding something back. But, feeling also that this pair knew what they were about, he bided his time. When all had eaten and tobacco smoke was blending with that of the burning wood, Lourenço drew the arrow from the ground and studied it. Then he passed it to Pedro, who, after a critical examination, held it in the blaze until the deadly head was burned away.

"A big-game arrow of the cannibal Mayorunas," said Lourenço. "The point, with its sawtooth barbs, is made from the tail bone of the araya, the flat devilfish of the swamp lakes. That fish, as you perhaps know, has a whiplike tail armed with that bone; and if he strikes the bone into your flesh it breaks off and stays in the wound, and you are likely to die."

"But in that case death comes from gangrene," McKay remarked. "This point has been dipped in wurali poison."

"You have seen such arrows before, Capitao?"

"Seen the poison before, yes. Over in British Guiana. The Macusi Indians make it from the wurali vine, some bitter root or other, a couple of bulbous plants, two kinds of ants — one big and black with a venomous bite, the other small and red — a lot of pepper, and the pounded fangs of labarri and couanacouchi snakes. They boil all this stuff down to a thick syrup, and that's the poison. The man who makes it is sick for days afterward."

"Our cannibals make that poison in much the same way. Yet Guiana is many hundreds of miles from here, and our Indians know nothing of those Macusi people. Queer, is it not, that the same plan should be used by savages thousands of miles apart?"

"Rather odd. Must have started from some common source hundreds of years ago and spread around. Queerest thing is, though, that a poison so deadly doesn't spoil meat for eating."

"Huh?" exclaimed Tim. "Mean to say them cannibals can kill us by scratchin' us with a poison arrer and then stummick us afterwards?"

"Exactly. You'd taste just as sweet as ever, Tim — maybe more so. Cheer up! They say it doesn't hurt much to die that way; you're paralyzed so quick you just sort of fade out."

Tim shook his head, his abhorrence of poison strong as ever. Knowlton spoke.

"I've heard that this wurali poison is much overrated, that it will kill only birds and monkeys, not men."

"*Por Deus!* Whoever said that was a fool trying to appear wise!" Pedro snorted. "We have seen the poison death, and we know."

McKay also shook his head.

"Experiments have been made with the wurali of the Macusis," he stated. "It was tried on a hog, a sloth — and a sloth is mighty hard to kill — also on mules, and on a full-grown ox weighing almost half a ton. It killed every one of them."

A momentary silence followed. Tim gazed sourly at the arrow, now harmless but still sinister.

"Urrrgh!" he growled. "Cap, ye had a narrer squeak — come near gittin' it from in front, and behind, too. Wisht I could have drilled that guy."

The bushmen grinned. And Lourenço's next speech was amazing.

"Be thankful you did not. That bullet might have killed us all."

After enjoying their puzzled expressions a moment he continued.

"We are nearer to a Mayoruna *maloca* than I thought. Not the one I intended to seek, but a smaller one. It is about three days' journey from here, and to reach it we must go through the bush. The man who left this arrow here today is from that *maloca*.

"A week ago his brother went hunting, and he has not returned. So this young savage and three of his comrades now are searching the bush for some sign of him. Today they separated, each going in a different direction, agreeing to meet again tonight at a place less than half a day's journey from here. This man circled around and worked along this creek, knowing his brother would hardly go beyond the water. He spied our canoes, then sought the men who had come in them and found you.

"He watched you for some time, and if you had not rushed at him he would have slipped away without attacking you, for he was alone and he saw your guns. But when you, Capitao, suddenly leaped at him he darted away, then stopped long enough to send an arrow at you. After that he dodged out of sight and ran to the camp of his three friends. He is there now, telling about you."

"Great guns! You chaps are wizards!" cried Knowlton. "How do you know all this?"

"Because we met him while on our way back here. He was running hard, and we heard him, so we blocked him. After we convinced him that we were friendly we talked for some time — I can speak their tongue — and he told us about you. He was sure you were enemies to him and his people, and believed also you had killed his missing brother, and he was going first to rejoin his companions and then hasten to the *maloca* to bring all their fighters against you. It was well that we met him in time. It was well, too, that you did not shoot him — or even shoot at him. His companions would have learned of it, and then — death for us all."

"And now what?"

"Now, comrades, we all go to the *maloca* of that man. We meet him and the other three tomorrow at the place where we talked to him today. I told him we were going to visit that other chief whom I knew, and, though he was at first suspicious of a trap, he finally agreed to lead us to his own chief. So in the morning we march. Now let us sleep."

Knowlton and McKay glanced at each other and nodded.

"Luck's with us so far," said the captain.

"Right. We just march right into Jungle Town with bodyguard and everything. Pretty soft! Wonder if they'll turn out the tomtom band to drum us in."

Tim said nothing. He squinted again at the headless arrow, then inspected the breech bolt of his rifle.

XIII

THE WAY OF THE JUNGLE

Dawn came, dismal, damp, and chill. Moisture dripped drearily from the upper reaches, and under the dense canopy of leaves and limbs the gloom and the fog together made a murk wherein the early-rising bushmen were scarcely visible to the North Americans ten feet away. Yet day had come, or was coming; the noise of the animal world left little doubt of that.

By the light of a sullen smoky fire and oil-smeared torches Pedro and Lourenço made up their packs, cording them roughly with bark-cloth strips brought from headquarters. The Americans, after eating a more solid meal than the Brazilians seemed to require, also rolled their blankets, hammocks, nets, and other paraphernalia; strapped the outfits into the army pack harnesses which they had transported for thousands of miles and never yet used; crammed their web belts with cartridges; slung their sheathed machetes down their left thighs; looked to their guns; and announced themselves ready to go.

While the northerners made these final preparations their guides slipped away for a time. Pedro, on his return, announced that the canoes had been concealed. Lourenço, bringing back the freshly filled canteens of the ex-army men, delivered with them the marching orders of the day.

"If you thirst, comrades, drink only from your canteens. If the canteens fail, never fill them from flowing water unless the Indians also drink from the stream. There are always small pools to be found, and, though their water may be warm and stale, it is not likely to be poisoned, as the streams may be.

"Today, and every day after we meet the cannibals, make no suspicious moves. Do not speak harshly. Do not laugh or sneer at them. They are unreasoning and easily insulted, and lifelong foes when angered. Let me do the talking.

"Do not hold a gun in a threatening manner or draw pistols unless you must fight. Then kill.

"Above all, pay no attention to their women.

"Now we go. I lead."

He turned and strode away into the fog as easily and surely as if cat-eyed and cat-footed. Pedro swung nonchalantly after him. The others followed in order, hitching at their backstraps.

The ghostly haze about them now was paler, but through the interstices overhead came no glint of sunshine, nor even the glow of a clear dawn. The whole sky evidently was overcast, and around the marching men the gloom still lay thick. Yet Lourenço's eyes seemed to bore through the shades and the dark shroud blurring the trunks, for his steady gait did not falter. The little file hung close together, for all knew that any man straggling would be instantly lost.

Worming around gigantic columns, crawling over rotting trunks long laid low, changing direction abruptly when blocked by some great butt too high to be scaled, sinking ankle-deep in clinging mud, the venturesome band wound along through the wilderness. Repeated glances at his compass showed McKay that the general trend of the march was southeast; but the impassable obstacles encountered at frequent intervals necessitated not only detours, but sometimes actual back-tracking.

"Walk four miles to advance one," was his thought. And for some time it seemed that such was the case. But then the ground changed, the light improved, the trees thinned, and the undergrowth became more dense — and, paradoxically, the rate of progress improved.

This was because the smaller growth gave the two leaders a chance to cut their way straight onward instead of dodging about; and cut they did. Their machetes swung with untiring energy, opening a path through what seemed an impenetrable tangle. Now every yard of movement was a yard gained. But the ground was rising and the struggle up some of the sharp slopes winded more than one man.

Then the slope dipped the other way, and they slipped down into a ravine where water gleamed darkly. Here a halt was called while the leaders sought for a fallen tree. Tim squatted and mopped his face for the hundredth time.

"Gosh! This is what I call travelin'!" he panted. "Flounderin' round in mud soup, bit to death by skeeters and them what-ye-call-'em flies — piums — sweatin' yerself bone dry and totin' forty thousand pounds, on yer back, not to mention hardware slung all over ye — this ain't no place for a minister's son or a fat guy, I'll tell the world. And this is only the start!"

A call from Pedro forestalled any answer. The trio struggled along to the spot where the guides waited at the butt of a slanting tree trunk spanning the gulf. As they reached it Pedro walked carefully up the trunk, carrying a long slender sapling, which he lowered and fixed in the bottom of the stream. Then, steadying himself with the upper end of this pole, he continued his journey to the other side, where he flipped the sapling back to Lourenço. One by one the others crossed, slipping, almost losing balance, but managing to evade a fall. Tim, walking the precarious bridge and looking down, saw that the surface of the water was dotted with the heads of venomous snakes.

"Are you following your trail of yesterday?" demanded McKay.

"No, Capitao. Yesterday we circled. Today we go as nearly straight as possible."

"And you can find the appointed place by this new route?" The captain's tone was dubious.

"Certainly. Else I should go the other way. Come."

Up another bank they toiled, and on through rugged country which seemed momentarily to become higher and harder to traverse. In the minds of the Americans grew suspicion that, for the first time, the Brazilians were bluffing; it seemed impossible for any man to keep his sense of direction in such a maze. But they said no word and followed on.

At length the leader paused and sent the long call of the mutum floating through the trees. No answer came. After a moment the line moved on, each man peering ahead with sharper gaze, each holding a little tighter. To the Americans, at least, the thought of possible ambush loomed large.

Four man-eating savages, hidden in this labyrinthine tangle and armed with arrows whose slightest scratch meant death, could strike down every man of this expedition without even a wound in return; for of what avail were high-power guns, automatic pistols, and machetes against invisible enemies? Yet there was assurance in Lourenço's confident air, and reassurance in the thought that these tribemen would be unlikely to assail a band avowedly on its way to visit their chief. Besides — Knowlton smiled grimly — even if the Mayorunas hungered for human flesh it would be more economical of labor to let the meat travel to the slaughterhouse on its own legs than to kill it here and carry it home.

Again the mutum whistle drifted away. Again no answer came. For a short distance farther the file continued its march. Then, in a small opening where the uptorn roots of a tree rose like a wall at one side, it halted.

"The place of meeting," Pedro said. All peered around. None saw anything but the upstanding roots, the forest jumble, the misty serpentine lianas. None heard any sound but their own hoarse breathing, the solemn drip of water, the insect hum, and the occasional melancholy notes of birds. The place seemed bare of life. Yet upon McKay came again that feeling of being watched.

Slowly, deeply, Lourenço spoke. The words meant nothing to his mates. They were like no words they knew. His eyes roved about as he talked, and it was evident that he saw no more than did the silent men behind him. But they guessed that he said he and they were there as agreed, with peace in their hearts, and that he was telling the men of the wilderness to come forward without fear. And they guessed rightly.

As quietly as a phantom of the mist a man took shape at the edge of the tree roots. Tall, straight, slender, symmetrically proportioned, with unblemished skin of light-bronze hue, straight black hair, and deep dark eyes, he was a splendid type of savage. Face and body were adorned with glossy paint — scarlet and black rings around the eyes, two red stripes from temple to chin, wavy lines on arms and chest. He held a bow longer than himself, with a five-foot arrow fitted loosely to the string and pointed downward, but ready for instant use. Diagonally across his body ran a cord supporting a quiver, from which the feathered shafts of several arrows projected above his left shoulder. Around his waist looped another cord from which dangled a small loin mat. Otherwise he was totally nude — a bronze statue of freedom.

Lourenço spoke again in the same quiet tone. The savage stepped warily forward. At the same moment three other naked men appeared with equal stealth from tree trunks which had seemed barren of all life. Like the first, each of these held an arrow ready, but pointing downward; and each moved with the slow, velvety step of a hunting jaguar. Their eyes searched those of these strange men of another world who, wearing useless clothing, carrying heavy weapons of steel, burdening themselves with queer weights on their backs, now invaded the wilderness which they and their fathers had roamed untrammeled for centuries. The invaders in turn studied the faces of the Mayorunas, of whom so many gruesome tales were told. For long silent minutes primitive and civilized man probed each other for signs of treachery — and found none.

Tim, forgetting the orders of the day, spoke out abruptly. At the gruff jar of his voice the wild men started and raised their weapons.

"Say, are those guys cannibals? I was lookin' to see some ugly mutts with underslung jaws and mops o' frizzy hair, like them Feejee Islanders ye see pitchers of. Barrin' the paint, I've seen worse-lookin' fellers than these back home."

With which he gave the savages a wide, unmistakably approving grin.

"Shut up!" muttered McKay.

Lourenço, unruffled, made instant capital of Tim's remarks.

"My comrade of the red hair," he said in the Indian tongue, "has never before seen the mighty warriors of the Mayorunas, and is astonished to find them such handsome men. He says his own countrymen are not so good to look upon."

Slowly the menacing arrows sank. As the savages studied Tim's wholesome grin and absorbed the broad flattery of Lourenço a slight smile passed over their faces. They stood more at ease. The whites sensed at once that, for a moment, at least, a friendly footing had been established, and relaxed from their own tension.

Once more Lourenço spoke, motioning toward the farther distances. The Indian who had first appeared now replied briefly. Two of the others stepped back to their trees and lifted long, hollow tubes.

"What's them?" demanded Tim.

"Blowguns," Pedro answered. "They use them for small or thin-skinned game. See, the two blowgun men carry also short darts in their quivers, and small pouches of poison."

"Uh-huh. They like their poison a dang sight better 'n I do. Say, are them guys goin' to march behind us? I don't want no poison needles slipped into my back, accidental or other ways."

Two of the savages were walking toward the rear of the line. Knowlton, exasperated, snapped out:

"They'll walk where they like, and you'll do well to give us more marching and less mouth. You nearly spilled the beans just now, and if Lourenço hadn't said something that pleased these fellows we all might be in the soup this minute. Pipe down!"

"Aw, Looey, I only said these guys were good-lookin'. Ain't no fight in words like that."

"You heard the orders this morning. Let Lourenço do the talking. That goes! We're skating on thin ice — so thin that if it breaks we drop plump into hell. Less noise!"

"Right, sir," was the sulky answer. "I'm deaf and dumb."

"March," added McKay. The head of the column already was on the move, led by the tallest Indian and a blowgun man, behind whom walked the two Brazilians. The whole line took up the step in turn and passed on into the unknown.

Again McKay consulted his compass at intervals, finding that now the route led more to the south, though there still was an easterly trend. After a time, however, the telltale needle informed him that they were proceeding almost due east, and glances at the surroundings showed that on their right was a densely matted mass of undergrowth. Not long afterward another interwoven brush wall blocked the way, and this time the leader veered to the west. Not until an opening appeared did he resume his southward course. It dawned on McKay that the savages, having no bush knives, were accustomed to follow the line of least resistance. This obviously increased the distance traveled.

The men of Coronel Nunes, too, perceived this. A halt was called, during which Lourenço talked with the guide, tapped his machete, and evidently protested against needless detours. The leader, with a few words, pointed south. Lourenço nodded and replied. The march was resumed, and when the next impenetrable tangle was encountered the Indians in the van stepped aside, the machetes of the Brazilians flashed out, and a way was cut straight through. From that time on the long knives came into frequent play and a direct course was maintained.

Suddenly, with a grunt of warning, the tall tribesman stopped. The plan of chopping through instead of going around had brought the Indians into a part of the forest which they had not heretofore traversed in their search for the missing hunter. Now they stood in a small trough between the knolls, under good-sized trees around which grew little brush. The ground was soft, almost watery. In the damp air, faint but unmistakable, hung the odor of death.

The savages at the rear came forward at once. All four of them spread out and, sniffing the air, advanced up the trough. A cry broke from one of them. The others, and the white men, too, hastened to the spot whence the call had come.

Scattered about in the soft muck were bones, two skulls, bits of tawny fur, a long bow, several big-game arrows. Around them the ground was marked with many tracks. Most of the imprints were of the vultures which had stripped the bones, but there were others — those of a barefoot man, of a great cat, and of a couple of wild hogs. The peccary tracks went straight on, but those of the man and the cat showed that a fierce struggle had occurred. And one of the two grinning skulls was that of a jaguar.

The story was plain. The hunter, following fast on the trail of the hogs, had suddenly met the jaguar. He had shot it; one arrow, blood stained for more than a foot above the barb, proved that. But in the few seconds of life left to it the animal had sprung and fatally torn the man. Then, as usual, had dropped the black scavengers of the sky to rend them both.

Silently the men of the bush and the men of the north looked down at the brief history written in the mud — a story only a week old, yet ancient as human life itself — primitive man and ferocious brute destroying each other as in the prehistoric days when saber-toothed tiger and troglodyte hunted and slew for the right to live. And as it had been then, so it was now. The living read the tale of tragedy and passed on, leaving the bones behind them. Only, before they went, the Mayorunas threw the remnants of the jaguar aside and piled the bones of their dead comrade together in one place. Then, bearing with them his bow and arrows, they resumed their way without a word.

XIV

A DUEL WITH DEATH

Rain came and went.

The first night's camp of the strangely assorted company was a wet one, for well on in the day the skies poured down the watery weight which had been troubling them once morning. Yet even in such miserable weather the four tribesmen of the Mayorunas declined to sleep in the same camp with the whites. They accepted the food tendered them, but when it was eaten they withdrew to some covert of their own to spend the night. Whereby the whites knew that, though their guides now could no longer suspect them of killing the lone hunter, they still were not accepted as friends.

"Did ye say them guys had a trick of jabbin' men in their hammicks at night, Renzo?" was Tim's significant question after the Indians had departed.

"Have no fear," Lourenço assured him. "They have promised to take us safely to their chief."

"How much is the word of a cannibal worth?" asked Knowlton.

"Worth everything, so long as you do nothing to make them forget it, senhor. Being uncivilized, they are not liars."

The lieutenant eyed him sharply, half minded to regard the answer as insolent. But there was no insolence in the Brazilian's straightforward gaze, and McKay laughed approvingly.

"Well spoken!" was the captain's comment.

"Among those people there are but two great crimes," Lourenço added. "They are, to speak falsely or to be a coward."

"Wherein a goodly portion of the so-called civilized world would fail to measure up to the standards of these cannibals," McKay said. "By the way, have you asked them about the Raposa?"

"No, Capitao. It is as well not to put into their heads the idea that we are hunting anyone here. I shall say nothing of that matter until we reach the chief who knows me."

"Good idea."

With that the talk ended and all sought their hammocks, dog tired from the day's travel. No watch was kept, for, as Pedro quaintly phrased it, "We now are in the hands of God and the cannibals." Nor was any watch needed.

Daybreak brought sunlight. While the breakfast coffee was being boiled the four wild men appeared silently and simultaneously, one bringing a red howling monkey and another a large green parrot as their contributions to the morning meal. Neither bird nor animal showed any wound except a slightly discolored spot surrounding a skin puncture no larger than if made by a woman's hatpin — the marks left by poisoned darts from the ten-foot blowguns. When the meat was cooked they offered portions to the whites, of whom Tim alone refused.

"I'd as quick eat a rat killed with Paris green," he growled. "No poisoned meat gits into my stummick if I know it."

"Bosh!" scoffed McKay. "It's perfectly wholesome — though it's tough as a rubber boot."

"And I might tell you, senhores, that among these people it is an insult to refuse any food offered you," added Lourenço. "I advise you to forget about the poison hereafter and eat what is put before you, even if it stinks."

His advice was emphasized by the evident displeasure of the tribesmen, who, though saying nothing, looked rather grimly at the man who had despised their provisions. But Lourenço then smoothed over the matter by telling them that the red-haired man was sick at the stomach that morning — which, at that particular moment, was not far from the truth.

Soon the triglot column was once more on its way across the hill country, which hourly grew higher and rougher — a constant succession of ridges and ravines. Lourenço, pointing out the absence of water marks on the trees of the uplands, said that now the land of the great annual floods had been left behind; for even the sixty-foot rise of waters in the rainy season could not reach to these hilltops. With the entry into this terra firma the travelers had also found the sun again, the dank mist of yesterday having vanished. Nevertheless, the going was fully as hard as on the previous day, because of the density of the bush and of the labor of crossing the narrow but deep streams flowing at the bottom of nearly every clove. Few words were exchanged, every man needing his breath for the work of walking.

As before, the keen machetes of the Brazilians opened a direct route through all opposing undergrowth. When a brief halt was called at noon the Mayorunas, who seemed to know exactly where they were despite the fact that they had never before followed this straight course, informed Lourenço that much circuitous traveling had already been saved, and that by tramping hard until sundown they might succeed in reaching the tribal *maloca* that night. But McKay vetoed the idea of a forced march.

"This gait is fast enough and hard enough," he declared. "No sense in exhausting ourselves to save a few hours' time. Also, we don't want to go staggering into the Mayoruna village with our tongues hanging out and our knees wabbling. First impressions are lasting with such people, and they might get an idea we were weaklings."

To which all except the savages, who did not understand the language of the white man, assented approvingly.

Yet it was the Mayorunas themselves who delayed arrival at their *maloca* — the Mayorunas and a monkey. When the sinking sun was still two hours high, and while the leader was forcing the pace as if determined to reach home that night whether the rest liked it or not, the monkey upset any such plan.

He was a big gray monkey, and he was high up in the branches of a tall matamata tree, where he deemed himself safe from the many creatures laboring along the ground below. Wherefore he chattered impudently down at them and, as the tall Indian guide halted, showed his teeth derisively. The savage grunted. The man behind him also grunted and lifted his blowgun. But the leader growled at him and the blowgun sank.

With a swift sweep of the hand the guide drew from his quiver one of those long, poisoned arrows and fitted it to the bow cord, which he had laid on the ground. With two toes of each foot he held the cord firmly on the soil. His right hand lightly grasped the arrow and aimed it up at the insolent primate. His left drew the bow up, up, into an arc.

Twang! the cord thrummed as his lifted toes released it. The arrow whirred aloft. Then a snarl of chagrin from the marksman blended with the grunts of his mates. The arrow had failed to reach the quarry.

It had missed, however, by a mere hand's breadth — missed only because it struck the limb directly under the monkey, where it hung by the tip from the bark. Muttering something which may have been a Mayoruna malediction, the savage moved aside a step or two, drew another arrow, and set it to the cord with more care than before. But while he did this the monkey was not idle.

Chattering in rage, the animal leaned down, worked the arrow loose from the bark, and threw it aside. The deadly shaft turned in air, then plunged aimlessly earthward. At that instant all below were watching the guide, who in turn was looking at his toes and placing the new arrow in position. Unseen, the other missile hurtled down — and ripped across the back of the marksman's left hand.

For an instant the tall cannibal stood as if petrified, staring at his cut hand and the shaft now sticking upright in the ground beside him. Then, in simple symbolism, he reversed the new arrow and stabbed it also into the dirt. Dropping his bow, he lay down on his back.

"Yuara will draw bow no more. Yuara goes to join the spirits of the dead," he said, calmly.

Mechanically Lourenço translated the words. McKay sprang forward.

"No!" he disputed. "Not without a try for life, anyhow! Merry, sling a tourniquet! Quick!"

Knowlton jumped to the side of Yuara, tied a handkerchief above the elbow, twisted it tight. McKay whipped from a pocket a keen-bladed knife. In one swift ruthless slash he laid open the arm from elbow to knuckles.

"Keep that tourniquet tight!" he snapped. "If the blood once gets past it he's gone. Tim, get out the salt bag! Lourenço, tell this fellow to breathe deep and keep it up!"

While Tim burrowed into his pack for the salt, Lourenço spoke, as much for the benefit of the other tribesmen as for that of Yuara; for the three Mayorunas stood in ominous silence, watching the outrush of blood caused by the knife of the white man.

"The white man of the black beard, who is very wise, will save Yuara to draw many a good bow if Yuara will do as he says. Let Yuara breathe deeply, that the spirit of life remain in him to fight against the demon of death. Even now the poison rushes out of the arm of Yuara."

"Yuara cannot live," was Yuara's cool reply. "Where once the poison has entered, there follows death."

"Is Yuara then a coward, that he will die without a fight? Then he is no Mayoruna, for no Mayoruna is a coward. Let Yuara die if he will. His comrades shall carry to their *maloca* the tale that, although the white man would have saved him, he died like an old woman, because he had not the will to live!"

Fire shot into the eyes of the prostrate man. He ground his teeth and struggled to rise and throttle the insulting Brazilian.

"No, not that way," Lourenço went on at once. "Yuara can fight the death demon only by drawing into himself the air in which is the spirit of life. The wise white man has stopped the poison at the place where the cloth is tied, and he knows the air spirits will help Yuara if Yuara will breathe deep and long. If he will not, then the white man's medicine cannot save him. Yuara's life or death is in his own hands."

In his heart Lourenço had faint hope that the injured man would live. But he knew the rest of the cannibal tribe must soon hear the tale of this incident from the three now present, and he was preparing an excellent excuse for the failure of McKay to save him. Whether Yuara lived or not, the Mayorunas now would know that the whites had done their utmost for him, and that very fact might make a vast difference.

Yuara, though his eyes still flamed, sank back under McKay's restraining weight and obeyed orders. After the first couple of breaths he settled into his task and his chest rose and fell rhythmically.

"Here's yer salt, Cap. What'll I do with it?"

"You come here and hold this tourniquet. Don't let it slip! Merry, fill this chap's mouth with salt. Lourenço, tell him to hold it as long as possible, then swallow it. Now, Merry, fix up a good strong salt poultice. The rest of you make camp. We've got a stiff fight on our hands, and we can't go farther until we've either won or lost."

The Brazilians glanced at the sun shadows and remained where they were. According to their experience, Yuara should be dead within ten minutes at most. Time enough to make camp when they knew how this venture would result. The Mayorunas also stood fast and watched for the shadow of death to blanch the face of their stricken mate.

But the minutes dragged past and Yuara's eyes did not grow dim. His first resignation over and his fighting blood aroused, he was battling grimly against fate. At times his deep respirations were broken by sudden gasps, and spasmodic quivers shook his whole body. But he breathed on, paying no heed to the burning pain of his ripped and salted arm.

"By cripes! he's puttin' up a man's scrap!" blurted Tim. "Stay with it, old feller. Ye'll win out yet!"

And as more minutes passed and the wounded man still breathed, a murmur of wonderment passed among the cannibals and the men of Nunes. Yuara should be dead, yet he was not even paralyzed. Such a thing had never before been known in this bush.

Lourenço touched Pedro's arm.

"Find a spot where we can make camp," he said. "I must stay here to speak to the wild men if words are needed."

Reluctantly Pedro went away. Soon he was back with news of a suitable place. He found all bending closer over Yuara, whose breathing had become stertorous and whose eyes seemed fixed.

"Going!" was the bushman's thought. But the others would not have it so.

"How 'bout a shot o' booze to jolt his heart, Cap?" suggested Tim, whose whole soul was in the fight.

McKay nodded. Knowlton quickly produced brandy and poured a stiff dose down Yuara's throat. It took hold at once, and light came back into the Indian's eyes.

"Got a good chance yet," McKay asserted. "Don't loosen that tourniquet. Let the arm mortify, if necessary, but hold that blood away from the heart at all costs. I'll chop his arm off at the shoulder before I'll give in."

His hard-set face showed he meant it.

Lourenço spoke to the Mayorunas, urging that camp be made at once. He and Pedro strode away, and all three of the Indians followed.

"Really think he'll pull through, Rod?" Knowlton asked, then. "If he does you're a miracle worker."

"It's an experiment," McKay confessed, watching Yuara with unswerving intentness. "Never saw this done, but it's worth a try — and I honestly believe it will work. I saved an Indian over in Guiana once by cutting off his arm as soon as he was hit, but I want to keep this fellow's arm for him if possible. Feed him some more salt."

Time passed unheeded. Sounds of labor not far off told that camp was being built. Presently the absent five returned, two of the Mayorunas carrying a crude but strong litter constructed from saplings and giant-fern leaves. McKay rose stiffly on cramped legs.

"All right. You can move him," he consented.

Carefully Yuara was lifted to the litter and transported to the new camp. There the Americans found not only the open shed, or *tambo*, usually constructed by the Brazilians, but also a somewhat similar shelter erected by the Indians. In the latter stood two stout crotched stakes, firmly braced — the handiwork of Pedro and Lourenço. And to these, with tough bush rope, the Indians fastened the litter of Yuara, thus forming a rude but effective hammock.

While McKay and Knowlton continued their ministrations to the stricken man the rest of the camp work was completed, the Mayorunas making hanging beds for themselves from withes, leaves, and bush cord, and the Brazilians slinging the hammocks of their own party and opening packs.

Night fell and the wounded man lived on. Supper was eaten, pipes smoked, the regular activities of the early hours of darkness gone through — and Yuara lived on. His deep breathing had become automatic, and his eyes stared straight up in concentration on his battle with the death demon.

At length he was seized with violent nausea which convulsed him for a time. But when the spasms passed he lay back more easily, and a faint smile flitted over his face as he looked at the white men.

"Been expecting that," said McKay. "Might loosen that ligature now — just a few seconds.... Tighten it! All right." Alter watching the sick man a little longer he added: "Now I'm going to eat and smoke. Feel like taking a drink, too, but guess I won't. The Indian will pull through now, I think."

When he had returned to the Indian hut with pipe aglow, Knowlton asked him, "Now tell us how you doped out this cure."

"Combination of various things. Salt is a partial antidote to venom in the blood, and I got it into him in three ways — by mouth absorption, by the stomach, and by the salt poultice, which drew out some of the poison from the forearm and helped neutralize what remained. Ripping his arm of course let out a lot of bad blood. Ligature above the elbow stopped most of the rest — though some sneaked past that point, I'm pretty sure.

"Big thing, though, was the deep breathing. Remember I told you about the experiments that killed mules and an ox? Another experiment was this — opening the windpipe of a poisoned mule after the heart stopped, inserting a pair of bellows, and starting artificial respiration. After four hours of this the mule came to life and stayed alive — though he was a wreck for a year afterward.

"I just put all these together, made the Indian do his own breathing — and here he is. I'm going to sit up awhile longer and watch him, but the critical period is over. You chaps can turn in."

But none turned in until midnight, when no doubt remained that Lourenço's prophecy would come true — that Yuara would live to draw bow again. Then, when the slashed arm had been thoroughly cleansed and bound, Lourenço spoke once more to the savages.

"The medicine of the wise white man and the air spirits have saved Yuara from the death demon. Yuara has fought as a man of his tribe should fight, and so has lived when he would have died. Tomorrow Yuara shall once more see his people, the first man of the Mayorunas to come back from the death of poison. And he and his comrades shall tell of the white man's wisdom, without which he now would lie cold on the ground."

"So shall it be," Yuara himself faintly answered. "Yuara, son of Rana, second chief of the men of Suba, will not forget."

"*Por Deus!*" exclaimed Lourenço. "Comrades, this man is no common hunter, but son of a subchief. Capitao, you have done good work today."

X V

THE CANNIBALS

Through the long, dim shadows of early morning the little column passed on the last leg of its journey to the *maloca* of Suba, chief of this outlying tribe of the Mayorunas. At its head marched Yuara, his left arm incased in bandages, his face drawn and pallid, his stride stiff and springless, but still carrying his weapons and stoically setting the pace as befitted the son of a subchief. He had had no sleep; he had lain in the gates of death; his arm ached cruelly; yet a warm glow shone in his hollow eyes as he reflected on the fact that in all the unwritten history of his people he was the first man to survive the inexorable power of the wurali. As long as he lived this fact would lift him above the level of all his fellows. Even the chief could not boast of such a superhuman feat.

The undergrowth this morning was not so thick as it had been, and the machetes of Lourenço and Pedro stayed in their sheaths. The ground, too, was more level and the footing more firm. After some three hours of walking the Americans found that they had come into a faint path.

Somewhat to the bewilderment of the white men, who expected the Indians to increase their speed now that the way home lay under their feet, the leading pair slowed their gait. Moreover, they scanned the trail with intent care and watched the trees along the way. At length, with a warning grunt, Yuara stepped out of the path and began a detour. His comrade and the Brazilians followed. The Americans stopped.

"What's the idea?" demanded McKay, looking along the innocent-appearing path.

"Probably a man trap, Capitao," answered Pedro. "Follow us."

"Let's see the trap first."

Lourenço called to Yuara, who stopped and grunted two words.

"*Si*, it is a trap. A pit, Yuara says."

Yuara spoke again, and Lourenço added: "He says we must not touch it. It is there just before you, covered so cunningly that it looks exactly like the rest of the ground. The cover is a framework of sticks balanced on a pole, and the instant a man steps on it it gives way. He falls into a nine-foot hole whose sides are dug inward, so that they overhang above him. There the cannibals find him and kill him. I fell into one of those holes when I first came into this Mayoruna country, so I know just how they are made."

"So? How did you get out?"

"There were two of us, and I stood on the other man's shoulders while he lifted me high enough to jump out. Then I tied bush rope to a tree and he climbed up the rope. Come. Yuara waits."

After a short circuit around the danger point the party returned to the path, and as they went on Lourenço explained further concerning the pit:

"Every approach to the *malocas* has this kind of trap hidden in it, and others also. The Indians recognize the places by some secret signal known only to themselves — a certain kind of stick or vine or something of the kind, placed where it can be seen by those who understand. The traps are made to stop any enemies who try to sneak up on the *malocas* and catch these people unawares. Another kind of trap is a spring bow or a blowgun shot by a vine stretched across the path. Still another is a piece of ground studded with poisoned araya bones which pierce the bare feet of anyone walking on them. It is well for us that we now have friendly guides."

"Quite so," McKay agreed, dryly.

Some distance farther on the leader again left the path, and this time all filed after him without comment. Pedro pointed significantly at a thin, tight-drawn bush cord stretched across the path at the height of a man's ankle — the trigger which would discharge hidden death at anything touching it. At another point, perhaps a hundred feet farther along, a third and last detour was made, and this time the nature of the trap was not revealed by anything on the ground. No questions were asked.

With the passing of these three menaces Yuara resumed his former pace and abandoned his circumspection. Before long came sounds of communal life — the barking of a dog and shouts of children. Then suddenly the forest thinned, and after a few more strides the marchers found themselves in a clearing.

Before them rose a big round house, about forty feet high and a hundred feet in diameter, its sides composed of palm logs, and its roof a thick thatch of palm leaves, whence smoke oozed lazily through an opening at the peak. A single low door, not more than four feet high, opened toward a creek a few rods away at the right. Near this doorway a couple of naked children, boy and girl, were playing with the dog, while beyond them a number of women, also nude, were busy at some kind of work.

As Yuara and his fellow-tribesmen entered the open space the boy shouted a greeting and started running toward them. Then, seeing the white men filing from the bush behind the warriors, the youngster stood as if shocked motionless. After one long stare he screamed and bolted for the shelter of the *maloca*. Other screams echoed his as the women also saw the bearded outlanders. They, too, dived through the doorway.

Out from behind the house leaped three warriors, two of whom already had fitted arrows to their bows, while the third — a powerful fellow — clutched a four-foot war club. Weapons raised, faces contracted into fighting masks, they stared speechless at the spectacle of the subchief's son calmly leading gun-bearing whites among them.

Knowlton, though his attention was riveted on the astonished warriors, caught the quiet snick of Tim's safe-lock being turned off.

"None of that, Tim!" he warned. "Put that safety on again. And don't hold your gun as if you intended to use it."

"Aw, I was jest tryin' her to make sure she was all right."

"Put it on!" snapped the lieutenant. Another tiny click told him the order was obeyed.

Out from the doorway darted another warrior, stooping low to avoid hitting his head. Others followed instantly, all armed and ready for action. The opening was still vomiting tribesmen when Yuara and the rest reached it. But none made a hostile move when it was seen that the son of the subchief was in command and that the strangers seemed friendly. Yuara spoke, briefly but authoritatively, and the weapons sank. Then, with a word to his three companions, he ducked through the doorway. The other three remained where they were.

"We shall have to wait now, comrades, until Yuara tells his father and the chief about us," Lourenço said. "So let us take off our packs and rest."

He set the example by laying his rifle on the ground, unslinging his pack, squatting beside it, and coolly rolling a cigarette. Apparently he was paying no attention whatever to the savages, who watched his every move. But McKay, glancing at him as he followed suit, saw that, for all his seeming unconcern, the Brazilian bush rover was keenly watchful and that his gun lay within reach of his hand.

From within the tribal house sounded the monotonous voice of Yuara. After listening a moment Lourenço quietly addressed the nearest warrior. A slightly surprised looked passed over the cannibal's face. He replied, and a slow conversation ensued.

Meanwhile the others looked over the array of savage fighting men. Except for difference of stature, build, and expression, they were as like as brothers. All were light skinned — hardly darker than the river-tanned whites themselves; all had straight-set eyes, with no hint of the slant often found among the Indians of the Amazon headwaters; and the cheek bones of all were fairly low. Their average stature was a little under six feet, and most of them had an athletic symmetry of physique. Their feet, McKay noticed, were small and shapely.

All wore tall feather headdresses of parrot and mutum plumes. All had the scarlet and black rings around the eyes, the streaks from temple to chin, the wavy design on their bodies. And each wore in the cartilage of his nose a pair of small feathers slanting outward. At another time and under other circumstances the white men might have smiled at those nose feathers, which resembled odd mustaches; but as they studied the austere faces around them they found no occasion for merriment. Nor was the tension lessened by the sight of the weapons grasped in the strong hands of the warriors.

Great bows and arrows, such as the hunters had borne, were supplemented here by the long clubs of heavy wood and by ugly spears. The clubs terminated in balls studded with jaguar teeth. The spears were triple pronged, each prong ending in a saw-toothed araya bone and each bone darkened by the fatal wurali. Frightful weapons they were — the one designed to smash skulls and tear out brains, the other to stab and poison at the same thrust.

Lourenço stopped talking, and the others observed that now the wild men stood more easily, their holds on their weapons loosened.

"I have shown them, Capitao, that I can speak their tongue, and told them we go to visit the chief Monitaya as friend," he explained. "They tell me Monitaya has grown great since last I saw him. Another tribe which lost its chief and subchiefs by a swift sickness has joined his own, and he now rules two big *malocas* together. He is a powerful fighter, and if he is friendly to us we have a good chance of success. Ah! here is Yuara."

The son of the subchief came through the doorway as he spoke, followed by an older man whose facial resemblance and ornaments indicated that he was the subchief himself. His headgear was more elaborate than that of his men, and around his shoulders and down his chest hung a brilliant feather dress, while a wide belt of green, blue, and black plumes encircled his hips. Yuara himself had inserted feathers in his nose and donned a headband of tall parrot plumes a trifle more ornate than those worn by the ordinary fighters, and somehow the simple addition seemed to transform him into a bigger, fiercer man. Also, his eyes now held a smoldering light which had not been there before.

The older man, Rana, the subchief, glanced swiftly along the line of new faces. Then his gaze returned to McKay. His mouth set and his countenance turned hard. He spoke curtly to Yuara, who replied with one word. After another long, unpleasant look at McKay, who stared coldly back at him, Rana grunted a few words and re-entered the house.

Lourenço, nonplussed by the frigidity of the subchief where he had expected gratitude or at least hospitality, glanced questioningly at Yuara. But the young man stood mute, looking straight ahead.

"The subchief says we shall enter and see the chief. We must leave our guns outside."

"Don't like that," muttered McKay. "That subchief looks ugly."

"But we must obey or provoke a fight, Capitao. Besides, our rifles would be useless inside, as they would be instantly seized if we lifted them. So let us make the best of it. But I think you can carry your pistols with you; they are covered by the holsters, and I do not believe these people know what they are. And since Rana spoke only of guns, we will keep our machetes. Come."

"Wait a second."

McKay dived a hand into his haversack and brought forth a heavy hunting knife with a gaudy red-and-white bone handle, sheathed and attached to a leather belt.

"Brought this along as a present for some Indian who might do us a good turn," he explained. "Been thinking of giving it to Yuara, but now I'll pass it to the chief. Might make a difference. All right, let's go."

With confident tread, but with some misgiving, the five advanced, leaving guns and packs on the ground. One by one they bent low and got through the doorway. Yuara, with a word to a clubman and a motion to the equipment, followed the whites, trailed in turn by his three companions of the forest. The clubman, after a curious inspection of the packs, stood on guard among them, his bludgeon grasped loosely but suggestively, ready to prevent any undue inquisitiveness by the rest. But soon he found himself alone, for the other tribesmen transferred their attention and themselves to the interior of the *maloca*.

Within the house the soldiers of fortune halted a moment, adjusting their vision to the sudden diminution of light. Except for the sunshine pouring in at the smoke hole above and at the tiny door behind, the only light in the big room came from small cooking fires scattered about the place, and for the moment details were withheld from the newcomers' sight. Then they found themselves in what seemed a labyrinth of poles and hammocks.

Through this confusion Yuara passed with familiar step, and in his wake the travelers went to a central fire around which was a comparatively clear space. Beyond, in a big hammock dyed with the symbolic scarlet and black and tasseled with many squirrel tails, sat a fat, small-eyed, heavy-jawed man whose elaborate feather dress and authoritative air proclaimed him chief. Beside him stood Rana and another subchief, lean and somber-faced. Behind this bulwark of tribal might huddled the women and children, staring wide-eyed. As the visitors stopped and returned the chief's unwinking regard the warriors packed themselves at their backs, blocking all chance of exit.

When the shuffle of feet had died and no sound was audible, Yuara began to talk. In his deliberate way he told the complete narrative of his journey, which previously he had sketched only in outline. His three companions corroborated his tale from time to time by nods, and when the discovery of the slain hunter's bones was described one of those three stepped forward and laid the dead man's weapons on the ground before the chief. As Yuara went on he touched his bandaged arm and pointed to McKay and Knowlton. And as he concluded he motioned toward Lourenço.

Ignorant of the Indian language, but guessing the nature of his talk from his motions, the Americans stood patiently awaiting the next move. For a time all three of the chiefs remained silent; but all of them studied McKay, standing bolt upright with arms folded and the belt-wrapped knife partly concealed in the hollow of one elbow. Though it was evident that Yuara had given the captain full credit for saving his life, the faces of the head men showed no sign of friendliness. In fact, their expressions were distinctly ominous.

At length the chief turned his eyes to Lourenço. The veteran bush-man promptly stepped forward and said his say. At the end he turned, took from McKay the knife, unrolled the belt, and dangled the weapon before the eyes of the rulers. They stared at it in obvious ignorance of its character. Not until the Brazilian drew the blade from its sheath and the glint of steel struck their vision did they show recognition. Then Chief Suba grunted, his little eyes lit up, and he reached for it.

For a few minutes he sat gloating over the gift, admiring the bone handle, hefting the weight of the long blade, while the subchiefs gazed in envy. When he looked up his face was beaming. But then the sour-faced subchief at his left hand muttered something, and Suba's visage darkened. His eyes rested again on McKay, went to the bandaged arm of Yuara, dropped to his knife — the first steel knife ever owned by him or any man of the Suba tribe — and rose again to the black-bearded captain. Abruptly then he spoke out.

Lourenço stared in blank astonishment. After a puzzled moment he shook his head as if unable to believe he had heard aright. Suba, scowl-ing, repeated what he had said. Lourenço shook his head again, this time in vehement denial, and began to talk. But Suba, rising with surprising agility for a man of his weight, stopped him imperiously and spoke with finality. Slowly the Brazilian nodded and turned to his captain.

"I do not understand this, Capitao. But these are the words of the chief:

"'The white man with the black beard tries a trick, but it does not deceive the free men of the forest. The thing which he thinks to be hidden in his own heart is known to Suba and his chiefs. It is known also to the chief Monitaya, and to his chiefs, and to his men also. The white man is bold. And now his own boldness shall be his death.

"'Since the white man has said he goes to visit the chief Monitaya, and since by some demon's power the white man has saved the life of Yuara, who is a man of Suba, the men of Suba will allow him to go in peace from this place. But Suba will see that he and his companions go to Monitaya, who will know how to deal with his visitors. The men of Suba will take the strangers at once to the canoes and carry them to Monitaya.

"'If the white man of the black beard and the black mind thought the men of the jungle blind to the foulness he would do here, he is a fool. It is useless for him or his men to lie and say they know not what Suba means. Let him look into his own heart and he will know well.

"'Suba has spoken.'

"Something is wrong, Capitao, but I do not know what it is. It will do no good to argue. Let us go at once."

Suba snarled commands to the warriors. They trooped toward the door. Without another word or glance at the three chiefs Lourenço stalked after the Indians, and his comrades followed with stiff dignity.

Outside, the savages picked up the rifles and packs and carried them to the creek, where small canoes lay. The five strangers were allowed to crowd themselves together in a four-man canoe, but their guns and packs were distributed among four other dugouts, into which armed paddlers entered. Other Indians brought provisions to the outgoing craft. In a very short time the leading canoe started off downstream, followed by the boat of the white men, behind which the other craft pressed close and vigilant.

They swung in among the trees, and the *maloca* of Suba was blotted out.

XVI

BLACKBEARD

"Well," said Knowlton, after a period of silent paddling, "we have met the enemy and we are his'n. No harm done so far, though, and if old man Calisaya, or whatever his name is, wants to act nasty we can send him and a few others along the road to glory with our gats. We'll travel the same road, of course, but we'll take company with us."

"*Si*, senhor," Pedro agreed. "And besides your pistols we still have our machetes. Yet I believe Lourenço's words to the chief Monitaya will make all well. But I cannot help wondering —" He glanced at McKay.

"I'm wondering, too, Pedro," said the captain. "It's hardly possible that these people know why we're here, and hardly likely that they have any interest in the Raposa. Lord knows I've nothing else up my sleeve. It's a riddle to me."

It remained a riddle to the rest, for no explanation could be gleaned from the Mayorunas. At the first halt, which did not come until nearly sundown, the Americans discovered that one of the men in the fore canoe was Yuara, who had been lying in the bottom of the craft and sleeping all the afternoon. From him Lourenço attempted to get information as to the reason for Suba's enmity — but in vain. The tall fellow spoke not a word in reply, and his face remained unreadable.

Camp was made, and by Yuara's direction the packs of the adventurers were restored to them. The rifles, however, remained under guard of savages appointed by the subchief's son. When the night meal was out of the way nothing remained but to seek hammocks and sleep, for further attempts at conversation by Lourenço met with the same silent rebuff from every cannibal addressed. None showed active hostility by either look or manner, but it was plain that between wild and civilized men stood a wall — a wall not too high for the jungle dwellers to leap over in deadly action if occasion should be given. Wherefore the whites held themselves aloof, said little, and slept early.

"I am glad Yuara is with us," Lourenço said. "As he promised, he does not forget what was done for him. He will keep this band in control, and unless I am much mistaken he will tell Monitaya all he knows of us, which surely will not do us any harm. At any rate, we can sleep in safety tonight. And since it does no good to puzzle about what is gone by or to worry about what has not yet to come to pass, let us sleep now."

"Ho-hum!" yawned Tim. "Renzo, ye spill more solid sense to the square inch than any feller I seen in a long time. We're here because we're here; today's dead and to-morrer ain't born yet, and li'l' Timmy Ryan hits the hay right now. Night, gents."

So, surrounded by man eaters, the trailers of the Raposa slept far more securely than on any night down the river when their companions had been supposedly civilized Peruvians. Whether a watch was kept by their guards during the night they neither knew nor cared, since they had no intention of attempting escape.

They awoke to find the men of Suba diminished in number by half. Yuara, deigning to speak for the first time since leaving the *maloca*, explained that the absent men had gone hunting for their breakfasts. Before long the hunters came straggling back, bearing monkeys and birds, which were divided among their companions. None of this meat was offered to the prisoners, who ate unconcernedly from their pack rations. Tim, after watching the Indians sink their sharp-filed teeth into broiled monkey haunches and tear the meat from the bones, snorted and turned his back to them.

"Look like a gang o' bloody-faced devils gobblin' babies," he muttered. "I'll believe now they're cannibals, all right."

So uncomfortably apt was his simile that the others grimaced and turned their eyes elsewhere until the savage meal was finished. Then their attention became riveted on a queer proceeding at the canoe wherein Yuara had journeyed yesterday.

To the gunwales amidships two of the men fastened a couple of small crotched posts. In the forks was laid a pole, crosswise of the boat, and from this, by slender fiber cords, four slabs of wood were hung. Strolling down to the canoe, the travelers found that athwart its bottom had been laid a crosspiece supporting two shorter crotched posts, between which stretched another transverse pole; and from this pole in turn the lower ends of the four slabs had been suspended. Now the savages joined the tips of each pair of slabs by carved end sections, and the contrivance seemed to be complete — a sort of grate, its bars sloping at an angle of forty-five degrees.

As the Americans eyed the arrangement in perplexity, one of the crew picked up from the bow of the canoe a pair of mallets the heads of which were wrapped in hide. With these he struck the slabs in rapid succession. Out rolled four notes of astonishing volume — the first four notes of the musical scale. Again and again he ran them over, then stopped. The deep tones thrummed away along the creek and died.

"By George! a big xylophone!" Knowlton exclaimed, admiringly.

"It sure talks right out loud," said Tim. "Lot o' class to these guys, at that. Bet this is their brass band, and we'll go rip-snortin' into the next town like we was on parade. Oughter have some flags to hang up in the boats, and mebbe a drum corps to help out. Wisht I had a tin whistle or somethin' and I'd join the orchester. I can toot a whistle fine."

"My favorite instrument is the old-fashioned dinner horn," laughed Knowlton. "But I think you're wrong — this is some kind of signaling apparatus."

"You have it right, senhor," Lourenço affirmed. "I have heard this sort of thing used, though I never before saw the instrument itself. Those notes will carry at least five miles, and the cannibals send messages by striking the bars in different order. This run which we have just heard is always used first, and no message is sent until a reply is received."

"Bush telegraph," nodded McKay. "First call your operator and then shoot the message in code. Pretty ingenious for a bunch of absolute savages."

Lourenço turned to Yuara and asked a question. Yuara curtly replied.

"He says, Capitao, that this is to tell Monitaya we come. But we now are too far off for Monitaya's men to hear. The bars are made ready before starting so that they can be used as soon as we are within hearing. He says also that we start now."

The Mayorunas already were entering their canoes. With cool deliberation the whites gathered up their equipment and settled themselves for the journey at whose end lay either life or death. The boat of Yuara started, and once more the flotilla was on its way.

For an hour or more it swung on among the forested hills before the telegraph instrument was put to use. Then it paused, and the sonorous voice of the xylophone spoke to the jungle. A period of waiting brought no reply.

The canoe moved on for a mile. Again the mallets beat the wood in the ascending scale of the call. And then, faint, mellow, far off, sounded the answer.

While every man sat silent the bars boomed out their fateful news. Slow, brief, deep as a bell tolling a dirge, a reply rolled back. And with the solemnity of a funeral cortége the canoes once more moved on, unhurried, inexorable, the measured swing of the paddles beating like a pulse of doom.

At length the crew of Yuara held their paddles. Yuara himself turned toward the second canoe and talked a minute. A signal to his men, and his boat proceeded. All the others remained where they were.

"He goes to Monitaya to speak of us," said Lourenço. "He will return. We have only to wait."

"Yeah," grunted Tim, disgustedly. "We'll wait till night if he takes as long to go through his rigmarole as he done yesterday. If I got to fight I want to hop to it, not set round in the shade o' the shelterin' palm while them guys are heatin' up the stewpot. This waitin' stuff gits my goat."

"You might sing us a song, senhor, to pass the time," Pedro suggested, with a tight-lipped smile.

"Say, I'll do that, jest to show these guys I don't give a rip. And while their ears are dazzled by me melody I'm goin' to git me holster unbottoned and me masheet kinder limbered up. Git set. Here it comes:

> *"Ol' Hindyburg thought he was swell,*
> *Pa-a-arley-voo!*
> *He made the kids in Belgium yell,*
> *Pa-a-arley-voo!*
> *But the Yanks come over with shot and shell*
> *And Hindyburg he run like hell,*
> *Rinkydinky-parley-voo!"*

Under cover of his outbreak, which made the savages clutch their weapons and glare at him in mingled suspicion and amazement, there proceeded a furtive loosening of pistols and machetes.

"A noble sentiment, and more or less appropriate," grinned Knowlton. "But don't give them another spasm for a few minutes, or they may rise up and kill us all in self-defense. They're on the ragged edge now."

"Aw, them guys dunno how to appreciate good singin'. But I should worry; I got me gat fixed now like I want it."

Time dragged past. The Americans and Brazilians smoked and exchanged casual comments on subjects far removed from their present environment. The Mayorunas watched them with unceasing vigilance, as if expecting a sudden break for life and liberty. Their chief had intimated that Monitaya would kill these men; and now was their last chance to try to dodge death. But neither the black-bearded McKay nor any of his mates manifested the slightest concern. And at last the canoe of Yuara came back.

It came, however, without Yuara himself. The son of Rana had remained at the *malocas* ahead, whence he sent the command to advance. Closely hemmed in by the men of Suba, the white men's boat surged onward at a brisk pace. Around a bend in the creek it went, and at once the domain of Monitaya leaped into view.

Two big tribal houses, each considerably larger than the one of Suba, rose pompously in a wide cleared space beside the stream. Before them, ranged in a semicircle, stood hundreds of Mayorunas — men, women, children — all silently watching the canoes of the newcomers. In the center of the arc, like the hub of a human half wheel, a small knot of men waited in aloof dignity, four of them adorned with the ornate feather dresses of subchiefs, backed by a dozen tall, muscular savages, each armed with a huge war club. Before all stood a powerful, magnificently proportioned savage belted with a wide girdle of squirrel tails, decked with necklaces of jaguar teeth and ebony nuts, crowned by plumes which in loftiness and splendor surpassed all other headgear present — the great chief Monitaya.

At the shore, beside a row of empty canoes, Yuara was waiting. He mentioned for his men to bring their dugouts to the regular landing place, and when they obeyed he gave commands. Then he turned and walked toward Monitaya.

"I go," stated Lourenço, rising. "You stay here until called. Yuara has told his men to leave all weapons in the canoes."

He walked away after the son of Rana, and if any misgiving was in his heart it did not show in his confident step. Halting before the big chief, he began talking as coolly as if there were not the least doubt of welcome for himself and those with him. Monitaya gave no sign of recognition, of friendliness, or of enmity. Proud, statuesque, he stood motionless, his deep eyes resting on those of the Brazilian.

"Sultry weather," remarked McKay.

"Just so, Capitao," agreed Pedro, narrow eyed. "We shall soon know whether we shall have storm."

"Indications are for violent thunder and lightning soon," Knowlton contributed. "See those husky clubmen awaiting? Looks as if a public execution were about to be pulled off."

"Yeah. But say, ain't that chief a reg'lar he-man, though! No pot-bellied fathead like that there, now, Suby guy. Hope I don't have to drill him. I bet I won't, neither. He looks like he had brains."

Hoping Tim was right, but dubious, all watched the progress of the parley. Lourenço evidently was stating his case in logical sequence, re-calling to the chief's mind the time when he had led him to revenge against the Peccaries of Peru, then going on to tell of the arrival of the strangers and the object of their search. Yuara's sudden, quick glance at him showed that the Raposa had been mentioned for the first time. A little later his face became slightly sullen, and the watchers guessed that Lourenço was now referring in somewhat uncomplimentary terms to the treatment received in the *maloca* of Suba. Soon after that the Brazilian ended his speech.

In a deep, quiet tone Monitaya spoke first to Lourenço, then to one of his subchiefs. The bushman beckoned to his waiting companions. At the same time the subchief stepped out and called two names. As McKay, Knowlton, Tim, and Pedro arose and stepped ashore with the weaponless men of Suba, out from the great human arc came two men. All advanced toward the chief. And though the Americans were studying the central figures as they walked, they also noticed that the pair of Mayorunas who had been summoned were lame. One walked with a stiff knee, the other as if a whole leg was paralyzed.

"Squad — halt!" muttered McKay. A step and a half and the four stood aligned and alert, two strides from Monitaya.

The eyes of the chief dwelt long on McKay, and they were hard eyes. Without shifting his gaze he grunted a few words. The two crippled Indians stumped forward and stared into McKay's face. Through a long minute the Americans felt a sinister tension grow in the air about them. Then, slowly, the cripples turned about and faced their ruler. In the tones of men sure of themselves, they spoke one word.

With the utterance of that word the tension broke. Through the long line of watching tribesmen ran a murmur. The clubmen relaxed from their ready poise. The subchiefs glanced at one another as if disappointed. And the stern face of Monitaya himself was transformed by a wide, friendly smile.

A sweeping gesture and the cordial timbre of the chief's voice told the Americans plainly what Lourenço translated a moment later.

"We are welcome, comrades. We shall sleep in the *maloca* of Monitaya himself and a feast shall be made for us. Our lives have just hung on one word, but now that the word is spoken we are safe. I cannot tell you more now, for I do not wholly understand this matter myself as yet — but I shall learn. Now is the time, Capitao to give presents, if you have any for the chief."

"I have. But our packs are in the canoe, and I'll be hanged if I'll make a beast of burden of myself at this stage of the game."

"I will have all the packs brought up, Capitao. The men of Suba took them from us at their *maloca*; now they shall restore them before all these people."

He addressed Monitaya affably, then spoke more brusquely to Yuara. That young man, whose previous austerity now had dissolved into open friendliness, uttered four words. Immediately his men returned to the canoes and brought up not only the packs, but the rifles.

From his blanket roll McKay brought forth a cloth-wrapped package out of which he drew a half-ax, its blade gleaming dully under a protective coating of grease, which he swiftly swabbed off. From his haversack he produced a heavy chain of ruby-red beads. Under the bright sun the beads glowed like living things, and the glittering steel flashed back a dazzling beam. The two gifts together had cost considerably less than ten dollars in New York, but to the chieftain they were priceless treasures;

and as McKay, with a formal bow, extended them to him, his face shone with delight. Yet he made no such greedy grab for them as had been displayed by Suba when tendered the knife. His acceptance was achieved with a calm dignity which brought a twinkle of approval to the eyes of the white men.

In the same dignified manner he led the way to the *maloca* which evidently was the older of the two and which had always been his home. The semicircle of his subjects broke up into a disorderly crowd which streamed after him and his guests or surrounded the men of Suba with holiday greetings. Within the tribal house the adventurers proceeded to the central space where burned the chief's fire. There Monitaya ordered certain hammocks removed to make room for those of the visitors. Soon the travelers were seated at ease in their hanging beds, their packs and rifles lying on the ground beneath them, while near at hand clustered groups of Mayorunas, staring at them in naïve curiosity.

Pedro drew a long breath.

"Senhores, that was a very close call," he declared. "As Lourenço says, our lives have hung on one word. What was that word, comrade?"

"The word was, 'No,'" answered Lourenço. "Monitaya asked those two crippled men, 'Is this the man?' As you saw, they looked at the capitao, giving no attention to the rest of us. Then they said, 'No.' You will remember that the capitao was the one whom Suba also picked upon. As soon as Monitaya finishes talking with those men I shall ask him what all this means."

The big chief was giving directions to a score of young fellows, who presently scattered to various parts of the house and accoutered themselves for hunting. Thereupon Lourenço approached Monitaya with the familiarity of former acquaintance, being received with a good-humored smile. For a time the two conversed. As they talked the smile of the ruler faded and his face grew dark, while into the Brazilian's voice came a wrathful growl. Finally both nodded. Lourenço returned to his hammock, frowning.

"Capitao, it is all because of your black hair and beard. Through all the *malocas* of the Mayorunas, far and near, has gone the word to watch for a big, black-bearded man who is neither a Brazilian nor a Peruvian, but of some country unknown to these people; and when such a man is caught, to kill him and his companions without mercy. And the reason for such a command is this:

"For many moons the Mayorunas, especially those of the smaller and weaker *malocas*, have been losing women. From time to time sudden raids have been made by gangs of gun-carrying Peruvian Indians and *mestiços* — half-breeds — who shot down the defenders of the houses before they could reach their weapons, and carried off girls. This, of course, is nothing new here, for such things have happened occasionally for many years. But within the past five years there has been a difference in these attacks which has made them much more deadly.

"These raids used to be made always at night, and they were few and far between. But of late they have come about also in the day, at times when almost all the men of the small *malocas* were far out in the forest hunting meat and the women had little protection. Several chiefs have been killed by the raiders, who seemed to be acting according to an agreed plan, to be organized for this work, and to know when to strike and how to get away quickly. And what is more, the men who did this were not chance parties who came only to get women for themselves and then stayed away. The same men came back time after time.

"A few of these were killed, but only a few; and all the dead were Peruvians. Being dead, they could tell nothing. But the Mayorunas felt that all these raids were directed by one mind. And they became sure of this when one captured girl escaped by killing a Peruvian with his own knife and returned to her own *maloca*. She said the raiders took her and the other girls to the big man with the black beard, who waited at a safe place a day's march from the tribal house.

"A few weeks later another small *maloca* several miles from here was attacked at night while two men of Monitaya were there, having stayed out too late on a hunting trip and taken refuge with their neighbors until day. Both these men were hit and crippled by bullets in the wild shooting that opened the attack. One was struck in the knee, the other in the lower part of the back. But both caught a glimpse of the leader's face and saw that he was the black-bearded man himself.

"So you see, Capitao, why we have been near death. Suba and Monitaya both thought you were the man. We were lucky to escape alive from Suba, and still more lucky that hero were two men who knew the face of the blackbeard."

"Schwandorf!" barked McKay.

"Yes, Capitao, it must be the German —"

"I know it's Schwandorf! And I know his game! He's a slaver!"

"A slaver?"

"That's it. Knew I'd seen that sneak before. He worked the same game in British Guiana eight years ago on a small scale. Had a gang of tough bush niggers from over in Dutch Guiana to do his dirty work. Stole Macusi girls — they're the best-looking Indians in B. G. — and sold them like cattle to gold miners. Cleaned up quite a pot before the English got on to him, but had to get out of the country on the hot foot — didn't have time to take his gold with him. His name wasn't Schwandorf over there, and he had no beard; he was thinner, too, and posed as a Russian; but he's the man. Must have made his get-away by the back door — down the Branco to the Amazon. Now he's running Mayoruna girls into Peru. He could sell them to rubber men or miners and make good money, eh, Lourenço?"

"*Si.*"

"Sure. And that's why he wanted to kill off his Peruvians — they knew too much; probably were trying to bleed him for hush money. He must have a regular slave route and a gang of border cutthroats to do his raiding — men who don't go downriver. Murderer, slaver — wonder how many other crimes are on his soul."

"Them two are enough," growled Tim. "And he ain't got no soul."

"No soul," echoed Pedro. "You have said it, Senhor Tim. And if ever these people capture him he soon will have no body."

XVII

FEVER

In the *maloca* of Monitaya a feast was in the making.

Fires glowed all about the great room. Hunters came in, bearing birds or beasts which were placed before the tribal ruler for inspection and approval. Fishermen armed with tridents or crude harpoons arrived with sizable trophies of their skill. And at length two young bowmen advanced proudly with a freshly killed wild hog. After glancing at this the chief added to his usual nod a few words of praise which made the huntsmen grin with all their pointed teeth.

Lourenço, squatting comfortably on a jaguar skin beside the lavishly decorated hammock of Monitaya, carried on a lazy-toned monologue which probably dealt with his various experiences since his last meeting with these people and which appeared to interest and amuse the chief. The others, lolling back in mingled fatigue and relief from tension, studied the interior of the place and watched the activities around them.

As in the *maloca* of Suba, the small forest of poles and hammocks seemed a higgledy-piggledy maze wherein was neither beginning nor end. Yet, as the newcomers took time to observe it, they presently found that the confusion was only apparent and that there existed an efficient and orderly arrangement. The hammocks, seemingly slung from any available pair of poles in utter disregard of one another, really were arranged in triangles. On the ground under the hanging beds lay woven grass mats and hides of the sloth and the jaguar; and in the space inclosed by each trio of hammocks burned a small fire. The hammocks were the beds of men, the mats and furs the couches of women and children, and each fire was the focal point of the family residing in that triangle.

Above the hammocks, from transverse poles, were suspended the weapons of the men: the great bows, the long blowguns, the fighting spears whose deadly points now were sheathed in thick scabbards of grass, the unpoisoned fish spears and harpoons. From these poles also hung the quivers of arrows and darts and the small rubber-covered pouches wherein a little fresh poison was carried by warrior or hunter. Thus both the ground and the air were utilized, and by the compactness of the arrangement an entire family with its worldly goods, was enabled to live in a comparatively small space. Looking around the wide room and remembering the big half circle of Indians who had stood outside, the two ex-officers estimated that in this tribal house and its twin dwelt seven hundred people.

Tim and Pedro, less interested in the Mayoruna domestic economy than in the Mayorunas themselves, were scanning the figures moving about in the reddish haze of smoke. Most of them were women, all nude and naïvely unconscious of any need of clothing. Like the men of the tribe, they bore the red and black rings and streaks on face and body; but, unlike the males, each wore a facial ornament in the shape of an oval piece of wood thrust through the lower lip. From time to time those near by glanced up from their work and gave the new men unmistakably friendly looks — particularly several young but well-grown girls who obviously were still unmated. In fact, these last smiled openly at the lithe, handsome Pedro, and red Tim was by no means overlooked.

"I got me orders," said Tim, *sotto voce*, "and I'm danged if I crack a smile back at them girls. But I sure feel like grinnin'. Watch yourself, old-timer; they're tryin' to flirt with ye."

Pedro, mindful of watchful eyes, turned his gaze to Tim's face before allowing himself to smile. Then he laughed.

"Do not fear," he said. "My heart is still my own."

"Same here. Specially when I remember these females would grin jest the same if them club swingers had spattered our brains all over the front yard awhile back. But I wisht sombody'd give the girls a nightie or somethin' to wear. I been around some and I seen quite a lot, but I ain't used to bein' vamped by a bunch of undressed kids with goo-goo eyes the size of a plate o' fish balls. I'm only a bashful country kid from N'Yawk."

"Live and learn," chuckled Pedro. "And clothes really have nothing to do with modesty."

"True for ye. Clothes is mostly a disguise, anyhow, specially with women, and an awful expense, besides. These guys are lucky, I'll say; they ain't got to buy their wives no fur coats or silk stockin's or nothin'. All the same, I got all I can do to hold me face straight when I see these li'l owl-eyes givin' us the glad look. I'd oughter stayed back in Remate de Males, where a feller can wink at a woman without gittin' all his pardners massacreed."

"Perhaps it would not be fatal, now that we are guests of the chief. But it is best to take no chances."

"Safety first. That's us. Grin at one of 'em and another might git sore because she missed out, and first thing ye know ye've started somethin' without meanin' to. Let's look at somethin' harmless — one o' them poisoned spears, f'r instance."

At that moment Monitaya and Lourenço both arose, the chief to inspect in person the progress of the arrangements for the feast, the bushman to return to his companions with additional news.

"Monitaya tells me," he said, "that his people have lost girls in other ways than by the murderous attacks of the gunmen. A number of young women who have gone into the bush near their *malocas* to get urucu and genipapa, which they use to make the red and black body dyes, have disappeared. So have several who went to the creeks for their daily baths. Warriors who tried to trail them have found the footprints of a few men, but always lost them at water. The girls had been taken away in canoes. Even this tribe of Monitaya, which never has been attacked by night raiders because it is too strong, has not been safe from these stealthy woman stealings by daylight. Three girls have been taken from here within the past two moons, and others have disappeared from other *malocas*."

"Hm! And Schwandorf hasn't been here recently," said Knowlton.

"No. It must be that he has agents who work when he is not here, or else this is done without his knowledge. I have told Monitaya what I know of Schwandorf, and he agrees that the women are taken as slaves. I have also told him that when we return down the river we shall see that Schwandorf troubles the Mayorunas no more."

"Excellent," McKay approved. "Have you asked him about the Raposa?"

"Not yet. It does not pay to hurry business with these people. After the feast is out of the way I will talk further with him."

No more was said for a time. The five lounged at ease, sniffing the savory odors arising from the reddish clay pots and pans in which fruit, fish, or fowl was frying in tapir lard, or meat was stewing. At length a number of tall, shapely women, apparently the handsomest of their sex in the tribe, laid a number of small mats in a semicircle on the ground before the chief, and placed thereon a steaming array of edibles. Furs were placed outside the line of mats. From somewhere appeared all four of the subchiefs, accompanied by Yuara. Thereupon Monitaya, with a smiling nod to his guests, squatted within the arc. Forthwith the visitors advanced in a body, disposed themselves comfortably on the furs, and assailed the viands with a vigor that brought a delighted grin to the face of their barbaric host.

Fried bananas, tender fish, broiled parrot which was not so tender, a thick stew of somewhat odorous meat seasoned with tart-tasting herbs, roast wild hog, and other things at whose identity the whites could not even guess, all were chewed and washed down with generous draughts of a rather sour liquid resembling beer. Remembering Lourenço's previous warning, each man took care not to slight any portion of the meal or to show distaste with anything, whether it pleased the palate or not. Throughout the feast the tall women hovered near, bringing fresh supplies whenever a dearth of any edible appeared to threaten. And when at last the feasters were full to repletion Monitaya himself designated what he considered titbits to tempt them further.

"Gosh! if I eat any more I'll bust, and I'm danged if I'll bust jest to satisfy this guy," asserted Tim. Wherewith he put one hand under his jaw and patted his stomach with the other, signifying that he was filled to the throat. Pedro lifted his elbows, dropped his jaw, and made motions as if gasping for air. The chieftain grinned widely. The grin became a chuckling when Tim, after a vain attempt to rise, lay back at full length on his rug and begged some one to make a cigarette.

"Guess I'll have to follow Tim's example," confessed Knowlton. And he too stretched out. Pedro and Lourenço also sprawled back. McKay, after glancing around, compromised with his dignity by leaning on one elbow. The subchiefs and Yuara, with slight smiles, relaxed in various postures. Monitaya alone arose — not without some difficulty — and got into his hammock, where he beamed down at them.

"Suppose this is a compliment to the chief," smiled McKay. "He thinks he has eaten us helpless."

"Speakin' for li'l old Tim Ryan, that ain't no joke, neither. Lookit all the girls givin' us the laff. Who are them tall ones that's been rushin' the grub? Waitresses or somethin'?"

"Those are the chief's wives," Lourenço explained.

"Huh? Gosh! he's one brave guy, that feller! Two — four — six — eight — nine of 'em! Swell lookers, too. I s'pose he has his pick o' the whole crowd here."

"He does not have to pick them Senhor Tim. They pick him. He and the subchiefs are the only ones who can take more than one wife. When a girl wishes to become the wife of the great chief or of a subchief, she works for months making feather dresses and necklaces and hammocks, and when these are done she gives them all to him. If he likes her well enough he accepts the gifts and allows her to be a wife to him."

"Yeah? And she's flattered to death, I s'pose. Wisht they'd start some-thin' like that up home, or, anyways, fix it so's a feller could get an even break. Way it is now, a feller blows in every dollar he's got, and then when he's fixin' to git the ring the girl leaves him flat for some other guy that ain't spent his dough yet. Yo-ho-hum! I'm goin' to take a snooze right there on the table. Wake me up, somebody, when the next mess call blows."

And with no further ado he shut his eyes and drowsed.

His companions lolled for some time, smoking and watching the family life of the ordinary members of the tribe, nodding now and then to some friendly-looking young fellow, but ignoring the mischievous glances of the girls. Monitaya himself lay back in his hammock and dozed. His wives, stepping nonchalantly among the strangers, cleared away the remnants of the feast by the simple process of eating them. Then they carried off the clay vessels.

For another hour all hands rested. Then Monitaya sat up, stretched his big arms, looked casually around the house to see that all was well, and smiled down at his guests. Lourenço, rising to a squat, began a new conversation. After a while he turned to McKay.

"The Red Bones and the Mayorunas are neither friendly nor hostile toward each other, and there is little communication between them," he reported. "From those *malocas* to the town of the Red Bones is a journey of five long days, so the men of Monitaya hardly ever go there.

"The Raposa whom we seek is known to the men of Monitaya, but he never has come here to the tribal houses. Hunters from this place have met him at times roving the wild forests, and some of the younger men fear him as the bad spirit of the jungle. The Mayorunas believe in two spirits or demons, one good and one bad, and the bad one is said to roam the wilderness, seeking lone wanderers, whom he kills and eats; the people sometimes hear this demon howling at night in the dark of the moon. So the young men have thought the Raposa might be this demon and have avoided him — it would do no good to try to kill a demon, and it would only make their own deaths more sure and horrible.

"But the older men do not believe this. They say the wild man is of the Red Bone people, and that the reason why his bones are marked in red on his living body is that he is neither alive nor dead. If he were dead his body would be thrown into the water and left there until his bones were stripped by those cannibal fish, the piranhas, and then the bones would be dyed red and hung up in his hut, as is the custom among those people. If he were alive like other men he would not have those marks on his body, but would wear only the tribal face paint. The bone paint on him is a sign to all the *Ossos Vermelhos* that he is alive, but dead, and is not to be treated like other men."

"Crazy!" exclaimed Knowlton.

"Yes. I think that is it. His body lives, but his mind is dead. Death in life."

"Has he been seen lately?"

The Brazilian repeated the question in the Indian tongue. The chief looked toward a certain hammock some distance off, called a name, raised an imperative hand. A slender savage came forward. To him the chief spoke, then to Lourenço, who, as usual, relayed his information.

"This young hunter saw him six days ago while following a wild-hog trail far out in the bush toward the Red Bone region. He came on the fresh track of a man who was following the same hogs, and later he caught up with that man. It was the red-boned wild man, and the wild man was very lame, having a hurt foot. They stood and looked at each other, and then the wild man walked away, watching him closely and ready to shoot with his bow. After he disappeared in the forest this hunter heard a long, shrill laugh and words that sounded like 'Podavi.'"

"Podavi — Poor Davy!" ejaculated Knowlton. "That's he, sure enough! Then he's near his own town now — he won't go far with a bad foot. We'd better move as soon as we can. Ask about an escort."

Once more the bushman conversed with Monitaya. The ruler's smile disappeared. For some time he sat gazing out over the heads of all, evidently weighing matters in his mind. When he responded, however, it was without hesitation.

"There is neither friendliness nor enmity between the two peoples, as has been said," Lourenço stated. "Our business among the Red Bones is our own affair, not that of Monitaya, and Monitaya will make no requests for us. But in order that we may go safely and return without harm he will send with us twenty of his best men. These men will have orders to protect us at all times, unless fighting is caused by our making a needless attack on the Red Bones. In that case the Mayorunas will do nothing to help us. They will only defend themselves."

"Fair enough!" nodded McKay. "Tell him we'll start no fight. If any trouble comes it will be from the other fellows. We'll leave here tomorrow morning."

Lourenço translated the promise into Mayoruna. But the chief seemed not to hear. His eyes had narrowed and were fixed on the face of Tim, who still lay on his back and was giving no attention to what went on. Following his look, the bushman gazed critically at the red-haired man.

Tim's florid face had paled. His mouth was drawn and his eyes stared straight up, wide and glassy. Slowly he rolled his head from side to side.

"Gee! Cap," he whispered, hoarsely, "I et too much. My head aches so I'm fair blind, and I'm burnin' up. Gimme some water."

With a swift, simultaneous movement McKay and Knowlton put their hands on his forehead. Lourenço and Pedro leaned closer and peered into his face. All four glanced at one another. Pedro nodded. His lips silently formed one dread word:

"Fever!"

XVIII

FRUIT OF THE TRAP

Heavy hypodermic doses of quinine, aided by Tim's rugged constitution and the fact that this was his first attack of the ravaging sickness of the swamp lands, pulled him back to safety within the next two days. To safety, but not to strength. Despite his stout-hearted assertions that he was ready to hit the trail and "walk the legs off the whole danged outfit," he was obviously in no condition to stand up under the grueling pack work that lay ahead. Wherefore, McKay, after consultation with the others of the party, and, through Lourenço, with Monitaya, gave him inflexible orders.

"You'll stay here. Stick in your hammock until you're in fighting trim. Then watch yourself. Don't pull any bonehead plays that'll get these people down on you. Take quinine daily according to Knowlton's directions — he's written them on the box. If we're not back in a fortnight Monitaya will send men to find out why. If they find that we're — not coming back — you will be guided to the river, where you can get down to the Nunes place."

"But, Cap —"

"No argument!"

"But listen here, for the love o' Mike! I ain't no old woman! I can stand the gaff! I'm goin' with the gang!"

"You hear the orders!" McKay snapped, with assumed severity. "Think we want to be bothered with having you go sick again? You're out of shape and we've no room for lame ducks. You'll stay here!"

Tim tried another tack.

"Aw, but listen! Ye ain't goin' to desert a comrade amongst a lot o' man eaters — right in the place where I got sick, too. Soon's I git away from here I'll be all right —"

"That stuff's no good," the captain contradicted, with a tight smile. "You didn't get fever here. It's been in your system for days. You got it back on the river. These people don't have it, or any other kind of sickness. I've looked around and I know. As for the man eaters, they're mighty decent folks toward friends. We're friends. You'll be under the personal protection of Monitaya, and his word is good as gold. It's all arranged, and you're safer here than you would be in New York."

In his heart the stubborn veteran knew McKay was right, but, like any other good soldier ordered to remain out of action, he grumbled and growled regardless. To which the ex-officers paid about as much attention as officers usually do. They went ahead with their own preparations.

"Be of good heart, Senhor Tim," Pedro comforted, mischievously. "You will not lack for company. The chief has appointed two girls to wait upon you at all times."

"Huh? Them two tall ones that's been hangin' round and fetchin' things? Are they mine?"

"Yes. They are quite handsome in their way, and strong enough to help you about if your legs remain weak. In that case you will probably be allowed to put your arms around them for support. I almost wish I could get fever, too."

Tim's voice remained a growl, but his face did not look so doleful as before.

"Grrrumph! I always seem to draw big females, and I don't like 'em. Gimme somethin' cute like them li'l' frog dolls in Paree — sort o' pee-teet and chick. Still, a feller's got to do the best he can. Mebbe I'll live till you guys git back."

With which he availed himself of the prerogative of a sick man and grinned openly at the two comely young women who stood near at hand, awaiting any demand for services. They were not at all backward in reciprocating, and, despite the tribal paint and their labial ornaments, the smiles softening their faces made them not half bad to look upon.

"'O death, where is thy sting?'" laughed Knowlton. "Be careful not to strain your heart while we're away, Tim."

"Don't worry. It's a tough old heart — been kicked round so much it's growed a shell like a turtle. Besides, I seen wild women before I ever come to the jungle."

Notwithstanding his apparent resignation, however, Tim erupted once more when his comrades shouldered their packs, picked up their guns, and spoke their thanks and good-by to Monitaya. He arose on shaky legs and desperately offered to prove his fitness by a barehanded six-round bout with his commanding officer. When McKay, with sympathetic eyes but gruff tones, peremptorily squelched him he insisted on at least going to the door to watch his comrades start the journey from which they might or might not return. Nor did he take advantage of his chance to hug the girls on the way.

With one arm slung over the shoulders of a wiry young warrior who grinned proudly at the honor of being selected to help a guest of the great chief, he followed the departing column out into the sunshine, where the entire tribe was assembled. And when the stalwart band had filed into the shadows of the trees and vanished he stood for a time unseeing and gulping at something in his throat.

Straight away along a vague path beginning at the rear of the *malocas* marched the twenty-four, the two northerners bending under the weight of their packs, the pair of Brazilians sweeping the jungle with practiced eyes, the score of Mayorunas striding velvet footed, resplendent in brilliant new paint and headdresses, armed with the most powerful weapons of their tribe, and loftily conscious of the fact that they were chosen as Monitaya's best. Savage and civilized, each man was fit, alert, formidable. Nowhere in the loosely joined chain was a weak link.

Before the departure the Americans had been at some trouble to rid themselves of Yuara, who, with his men, had tarried at the Monitaya *malocas* during Tim's sickness. While Knowlton was giving his ripped arm a final dressing he had calmly announced his intention of joining the expedition into the Red Bone country, and it had taken some skillful argument by Lourenço to dissuade him without arousing his anger. All four of the adventurers would gladly have taken him along had he not been hampered by his injury, but, under the ruthless rule barring all men not in possession of all their strength, he had to be left.

Now, as on the previous jungle marches, the way was led by two of the tribesmen, followed by the Brazilians and the Americans, after whom the main body of the escort strode in column. The leader and guide, one Tucu, was a veteran hunter, fighter, and bushranger, who had been more than once in the Red Bone region and withal possessed the cool judgment of mature years and long experience; a lean, silent man who, though not a subchief, might have made a good one if given the opportunity. With him Lourenço had already arranged that a direct course should be followed, and that whenever dense undergrowth blockaded the way the machete men should take the lead.

For some time no word was spoken. The path wound on, faintly marked, but easy enough to follow with Tucu picking it out. It was not one of the frequently used trails of the Monitaya people, but a mere *picada,* or hunter's track; yet even this had its pitfalls to guard the tribal house. Soon after leaving the clearing Tucu turned aside, passed between trees off the trail, went directly under one tree whose steep-slanting roots stood up off the ground like great down-pointing fingers, and returned to the path. All followed without comment.

A considerable distance was covered before any further sign of the presence of ambushed death was shown by the savages. Then it came with tragic suddenness.

Tucu grunted suddenly, and in one instant shifted his gait from the easy swing of the march to the prowl of a hunting animal. Behind him the line grew tense. The click of rifle hammers and of safeties being thrown off breech bolts blended with the faint slither of arrows being swiftly drawn from quivers. Eyes searched the bush, spying no enemy.

Two more steps, and Tucu stopped, head thrust forward, eyes boring into something on the ground. The rest, taking care not to touch one another's weapons, crowded around and looked down at the huddled form of a man.

A matted mass of black hair, a neck burned copper brown by sun, tattered cotton shirt and trousers, big, bare dirty feet, a rusty repeating rifle of heavy caliber — these were what they saw first. The man lay straight, his face in the dirt, his hands a little ahead as if he had been crawling forward at the moment of death. Tucu turned him on his back, revealing a blanched yellow-brown face which was proof positive of his race.

"Peruvian," said Pedro.

"What got him?" demanded Knowlton. "No wound on him."

Lourenço questioned Tucu. The leader, who evidently knew just where to look, tore open the thin shirt at the left side and pointed to a tiny discoloration surrounding a red dot under the ribs. He muttered a few laconic words.

"A blowgun trap," Lourenço explained. "The gun is set a little way beyond here. This man, sneaking along the path, broke the little cord which shot the gun. The poisoned dart struck in his side. He must have pulled out the dart, but he could not go far before his legs became paralyzed, and he fell. Then, still trying to crawl, he died."

Pedro picked up the dead man's gun and worked the lever. The weapon was fully loaded and showed no sign of recent firing. Pedro coolly pumped it empty, gathered up the blunt .44 cartridges, and pocketed them for his own use.

Tucu watched the proceeding in satirical approval. Then, leaving the body where it lay, he went stooping along the path ahead, his keen eyes searching the undergrowth. In a few minutes he returned with the blood-stained dart which, as Lourenço had guessed, the stricken prowler had pulled from his flesh and dropped. This he passed to a blowgun man. The latter carefully opened his poison pouch, redipped the point of the dart, held it a moment to dry in a shaft of sunlight, and slipped it into his dart case among a score of unused missiles.

"No waste of ammunition here," was McKay's dry comment. "What happens to this corpse now?"

Through Lourenço's mouth Tucu answered.

"It will be left here until police warriors come from the *malocas*. Certain men travel the paths daily to inspect the traps. When they find this man they will cut off his hands and feet with their wooden knives and throw the rest aside to be eaten by the animals. He has not been dead long or he would have been devoured by some wild thing before we came. The trail travelers will set the trap again and take the hands and feet to the *malocas*, where they will be washed, cooked, and eaten."

The faces of the Americans contracted slightly. A simultaneous thought made them flash startled glances at each other.

"Tim —" Knowlton said, and paused. Lourenço smiled.

"No, Senhor Tim will not be expected to eat man meat," he assured them. "I thought of that before we left — one never knows when these traps will yield human flesh. So, without letting Monitaya know why I spoke, I told him you North Americans believed the flesh of an enemy to be poisonous, and that you would not eat it on that account. Monitaya will remember that."

"By George! you have a head on your shoulders, old scout! I was worried for a minute. If they offered Tim a broiled foot or a stewed hand he'd go for his gun."

Briefly Tucu spoke. The Mayorunas separated and went into the forest, seeking any sign of other enemies.

"Queer that this chap should come here alone — if he was alone," added Knowlton. "Suppose he's the fellow that's been swiping stray girls? Or a spy?"

"Neither, I think, senhor. The girls were captured by more than one man, and I doubt if this one had been here before. Probably he was one of those lone prowlers of the bush whose hand is against every man. He is a half-breed, as you see, and came, perhaps, to steal a girl for himself. The jungle is well rid of him."

"Uh-huh. Guess you're right. Say, I'd like to see how that blowgun trap operates. Can't understand what blows the dart when nobody is here."

"I do not know, either, senhor. Perhaps Tucu will show us."

The savage guide, after a moment's hesitation, pointed along the trail and stalked away, the others at his heels. At a spot some fifteen yards farther on he turned into the bush at the right, walked a few paces away from the path, turned again sharply to the left, advanced once more, and halted. Before them, not easy to discern in the masking brush, even though they were looking for it, hung the long barrel of the blowgun, lashed to a couple of small trees and pointing toward the path.

Tucu stepped to the mouthpiece of the slender tube and pointed to a sapling, just behind and in line with it, which had been cut off about shoulder-high from the ground. From the tip of this thin trunk dangled a wide strip of bark. The savage, having indicated this, stood as if the action of the device were perfectly clear.

"Too deep for me," admitted McKay, after a puzzled study of the tube and the trunk. The others nodded agreement. Lourenço confessed to the Indian the blindness of all.

Thereupon Tucu bent the sapling far over and released it. As it sprang erect the bark strip slapped the end of the gun. Also, the watchers saw something hitherto unnoticed — a thin, flexible vine attached to the top of the thin stump. Lourenço's face showed understanding.

"See, comrades, this is it: The little tree is bent far down and held by the long vine. The vine passes around a low branch, then up over other limbs, and out across the path, where it is fastened to a root near the ground. A man following the path breaks the vine. The little tree then flies up and the bark sheet strikes the wide mouthpiece of the gun. The air forced into that mouthpiece by the blow of the bark shoots the little dart. The dart does not fly as hard as if blown by a man, but it goes swiftly enough to pierce the skin of anything except a tapir. As soon as the poison is in the blood the work is done."

"It sure is done," Knowlton echoed, thinking of the short distance covered by the dead Peruvian after passing this spot. "Mighty ingenious apparatus. These people are no fools, I'll say."

"You say rightly," Pedro muttered. Turning, they went out to the path, looking askance at the thin death tube as they passed along it.

The scouting Mayorunas returned, having found nothing. Tucu resumed his place at the head of the line. Without a backward glance at the body sprawling in the trail at the rear, the column swung into its usual gait.

The Americans, silent before, were silent again. They had looked for the first time on the work of the Mayoruna traps; had observed the cold-blooded way in which the Indiana handled the still form on the ground; had visualized the forthcoming mutilation of that body and the resultant cannibal rites. More vividly than ever before they realized that these men and Monitaya himself were relentless creatures of the jungle, and that, despite the present existent friendliness, there yawned between them and their barbarous allies an impassable gulf.

For the moment the jungle itself seemed a poisonous green abyss of creeping, crawling, sneaking death. And though they had faced death too often in another land to fear it in any form, though they marched on with unwavering step, their eyes were somber as in their hearts echoed the last appeal of the man they had left behind them:

"Ye ain't goin' to desert a comrade amongst a lot o' man eaters —"

X I X

THE RED BONES

Four days the expedition tramped steadily onward through the rugged labyrinthine hills. Four nights its members slept in utter exhaustion. Neither by day nor by night was any sign of the Raposa seen, nor of any other human being.

So tired from the constant struggle did the Americans become that their jaded brains began to picture the mysterious wild man as a mere legendary creature, which they never would find even though they searched the inscrutable forests until the end of time. Yet when, on the fifth day, Tucu informed them that they now were nearing the principal settlement of the Red Bones, the announcement cheered them as if they were about to enter a civilized city and there meet David Rand safe and sane.

Not that any chance of striking his trail had been neglected in the meantime. It was thoroughly understood that if he were met anywhere he was to be made prisoner, and that thereafter the back trail should be taken. Lourenço had impressed on Tucu the fact that the whole journey had for its object the finding of the wild man, and that he must not be killed if found. Since the Indians were not in the habit of hunting so assiduously anyone but a bitterly hated foe, it is quite possible that they misunderstood the spirit of the quest and believed the "dead-alive" prowler would, if captured, undergo some extremely unpleasant treatment at the hands of the white men. But so long as it was made clear that the Raposa must be caught alive, if caught at all, Lourenço did not trouble about what the Mayorunas might surmise.

Now, as the end of the long, pathless trail approached, arose a question of which McKay had previously thought but had not spoken — how he was to converse with the Red Bone chief. Lourenço asked Tucu whether the Red Bones spoke the Mayoruna tongue. Tucu replied that they did not. He added, however, that the languages were not so dissimilar as to prevent some sort of understanding being reached between members of the two tribes. The veteran bushman nodded carelessly.

"When the tongue fails, Capitao, the hands still can talk," he said. "It takes more time and work, that is all. Ah, here is a path!"

It was so. For the first time since leaving the Monitaya region a path lay under their feet. And for the first time Tucu and his fellow Mayorunas, glancing along that faint track, showed hesitation.

"Why the delay?" snapped McKay.

"They suspect traps. I will go ahead and feel out the way. I have done it before on other paths."

After a few words to Tucu, Lourenço cut a long, slim pole. With this in hand he preceded the column, walking slowly, pausing sometimes, continually prodding the path, studying it with unswerving gaze as he progressed. The thin but rigid feeler, strong enough to tip the cover of any pit or to spring any concealed bow or blowgun, was at least ten feet long, and between the scout and the head of the line Tucu preserved another ten-foot interval. Progress was necessarily slow, but it was sure.

In this fashion they advanced perhaps half a mile. Not once did they have to leave the path, but Lourenço's caution did not diminish. Rather, it increased as they neared the Red Bone town. At length another path joined the one on which they were traveling. Here Lourenço paused for minutes, inspecting with extreme care the ground and the bush.

Suddenly he cocked his head as if listening. Then, with a backward motion of the hand to enjoin silence, he faced down the branch path and stood calmly waiting.

To those behind came a light rustle of leaves and a scuffle of moving feet; a sudden cessation; then Lourenço's voice speaking to some one concealed behind the intervening undergrowth. His tone was slow, quiet, easy — the tone which, even if the words were not understood, would soothe suspicious and abruptly alarmed minds. After another short silence he resumed talking, pointing carelessly to the place behind him where stood the silent file of Mayorunas. A guttural voice replied. A head peered cautiously from the edge of the bush, stared fixedly at Tucu, and withdrew. The voice sounded again. Immediately three Indians stepped into view, poised for action. Another interval of staring, and they relaxed.

"Come forward, comrades," said Lourenço. They came, halting again at the junction of the trails. Tucu spoke to one of the newcomers, who scowled as if only partly understanding, but grunted some sort of answer. Those behind the Mayoruna leader craned their necks and scanned the Red Bone men, who continued to eye with evident misgiving the tall-bonneted cannibals and the broad-hatted pair of whites.

Man for man, these Red Bones were in every way inferior to the emissaries of Monitaya. Their bodies were more gaunt, their skins more coppery, their foreheads lower, and their expressions much less intelligent. Furthermore, they wore not even the bark-cloth clouts which formed the sole body covering of the Mayorunas — they were totally naked. The one point of similarity between the two tribes was that the faces of the Red Bone men were streaked with red dye. But the facial design was much different: two short transverse stripes on the forehead, and three lines on each cheek, running from the eyes, the end of the nose, and the corners of the mouth, straight back to the ears. Studying those visages, Knowlton and McKay recalled Schwandorf's statement that these people not only ate human flesh, but tortured prisoners of war. It was easy to believe that he had told truth.

McKay, standing behind Pedro, shifted his position a bit. At once the eyes of the three Red Bones widened and riveted on his face. Heretofore they had seen only his hat and eyes, the rest being hidden from them by Pedro's neck and an intervening palm tip. Now that they saw his black-bearded jaw, they started slightly and peered intently at him.

"I think, Capitao, you would do well to shave," Pedro suggested, with a smile.

"'Fraid so," the captain granted. "Black beards evidently are *de trop* in the jungle social set at present."

But then one of the Red Bone men came forward, still squinting narrowly, and his expression was not hostile. In fact, it was more friendly than it had yet been. After a closer scrutiny, however, his face turned blank. Slowly he stepped back and muttered something to his companions.

At this Pedro's eyes narrowed speculatively. But his expression did not change, and he said nothing.

A lengthy conference took place between Lourenço and Tucu on the one hand and the three Red Bone tribesmen on the other; a difficult talk in which words and sign language both were used and frequently repeated. Eventually an understanding was reached. The three stepped back, picked up some small game which they had dropped on beholding Lourenço, returned, and led the way along the path. Lourenço cast aside his poke stick and resumed his usual place in the column. The whole line moved ahead at a much smarter gait than before.

"Note — this path is not mined," thought Knowlton.

This proved true. Moreover, the way now was more broad and firm, so that travel on it was much easier. After twenty minutes of rapid tramping it debouched abruptly into a cleared space. Here all halted.

Before them lay a town of small, low huts, crowded closely together in two parallel rows which curved together at one end. The other end lay open, giving access to a sizable creek whereon floated canoes. At the water's edge, along the crude street studded with charred stumps, and among the damp-looking huts moved naked figures of men and women occupied with various sluggish activities. Some of the men already had spied the invading party and were standing at gaze.

"Comrades, we have reached the end of our trail," said Lourenço, running a cool eye over the place. "Now all we have to do is to find your Raposa and get him and ourselves away alive."

"That's all," Knowlton echoed, unsmiling. "The reception committee is forming now." And with the words he unbuttoned his holster.

A shrill yell had run along the double line of houses, and out into the stumpy street now swarmed men armed with hastily seized weapons. Hands pointed, confused exclamations sounded, and a compact detachment of warriors came jogging toward the newcomers. The three guides drew away from the Mayorunas. The latter promptly fitted arrows to their bows, inserted darts in their blowguns, lifted spears or clubs, and with eyes glittering awaited whatever might befall.

A couple of rods away the Red Bones halted, bows ready. A hatchet-faced savage who seemed to be in command rasped something at the three hunters, who quickened their pace toward him. Tucu strode out four paces beyond his own men and stopped. Then both parties waited while the hunters reported what they knew to the hatchet-face.

"What did you tell them, Lourenço?" asked McKay.

"That we came on a friendly visit to the chief, for whom we had important words."

"Nothing of the Raposa?"

"No. They wasted much time arguing that we must tell them all our business and let them inform the chief, while we were to stay back on the path until permitted to enter the town. We told them our talk was for the chief alone, and that we should come here whether they liked it or not. So, having no choice, they led us in."

McKay made no comment. None was necessary. Furthermore, his steady eyes had caught a simultaneous head movement of the Red Bones — a peering movement, as if all were seeking some one man among the new arrivals. Pedro observed this. He spoke softly to Lourenço.

"Lourenço, tell Tucu to say to the Red Bones that we come led by a black-bearded white man; that this blackboard comes from the far-off country where all men wear black beards; that the blackbeard will speak with the chief only."

The Americans looked queerly at the young Brazilian, as did Lourenço himself. But without question Lourenço obeyed. Calling to Tucu, he gave the message. Tucu moved his head slightly, but gave no other sign of having heard.

"Now, Capitao, step forward a little and show yourself more clearly," prompted Pedro.

With another puzzled glance McKay did so. He saw that the brown eyes of the younger man held a dancing gleam, but he could not read the thought behind those eyes. Yet he noticed that as soon as he stepped out the Red Bones all focused their gaze on him. More than that, the spokesman of the three hunters pointed at him and said something to the sharp-featured leader.

Now that leader came forward alone. Six feet from Tucu he halted again and talked in a growling tone. The Mayoruna leader, cool and dignified, made answer. After a somewhat protracted exchange Tucu turned his head and motioned to Lourenço, who went forward, listened, replied shortly, and came back. Meanwhile the first detachment of Red Bones had been strongly reinforced by others who had come up singly or in small parties. Now the expedition was outnumbered at least four to one by hard-faced, brute-mouthed, naked men ready, if not eager, for trouble.

"The Red Bone says we shall see the chief," Lourenço stated. "At first he said only you, Capitao, should go to him. Then he insisted that we all lay down our arms. Tucu has told him we lay down our arms for no man or men; that we come in peace — otherwise there would be many more of us; that we leave in peace unless the Red Bones themselves bring on a fight. In that case, though we are few, there lies behind us the power of Monitaya, and behind Monitaya the power of the Mayoruna chiefs, all strong enough to wipe the Red Bone nation off the face of the ground."

"Strong stuff, that," said Knowlton.

"Strong, yes. But no stronger than is needed to impress these people. Tucu intends to prevent trouble if he can; and often the best way to prevent trouble is to make the other man realize what may happen to him if he starts it. Also he has his orders from Monitaya to stay with us at all times, and he will follow that order even if you, Capitao, try to change it. Now we go together to the chief."

He nodded to Tucu, who grunted to the Red Bone leader. The hatchet-face in turn shouted something to the men behind. Slowly they drew apart into two groups.

"You are the leader, Capitao," suggested Lourenço. Promptly McKay marched forward, head up, eyes front, face bleak. The rest followed, Tucu falling in behind McKay when the captain passed him. Preceded by the Red Bone spokesman, the line advanced between the two bodies of copper-skins and swung along the evil-smelling avenue to its upper end.

There, in the very center of the loop joining the two rows of huts, was a house twice as big as any other. From its doorway the inhabitant of that house could watch the whole life of the Red Bone town. Obviously it was the home of the chief. At its door a pair of warriors stood guard, but of the ruler himself there was no sign.

Ten paces from it the thin-featured leader stopped and motioned to McKay to halt. As the captain and the line behind him did so he stalked onward, passed through the doorway, and faded from sight in the dimness beyond. With one accord the members of the visiting party looked around them.

The street behind now was filled with the mass of Red Bone warriors who had trooped after the column. All exit in that direction was blockaded. But the ex-officers noted that between the houses were spaces each wide enough to hold a couple of men, and in an undertone McKay gave defensive instructions to Lourenço.

"If fighting starts, have the Mayorunas take cover along these houses on each side. We who have guns will use the chief's house. We can sweep the whole street from there. You two fellows capture the chief alive if possible. He'll be more useful as a hostage than as a corpse."

Pedro beamed approval of this swiftly formed plan. Lourenço muttered to Tucu, who in turn passed the word down the line. Then all stood waiting.

Presently the Red Bone man came out. He shouted a name. From the doorway near at hand, where he had been standing and peering at the small but formidable body of newcomers, an old man now stepped forth and advanced, limping a little, to the hatchet-face. The latter talked briefly to him, then to Tucu. The Mayoruna leader pointed to Lourenço. The old man spoke to the Brazilian, who answered at once. Thereupon the wizened old fellow entered the chief's house.

"That old man speaks the Mayoruna tongue quite well, Capitao," said Lourenço. "He says you and I shall enter and talk through his mouth with the chief. All others remain outside, and we must leave our rifles here."

"All right. Glad we can leave Tucu out here to control these fellows. Here, Merry." He passed his rifle to Knowlton. Pedro took Lourenço's gun. With packs still on their backs the chosen men proceeded to the doorway and entered the house where waited the ruler of the Red Bone tribe.

Behind them the line settled into easier postures of waiting. The Red Bones, though so compactly ranged as to cut off any chance of escape, held their distance, obviously neither inclined to fraternize nor ready to precipitate conflict by crowding. Thus, while keeping their ears open for any sound of a concerted movement from behind, the visitors could use their eyes to inspect the huts nearest them.

In some of these, women stood near the doorways, staring with unwinking absorption at the light-skinned, athletic men outside who were so much better to look upon than their own mates. The Mayorunas returned the stares with the brief glances of men accustomed to noticing everything but totally uninterested — as well they might be, for these poorly shaped, heavy-mouthed, mud-skinned females were not to be compared with their own women. Knowlton and Pedro, too, looked them over, but with the same expression as if inspecting a family of lizards. Then they glanced into other huts now empty of life, and in a couple of these they saw rigid red-hued objects hanging from the roofs.

"The red bones of the dead, senhor," Pedro muttered, and his blond companion, peering again at the sinister decorations, nodded without reply.

Voices came to them from the chief's house, talking with droning deliberation. Evidently no cause for friction had yet arisen. They let their eyes rove on beyond the guarded doorway, to pause at a house a short distance away at the right. There stood a clubman, who leaned idly on his weapon, but showed no intention of moving from his place. The door of that house was closed. Not only closed, but barred on the outside.

"Hm! Looks like a jail," said Knowlton. Pedro smiled, but an intent look came into his face and he studied the closed house.

Suddenly both started. At one corner of the house, unseen by the clubman, a head had cautiously slipped forth. For only an instant it hung there before dodging back out of sight. But both the watching men had seen that the face, though half masked by long dark hair and a thick beard, was much lighter than that of any Red Bone savage. And in the hair above one ear was a white streak.

X X

THE RAPOSA

McKay and Lourenço, in a broad, low, musty-smelling room, faced a man who stood and a man who sat. The man who stood was the old savage who could talk in the Mayoruna language. The man who sat was the chief of the Red Bones.

In his first words to the visitors the old interpreter revealed that the name of the Red Bone ruler was Umanuh. Later on Lourenço informed

McKay that in the Tupi *lengoa geral* of the Amazonian Indians (which, however, was not spoken by this tribe) the word "umanuh" meant "corpse." And whatever the name may have signified in the language of the Red Bones, its Tupi definition fitted with disagreeable precision. For Umanuh was a living cadaver.

Gaunt, gray skinned, lank haired, hollow of cheek and eye, with thin, cruel lips so tight drawn that the teeth behind seemed to show through, ribs projecting, clawlike hands resting on bony knees, his whole frame motionless as that of a man long dead, the head man of the bone-dyeing tribe was the antithesis of both the piggish Suba and the herculean Monitaya. Only his eyes lived; and those eyes were cold and merciless as those of a snake or a vulture. A man who ruled by ruthless cunning, who would gaze unmoved on the most ghastly tortures, who would devour human flesh with ghoulish relish — such was the creature who sat in a red-dyed hammock and contemplated the impassive face of McKay.

"Umanuh, great chief, eater of his enemies, with fangs of the jaguar and wisdom of the great snake, awaits the greeting of the one-whose-hair grows-from-his-mouth," droned the old mouthpiece of the chief.

"Makkay, leader of the fighting men of the Blackbeards, whose voice is the thunder and whose hand spits lightning and death, gives greeting to Umanuh," responded Lourenço in a like droning tone.

A pause. Umanuh gave no sign of life. McKay, straight and cold, met the unwinking stare of the chief with his own chill gray gaze. Between the two who spoke not was a testing of wills.

"Makkay brings with him none of the Blackbeard warriors," pointed out the interpreter, who seemed to know his master's thought. "He comes with only the jungle men of light skins."

"Makkay needs none of his own warriors when he comes in peace. If he came in war the terrible Blackbeards with him would cause the whole forest to fly apart in smoke and flame. Since he walks in peace to visit his friend Umanuh, of whose wisdom he has heard, he brings only his friends the Mayorunas, who are friends also to the men of the Red Bones."

Another pause. The old man now seemed somewhat uncertain of himself. The silent duel between McKay and Umanuh went on. At length the chief's eyes flickered a trifle. In a hissing whisper he said something.

"The men of the Mayorunas never come to this country unless seeking something," the interpreter promptly spoke up. "What do they seek?"

"Only that which Makkay seeks."

Then, turning to the captain, the Brazilian added: "Capitao, we now have reached the point to talk business. Have you any presents? And is it your wish to give them now or later?"

"I have a few things. But I'll give them later — if at all. This chief is hostile. Tell him what we're here for and see how he acts."

"It has come to the ears of Makkay," Lourenço informed the man of Umanuh, "that a man of the Blackbeards lives among the men of the Red Bones. Makkay would see that man."

Again the interpreter awaited his master's voice before answering.

"No man of the Blackbeards is among the men of Umanuh," he then denied.

"If he is not among them he is near them," was Lourenço's certain reply. "He has been seen both by other Blackbeards and by the Mayorunas. I, too, have seen him. He bears on his bones the sign that his mind is out of his skull. His eyes are green and his hair touched with white. Umanuh and his men know well that I speak true."

The pause this time was longer than before.

"There was such a man, but he is gone."

"Then Makkay asks his friend Umanuh to find that one. A chief so wise can easily find him where others would see only water and mud."

"If he could be found what would the great Blackbeard leader do with him?"

Lourenço thought swiftly. To say the Raposa was McKay's friend would do little good. Friendship meant nothing to this unfeeling brute. Therefore the bushman insinuated something which his cruel mind could comprehend.

"If a Red Bone man abandoned his people and went to another tribe, what would Umanuh do to him when he was found?"

A cold glimmer in the chief's eyes showed that he thought he understood. Moreover, he would much like to see what sort of torture this hard-faced Blackbeard would use on a fugitive. It might be something even more fiendish than his own pastimes. So the next reply came promptly.

"If that man is found the blackbeard will pay for him?"

"There are gifts of friendship for Umanuh," Lourenço nodded.

"The Blackbeard leader will pay more than the other Blackbeard?"

Lourenço almost blinked. What other Blackbeard? The Raposa himself? But the Brazilian repressed his bewilderment.

"Makkay will first see the man to make sure he is the Blackbeard whom Makkay wants," he dodged. "Then he will pay well."

"Umanuh will see the gifts now."

"The gifts cannot be shown now. They are packed away. When Makkay has looked on the man Umanuh shall look on the gifts."

Another eye duel between the chief and McKay. As before, the captain's eye proved the harder.

"Umanuh will think of the matter. Night comes. The man hunted by the Blackbeard is not here. The Blackbeard and his men may stay tonight across the water. When the sun rises again Umanuh will talk further."

"It is well. Let Umanuh tell his men to stay on this side of the water, that we may not mistake them in the night for enemies."

When Umanuh had hissed assent the old man stepped to the doorway and summoned the hatchet-faced warrior. To him instructions were given. He turned and carried the commands to the tribesmen.

"Makkay wishes Umanuh peaceful rest," said Lourenço. With which he flicked his eyes toward the door. McKay, with stiff stride, stalked out. Lourenço followed. Both felt the snake eyes of the cadaverous chief dwelling on their backs.

To the waiting Knowlton, Pedro, and Tucu it was briefly explained that preliminary negotiations had been concluded and that camp now would be made on the farther side of the creek. Tucu, observing that the Red Bone mass behind was dividing again to let the visitors pass through, gave the word to his men. The column began to move out, marching in reverse order. Pedro muttered swiftly to his partner.

"Lourenço, see that house with the barred door where the clubman stands guard. Remember where it is."

The other swept the loop in one quick glance, located the house, and fell into step without a word, the guarded structure fixed on his brain as clearly as if he had studied it for an hour. Walking down the malodorous street, he said, quietly, "There will be a small moon tonight."

"You are becoming a reader of the mind, comrade," Pedro grinned. No more was said.

Down to the shore of the creek trooped the party, followed closely by the hatchet-face and a score of tribesmen. The whites and the Mayorunas got into half a dozen of the waiting canoes and paddled across. In other dugouts the Red Bone men also crossed, but they did not land. As soon as the borrowed boats were empty the tribesmen took them in tow and returned to their own bank. The visitors were left on a partly cleared shore, separated from their uncordial hosts by some twenty yards of deep water. Not one canoe was left them. Furthermore, the Red Bones now began activities indicating an intention to establish a night-longwatch on the irside of the stream.

"Taking no chances of our raiding them tonight, or even snooping around town," said Knowlton. "Keeping everything in their own hands. Reckon we'd better post sentries tonight, Rod, just to keep an eye on that outpost of theirs."

McKay nodded.

"We four will take it in turn," he agreed. "Lourenço — Pedro — you — I. Three-hour tours."

"Pardon, Capitao," interposed Pedro. "It would be well to change that. You two senhores take the first two watches."

"Why?" frowned McKay.

"Because Lourenço and I wish to go visiting. We are much smitten with the charms of the ladies here."

The captain's frown deepened, but he studied Pedro's devil-may-care face keenly before answering.

"Humph! What's up your sleeve? Out with it!"

Pedro glanced around him and across the water. The tribesmen, both of the Mayoruna force and of the Red Bones, were watching the colloquy.

"We are watched, Capitao. Let us make camp now and talk later. These men do not understand our words, but we cannot tell what they may see in our faces. Now speak harshly, as if I had been insolent."

McKay did. He thundered at the young bushman as if about to do him bodily injury.

Pedro retreated a step, as if taken aback by the storm he had unleashed. When McKay stopped he replied: "Excellent, Capitao. Now I go to start work on the *tambo*."

He trudged away with a sullen gait. On both sides of the stream the Indians muttered and looked at the tall commander with increased respect. Truly, the Blackbeard was a fierce ruler and one who must not be angered; he had the voice of a great gun and the temper of a jaguar. That other man was lucky to have his head still on his shoulders!

When the camp was made at the edge of the bush and the four comrades were grouped in their hammocks, Lourenço narrated in detail the conversation with Umanuh. Knowlton reciprocated with news of what he and Pedro had seen at the corner of the barred house.

"I almost jumped after him, Rod," he admitted. "Had all I could do to hold myself. But I knew anything sudden like that might start war right there, and we wouldn't have a Chinaman's chance of getting away with him, so I stood fast. But he's here, and old Umanuh's a liar by the clock if he says otherwise."

"He is the same man we saw in the forest, Lourenço, or my eyes are twisted," added Pedro.

"Hm! Something very fishy here," commented McKay.

"Very fishy indeed, Capitao," Lourenço echoed. "The man is within call, yet Umanuh says he is not here. And Umanuh wants us to buy the man. What is more, he asks if we will pay more than the other Blackbeard. What other Blackbeard? The man himself has a dark beard, and since we left headquarters Pedro and I have grown black whiskers, too. Yet Umanuh cannot mean the crazy man would pay him to stay here, or that either of us Brazilians would try to buy him. There are no other men with black beards — except the German woman-stealer; and of course he cannot be the one."

"No?" Pedro asked, softly.

"No, certainly. Why? Of what were you thinking?"

Pedro's brown eyes twinkled, but he made no answer. He only inhaled a long puff from his cigarette and looked across the water at the hairpin-shaped town.

"What about that visiting trip of yours tonight?" McKay asked.

"I wish to see what is in that house with the barred door, Capitao. When I am curious about such a matter Lourenço always becomes curious, too, so I shall have to take him with me. If I did not he would say I was making love to the chief's wives."

"*Por Deus!* That may be all the barred house holds — the wives of the chief," guessed Lourenço. "Why waste time and risk death to look into that place?"

"*Quem nao arrisca nao ganha*, as the coronel would say — he who risks nothing gains nothing. I feel that we should visit that house. Something calls me back to it."

Lourenço studied his partner a moment, then nodded slowly. But McKay interposed decided objection.

"Too dangerous. Also unnecessary. We'll get Rand — if the man is Rand — through the chief. Your night spying might ruin everything and get you killed into the bargain. Nothing to gain and all to lose. Stay here."

Pedro's eyes hardened. But it was Lourenço who answered.

"Capitao, I think we had best do as Pedro says. It is a queer thing and I cannot explain it, but I have known him to have such ideas in the past and they have always worked out for the best. He himself does not know why he does some things — things which look totally foolish and which often are very dangerous — except that he feels like doing them. Yet I have never known this foolishness to fail to turn out well. He and I will go over tonight and see what we may see."

The captain's brows drew together. Flat insubordination! Then he remembered that these men were not subordinates at all; remembered also what Coronel Nunes said concerning their ability to get into and out of dangerous situations. When Knowlton sided with them he capitulated.

"Up in the States we'd say Pedro was 'riding his hunch,'" was the lieutenant's remark. "And I've known a hunch to bring all kinds of good luck. Gee! I'd like to go across with you lads myself! But I'm no jungle expert, especially after dark, and I'd only be in the way. Besides, we'll sure have to stick here and keep up appearances while you're gone. How will you get over? There's no way but swimming, and this creek's probably inhabited by the usual 'gators and snakes and things."

"When one can travel only by swimming, one swims," Pedro smiled. "Leave that to us, senhores. Now the sun sinks fast and I have hunger. Let us eat."

Night was at hand. While the whites talked some of the Mayorunas had quietly slipped away into the bush, seeking whatever fresh meat might be obtainable without straying too far from camp. Naturally, the hunting was poor so near an inhabited place, but now the absent men came stealing back with a few small birds and one monkey. Though the savages asked nothing and evidently expected nothing from the whites to eke out this scant provision, the latter opened their meager larders to Tucu, ordering him to see that every man had at least a few mouthfuls to eat. Tucu, like a good commander, made no bones of accepting the invitation for the good of his men. When all hands had stowed away the last meal of the day the rations were reduced almost to the vanishing point.

"Those miserable whelps over there might have had the decency to give us a few bites," Knowlton growled, looking at the Red Bone men on the other bank, who were gorging themselves on meat brought by their women.

"It is quite possible that they intend to give us several bites later on," Pedro suggested, with a mirthless smile.

"Uh-huh. Shouldn't wonder. But it's also possible that they'll have to assimilate a few lead pills before chewing us up. Rod, we'll have our work cut out standing guard tonight. I wouldn't put it past that lying old Umanuh to try rubbing us out before morning."

"Nor I," concurred McKay. "Only question is whether he dares take a chance against our guns and against the likelihood that Monitaya will send other men to investigate our disappearance. Better keep well out of sight."

As he spoke the last light of day vanished. Stars and a quarter moon leaped out in the swiftly darkening sky. The small fire of the expedition threw dim shadows against the poles of the night shelters. Lights glimmered in the Red Bone huts, and other lights began to streak across the gloom — the bright little lanterns of fireflies coasting along the stream. But at the point where the Red Bone night guard lurked no light shone. They had built no fire, and now they were almost invisible in the faint moonshine — sinister shadows which even now might be meditating murder or worse.

Lourenço lounged over to Tucu, who was watching those shadows with a fixed cat stare, and informed him that until morning a man with a gun would be always on guard while the rest slept. The Indian grunted approval. By way of precaution against being killed by his own men, the Brazilian added the information that later on he and his comrade would leave the camp and go upstream for a time. At this Tucu's eyes dwelt on his, veered to the lights of the town, and returned. In them was a plain, though unspoken, question. The bushman ignored it and strolled back to his *tambo*.

The moon sailed higher. The animal uproar of early night began to diminish. The fire, almost buried under slow-burning wood whose acrid smoke alleviated the insect pests, smoldered dull red. McKay and Knowlton drew lots for the first sleep, the captain winning and promptly getting under his net. In the Mayoruna shelter all was dark and silent, each man sleeping lightly with one hand on a weapon. The two Brazilians also were out of sight in their hut.

Up and down, a barely distinguishable figure, Knowlton passed slowly with holster unbuttoned and rifle cocked, eyes turning periodically to the Red Bone outpost and ears intent to pick any unusual sound out of the night noise. Gradually the small lights of the town faded out. To all appearance, sleep had whelmed it for the night. The watchers on the farther shore stirred a little at times, but the blot they made in the moonshine remained fixed in the same spot. The only moving things were the khaki-clad sentinel and the blazing fireflies.

Another hour rolled slowly by. The sentinel stopped and stood at a corner of the *tambo*. Now was as good a time as any for the Brazilians to start their perilous reconnaissance. Perhaps they had gone to sleep. He squinted at their hammocks. Yes, they were occupied. Stepping softly to the hammock of Pedro, he lifted the net to whisper to the occupant. Then he stared, dropped the net, and lifted Lourenço's curtain. A soft, self-derisive chuckle sounded in his throat as he stole out again.

The hammocks were occupied, yes; but only by packs and rifles. Armed only with machetes, the two bushmen now were — where? He did not even know when or which way they had gone. Fine sentinel, wasn't he, to let two full-grown men sneak away right under his nose? And if they could get out so slick, why couldn't somebody else — a murderous Red Bone, for instance — get in with equal facility?

Wherefore he became all the more alert. Instead of resuming his slow pace, he stood quiet at a corner, scrutinizing everything within his range of vision, listening more intently than ever. Two or three times he leaned forward and lifted his piece as some splashing noise in the creek came to him; but each time the cannibal guards on the other bank also sprang to see what caused the sound, then grunted to one another and relaxed, so he knew it was made by piscatory or reptilian life. Near him nothing moved. And the moon sailed on westward, smoothly, steadily measuring off the silent hours of the night watch.

Then all at once every nerve in him strained toward the back of the *tambo*. Something was there! He had not heard it — seen it — smelled it — but he felt it; a nameless thing that did not belong there. With smooth speed he pivoted, looked, listened. Nothing there.

Motionless, feeling slightly creepy, concealed under the roof corner, he waited. A sound came — a stealthy sound. Something was creeping in. Lourenço and Pedro, perhaps? Stooping low, he peered along the ground under the hammocks.

A man was coming — coming on all-fours like an animal. He was too stealthy to be either of the Brazilians. Knowlton glimpsed him only dimly, but he was sure this was no man who belonged here. And now, as on a previous occasion almost identical in its circumstances, the watchman acted in accordance with Tim Ryan's General Order Number Thirteen.

In three jumps he was upon the invader. His gun butt crashed down on the rising head. The other collapsed on the ground.

Swiftly Knowlton snapped a match with his thumb-nail. The sudden flare half blinded him, but what he saw made him suck in his breath. When the match went out he turned the senseless body over, drew his pocket flashlight, stabbed its white ray downward. Then he committed the unpardonable sin of the army — he dropped his rifle.

Dark haired, dark bearded, streaked with red dye and bleeding slightly at the nose, at his feet lay the man for whom the indomitable trio had traveled thousands of miles and dared all the deaths of the jungle — the Raposa.

XXI

SHADOWS OF THE NIGHT

"Rod! Wake up!"

The tense whisper aroused McKay instantly. With one sweep of the arm his net was torn aside and he leaped out with pistol drawn.

"Right, Merry. What is it?"

"We've got him! Look!"

The electric ray again streaked the gloom. The astounded captain did not drop his gun, but he came near it. For a long minute he stood as in a trance. When he attempted to holster his weapon he fumbled three times for the sheath before he found it.

"Whew!" he breathed. "Have you killed him?"

"Nope — don't think so. Lord! I hope not! Now that I think of it, I did give him a mighty solid smash. Used the butt. He was crawling in here, and naturally I didn't stop to ask for his card. Feel his head."

McKay complied. His exploring fingers found only a huge bump under the thick hair.

"No, his skull's whole. Didn't even split the scalp. You crowned him hard, but unless he got concussion he's still useful. His nosebleed comes from hitting the ground, I think. Turn off the light. Are you still on guard?"

"Yes. The Brazilians are out."

"Take a turn and see that all's clear. Can't tell what might break any minute now. Leave your flash here."

Passing the flat, nickel light-box to the captain, Knowlton retrieved his gun from the ground and resumed his patrol. Slight as the disturbance had been, uneasiness was in the air. The savages on the far shore were up, peering at the *tambo* and muttering to one another. Measuring the distance, the lieutenant saw that, though they had undoubtedly seen the flashlight switched on and off and made out the movements of men, they could not have discerned what lay on the ground beyond the hammocks. Nearer at hand, Tucu and a couple of the Mayorunas were awake and looking out. But the sight of the sentinel strolling up and down in apparent unconcern and the absence of light in the *tambo* gradually quieted the suspicions on both sides of the water. Soon the Red Bones squatted again and the Mayorunas lay back with minds at ease.

Then a dim sheen of light showed for a time at the back of the white men's shelter, fading out after a few minutes into the usual gloom. McKay had pulled a blanket over himself and the unconscious man, masking his torch glare from any watching eye while he studied the face and form of the invader. After the faint radiance vanished certain sounds came to the sentry's ears. Then McKay's tall figure loomed in the vague moonshine. Knowlton stopped beside him.

"It's Rand," the captain vouchsafed in an undertone. "No question of it. Features identical, though face is drawn. White hair mark, broken nose, green eyes. I opened one eye. Got a bad foot, partly healed; looks as if he'd torn it on a stub. Poor devil seems nearly starved."

"So? Then that's why he sneaked in like that — wanted to steal some grub. Those mutts over yonder probably haven't fed him since he got hurt."

"That's it. He's had to do his own foraging, and his foot has given him mighty little chance. Damn those brutes!"

"Right! But now what? Look out that he doesn't sneak away again."

"He won't. I tied his feet. He's in Pedro's hammock, still dead to the world. If he wakes up and starts to yell I'll gag him. We've got to get away now as soon as we can."

"How?"

"Don't know. By water, perhaps. Wish those bushman were here. Haven't heard any noise over there, have you?"

"All quiet. They're safe — or dead."

"Hm! Confounded foolishness, anyway. But we've no means of getting out until they're back. Couldn't desert them, besides. What time is it?"

"Ten-thirty. You go on watch at midnight."

"I'm on watch now, inside. They may be back any time. If they don't show up in the next couple of hours I'll send Tucu to find out why. We'll have to get those canoes over here, too. Water leaves no trail."

He turned back into the hut, leaving Knowlton figuring chances. To obtain those canoes was a man-sized job. To put the Red Bone guards out of action without arousing the whole tribe was an even bigger job. But no boats could be brought over until the outpost was silenced, that was sure.

Another half-hour crept past. Still no noise from the town, no suspicious move on the other shore. Then from the *tambo* itself came a low mumble of voices. Knowlton stepped swiftly into it. As noiselessly as they had gone the two bushmen had returned.

In his usual concise phrases McKay was informing them of the capture of the Raposa. With his back to the stream and the flashlight held close to his body, he played the light for an instant on the face of the still unconscious man. Then, once more in darkness, he asserted:

"Now that we have him, we must get out of here. Only chance to do that is to get the canoes. With them we can at least be away from this town by sunrise, and it will take the Red Bones just so much longer to find our trail where we take to the bush. We'll get a flying start that way. Anything else to suggest?"

"That is the best plan, Capitao," Lourenço agreed. For the first time since the Americans had known him his voice held a note of suppressed excitement. "It is the only plan worth while. And I do not think we shall have to take to our legs soon — if at all. I believe this creek connects with that which flows past the Monitaya *malocas*. We have learned some things. *Por Deus!* If only we had known the Raposa was here!"

"Why?"

"Because then we could have brought company with us. Senhores, guess what the barred house holds."

"Well?"

"Women of the Mayorunas! Girls stolen from Monitaya and other settlements!"

"Jumping Judas!" ejaculated Knowlton. "Are you sure?"

"Sure, comrades! These foul Red Bones are the men who have been lurking around the Mayoruna tribe houses and capturing girls who went into the bush. They have taken the prisoners to the water, where the trails always were lost and where they could find hiding places until night, then drive their canoes past the clearings and get out of that country. So there must be some water connection by which these men travel, and by which we too can travel. If we go downstream we are almost sure to find it by daylight."

"But why — what's the idea of their stealing the girls? For victims? If so, how are the girls still alive?"

"Do you not see, senhor?" Pedro broke in, impatiently. "Did not Umanuh ask if we would pay more than the other Blackbeard for the Raposa? What other Blackbeard?"

"Schwandorf!" the Americans blurted, simultaneously.

"Not so loud! Schwandorf, of course! Umanuh works with the German. He catches girls by stealth and sells them to the German to add to his slave gangs. While the Mayorunas all blame the Peruvians for the disappearances, Umanuh works unsuspected. He is holding these women until Schwandorf comes again — and it may be that Schwandorf is not far off at this moment. Now that we have come seeking the wild man, Umanuh at once thinks of selling him also; and he wonders whether we or Schwandorf will pay the more for him."

"By thunder! I believe you're right!" Knowlton coincided. "He's stalling for time, holding us here while Schwandorf comes up, I'll bet. No wonder he and his men are wary of the Mayorunas — they thought we'd come to snoop around and catch 'em with the goods. You fellows must have done a mighty slick job to find out this stuff without getting caught. Isn't the house guarded at night?"

"Indeed it is! Two clubmen are there now, and there is only the one door. Not even a window. But Lourenço worked a small hole between two logs at the back while I watched the clubmen, and through the hole he whispered with one of the women inside. If only we had known the wild man was here we could have jumped the guards and tried to bring back the women. But of course your business about the Raposa had to be thought of first, so all we could do was to tell them friends were here."

For a few seconds there was the silence of thought. Then Knowlton chuckled.

"I'll say we have our hands full this night. Now we not only have to get ourselves and Rand out of here, but also rescue the fair damsels from the clutches of the ogre. 'Twon't do to leave them here while we go back to Monitaya and get the rest of his army. By the time we could come back they'd be gone — one way or another. What's done has to be done now or never."

"Right!" McKay commended. "We'll have to save the women, of course. Question is — how?"

Lourenço answered at once.

"My idea, Capitao, is this: We two will return. With us we will take Tucu. The three of us can handle those guards quietly. We must have Tucu, because the women do not know us and might balk at the last moment. Women are queer creatures, and these might think themselves safer inside prison walls than following two strange men through the night; but Tucu can handle them. When once we are clear of the houses Tucu can lead the women to the bank above here, and we shall try for the canoes. Then it will be fast work to get away, but if we have good fortune it can be done."

"Confound it! You fellows are taking all the risks! Can't you take more men —"

"No. No man but Tucu. He has a cool head. These others, if they knew, would go blood-mad and attack the Red Bones to avenge their lost women, and so would get us all killed. Now I will talk with Tucu."

He slipped into the Mayoruna shelter and returned with the cannibal leader, whom he led to the far side of the *tambo* before speaking. Then, in whispers which the other tribesmen could not overhear, he explained the situation. Knowlton took another turn or two along his post, finding that the Red Bones across the water were stirring about and evidently aware that something was going on; but they made no move either to get into a canoe or to send a man to the houses beyond. As he stopped again at the corner near the whispering pair he heard Tucu grinding his teeth, and as the savage turned his face toward the Red Bone outpost it was a mask of murder. But he spoke no word as he slipped back to his own men.

"He will wake another man and tell him what to do," Lourenço explained. "But only we four shall know of the women until they are freed. Will one of you lend Tucu a machete? He may need a weapon, and he cannot carry his big bow on this trip."

A few minutes later the three crept out behind the *tambo*, Tucu gripping McKay's machete. As a final word Lourenço said: "Our men here may move about a little after a time, but do not try to keep them quiet. It is a part of the plan."

With that he was gone. Listen as they might, the Americans could hear no sound to indicate that three men now were traversing the black tangle beyond.

McKay took up his rifle and assumed the sentry work. Knowlton sat in his hammock, grateful for the chance to rest his weary legs. From the hammock where the Raposa lay no sound came. With a worried frown the lieutenant leaned over him and laid hand on his heart. After a while he sat up again in relief.

"Lord! I sure knocked him cold!" was his thought. "But he's still with us, and there's no use in reviving him now; the less noise over here the better. Hope I didn't jar his brains loose altogether; he might wake up a murderous maniac. Poor devil! A millionaire, yet half starved and more than half nutty."

He glanced at the dim scene before the hut. The moon now had journeyed so far westward that the creeping shadows of the tall trees had moved out almost to the creek, and the two crude shelters and the sentinel were surrounded by dense gloom. The Red Bone men opposite must rely on their ears alone hereafter, for they could not see through this darkness. McKay was visible enough to his own party, but not to the enemy. The blond man in the hammock watched the somber figure of his comrade, followed the flight of a big firefly whose light floated near, thought of the two bushmen out in the dark, and looked again at the still form of Rand.

"Drifters all," he soliloquized. "The fireflies and Rod and Tim and I and those Brazilian dare-devils — all floating around because we can't keep still, and never getting anywhere. And you, you silly-ass Rand, have a mint waiting for you up home, and we have to come find you and lead you up there and shove your nose into it. And if you get your brains back you'll be a nine days' wonder and a hero of the jungle and all that, and the girls will all tumble over you — because you've got a couple of millions in your sock. And we fellows who yanked you out of hell by the left hind leg can pocket our pay and go jump off the dock, for all anybody cares. Ho-hum! All the same, I'd rather be me than you, old thing. Free to drift and able to handle myself. You can have the money and the moths that hang around it."

With which he yawned, squinted again at the sinister figure squatting out yonder in the moonshine, arose, and made himself useful. Working very quietly, he took down three of the hammocks, rolled them up, laid them at the corner nearest the creek; made up the packs by sense of touch and placed them and the rifles of the absent pair in the same place. Then he lifted the Raposa from the one remaining hammock, laid him on the packs, rolled up the hammock itself, and put it under the unconscious man's head. If given time when the crisis came, he meant to save all equipment. If not, Rand lay where he could be grabbed without delay.

Before he completed the work he became aware that the Mayorunas all were awake. Not only awake, but moving stealthily about, as Lourenço had predicted. McKay also knew it and stepped back into the hut, where Knowlton told him what he had done. But so softly did the men of Monitaya move that the Red Bone watchers showed no sign of alarm. Both the Americans observed, however, that the cannibals across the stream had their heads together and that occasionally one looked up at the little moon.

"Get that, Rod? They're waiting for the shadows to crawl over there and cover them and the water. They know that then we can't see what they're up to. I'm betting they intend to pull some dirty work after that."

"Yep. But intention and accomplishment are two different birds. Wonder what these Mayorunas are fixing to do. Wish I could talk their language."

"Tucu evidently left orders for them to get up at a certain time, but why I don't know. We'd better let them alone."

The shadow line passed out upon the water, slipping by infinitesimal gradations across its mirror surface. The Mayorunas had become quiet. The whites waited in silent suspense for they knew not what. Far out in the forest a jaguar gave his coughing roar at intervals. Little by little the Red Bone men arose from their squat until they stood erect. A tense stillness held both forces. And the shadows crawled on — on — and reached the farther bank.

Then a Red Bone man shoved his head forward, squinting upstream as if he had heard something move in the rank grass. He began to sneak softly in that direction. At that moment, from the water's edge a little above the camp, sounded a loud hiss.

Before the sound died a sudden thrum of bow cords filled the air. A whisper of five-foot shafts speeding over the water — a rapid-fire series of tiny impacts — a couple of short groans — the thumps of falling bodies — and the Red Bone outpost was no more. Shot through and through by the deadly war arrows of the Mayorunas, they were dead before they struck the ground. And from the men of Monitaya sounded one short, subdued "Hah!" of savage satisfaction.

Up from the ground where that hiss had sounded rose a tall figure which waved its arms and danced about in impromptu signals. Then it ran for the canoes. Out from the gloom upstream other figures took shape, running fast for the same point. With one simultaneous movement Knowlton and McKay seized the Raposa and rushed with him to the stream.

"Senhores!" sounded Pedro's voice, low but tense, across the water. "Be ready!"

"Ready and waiting!" snapped McKay. "Who are those people. Your women?"

"*Si*. We are not discovered —"

Across his words smote a long shrill yell from the town.

"*Por Deus*. We *are* discovered! Get our rifles, for the love of *Deus Padre*."

He leaped into a canoe, drove it headlong across, and dived for the *tambo*. Behind him the other figures dashed panting up to the landing. Tucu's voice rasped in swift commands. The fugitives swarmed into other dugouts. The Mayoruna men, still ignorant of the identity of these people, but assured by Tucu's voice and manner that they were not enemies, lowered their weapons and rushed for the water. Up in the town the yelling swiftly grew into a roar, and running figures came pelting toward the creek.

The canoes struck the bank. Some were partly filled, some empty and in tow. Into Pedro's canoe the whites bundled the Raposa, while the Mayorunas got into anything within reach. Lourenço appeared from nowhere and urged the Americans to open fire. As he spoke, arrows thudded into the ground and the water.

"Take this man and go!" rasped McKay. "We're losing our equipment, but —"

His rifle leaped to his shoulder. Flame spat from it. From the van of the charging Red Bones shrilled a death scream.

Again and again the captain's gun cracked. Knowlton's joined in. Before their rifles grew silent the blunt roar of Pedro's repeater broke out. And with the emptying of their long guns the Americans drew their short ones, and in a concerted ripping crash the forty-fives volleyed death and dismay into the oncoming cannibals.

The rush was checked. For a few seconds the Red Bones wavered and milled about. Into their mass poured a cloud of arrows and blowgun darts from the silent but no less deadly weapons of the Mayorunas. As the whites paused to reload, Pedro opened a new blast from Lourenço's rifle, which his comrade had passed to him on the run. Lourenço was not shooting, but working madly and alone to save the equipment. And, thanks to the renewed deadly fire of the guns, he saved it.

Before the wicked belch of the three rifles and the two automatics the Red Bones gave back more and more. Their arrows plunged all around the fighting men, but they fell at random, for the gunmen and the canoes were virtually invisible in the deep shadows. Downstream, Tucu's harsh voice jarred in commands as he straightened out the line of boats.

At the next lull in the firing Lourenço panted: "In, comrades! We are loaded. In!"

"Great guns! Are you still here?" snapped McKay. "I told you —"

"In! Talk later. Come!"

The three gun fighters swiftly obeyed. With a powerful heave Lourenço sent the canoe after the others. Americans, Brazilians, and the Raposa hunched up among the packs, all went sliding down a jungle Styx.

A moment later the Red Bone warriors, taking heart from the cessation of firing, poured an avalanche of arrows into the spot where they had been. And as the canoe, last in the escaping line, was swallowed up in the impenetrable blackness of the forest a hair-raising screech of diabolical fury blended with a swift succession of splashes back where the cannibals were plunging headlong into the stream to reach the dead or wounded men whom they vainly hoped to find on the farther shore.

"I told you to take this man and go!" McKay fumed. "By disobeying orders you risked losing him."

"Oh, pipe down, Rod!" remonstrated Knowlton. "If they had, where'd we be now? This was the last canoe."

"*Si.* It is so," added Lourenço, his voice hard edged. "As it is, the man and the equipment and you also are here. And let me tell you this, Capitao Makkay, whether you like it or not: Pedro and I would see this wild man and a million others like him in a hotter place than this before we would abandon fighting comrades."

To which McKay, finding no adequate answer, made none whatever.

XXII

THE SIREN OF WAR

Like a fleet manned by sightless sailors the line of boats blundered on through the blackness. With no guiding light, the canoes bumped the banks and collided with one another in perilous confusion. Speed was impossible, yet speed was imperative. Knowlton and his little flashlight solved the problem.

"Say, fellows, let's take the lead," he suggested. "This little light isn't much, but it's something, and there are some extra batteries in my haversack when this burns out. We can see a little way ahead, and pass back the word to the rest. What say?"

"*Na terra dos cegos quem tem um olho e rei* — in blindman's land he who has one eye is king," said Pedro. "That little white eye in your box may save us all. Lourenço, tell those ahead to let us pass."

Without question the preceding dugouts swerved, and the boat of the white men slipped by. At the head of the line they found Tucu and his crew struggling manfully to make progress without wrecking the whole fleet at the turns. Vast relief and instant acceptance of the new leadership followed Lourenço's explanation. At once the floating column began to pick up speed. And it was well that it did.

Howls of baffled hate came faintly through the tree mass from the Red Bone town. Some time later more yells of rage sounded, much nearer — back at a place on the creek which the last boat had cleared only a few minutes previously. Some of the Umanuh men had made torches and run along one of the Red Bone trails to a bend in the stream, only to find the water bare of everything but dying ripples.

Whether the enemy attempted to follow in canoes the escaping party never knew, for none succeeded in overtaking the rearmost boat. And after that one snarling uproar on the creek bank they heard no more of the land pursuit. The narrow margin of safety gained by the aid of the flashlight proved enough to give a commanding lead, and from that time on the only obstacles to their retreat were those of darkness and winding waters.

Hour after hour Knowlton squatted in the extreme bow, picking out the turns and snags just ahead and passing the word back to Lourenço, who, in the stern, steered in accordance with his orders and relayed the course to Tucu, just behind. Amidships, Pedro and McKay plied steady paddles and the Raposa lay all but forgotten on the baggage. There were no halts. If any boat back in the blackness got into difficulties it extricated itself as best it could, unaided by the rest, and fell into a new place in the column.

At last a wan light, which was scarcely a light, but rather a lessening of the density, came about the stream. The renewed racket of birds and beasts announced that up overhead the sky had paled into dawn. Slowly the nearest tree trunks began to take shape in the void, and presently the shore line became visible to all eyes. At the same time Knowlton's tiny lamp dimmed and faded out.

"Another battery gone," he announced, opening the case and dropping its contents into the creek. "Ho-yo-ho-hum! Gee! I'm all in! Eyes feel like a couple of burnt holes. Well, gents, I move that at the first available spot we go ashore, feed our faces, look at the ladies, and perform our morning salute to Umanuh — said salute consisting of applying the right thumb to the end of the nose and snappily twiddling four fingers."

"Motion carried." McKay's set face relaxed. Then, his glance dropping to the Raposa, it tightened again. "Oh, hullo, Rand! How you feeling?"

The unconscious man was unconscious no longer. Moreover, his expression was not that of one just emerging from a stupor and bewildered as to his surroundings. Though he had made no movement to change his position, his eyes indicated that he had been awake for some time. They dwelt steadily on McKay, then strayed past the captain to Pedro, Lourenço, and the first Mayoruna crew following a few feet behind. His face was inscrutable, and he spoke no word.

"You're with friends. Understand? Friends. You're going home. These Indians are friends, too. Get that? *Friends!*"

The green eyes hung on McKay's face again; but, as before, no answer came in word, movement, or expression.

"No good, Rod," said Knowlton, who could not see the rescued man's face, but watched McKay's. "'Fraid I knocked his last brains down his throat. Dead from the neck up."

"I don't know about that. He doesn't look vacant. See here, Rand. We're going to land and eat! You hungry? Uh-huh. Thought you'd understand that. He's alive, Merry. Maybe not all here, but enough to get us."

"Good!"

The blond man turned his attention downstream again. Soon he suggested, "How about landing at that little open space down there at the left, Lourenço?"

"Very good, senhor. It looks dry."

The canoe swerved and floated down to a spot on the left shore where bright light poured down from an opening in the overhead wall of foliage.

"Now look here, Rand," warned the captain. "We'll untie you. But if you try to duck into the bush, now or later, you get shot. Shot! Understand?"

He tapped his pistol, and the gray eyes boring into the green ones were hard as chilled steel. For the first time Rand responded — a slow, short nod.

McKay cut the cord around the wild man's ankles, then stepped ashore and held out a hand. Rand arose quietly, jumped to the earth unassisted, lifted his bad foot and stared at it, then limped onward into a spot where the sun now shone bright and warm, and sat down to bask.

"Have to fix that foot, I expect," yawned Knowlton. "But my eyes right now are one solid ache, and I'm going to rest them. Watch him, will you, Rod? Can't tell what he might do. Of course you wouldn't shoot him, but —"

"Wouldn't I? Not to kill, no. But if he makes one break I'll drill a leg for him. He's going to the States!"

"Sure. I'm with you all the way. Now beat it and let me repose myself."

He bathed his eyes, then lay down in the canoe with a wet handkerchief across them. Pedro and Lourenço already were ashore and raiding the slender packs for food. The Mayorunas were debarking and watching each new boat as it drew up, their eyes on the women who had wielded paddles with them but whose faces they now saw closely for the first time. In the shaft of sunlight McKay stood tall and forbidding, rifle in the crook of one arm, hat pulled low, guarding the gaunt man at his feet and viewing the landing of the expedition.

The women, all young, numbered eleven. Their skins looked slightly pallid, their eyes too big and black, their faces somewhat drawn — the results of close confinement and anxiety; but none showed any sign of abuse. For commercial reasons alone, Umanuh had seen to it that the woman flesh he held for sale should remain uninjured. Now, saved from the slave trail or worse, the girls showed no more emotion than if on a mere journey after turtles or fish. A few spoke to men whom they evidently knew. Others gathered in a dumb cluster and awaited whatever might come next. With these Tucu talked in gruff monosyllables.

When all were ashore, a dozen of the men went into the jungle to hunt. The others sought firewood, inspected weapons, talked with one another and with the girls, who stared at McKay and asked who he was. A number of the warriors looked sourly at Rand, whose face still bore the Red Bone tribal streaks which now, to Mayoruna minds, was the insignia of the enemy. All knew he was the man who had been sought, all saw that he was not a Red Bone, but a white man; yet their mental reaction to the sight of the sinister red cross on the forehead and the straight cheek lines was rabidly hostile. McKay, all-seeing, decided to wash Rand's face for him before journeying much farther. But Rand himself gave no sign that he either knew or cared what the feeling of the Mayorunas might be. Utterly impassive, he stared back at them.

Then one of the women pointed at him and said something to Tucu. The tall watchdog's jaw set a little harder as he waited the effect. Somewhat to his surprise, Tucu and a couple of the other men now gave Rand a more friendly look. Soon afterward Tucu passed Lourenço, who talked with him a few minutes. Catching the Brazilian's eye, the captain motioned him nearer and asked for any news.

"Tucu says, Capitao, that most of these girls are from *malocas* other than that of Monitaya, though some of Monitaya's women also are here. And one of them says this man, the Raposa, tried to release them a short time ago and was nearly killed by the Red Bones for it. They let him live only because he is crazy, and they fear to kill a crazy man."

"What! He tried to get them clear?"

"Yes. He opened the door and motioned for them to run, but before they could escape they were caught. He was badly beaten. You will remember that he was hiding behind that same house when Pedro and Senhor Knowlton saw him. Perhaps he meant to try again."

"Hm! Crazy and wild, but a white man for all that. How did you manage to free the women?"

"Very simple," was the cool answer. "We stabbed the guards, opened the door, and came back to the creek with the women."

"Just like that, eh? And the guards made no resistance, I suppose."

"Not much," grinned the bushman. "They were not allowed to."

"I see. Very simple, as you say. About as simple as our calm and unhurried departure."

"Something like that, Capitao. What do you desire for breakfast — salt fish and coffee, or coffee and salt fish?"

"A little of everything, thanks. Here comes some monkey meat, too."

The first of the hunters had returned, bringing two big red howlers. Others drifted in at intervals, and not one returned empty handed; for here in the virgin jungle the game was plentiful, particularly at this early hour. Soon the air was heavy with the odor of broiling meat, and from the fire of the Brazilians the fragrance of coffee was wafted to the nostrils of the recumbent Knowlton. He arose, swallowing fast.

"Gee! I'm half drowned!" was his humorous complaint. "The smell of eats makes my mouth water so fast I have to gasp for air. Must tickle your nose, too, eh, Rand, old top?"

Rand, famished though he was, gave no sign of assent or of hunger. In fact, he gave no sign of anything. Stoically he sat, eyes front.

"By thunder! the man's got pride!" the lieutenant added, in a lower tone. "Almost ready to keel over from lack of food, but stiff as a cigar-store Indian. Darned if I'm not beginning to respect him!"

Tucu approached, carrying two big monkey haunches. One he offered to McKay, the other to Rand. The latter's immobility vanished in a flash. With a lightning grab he seized the proffered meat and sank his teeth in it. As he wolfed down the tough flesh the three men standing over exchanged glances. Tucu laid a hand on his stomach and pressed inward, signifying that the man had long gone hungry. The others nodded. Then they split the other haunch between them and fell to gnawing.

Lourenço, bringing coffee to the captain, asked Tucu in what direction the Monitaya houses lay. Without hesitation the Indian pointed off to the left. The Brazilian glanced at the creek, estimating its general direction and rate of flow, then returned to his fire.

Offered coffee, Rand took it and sipped it with evident relish. Likewise he accepted a cigarette, which he puffed like a man just learning to smoke — or one who has not smoked for years. For his meat, his drink, and his smoke he gave no indication of gratitude. His attitude was as indifferent and matter-of-fact as if he were one of the Mayorunas. When his smoke was ended he began inspecting his bad foot.

"Let's see that," said Knowlton, dropping on one knee. "Looks pretty sore. Yes, it's more than sore; it's infected. How'd you get it, anyway?"

No answer. Knowlton probed his face keenly. Rand straightened out his legs, wriggled his toes, and scowled.

"Queer!" muttered the lieutenant, rising. "He looks as if he actually didn't know how he got that wound. You'd think he'd remember that much, anyhow. I sure am afraid his head is all scrambled up."

He went to the canoe, returned with his meager medical kit, and knelt again.

"Now listen here, Rand. I don't know how well you understand me, but I'm taking the chance. This foot has to be opened up and cleaned out. Otherwise you're going to have serious trouble with it. I'm going to hurt you. If you raise a row you'll get an anæsthetic — a swift punch under the ear. Better sit still and make no fuss."

With which he went to work. He did a thorough job, and there was no doubt that it hurt. But Rand gave no trouble, nor even a sign of pain — except that he dug his fingers into the dirt.

"Good boy!" the amateur surgeon approved, when he finished. "You're a Spartan — if you happen to remember what that is. Now we'll move on. But before we go, wash your face good and hard. Get that tribe paint off. These Indians with us don't like it. You're no Indian, anyhow; you're white, like us. Savvy? White man. Wash off paint!"

He rolled up his kit and returned to the canoe. The Mayorunas, men and women, were entering their own craft. Rand sat motionless a moment, McKay and the Brazilians watching him keenly. Slowly then he got up of his own accord, limped to the water's edge, and began to scrub his face.

When he desisted the marks still showed, for the red dye clung stubbornly to his skin; but they were fainter than before. The other men eyed him thoughtfully, none speaking. He settled himself in his former place, curled up, and began to doze.

"A queer fish!" Pedro said, softly. "Is he crazy or not?"

"Hanged if I know," replied McKay. "He's no maniac, anyhow. I'd give real money to know just what his mental condition is. But we can forget him for a while. I'm going to let you fellows sleep by turns now. I had some sleep last night; you've had none at all. Merry, your eyes need rest. You curl up in the bow and snooze one hour. Then another man, and so on. And how about letting Tucu lead the parade again?"

"Excellent, Capitao! I was thinking of that." Lourenço talked to Tucu, who swung out into the current. The boat of the white men followed, then the others. At a steady cruising speed the brigade surged on downstream.

Knowlton's allotted hour passed. Pedro took his place and was instantly asleep. In turn he was aroused, and Lourenço laid down his paddle. But just then Tucu's canoe slowed and floated in to the left bank.

The others backed water and looked at a very narrow ravine — almost a cleft — in a rising hillside. Through it led a lane of water. From the third boat, in which were two women of the Monitaya tribe, now came voices carrying information to the Indian leader. At once he turned his boat into the cleft.

"This is the connection we have been seeking." Lourenço explained. "The women say the boats of their captors came through this crack in the hill. At the end we shall find the creek of Monitaya."

The women spoke truth. After threading their way along the weedy water-path, which was barely wide enough to give passage for the boats, they emerged at a slant into another stream. Down this, with the sure instinct for direction of the hereditary jungle-dweller, Tucu turned his prow without asking the women whether to go with or against the current. Once more on the waters of their home creek, the Mayorunas quickened their strokes and howled merrily on toward their *malocas*.

Lourenço took his nap and resumed his place. Hour after hour the fleet sped on. Noon passed without a halt, the paddlers munching at whatever fragments remained from breakfast. By turns the Americans and Brazilians each got another hour's sleep, McKay consenting to relax when all his mates had rested. Rand dozed and awoke at intervals, seeming content and comfortable despite his cramped position.

By four o'clock even the Mayorunas began to lag in their strokes. Excluding the halt at sunrise, they now had been journeying for fifteen hours, in the last nine of which they had covered many miles of serpentine water. The heat of the day and the constant drive of the paddles had taken their toll, and now the body of every man fiercely demanded more food. McKay, knowing that in jungle travel distance is not a matter of miles, but of hours, had begun to figure that the journey which had taken nearly five days of overland work might be completed that night by the swiftly moving canoes. But now, recognizing the signs of exhaustion, he realized that without some powerful spur the Indians would not attempt to reach the home *malocas* until the morrow.

Then the spur came. Even as Tucu began scanning the shores for a good camp site, he and every other Mayoruna suddenly ceased paddling and threw up his head. Faint and far, a xylophonic call of beaten wooden bars rapped across the jungle, rising and falling in swift, regular cadence — a sirenical flow and ebb of sound waves. Over and over it undulated, rapid, incessant, imperative.

A chorus of excited grunts broke from the canoe brigade. The dugout of Tucu leaped away like a roweled horse. Lourenço and Pedro buried their paddles in mighty strokes, hurling their boat ahead to keep from being run down by those behind.

Lourenço barked at Tucu, who flung back an answer.

"Paddle hard, Capitao! If we do not keep up we shall be wrecked. That message is the war call of the Mayorunas — calling in the hunters from the forest to take arms against an enemy. We must race now with these madmen around us, or we go under. Paddle!"

XXIII

STRATEGY

In the last light of the fast-fading day the canoes darted from the forest into the clearing where stood the Monitaya *malocas*.

Long before their arrival the siren call had ceased, but there had been no lessening of speed by the racing dugouts. On the contrary, the last long mile had been covered in a final desperate spurt, the paddles swinging in swift unison to the accompaniment of a ferocious chant of one syllable: "Hough! Hough! Hough!" This explosive cadence had echoed down the stream ahead of them; and now, as the panting crews emerged from the jungle, they found themselves flanked by a long line of their fellow-warriors, bristling with drawn arrows and ready spear points. But of the enemy whose presence that great xylophone had betokened there was no sign.

At sight of the familiar feather bonnets of their own men the tense Monitayans let their weapons slowly sink. And when Tucu, leaping ashore, gaspingly demanded news of the fight, the line dissolved into a mob which rushed to welcome him and his mates. In the first few breaths it was learned that no fight had yet taken place, but that all the warriors had been brought in and ordered to prepare to march at the next sunrise; and that the sudden war call had been sent out as the result of the arrival of a stranger.

Then the crowd parted, and through it came striding two men whose appearance caused the white men to erupt into hoarse shouts of greeting. One, whose hard face swiftly relaxed into a half smile of relief, was the great chief himself. The other, whose jutting jaw suddenly dropped and whose blue eyes opened in incredulity, was Tim — Tim, once more strong and florid and aggressive, gripping his rifle, astounded at the sight of his comrades standing there alive and alert. They soon learned why.

Dropping his gun, he sprang at them with an inarticulate roar of welcome. He wrung their hands, pounded their shoulders, laughed, cried, swore, all at once. Then he burst out:

"Glory be! Ye're alive, homelier 'n ever and tough as tripe! We thought ye was wiped out sure! We was all set to start in the mornin' and pull them Red Bones to pieces. Mebbe we'll do it yet, too. How'd ye break through? Did ye kill Sworn-off and his gang?"

"Schwandorf? Gang? Haven't seen anybody but Red Bones — though we sure saw plenty of them," replied Knowlton. "What are you talking about?"

"Then ye missed him by about one point windage. When'd ye leave? Last night? I bet he's there by now. Gee! Where'd ye git them girls? And who's this guy? Great gosh! Is he the Raposy? Wal, for the love o' Mike —"

"Tim!" broke in McKay. "What's all this about? Now wait. This is the Raposa. These girls are Mayoruna women held prisoners by the Red Bones. We got them last night and lit out in the middle of a general engagement. Now open up with your news."

"Right, Cap. We got a visitor today — old friend of ourn — li'l' old Hozy, the only white guy in that Peruvian crew we had. He's all dolled up like an Injun — shaved face, tribe paint, and so on. He come through the Injun country that way — I dunno yet how he done it, him bein' a Peruvian and all, but he got through, and he says Sworn-off and a whole gang of bad eggs is back here to git this Raposy guy and all the girls they can lay hands on. He says Sworn-off's got them Red Bones workin' for him, and you fellers must be massacreed sure by now.

"Good thing I was here when he come, or he'd be cut up and in the stewpot. Monitaya's a good skate, but he sure is poison to anything Peruvian, and soon as Hozy begun to try to talk he got wise and dang near bumped him off. I got him to cool down some, and he believes Hozy's tellin' the truth, but even at that they got Hozy tied up like a dog. Come look at him."

But it was necessary to wait awhile for Tucu and Lourenço to tell Monitaya the tale of what had taken place; for the chief demanded immediate and full details, and not until he had them would he return to his *maloca* and his hammock throne. By that time the little moon was again ruler of the sky and the keen hunger of the voyagers had grown ravenous.

Followed by the rescued and the rescuers, he then stalked into the tribal house and to his usual place, where he commanded that food be brought.

On the ground, directly in front of the chief's hammock, sat a gaunt, painted Indian around whose neck was a stout noose, the other end of the cord being held by a muscular savage whose skull-smashing club was gripped loosely in his other fist. As the whites reached them the noosed man's face cracked in a grin.

"Greetings, señores," said the voice of José. "You will pardon me for remaining seated, yes? The man behind me is itching for an excuse to crush my head."

"José!" exclaimed both Knowlton and McKay. Though Tim had said José was "tied like a dog," they had not thought to find the expression literal truth. The sight angered them and they turned to Lourenço.

"Tell Monitaya we want this man freed!" McKay snapped. At his peremptory tone the cannibal chieftain looked oddly at him, and when Lourenço translated the demand — though in a more diplomatic manner — he scowled. But he gave the clubman the word and the rope was lifted from the prisoner's neck.

"*Gracias, amigos*," he bowed. "If I still remain seated, it is because I am very weary — and I have not eaten since yesterday."

His thin face and his projecting ribs not only corroborated his simple announcement, but indicated that for more than one day his food and rest had been almost *nil*. Naked, painted, minus his fierce mustache and flamboyant headkerchief, he appeared a far different man than the domineering *puntero* of a short time back. But his bold black eyes, his reckless grin, and his mocking tone proved him the same swashbuckling José, undaunted by hunger, exhaustion, or his position as prisoner of man eaters whose enmity was implacable.

"Well, you're going to eat now, or we'll know why not!" vowed Knowlton. "We understand that you brought a warning to Monitaya. Is this his way of treating men who risk their lives to befriend him?"

José shrugged.

"Once an enemy, always an enemy. That is their rule. And do not think that I traveled the bush and threw myself into this snake heap from love of Monitaya. I do not care if he and all his race are blown to hell. I am here because, as I once told you, José Martinez never forgets. Thank you, señor, I will eat now and talk later."

Deftly he extracted a chunk of meat from a clay pot which had been placed before Knowlton and in turn tendered to him. Monitaya watched him eat, but gave no sign of disapproval; and the Americans, and even the Brazilians, made an aggressive show of friendship toward the lone Peruvian for the express benefit of the chief. They knew well that by their rescue of the Mayoruna women they had made their own position among these people virtually impregnable, and that their recognition of José as a friend probably would be his only bulwark. Wherefore they left no doubt in the minds of the watchers as to where he stood in their regard.

Monitaya, sitting in regal dignity, looked down upon two parties of seven feasting with famished speed — the rescued women who were not members of his own tribe, and the four Americans, two Brazilians, and one Peruvian. All the others had scattered — Tucu and his band to their own family triangles, and the four Monitaya girls to become the nuclei of feminine groups which demanded intimate accounts of their capture and treatment by the captors.

To the strange women at his feet the chief paid scant attention now, though he meant to interrogate them after their hunger was satisfied. His eyes dwelt on Rand, the strange combination of white man, Indian, and jungle demon of whom he had heard so much and on whose tanned skin the red skeleton streaks told the tale of a "mind out of the skull." José and Tim stared in frank curiosity at the dead-alive newcomer, whose silent composure remained totally unperturbed. But the seven new girls, though ignored by the chief and his guests, were by no means neglected by the other men of the *maloca*, being thoroughly stared at by most of the young bucks — and, it must be confessed, by a goodly proportion of the married men also.

When at length the meal was finished Monitaya commanded the girls to stand before him and narrate their experiences. The men lit smokes, José seizing the proffered cigarette with avidity, Rand accepting his with the usual odd deliberation.

"Wal, Hozy, old feller, ye're in right with the chief now," asserted Tim. "Ye got all our gang with ye, and she's some li'l' old gang, I'll tell the world. This feller Renzo can talk cannibal so good he makes Monitaya hunt for the dictionary, and he'll tell the chief in ten seconds what I tried half an hour to say this afternoon — that ye belong. I ain't been here long enough to learn much o' their lingo, ye understand. If I could spout it like French, now, there wouldn't been no trouble."

McKay and Knowlton snickered. They knew Tim's French was several degrees worse than the usual American doughboy's "frog" talk.

"Good thing you couldn't," derided Knowlton. "You'd have had José crucified before we got here."

"That's right, gimme the razz! Course, I did have a li'l' trouble makin' some o' them frogs understand, but that was because they was so ignorant they didn't know their own language when they heard it spoke right. Anyways, ye got to admit Hozy's still with us and sassy as ever, and he wouldn't been if Timmy Ryan hadn't been round to powwow for him."

"You have it right, señor," José agreed, gravely. "Without you I should now be dead. I can speak the Mayoruna tongue quite well, but of what use is it to talk any language when men will not listen? It was you and your gun that saved me."

"Gun? Good Lord! Did you pull a gun on Monitaya?" ejaculated the lieutenant.

"Aw, no. That is — I guess mebbe I did wave me piece around while I was arguin' — I can always convince a guy better if I got somethin' in me hand. But I didn't git real rough."

"You are lucky to be still alive, Senhor Tim," said Lourenço. "If Monitaya were not the man he is you would not be alive. I am glad we have returned."

"Meanin' I need a guardeen? Say, lookit here now —"

"As you were!" clipped McKay. "We're all wasting time. José, let's hear your report. I thought you were going to put Schwandorf out of action for good?"

"And I am, Capitan! That is why I now am here. If I had reached him immediately after leaving the Nunes place it would have been done at once. But a man travels slowly when he is alone and has lost much blood, and before I met Schwandorf again I had time to think coolly. Then when I saw him I changed my plans.

"Some days down the river I met him traveling fast in a canoe paddled by hard men whom I know. He pretended to be greatly grieved when I told him you all were dead. Oh yes, señores, I told him that! I was play-ing with him, and it amused me to see how he thought he was deceiving me when I was really fooling him. I said we were attacked by Indians a short way above the Nunes place and that I alone escaped. Then he said something that made me decide not to kill him for a time.

"He told me he had learned that this man here — his name is Rand, yes? — that the man Rand was a bank thief who had run away from North America, and that a reward would be paid for him. He said your real reason for coming here was that you were detectives trying to earn the reward. That is false, is it not, señores?"

"We're no detectives. Rand's no thief."

"Ah, so I thought. But Schwandorf often tells truth to conceal his lies, so that it is sometimes hard to know which is true and which untrue. He went on to say he had warned you not to come into this Indian country, and he was sorry you had been killed — the snake — but since you were dead we might get the money for ourselves. If we succeeded in catching the man Rand and taking him out alive I should get half the reward, or five hundred dollars.

"I saw plainly what his plan was. I might be useful to him in catching Rand if Rand was out in the bush, for I have traveled this country alone more than once and am a far better bushman than the German. But whether I got Rand or not, I never should live to demand my part of the money. I know too much about Schwandorf — things which I shall not tell now. So when the right time should come, José would meet with a fatal accident, such as a bullet in the back, or a knife in the throat while sleeping. But I did not let him know I saw this. I pretended to fall in with his plan like the fool he thought me to be.

"It was not Rand alone that brought him here. You have brought back Mayoruna women from the Red Bone country, so you know the Red Bones are women stealers. And they steal for Schwandorf. You may believe me or not, señores, but I did not know this until the German told me. Oh yes, I knew he dealt in women, but of the Red Bone part of his business I was ignorant. As soon as I learned it I saw how I could put the illustrious Señor Schwandorf out of action, as you say, and at the same time try to save you.

"I sharpened my knife to a razor edge, deserted the German when we reached the right place, shaved with my knife, painted myself with the red and black plant dyes, and came overland to this place, thinking you would be here if still alive. But you had traveled faster than I expected and had gone into the Red Bone country, so my chance to save you seemed to have passed. I could only try to tell this chief the Red Bones were stealers of his women and that the German was with them, knowing that if he believed me he would go on the war trail against them and kill them all. But if Señor Tim had not befriended me I should have died too soon to tell my tale. That is all, señores. Now can you spare a little more tobacco?"

They could and they promptly did. With a new cigarette glowing he lay back and looked quizzically at the women lined up before Monitaya.

"How many men has Schwandorf?" asked McKay.

"About twenty in all, Capitan. There were eight in his crew, and they were to meet a dozen more at a place on the Peruvian side."

"All riflemen?"

"*Si*. He brought many cartridges for them. They are to raid tribe houses of these people."

"Capture women and run them into Peru?"

"*Si*." José yawned as if speaking of a deal in salt fish.

The Americans looked thoughtfully around the big house. They saw that every man near them was inspecting some kind of weapon — making sure that bow cords were unfrayed, that arrow heads and spear points were firm, that the long blowguns had received no cast from suspension, and that darts were absolutely straight and true. The strong but cruel faces of the warriors were stamped with malignant hatred of the Red Bone tribe and the Blackbeard who enslaved their women. The command to prepare for a march at dawn had not been withdrawn.

"We'll be expected to go, too, and I'd sure like another crack at Umanuh, not to mention the Schwandorf outfit," said Knowlton, "but we have friend Rand on our hands now, and our first duty is to get him out of here safely."

"Aw, Looey, have a heart! I ain't had no action since that li'l' scrap down the river, and I got to have some excitement before we blow. What's more, we can't beat it now, with Monitaya dependin' on us to fight on his side. He'd git sore, and I don't blame him."

His superior officers and the Brazilians frowned. Every man of them itched to close with the enemy in one final decisive battle. Yet —

"What'll we do with Rand?" Knowlton voiced the general thought.

The green eyes of the Raposa turned to him, rested long on his, traveled deliberately along the other faces. And then, to the utter astonishment of all, the dumb spoke.

"I'll fight," said Rand.

Speechless, the men around him stared. His face was inscrutable as ever, his eyes fathomless, his voice flat and toneless. But slowly he raised his hands as if holding a bow; twitched his right thumb and forefinger in the motion of loosing a shaft; let the hands sink. His gaze calmly lifted from theirs and dwelt on the farthest wall. Not another word did he speak.

"Begorry! there's yer answer!" triumphed Tim. "He says, 'Fight!' And I bet he can sling a wicked bow and arrer, at that. Don't ye s'pose he wants a crack at them Red Bones, after the way they used him?"

"I think, comrades, that the man has settled the matter for us," Pedro seconded. "None of us wants to run away; and, as Tim says, we are expected to help Monitaya. We should be considered cowards, worse than dogs, if we refused. If we do not fight the Red Bones we may have to fight these Mayorunas, who now are our friends. We must stay."

McKay nodded, still studying the expressionless countenance of Rand.

"That's settled," he announced, crisply. "Now, Lourenço, find out Monitaya's plan of battle."

The chief had finished his examination of the women and Lourenço promptly put the question. Monitaya laconically replied.

"His purpose is not changed by our arrival, Capitao. He and his men go tomorrow to attack and destroy the Red Bones. When they reach the town of Umanuh they will surround it, and all will rush in when the chief gives his yell of war."

"About what I expected. An Indian has a single-track mind always. But his strategy is rotten. Might be good enough if he had only Umanuh to deal with, but with Schwandorf in the game it's different. Ask him how he expects to protect his women while he's gone."

"He says," Lourenço reported, "that there will be no danger to the women, because his warriors will be between the women and their enemies until those enemies are dead."

"Very simple. So simple that it's foolish. He doesn't figure on the other fellow's mind at all; doesn't realize that a man like Schwandorf is bound to outguess him on such straightaway tactics and isn't at all likely to play into his hands. But that's the exact situation. The German will outguess him, and it's up to him to outguess the German in turn. We'll do his guessing for him.

"Schwandorf goes into Umanuh's town, learns what's happened, finds the Red Bones frothing at the mouth, and is sore himself. He figures that we've returned here with the women, that Monitaya's men are blood-mad against the Red Bones, and that they'll do just what they are planning to do — march on Red Bone town and leave their women unprotected except by the old men, whose defensive power is negligible. He is in this country for the express purpose of getting girls, and with Monitaya's men away from their *malocas* he has a wide-open chance to make the biggest slave haul of his life. So he plans to outmaneuver Monitaya, attack this place, capture all the young women, allow the Red Bones to massacre everyone else and burn the houses, and then move on without the loss of a man. After that perhaps he intends to find us and get Rand, or perhaps to attack other Mayoruna *malocas*. At any rate, his first objective is this place. Am I right so far?"

"Dead right," Knowlton nodded.

"Very well. Now he may figure that, having found the water connection between the two creeks, the Mayorunas will come against Umanuh by the canoe route. Or he may think they'll make the overland trip. In either case, the Red Bones have to come through the bush, for the simple reason that they haven't boats enough to carry all their force. Their canoes were rather few when we were there, and we commandeered several of them for our own use. If they decide to come part of the way in canoes they'll have to work a come-and-go transport service, bringing the fighting men down in batches to some rendezvous from which they must finish the journey on foot. Chances are that they'll disregard the canoes and all march overland by some route that would dodge the Mayoruna line of march. But in either case they're coming here. And it's here, in the place where he's not expected to be, that Monitaya should meet them. Let him fortify himself and await the assault. It will come."

"And we shall be saved many weary miles of leg work," José smiled. "Capitan, your strategy is magnificent."

"Begorry! it ain't so bad at that!" Tim approved. "Hozy, me and you will have our hammicks slung out front here when the show starts and do our shootin' prone. Suits me fine. Put it up to the chief, Renzo."

Lourenço did. Very carefully he explained it all to Monitaya, dwelling on the fact that McKay himself was a warrior chieftain and familiar with the fighting methods of such men as the atrocious Blackbeard, and depicting graphically the horror of an attack by the barbarous Red Bones on the defenseless women. It took him some time to divert the chief's stubborn mind from the original plan, but in the end he succeeded.

To the vast astonishment and disappointment of the vengeful warriors, Monitaya curtly announced that the projected march would not take place. They stared as if disbelieving their ears, and more than one black look was given Lourenço. But not a man questioned the countermanding of orders, not a mutter was heard. The great chief had spoken, and his word was final.

Reluctantly they laid aside the weapons on which they had been toiling with such purposeful zeal. The chief watched them with a little smile of pride — pride in their zest for war, pride in their unquestioning acceptance of his dampening order. Then he coolly told them to continue their work; told them, further, that the next morning all the streams were to be poisoned, new traps set, and scouts stationed far out on every trail to await and report the approach of foes. Instantly their faces flamed again and from every quarter of the wide house rose an excited hum. They were to fight, after all!

"Tough eggs, these lads, if ye ask me," yawned Tim. "Bet ye we'll see a row worth lookin' at when she does break."

He forebore to mention the fact that in rifle power their assailants would outnumber them four to one.

XXIV

THE BATTLE OF THE TRIBES

The next four days, though they were days of waiting, were busy enough to satisfy the most impatient Mayoruna warrior.

Outposts were established on every route by which the attacking force would be likely to approach the twin *malocas*, the watchmen being given the strictest commands not to fight, nor even to allow themselves to be seen, but to run at top speed with the warning.

Poison detachments went forth to collect the ingredients for making deadly the water and the weapons. Those detailed to the work of polluting the streams gathered quantities of blue-blossomed, short-podded plants with yellow roots, the roots being pulped and thrown into the slow currents, which straightway became fatal to man or beast The wurali squad procured their favorite materials and, in a flimsy shed well away from the houses, prepared a plentiful supply of the venomed brew.

New traps were set at points where a man or two might be picked off, though it was realized that these would have little effect on the final result. And inside the big houses men especially skilled in the manufacture of arrows and darts toiled swiftly and steadily from dawn till far into the night.

These activities, however, were only the usual defensive preparations made by the warriors whenever they knew a sizable body of foes was somewhere in the vicinity. It remained for the brains of the white men to devise additional features, simple enough in themselves, but astounding to the savages, who were accustomed only to the primitive battle tactics of their ancestors. For the first time in their lives the cannibals found themselves digging in — and also digging out.

After a survey of the terrain and a catechism of Lourenço and Monitaya as to the usual methods of attack and defense, the two officers broached an idea born of the exigencies of the situation. As they expected, the great chief was somewhat slow to approve it, for it involved a literal undermining of the walls of his fortresses. But despite the natural inflexibility of his mental processes he was an unusually intelligent savage, and eventually the patient reiteration of the advantages of the scheme won him first to assent and then almost to enthusiasm. Wherefore the amazed tribesmen were set to work, armed with crude wooden shovels, in digging holes under the logs which sheltered them from man, beast, and jungle demon.

All along the walls, at intervals marked by McKay and Knowlton, the tunnels were dug. At the same time another large gang excavated before each of the *malocas* a deep, curving trench, the two long pits being separated by a ten-foot space of solid earth affording free passage from the houses to the creek. Meanwhile the women and the older children were weaving flimsy covers from withes and vines. As soon as a tunnel was completed it was masked outside the walls by one of these covers, on which a thin layer of earth and grass was laid. The two trenches were likewise concealed, and the loose earth was carried inside the house and packed solidly against the walls flanking the doors.

At sundown of the fourth day the work was ended. And so well was it done that when the great chief, his subchiefs, and his foreign allies went on a final tour of inspection they could find no sign that the houses were honeycombed with exits or that the ground in front of the little entrances was not solid at all points.

"Rod and I took the idea from those pit traps out on the trails," Knowlton explained for the dozenth time. "Holes are covered to look exactly like the rest of the ground. Every man of us has to be inside when the enemy arrives, but we have to get out quick when the right time comes, so we go under the walls. And can't you see those brave women stealers go kerplunk down into the trenches? Oh boy!"

Whereat Lourenço and José smiled as if enjoying a secret joke. They were. For they knew something of which the Americans were not aware — that Monitaya had improved on the trench-trap idea of the whites by studding the bottom of those trenches with barbed araya bones smeared with wurali.

"Yeah, and I figger them guys'll git some jolt when these houses, which ain't got nobody in 'em but women and kids, begin to spit lead out o' loopholes and spew screechin' cannibals up out o' the ground. Gosh! I wouldn't miss seein' Sworn-off's face for a keg o' beer — and that's sayin' somethin'."

Wherein Tim expressed the general sentiment.

So ended the fourth day. When the fifth broke no man showed himself outside the walls. Except the few outposts, every male of the Monitaya *malocas* bided within, awaiting with growing tension the arrival of the enemy. It was more than likely, McKay had pointed out, that the main body of the barbarous force led by Schwandorf would be preceded by a handful of scouts, and quite possible that one or more of these would slip past the outguards and spy on the tribal houses. The sight of even one warrior would instantly apprise any such spy that the others must be near, and the word would go back at all speed to the Red Bones. Wherefore the only Monitayans to pass through the tiny doorways that morning were a few young women sent out as bait. These, naturally, took good care to stay near the entrances.

Within, the men waited at their appointed places. Each tunnel had its quota of warriors, the number being divided evenly to assure a speedy and simultaneous exit. The Americans had elected to fight from the *maloca* of the great chief, while the Brazilians and José were to garrison the doorway of the other house as soon as the warning came. Rand, wordless and imperturbable as ever, now was armed with a strong bow and plenty of new arrows with unpoisoned heads; and he, of course, would remain with his own countrymen. Thus, preparations completed, all settled themselves to the interminable hours of waiting.

Up on the heaped earth near the doorway, which made the walls practically bullet-proof to a height of six feet and thus would protect the women and children, one or more of the Americans was constantly on the lookout through some inconspicuous loophole. Hour after hour dragged past, and no unusual movement or sound came to reward their vigilance. Under the glare of the sun the roof and walls grew hot; under the silent strain of endless anticipation the impatience of the fighting men became a ferment. At length Pedro, unable to keep still, mounted to a peephole near Knowlton. Scarcely had he put his eye to the opening when both men sucked in their breath.

At the edge of the bush a man's head peered from behind a tree. And at the same moment a single canoe came creeping out of the bush and up to the landing place. The head behind the tree was that of a Red Bone spy. The two in the small canoe were Yuara and a companion from the Suba tribe.

"Lourenço!" hoarsely whispered Pedro. "Yuara comes. Tell girls to run to welcome him and guide him between the pits. A spy is watching. If Yuara walks on the pits he dies and our trap is revealed. *Por amor de Deus*, send girls quickly!"

Lourenço acted instantly. Seizing two young women, he propelled them doorward, talking swiftly the while. Yuara and his mate were already advancing innocently toward the few girls outside, none of whom had wit enough to warn him. But the two whom the Brazilian had grasped happened to be of quick intelligence, and now they darted out. Before the visiting pair could reach the death trap the girls were upon them, laughing as if delighted to see a man once more, and deftly turning them aside to the point where two unobtrusive stubs marked the bridge of safety.

Vastly astonished by such effusive welcome from two girls whom they did not know, but by no means displeased thereby, the young warriors of the Suba clan were piloted to the door and inside. As they disappeared, the head of the spy also vanished.

"Woof!" muttered Knowlton, wiping sweat from his brow. "That was close! Here's hoping we have no more visitors."

Yuara and his companion meanwhile were being interrogated by both Lourenço and Monitaya, who in turn enlightened them as to the present state of affairs. At the promise of war the faces of the Suba men lit up.

"Yuara comes only on a visit to learn news," Lourenço told the rest. "You remember that the day after our return a canoe was sent downstream to a point where the wooden bars could be beaten and heard by

Suba's men, and that a warning against the Red Bones and Schwandorf was given in that way. Yuara has become anxious to know more, so he is here."

"If he sticks around he'll learn a lot," predicted Tim.

With no waste of words or motion Yuara coolly attached himself and his fellow-tribesman to McKay. Monitaya and his subchiefs were informed of the arrival and departure of the enemy scout. The word passed among the warriors, who, despite their innate equanimity, began to grit their pointed teeth and quiver like dogs held in leash. But another hour passed, and yet another; and still no word from the outposts arrived.

Suddenly a chorus of screams shrilled from the women outside. In a frenzy of fear they plunged through the doorways. Blending with their outcries, a hoarse yell of ferocity rose raucously from the direction of the creek. At once a louder ululation burst forth at the rear and sides of the clearing. Monitaya's outguards had failed and the *malocas* were surrounded.

Loping from the bush fringing the stream came a score of yellow-faced, shirtless, barefooted brutes crisscrossed with cartridge belts and gripping rifles. At their head loomed a burly black-whiskered creature with a revolver in each hand — the malignant Schwandorf himself.

Grinning like a pack of yellow-fanged wolves, they doubled toward the low entrances, their guns spouting wantonly at the upper walls — a ragged volley meant to terrorize the defenseless women within, none of whom were to be killed until the handsomest had been cut out and set aside for slavery. Some of the heavy bullets bored through between logs and thudded wickedly into rafters and roof poles within. But from the loopholes where the defending rifles lurked no shot cracked in reply.

The fiendish howling of the Red Bones, sweeping in from all sides to the butchery, swelled into a feline screech that almost drowned the roar of the rifles. Into the view of the watchers at the loopholes streamed hideous faces and naked brown bodies swerving inward from left and right to follow at the heels of the Blackbeard and his gunmen. In a few seconds more the trotting line of Peruvians was backed and flanked by a horde of demons hungering for the taste of women and babes. On they came —

With the suddenness of a cataclysm the ground opened. Riflemen vanished in midstride. Savages screaming triumphant hate were gone in the flick of an eye. Others, instinctively digging their heels into the ground the instant those ahead of them disappeared, were hurled forward and down by the momentum of the following mass. Before the rush could be checked the trenches were packed with men struggling in frenzy to get out, wounding themselves and one another with the deadly points of their poisoned weapons.

Of the twenty gunmen only four remained. They were the four immediately behind Schwandorf. By blind chance the German had set foot on the narrow isthmus separating the twin trenches, saving himself and the henchmen at his heels from being engulfed. Now, as the Red Bones fought back from the trap yawning before them, he and the surviving Peruvians stood staring in momentary stupefaction at the welter of death on their flanks. The malevolent yells of the savages had been cut short by the catastrophe, and for the moment no sound was heard but the grunts and snarls of struggling men.

Then into the semisilence burst a mighty voice — the battlefield voice of McKay.

"Now! Fire at will!"

The walls spat flame and lead. A scythe of death swept above the ground where stood Schwandorf and his riflemen. The Peruvian half-breeds collapsed and lay still. But Schwandorf, shocked into activity by the impact of that first word, dodged death by an infinitesimal fraction of a second. Hurling himself backward, he struck the earth just as the bullets sped through the air over him. With a lightning rebound he was up while fresh cartridges were jumping into the rifle barrels menacing him. Headlong he dived into the mass of Red Bones just behind. And the next bullets darting after him killed the savages, leaving him unharmed.

The command of McKay and the crack of the rifles sent the quivering Mayorunas into the fight. In a flash every masking tunnel cover was thrown bodily into the air. Before the thunderstruck Red Bones had recovered from the shock of finding their gun-armed leaders annihilated and their mass being swept by swift-shooting rifles hidden in the walls, they beheld a horde of vindictive foes erupting from under those walls like warrior ants rushing from subterranean galleries. A blood-chilling yell of concentrated fury smote their ears; a hastily loosed storm of war arrows and short throwing-spears ripped into their flesh; a swift-running arc of light-skinned men swerved around them, shooting and stabbing as they went. They, who had so exultantly surrounded the homes of women and children, now were surrounded in turn.

From the doorway of Monitaya's *maloca* the two Brazilians and José now leaped forth and, firing as they ran, dashed to hold the entrance of the other big house. A few arrows whirred around them during their transit, but the shafts were shot hurriedly and missed. Meanwhile the three bushmen were striking down enemies at every flash of their guns, firing with the swift surety of veterans of many a running fight. They reached their objective unwounded; and when they reached it a fringe of dead foes marked their passage along the face of the hostile array. Once within the door, they rapidly reloaded and sprayed lead along the trenches, which, though now nearly full, had become a dead-line past which no Red Bone sought to go.

Up on the earth embankments within the chief's house the four Americans fought steadily on; the soldiers shooting as coolly as if engaged merely in rapid-fire target practice, the silent Rand methodically driving arrows in swift succession from his wall-slit. Arrows thudded thickly into the logs masking them. Bullets, too, slammed into their rampart — bullets from the heavy revolvers of Schwandorf, who, ever keeping himself protected by the bodies of his cannibal allies, shot with both hands as the chance came. And the German could shoot. With only the small gun muzzles as targets, he planted bullets so close as to knock dirt more than once into the eyes of the riflemen and render them momentarily useless. After a time he got a bullet fair into a loophole.

Knowlton grunted suddenly, swayed back, toppled, fell down the parapet. For a few seconds he lay still.

"Looey!" howled Tim. "How ye fixed? Hurt bad?"

The lieutenant heaved himself into a sitting position, stared around, clapped a hand to his right shoulder, looked at the red smear his palm brought away, reeled up, and scrambled back to his rifle. Schwandorf's bullet had drilled clear through the shoulder, and in falling his head had struck one of the upright poles. Without a word he got his gun into action once more, shooting now from the left shoulder. Tim, with a tight grin of relief, devoted himself once more to trying to shoot down the dodging German.

The encircling Mayorunas, their first paroxysm of fury vented, now settled in cold hate to their work. On all sides their clubmen and spearmen were bludgeoning and stabbing at the close-packed Red Bones, leaping in, killing, springing back and onward with terrible efficiency. Beyond these a thin but deadly line of bowmen poured arrows in high-looping curves over the heads of the hand-to-hand combatants, the shafts whizzing far up, turning, and plunging down unerringly into the center of the enemy force. Each of those arrows could, and many did, end the lives of two or three adversaries by gouging their skins and letting the fearful wurali into their blood. The blowgun men too were darting into every opening, handling their clumsy weapons like feathers and constantly moving to spy out fresh targets.

But the men of Monitaya were by no means escaping unscathed. The Red Bones, assailed from every quarter and milling about in hopeless disorder, were fighting now with desperate frenzy. Their own clubbers and stabbers were charging out and smashing skulls or piercing abdomens, their arrows rose in all directions at once, and some into whose veins the wurali had struck sprang in the last moments of life on nearby foes and bit like mad dogs. With a leader and a chance to form into any sort of flying wedge they might have broken through with comparative ease and taken a far heavier toll. But they had no leader: for Umanuh, whose name meant "corpse," now was a corpse in truth, his merciless brain oozing from a skull shattered by a Mayoruna clubman; and Schwandorf was very busy looking out for Schwandorf. So it was every man for himself, with the devil rapidly taking not only the hindmost, but the foremost as well.

Thicker and thicker fell the dead. The trenches now not only were filled to the level of the ground, but piled with a windrow of bullet-torn bodies knocked down by the ever-spitting rifles. José, Pedro, and Lourenço abandoned all shelter and knelt in plain sight before the door which they had kept clear of all close attack. Monitaya, until now a field general who strode up and down roaring commands and encouragement, suddenly cast away his regal role and, seizing a club from one of his bodyguard, hurled himself on the nearest Red Bones — a raving, ravening demon of destructiveness whose glaring eyes smote terror into those fronting him and whose weapon swung like the club of Hercules. His bowmen and blowgun men, at last out of missiles, came charging in with bare hands or weapons seized from fallen warriors. Maneuvering had ended. Henceforth the fight was a grappling mêlée.

Then the gunfire dwindled and died. The rifle cartridges were spent.

XXV

THE PASSING OF SCHWANDORF

The three soldiers flung down their hot, empty guns.

"Nothin' left but the gats and the steel," rumbled Tim. "Me, I'm goin' out and git some fresh air."

With which he drew pistol and machete, leaped down, and lunged through the door. McKay bounded at his heels.

"Merry! Rand! Stay here!" he commanded. Then he was outside, his pistol roaring in unison with Tim's.

Knowlton and Rand looked at each other. The lieutenant fumbled his pistol from its holster, got it firmly in his left hand, slid down the embankment, and staggered out. Rand coolly walked over to Tim's discarded gun, picked it up, and followed.

Over at the other doorway the bushmen threw aside their useless guns and drew their machetes. José, grinning like a death's-head, whirled the bush knife aloft and mockingly dared the Red Bones still fronting him to come and take it from him. Pedro and Lourenço indulged in no such bravado, but leaped like jaguars at their foes. Whereupon José, muttering a curse on them for getting the jump on him, dashed forward with furious abandon.

Their pistols emptied, the Americans also drew machetes — all except Rand, who had no weapon but the bulletless rifle — and waited. Few unwounded Red Bones now were left; but among those few Schwandorf still lived.

"Schwandorf!" bellowed McKay. "You yellow cur — you *Schweinhund*! Come and fight!"

"Yeah!" taunted Tim. "The women and kids are inside. Come and git 'em!"

Schwandorf came. He came not because he wanted to, however, for his guns, too, were empty. He came because the Red Bones, sensing the challenge and loathing the Blackbeard who had shielded himself so long among them, threw him out bodily. They had no time to stand and watch what might happen to him, but they took time to cast him out where he must stand on his own legs. Then, snarling, they resumed their now hopeless battle against their encompassing executioners.

For a moment the German stood glowering at McKay. Then, with a dramatic gesture, he threw aside his useless revolvers and advanced empty handed.

"Man to man?" he growled.

"Man to man!" echoed McKay, passing his pistol to Tim and sheathing his machete. Fists clenched, he sprang forward.

Schwandorf halted. His hands remained empty — until the captain was within eight feet of him. Then he leaped back, his machete jumped into his fist, and its point stabbed for his antagonist's abdomen.

An instantaneous side-step and twist of the body saved the captain from evisceration. The blade ripped through breeches and shirt and scraped the skin. As Schwandorf yanked it back for another thrust McKay struck it away with one hand and, without drawing his own steel, jumped again at his assailant. An instant later the two blackbeards were clenched in a death grapple.

Schwandorf found his long knife useless and dropped it. He strove for a back-breaking hold, but found it blocked. McKay, though an indifferent swordsman, was a formidable wrestler and fist fighter, and the German's advantage in weight was more than offset by the American's quickness and wiry strength. Science was thrown to the winds. A heaving, choking, wrenching man-fight it was, stumbling over bodies, each straining every muscle, trying every hold to twist and break the other and batter him down to death.

Smashing fist blows brought blood dripping from their faces. Bone-wringing grips forced gasps from their lungs and superhuman spasms of resistance from their outraged nerve centers. They fell across a corpse, rolled on the ground, throttled, kicked, struck, and tore. Finally, in a furious outburst of energy, the American fought his enemy down under him, clamped his body with iron knees, and crashed a terrific punch squarely between the German's glaring eyes. Schwandorf went limp.

At that instant a backward eddy of the battle surged over the pair. The maniacal Red Bones, fighting to the last bitter drop of doom, found two white men under their feet. Screeching, snarling, they fell on them like wild beasts, tearing with tooth and nail. Their arrows were gone, their darts exhausted, and no spearman was among them; they fought with nature's weapons, while above them one lone clubman struggled to swing down his lethal bludgeon without killing his fellows.

McKay, wrenching his machete loose and gripping it with both hands, got its point upward and jabbed blindly at the weight of flesh bearing him down. Faintly to his ears came yells of rage and the impact of blows — the battle roars of Tim and Knowlton, who with their machetes were cleaving a way to their captain. But the beastly demons over him still crushed him down on Schwandorf, smothering him under the burden of bodies dead and alive. His stabs grew weak. Exhaustion and lack of air were killing him more surely than the savages.

Pedro, Lourenço, José and the inexplicable Rand came slashing and clubbing a path of their own to the beleaguered Scot — the Brazilians cutting straight ahead with deadly surety, the painted Peruvian chopping and thrusting with a fixed grin, Rand swinging the gun butt down on head after head. From still another direction Yuara and his satellite came boring in with spears snatched from dead hands. The three rescue parties reached the squirming heap at almost the same moment. But Yuara was the one whose arrival counted most.

In one last convulsive struggle McKay heaved himself up until he was once more on his knees. His head came out of the welter, his mouth wide and gulping for breath. The lone clubman grunted, swung his weapon high, and with all the power of his muscular body drove it down at that upturned, unprotected face.

With a mighty plunge Yuara threw himself over the captain. His spear sank into the stomach of the clubman. But the heavy wooden war hammer fell with crushing force. As the Red Bone collapsed with the spear head buried in his middle, his slayer also dropped under that terrible stroke with head mangled beyond recognition.

Yuara, son of Rana, warrior of Suba, who owed his life to McKay's rough surgery, had paid his debt.

Under the impact of his body McKay also slumped forward, senseless.

Over them now burst the bloodiest berserk battle of that bloody day. The soldiers, the bushmen, and the reclaimed Raposa, already smeared from head to foot with red stains from their own veins and those of foemen, went stark mad. Before their united ferocity the men of Umanuh dropped as if rolled under by an inexorable machine of war. Backward they reeled, striving now to escape the red wall of cold steel surging at them — only to fall under a fresh attack of ravening Mayorunas who came pouring in upon them from the sides. The last of the group lurched headless to the ground under a decapitating side-swing from the awful club of Monitaya himself.

Then Knowlton, his lifeblood still draining slowly but surely away through his wounded shoulder, pitched on his face and was still.

"Back!" gasped Tim. "Git looey and cap out o' this! Here, you Raposy! Lend a hand!"

The Raposa, his green eyes ablaze and his obdurate calmness totally gone, glared around as if seeking one more Red Bone to kill. Then, as Tim heaved the lieutenant across his shoulders and went lunging across contorted bodies toward the *malocas*, he ran back to the heap where McKay lay and dug him clear. Lourenço aided him in lifting the captain, and they bore him off after Knowlton.

Pedro and José shoved the other bodies aside until they uncovered the prone figure of Schwandorf — a ghastly form dyed from hair to heels with the blood of the cannibals whom he had led there. To all appearances he was dead. Yet the Brazilian and the Peruvian looked keenly at him, then at each other.

"There is a saying, is there not, that the devil takes care of his own?" grinned José. "It would be sad if this man should yet live and escape. See! What is that tall Red Bone doing over yonder?"

Pedro followed his pointing finger. He saw no such Red Bone as José had mentioned. But when he looked back at Schwandorf he noticed something that made him glance quickly at José once more.

"Ah yes, Señor Schwandorf is truly dead," the Peruvian added, wiping his machete carelessly on one bare leg. "Whether or not the devil takes care of his own, as I was saying, there is no doubt that *el Aleman* now is with the devil. So, since we can do nothing for him, let us look after the two North American señores."

Pedro, with a grim smile, turned with him toward the tribal houses. There was nothing else for them to do, for the Mayorunas now were dispatching the last survivors of the attacking force. Before the pair entered the low doorway a long, triumphant yell burst from the hoarse throats of the men of Monitaya. Of all the Red Bones who had swept in such ghoulish glee into that clearing not one now remained alive.

At that shout of victory and the entrance of the men to whose precautions and prowess they owed so much, the women flocked again into the center of the *maloca* and the children dived out through the tunnels to behold the battlefield. Though bullets and arrows had come through the doorway, those inside had escaped all injury by hugging the protective earth embankment or taking refuge in the vacant shafts under the walls. Now the older women, experienced in treatment of wounds, busied themselves with the white warriors, while the younger ones fetched water and pieces of isca — a natural styptic made by ants — or made up pads of poultices of healing herbs.

Tim, who had expected to play surgeon with his crude knowledge of first aid, found himself not only relieved of his job, but being bathed and plastered with the others. He, José, Pedro, Lourenço, and even Rand were gashed by thrusts from broken spear hafts, bleeding from open bites, ripped by glancing sweeps of tooth-set clubs, bruised by fierce blows — minor injuries all, but such as might easily have resulted in blood poisoning unless given prompt attention. Later on they were to be thankful for those ministrations, but now they tolerated them only because they could do nothing for the captain and the lieutenant.

McKay and Knowlton were under the direct and capable treatment of the wives of the great chief. Of the two McKay looked by far the worse, but actually was in much better condition. From the waist up he was clawed, bitten, and bruised so badly that he was a fearsome spectacle; his left arm was dislocated, three fingers of his right hand were broken, and his muscles were so wrenched that for a week afterward he moved like a cripple; but his present unconsciousness was largely due to exhaustion and partial asphyxiation. Knowlton, whose skin was comparatively unmarked, but whose veins had continued to pour vital fluid from his gaping bullet wound during his stubborn fight, now was badly weakened. But whatever could be done for him was being done, and the others could only stand by.

The women not engaged in caring for the fighting visitors soon found themselves busy with their own male relatives, who came stumbling in by themselves or were carried by others. The Red Bones, though finally annihilated, had made their mark in the Mayoruna tribe. At that moment thirty-six of Monitaya's warriors lay dead among the bodies of their enemies, and before the next sunrise several more passed on to join the spirits of their comrades in arms. Yet all who survived, though some were crippled for life, thought only of the victory and gloated on their scars of combat. As for those who had fallen, they were dead, had died as Mayorunas should, and so needed no sympathy or regret. Even now their bodies were being collected for immediate transportation into the forest, where, in accordance with the tribal custom, they would be burned.

Some of the men who brought in the wounded men continued on to the bushmen and, in significant sign manual, requested a loan of their machetes. Having received them, they hastened out to join those who, equipped with hardwood knives, were gathering the sinister trophies of triumph before heaving the dead Red Bones out to the waiting vultures.

"Urrrgh!" growled Tim. "'Twas a lovely scrap, but I wisht I was somewheres else, now it's over. While ye was away they brought in the fists and feet o' some guy they caught in a trap —"

"We know," nodded Pedro.

"Yeah. Wal, I s'pose we got to look pleasant. Dog eat dog, as the feller says. Long as somebody has to git et, I'm glad it ain't us." Wherewith he turned to the Raposa and changed the subject. "Raposy, old sport, ye sure done some good work, for a crazy guy. I'll tell the world ye cracked heads like a Bowery cop full o' bootleg booze."

The Raposa's green eyes glimmered. In fact, they almost twinkled. And for the second time the wild man spoke.

"I am not crazy."

"Huh? My gosh! Ye spoke four whole words! That makes six in a week. Be careful, feller, or ye'll strain yerself. And as far's bein' crazy's concerned, don't let it worry ye none. We're all crazy, too, or we wouldn't be here."

Under cover of his banter the veteran eyed the other sharply. As he turned his gaze aside to the moving figures about him he thought: "Begorry! he don't look like a nut, at that. Mebbe somethin's unscrambled his brains again. Here's hopin', anyways."

The big tribe house now was full of life. Small groups of warriors, their hurts dressed with primitive poultices, gathered around the hammocks of those more seriously injured and discussed the battle. Others came in bearing armfuls of severed Red Bone hands and feet, which were distributed among the family triangles. The women, their remedial work done, now turned to the clay cooking vessels, freshened the fires, stripped the flesh of their enemies from the bones, and set it to boil. Among the hammocks moved the subchiefs, their eyes still shining with the light of battle, examining the wounded men and glancing at the preparations for the dire feast to come.

Over all drifted a steadily thickening smoke which rolled up and out through the vent in the peak of the roof, where the setting sun smote it with rays of gleaming red. Around the *maloca* gleamed the red light of the cooking fires among whose burning fagots bubbled the red pots and pans. Red men and women passing about in a crimson setting — the scene formed a fitting end to the reddest day in the unwritten records of the tribe, who since noon had proved themselves worthy champions of the ancient god whose name they never had heard, but who nevertheless ruled their lives — the red god Mars.

Monitaya himself, head high and chest swelling with pride, now came striding lithely in, followed by a young warrior carrying something. He stopped between the hammocks of McKay and Knowlton, studied their faces gravely, listened as his wives told of what had been done. At almost the same moment the eyes of the pair slowly opened and stared up at him.

The face of the great chief melted in one of its transforming smiles. The captain and the lieutenant grinned pluckily back. With a nod of silent comradeship the big savage turned to his own hammock and sat down. Two of his women built up the royal fire and fell to work on the things handed over by the young warrior. Tim and his mates took one squint at what they were doing. Then they moved between the fire and the two officers, blocking the view.

"'Bout time ye woke up and listened to the birdies," Tim chaffed. "Fight's over, and we been hangin' round waitin' for ye to quit snorin' so's we could hear ourselves think. Lay still, now! Ye're all plastered up nice and comfy — and don't preach to me no more about the girls. Ye had every dang one o' the big chief's wives hangin' over ye and kissin' ye so hard it sounded like a machine gun. Ain't that right, fellers? Me, I'm so jealous I could bite the both of ye."

"Schwandorf dead?" hoarsely queried McKay.

"Huh? Oh, him? Sure. Ye fixed him right, Cap. The pretty li'l' black-birds has flew away with him by now. Say, ye mind that feller Yuarry? Know what he done? Wal —"

And while he talked, behind his back the wives of Monitaya completed their task and dropped into the great chief's stewpot the flesh of the black-bearded slaver and slayer who would menace them no more.

XXVI

PARTNERS

Seven men squatted around a camp fire on the river bank. Beyond them, half revealed by the flickering light of the flames, rose the poles of a *tambo* wherein empty hammocks hung waiting. At the edge of the water lay two canoes.

Five of the men wore the habiliments of civilized beings, though their shirts and breeches were so tattered and stained that a civilized community would have looked askance at them. The other two were nude as savages, but their beards and tanned skins were those of white men. Beards of varying length seemed, in fact, to be the fashion, for everyone present wore one, and all but two were very dark. Of the odd pair, one's thin face was partly covered by stubby, blond hair, while the other's jaw was masked by a growth of unmistakable red.

Lifting their cigarettes, the blond man and a tall, eagle-faced comrade moved their arms stiffly, as if still hampered by injuries. Newly healed scars showed on the skins of the rest.

"Injuns are a funny lot," declared the red-haired one. "There's Monitaya, now. Keeps us a couple weeks, doctors us half to death, feeds us till we gag, gives us new canoes, sends a platoon o' hard guys with us to see that we git to the river safe — and don't even say good-by. No handshake, no 'Good luck, fellers' — jest a grin like we was goin' to walk round the house and come right back. And the lads that come out with us done the same — turned round and quit us without a word. I bet if we lived amongst 'em long we'd git to be dummies, too."

For a moment there was silence. For no apparent reason all glanced at one of the naked men, on whose skin faintly showed reddish streaks.

"You would," he said.

"Huh! Gee! Rand's talkin' again! First time since we licked them Red Boneheads. Two whole words. Go easy, feller, easy!"

"I will be easy. But it's time I talked. I am not dumb. I am not crazy."

The green-eyed man spoke slowly, as if forming each word in his mind before pronouncing it. The rest squatted with eyes riveted on his face.

"I have not talked before because I had to find myself. I had to hear English spoken and become used to it. I had to put things together in my mind. Even now some things are not clear. But I can talk and make sense of my talk. I will tell what I can remember. First tell me one thing. McKay, am I a murderer?"

"A murderer? You? If you are we never heard of it."

"A man named Schmidt. Gustav Schmidt. German merchant at Manaos."

"Gustav Schmidt? Piggy little runt, bald and fat, with a scar across his chin?"

"Yes."

"He's dead, but you didn't kill him. He was shot a little while ago by a young Brazilian for getting too intimate with the young fellow's wife. We heard about it while we were in Manaos, and saw his picture. What about him?"

"I thought I killed him. I struck him with a bottle. I was told he was dead. How long have I been here?"

"You left the States in 1915. It is now 1920."

"Five years? My God! What has happened in that time? Is my mother well?"

The others looked pityingly at him. Slowly Knowlton spoke.

"Your mother died two years ago from heart trouble. Your uncle, Philip Dawson, also is dead."

Rand's jaw set. The others shifted their gaze and busied themselves with making new cigarettes, spending much time over the simple task.

"Poor mother!" Rand said, huskily. "Uncle Phil — he was a good old scout. And I was here — buried alive — only half alive! My head — Tell me, what happened on the night before you dressed my lame foot? I remember clearly everything from the time I woke in the canoe before daylight that morning. Before that there is a blur."

Knowlton sketched the events of that night, and told also of the glimpse which he and Pedro had caught of the "wild man" while waiting outside the house of the Red Bone chief. A flash lit up Rand's face.

"So that is how I got my sore head. You struck me with your rifle butt. That explains much. Before I became a wild beast I was shot in the head. The bullet did not go through the skull. It struck me a terrible blow on the crown. When I recovered consciousness I was not myself. I have never been the same until —"

"Gee cripes!" exploded Tim. "That's it. I seen that same thing up home. Bug Sullivan, it was. When he was a li'l' feller he tumbled downstairs and hit his head, and for 'most ten years he was foolish. Then a brick fell off a buildin' and landed on his bean. It knocked him for a gool, but when he come out of it he was bright as a new dime. Looey, when ye busted Rand with yer gun ye jarred somethin' loose inside, and now he's good as any of us."

"By George! You're right!" cried the lieutenant. "Things like that do happen. I've heard of them. Haven't you, Rod?"

McKay nodded.

"That is it," affirmed the Raposa. "I have not been insane. But much was gone from me. My mind was a house full of closed doors which I could not open. I knew who I was and why I was here, but I knew also that something had happened to my brain; knew I was defective; believed I was wanted for murder. So I could not go out. I could only stay here, prowl the jungle, live the jungle life.

"Now that the closed doors have opened again, others have swung shut. I cannot remember much of my wild-beast life here. Some things are clear. Too clear. Torturings and horrible feasts. Perhaps I should be grateful that some things are forgotten.

"But now my life up to the time I was shot is plain again. I talked with a man who had traveled the Amazon and the Andes. I never had seen either, and I was ripe for something new. A steamer was just sailing south, and I got aboard in a hurry. No baggage but a suitcase and five thousand dollars. I had traveled a good deal — Europe, Canada, Japan — and always found that plenty of money was all a man needed. Thought it was the same way here. I've learned better.

"I visited Rio — a few hours — and then came up along the coast and inland. At Manaos I got into trouble. Went ashore and got to drinking with two Germans. One of them — Schmidt — grew ugly and said a lot of rotten things about the States. Tell me something, men — is the war over and did our country get into it?"

"It is, and it did." And Knowlton outlined the epochal occurrences of the world conflict.

"And I missed that, too!" mourned Rand. "But I started a war of my own down here, anyway. When I quit seeing red I had a bottle neck in my hand and both the Germans were down. Somebody said Schmidt was dead. A couple of men tried to grab me. I fought my way clear, hid awhile, got back on the boat without being noticed, and paid one of the crew well to hide me in the hold and feed me. Nearly died from heat and suffocation down there, but lived to reach Iquitos, where my man smuggled me ashore. I thought I was safe there. But before I could make a move to travel on I fell into the hands of that cursed Schwandorf."

"Schwandorf!"

"Schwandorf. He was in Iquitos. The sailor who hid me must have sold me out to him. Schwandorf told me he was a police officer in Brazilian employ. Said he would take me back to stand trial for murdering Schmidt. The dirty blackmailer took all my money to keep his mouth shut and take me to a 'safe place.' The safe place was up this river. I came up here with him in a canoe paddled by some tough Peruvians. Then he began trying to bully me into doing dirty work for him — running women into Peru. I saw red again and jumped for him. He gave me that bullet on the head.

"After that things are badly blurred. I found myself among savages. How I got there, why I wasn't killed, I don't know. Schwandorf was there awhile. Then he went away with his gang, leaving me very sure of only one thing — I was a murderer and would be executed if caught. And — well, that's about all, except that the savages seemed rather afraid of me and didn't want me around."

There was another silence. Then Lourenço remarked:

"Between Schmidt and Schwandorf you have suffered much. It is possible that there was a connection of some sort between them. But neither can ever trouble you again. I do not see why Schwandorf took the trouble even to put you among the Red Bones. One more bullet would have ended you."

"Any ideas on that subject, José?" asked McKay.

"Only a guess, Capitan. I was not here five years ago, and I knew nothing of Schwandorf then. But I know he always schemed for his own good and overlooked no chances. So perhaps, finding this man not dead, but darkened in mind by his bullet, he thought he might be able to use him in some way at some future time. A dead man is not useful to anyone. If this man should never become valuable he could live and die forgotten among savages, where he could do Schwandorf no harm. If worth something he could be found again."

"Cold-blooded Prussian efficiency," nodded McKay. Then he spoke directly to Rand.

"Since you're mentally sound," he went on, "we may as well tell you how you happen to be among us. We three — Merry, Tim, and I — came here to find you. The settlement of the Dawson estate hinges on you."

"On me? How? I've no claim to it. Paul Dawson, Uncle Phil's son —"

"Is dead, too. Killed in action in the Argonne, You're next in line."

McKay watched him keenly. So did Knowlton. The half-expected jubilance did not come.

"So Paul's gone," was Rand's reply. "Hard luck. Suppose I hadn't been found — then what?"

"In due time the money would go to a school. Boys' school."

"Orphans? Blind? Cripples?"

"Hardly." McKay's mouth curved sardonically. He named a preparatory school of the "exclusive" type. Rand's mouth also twisted.

"That hotbed of snobbery? That twin sister to a society girls' finishing school? Might have known it, though. Uncle Phil was fond of the sort of education that doesn't educate. I'm glad you fellows found me. I'll go home and collect every red cent, just to keep it out of the hands of the supercilious bunch of bishops that run that sissy-spawner."

Knowlton chuckled appreciatively.

"It's not the sort of school that breeds he-men, for a fact," he agreed. "But you don't seem much enthused over having a couple of millions dropped into your lap."

Rand sat still. His face remained cheerless, impassive.

"What is money?" he said, presently. "I've always had plenty of it. What's it done for me? When you have it you can't tell whether people are friends to you or only friends to your money. It makes you cynical, suspicious. What's worse, you depend too much on it. You think it will do everything. Then if you land in a place where it's no good and you haven't got it, anyway, you're up against it a good deal harder than the fellow who never had it but knows how to handle himself without it."

"True for ye," Tim concurred, heartily. "All the same, I bet ye'll change yer tune after ye git home."

"Will I?" The green eyes impaled him. "Maybe. But I don't think so. I've had my run at blowing in money on myself alone. Now I'm going to blow some on other folks. I missed out on the war, but — There must be quite a few of our fellows lamed and crippled by that war. And I'll gamble that the government isn't treating them all like princes. I know something about governments."

"Princes? Say, feller, there's many a dog that's took better care of than some of our boys back home!"

"So I thought. The income from a couple of millions, along with some of the principal, will do a lot of good if used right. And —" His eyes turned to the three bushmen.

"Do not look at us in that way," said Lourenço, reading his thought. "We can make all the money we need, and we came with the capitao and his comrades only because we wanted excitement. Use your money for the crippled men who need it."

"And José Martinez also is well able to provide for his wants," coolly added the other naked man. "I am here only to settle old scores, and now they are settled. Each man is goaded by his own spur — money, wine, women, excitement, revenge. Money is not mine."

He yawned, arose, stretched like a cat, and stepped toward his hammock. The two Brasilians also moved toward the *tambo*. The others stood a moment longer beside the fire.

"Well, since we three didn't come here because of wine, women, or revenge," Knowlton said, whimsically, "it must have been for money and excitement. Don't know which was the stronger lure, but if we could have only one of the two I think we'd let the money slide. How about it, Rod?"

"Right! And, Rand, let me say this: Before we knew you we had an impression that you were more or less of a worthless pup. We've changed our ideas. If you ever go broke and want to hit a trail into some new place to make a strike of your own, and you need partners, let us know."

And he held out his hand.

The naked millionaire took it. For the first time a faint smile lightened his face.

"I'll do that, partners!" he promised.

"Yeah! That's the word. Pardners! Only, li'l' Timmy Ryan bucks at ever travelin' back into this here, now, Ja-va-ree jungle. I got enough of it. Right now I'm homesick."

"So say we all," affirmed Knowlton. "Now let's turn in."

But Tim stood a little longer looking out at the moonlit river and the two waiting canoes. His gaze roved along the stream, northward. He lifted his head, opened his mouth, expanded his lungs, and then the astounded denizens of forest and stream cut short their discordant concert to listen to something they never had heard before and never would hear again — a great voice thundering a censored version of a North American army song.

> *"Home, boys, home! Home we want to be!*
> *Home, boys, home, in God's countree!*
> *We'll raise Ol' Glory to the top o' the pole*
> *And we'll all come back — not a dog-gone soul!"*